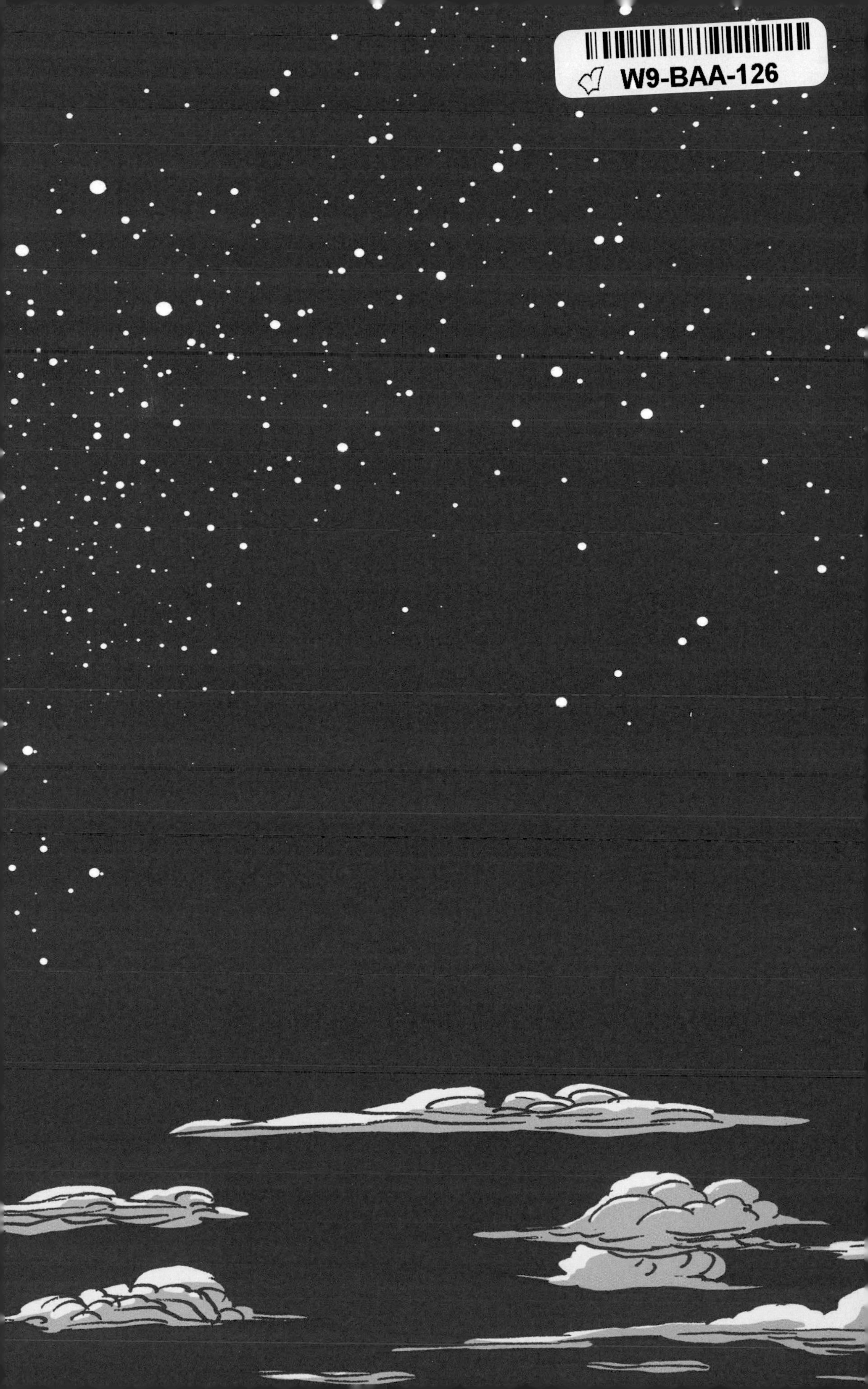

PRAISE FOR
ILLEGAL

★ "Moving and informative, *Illegal* puts an unforgettable human face to the issue of immigration; it is recommended for all readers of middle school level or higher."

—*Foreword Reviews*, Starred Review

★ "[An] achingly poignant graphic novel."

—*Publishers Weekly*, Starred Review

★ "Action-filled and engaging but considerate of both topic and audience, Ebo's story effectively paints a picture of a child refugee's struggle in a world crisscrossed by hostile borders."

—*Kirkus Reviews*, Starred Review

★ "The horrors Ebo witnesses, the impossibilities he survives, are haunting testimony to the human spirit. Artemis Fowl series creator Colfer (who taught elementary school in Italy, Saudi Arabia, and Tunisia) leads the team…in transforming staggering statistics into a resonating story about a single boy and what remains of his family. Italian artist Rigano's gorgeously saturated panels—rich in details, affecting in its captured expressions, landscapes made spectacular as if a reminder of everyday beauty despite tragedy—prove to be an enhancing visual gift to the already stirring story. A creators' note and quotes from real refugees close out this illuminating, important volume."

—*Booklist*, Starred Review

★ "The narrative…[moves] back and forth through time, depicting every new, painful trial—murder, poverty, dehydration, repeated dehumanization—with sensitivity and nuance. Rigano's illustrations show the beauty of the unforgiving landscapes and the individuals desperately seeking a better life; Colfer and Donkin's text is deep and evocative. *Illegal* is not an easy read, but the creators have made the story both approachable to and captivating for a young audience. With the timely subject material and back matter dedicated to both the refugee experience and the art of creating a graphic novel, *Illegal* is sure to be a bookseller, librarian, and teacher favorite."

—*Shelf Awareness*, Starred Review

For Jackie, Finn and Seán. —EC

For Viv, Lexie and Fisher. —AD

For Paola, always. —GR

ILLEGAL

EOIN COLFER
ANDREW DONKIN

ART BY GIOVANNI RIGANO

LETTERING BY CHRIS DICKEY

sourcebooks
jabberwocky

Written by Eoin Colfer and Andrew Donkin
Lettering by Chris Dickey

Published by Sourcebooks Jabberwocky, an imprint of Sourcebooks, Inc.
P.O. Box 4410, Naperville, Illinois 60567-4410
(630) 961-3900
Fax: (630) 961-2168
sourcebooks.com

Originally published in 2017 in Great Britain by Hodder Children's Books, an imprint of Hachette Children's Group, part of Hodder and Stoughton.

Source of Production: RR Donnelley Asia Printing Solutions Limited
Date of Production: December 2018
Run Number: 5013963

Printed and bound in China.
RRD 10 9 8 7 6 5 4 3 2

You, who are so-called illegal aliens, must know that no human being is illegal. That is a contradiction in terms. Human beings can be beautiful or more beautiful, they can be fat or skinny, they can be right or wrong, but illegal? How can a human being be illegal?

—Elie Wiesel
Nobel Laureate and
Holocaust survivor

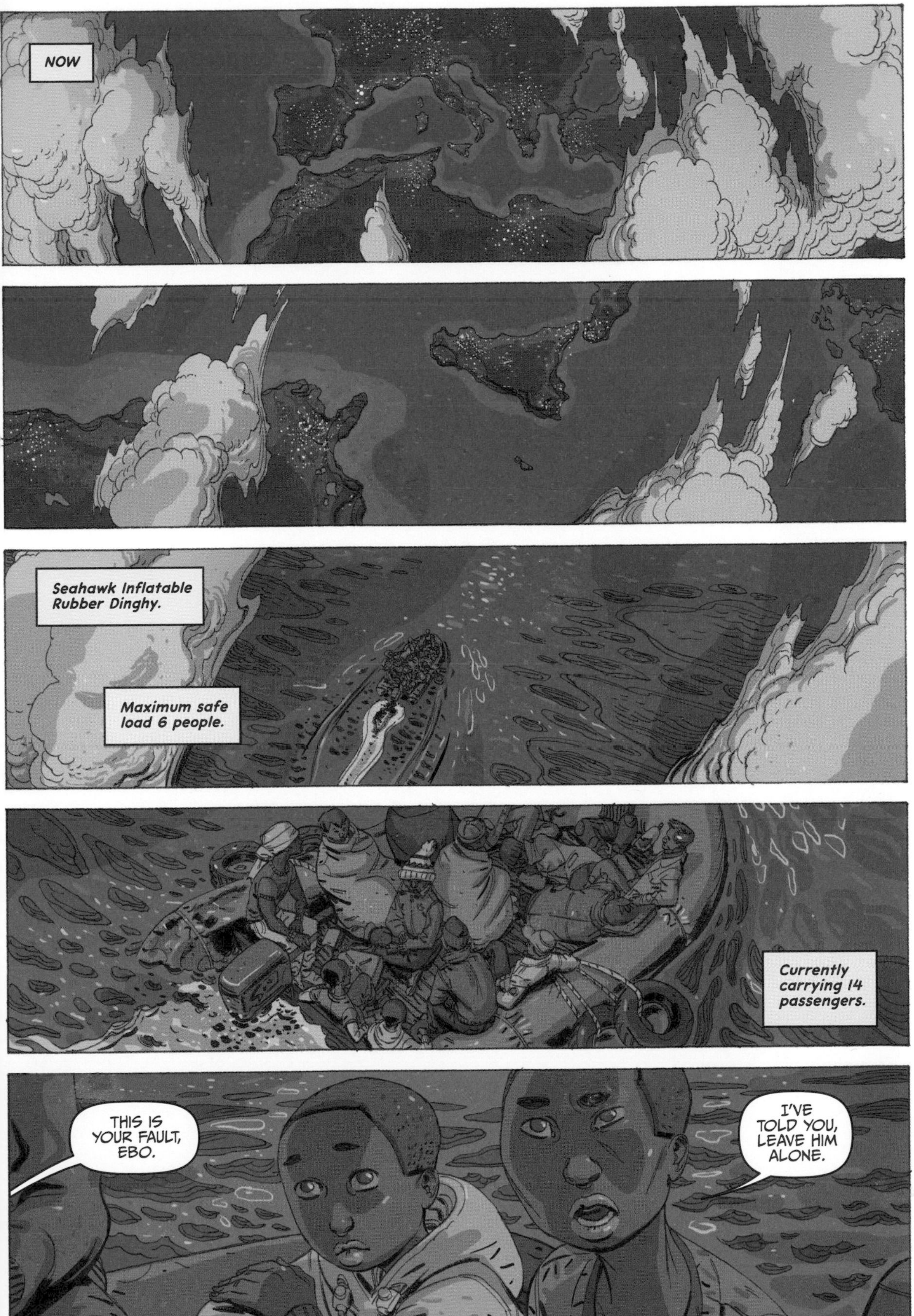
NOW
Seahawk Inflatable Rubber Dinghy.
Maximum safe load 6 people.
Currently carrying 14 passengers.
THIS IS YOUR FAULT, EBO.
I'VE TOLD YOU, LEAVE HIM ALONE.

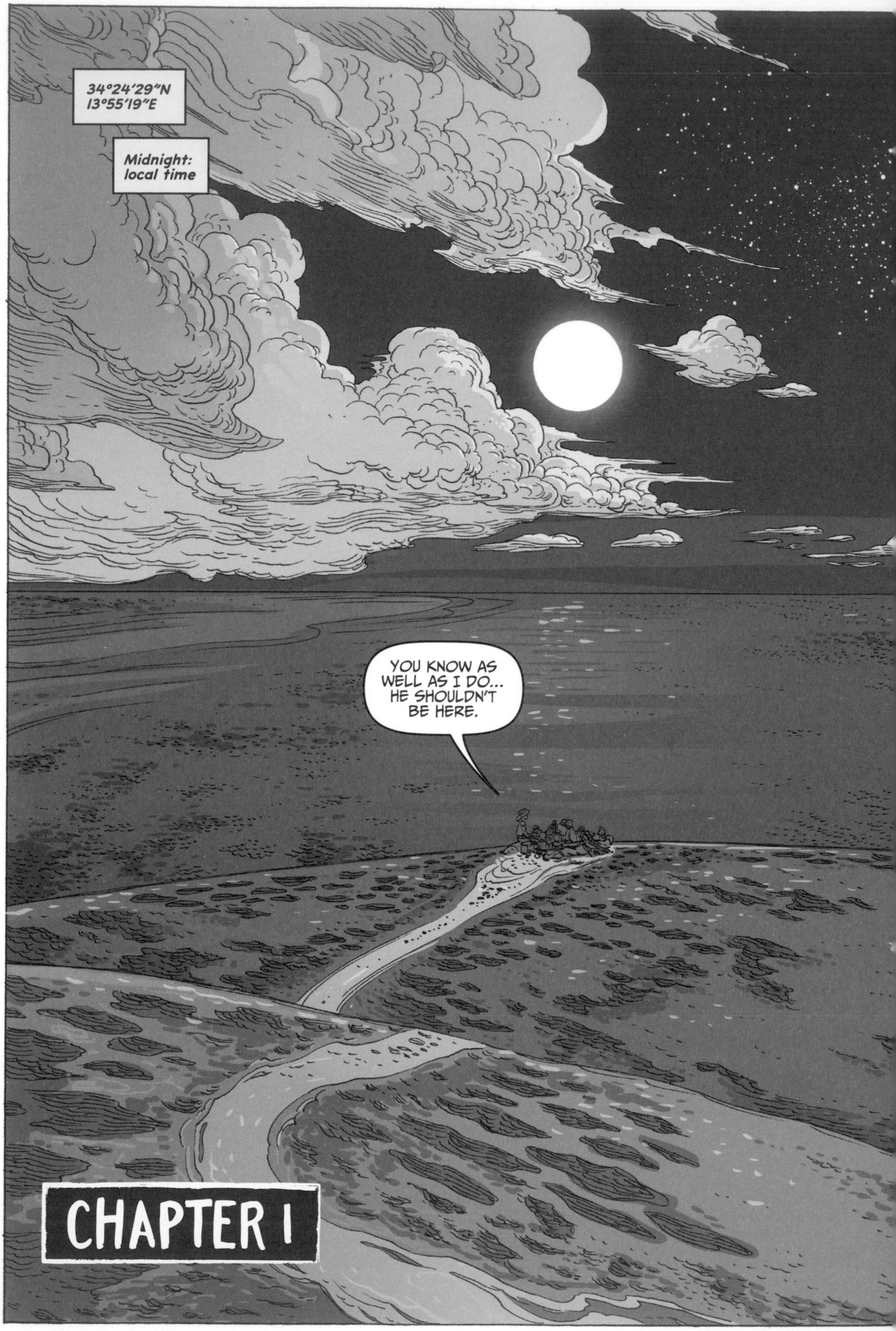
34°24'29"N
13°55'19"E
Midnight:
local time
YOU KNOW AS WELL AS I DO... HE SHOULDN'T BE HERE.
CHAPTER 1

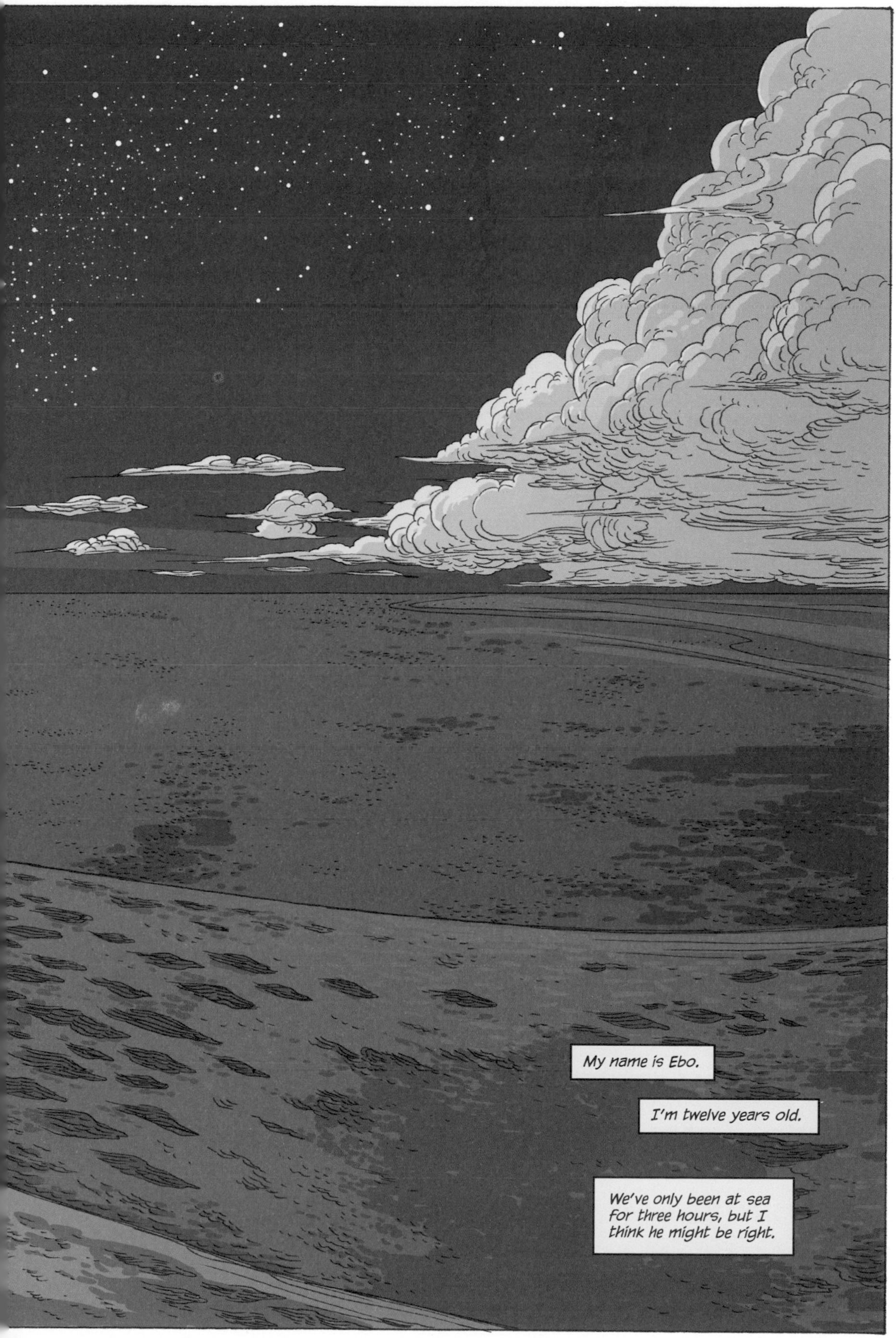
My name is Ebo.
I'm twelve years old.
We've only been at sea for three hours, but I think he might be right.

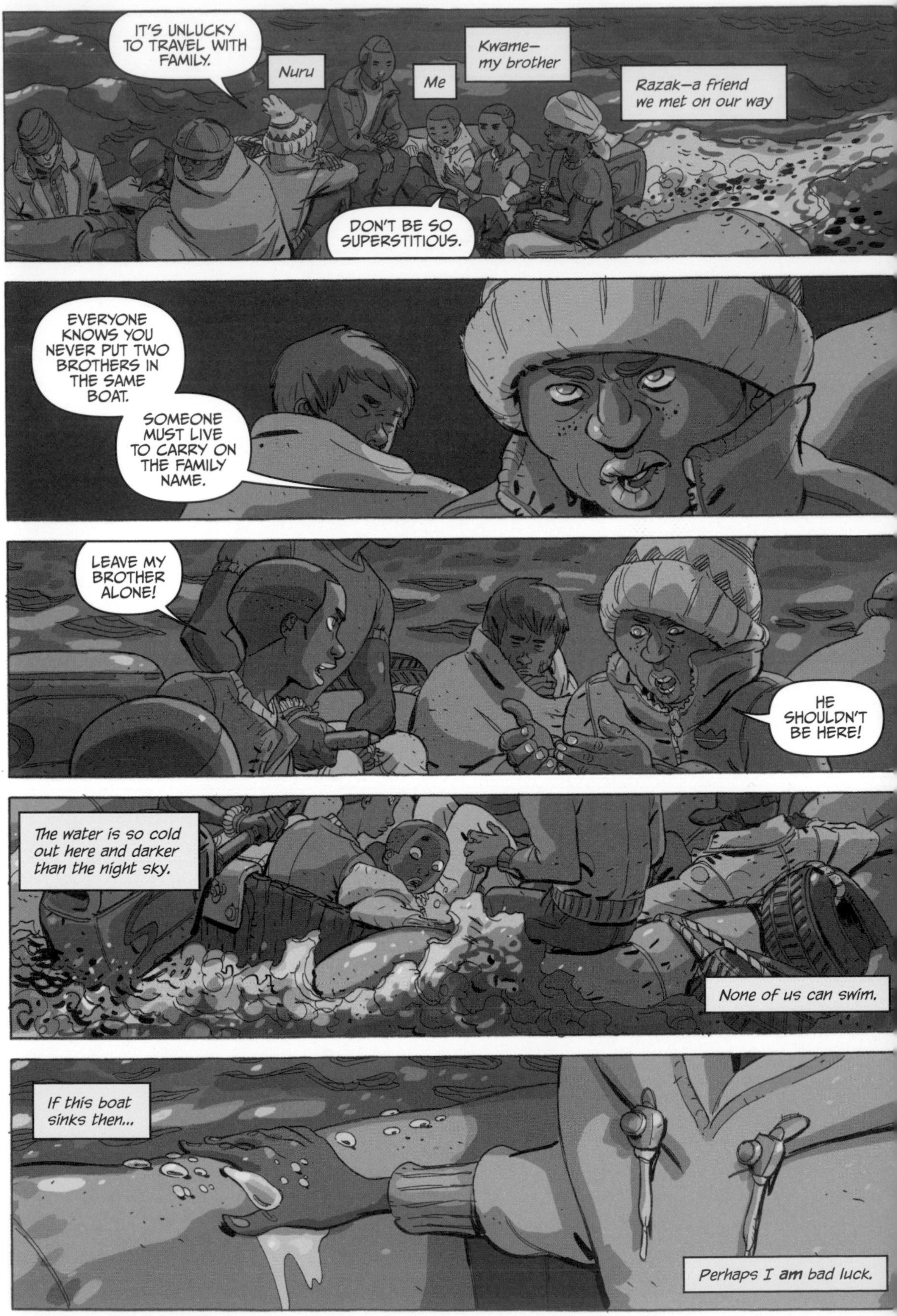
IT'S UNLUCKY TO TRAVEL WITH FAMILY.
Nuru
Me
Kwame—my brother
Razak—a friend we met on our way
DON'T BE SO SUPERSTITIOUS.
EVERYONE KNOWS YOU NEVER PUT TWO BROTHERS IN THE SAME BOAT.
SOMEONE MUST LIVE TO CARRY ON THE FAMILY NAME.
LEAVE MY BROTHER ALONE!
HE SHOULDN'T BE HERE!
The water is so cold out here and darker than the night sky.
None of us can swim.
If this boat sinks then...
Perhaps I am bad luck.

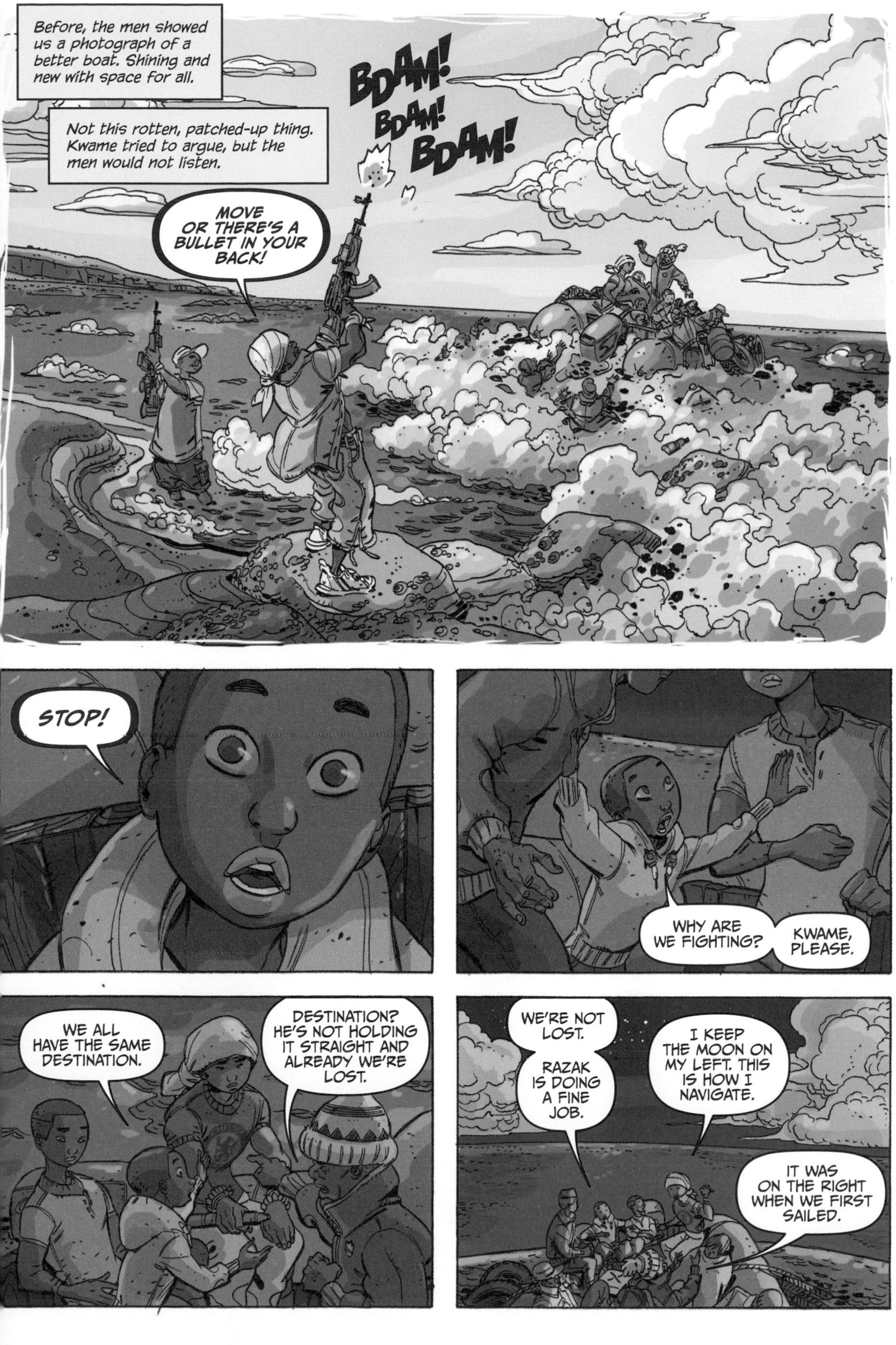
Before, the men showed us a photograph of a better boat. Shining and new with space for all.
Not this rotten, patched-up thing. Kwame tried to argue, but the men would not listen.
BDAM! BDAM! BDAM!
MOVE OR THERE'S A BULLET IN YOUR BACK!
STOP!
WHY ARE WE FIGHTING?
KWAME, PLEASE.
WE ALL HAVE THE SAME DESTINATION.
DESTINATION? HE'S NOT HOLDING IT STRAIGHT AND ALREADY WE'RE LOST.
WE'RE NOT LOST.
RAZAK IS DOING A FINE JOB.
I KEEP THE MOON ON MY LEFT. THIS IS HOW I NAVIGATE.
IT WAS ON THE RIGHT WHEN WE FIRST SAILED.

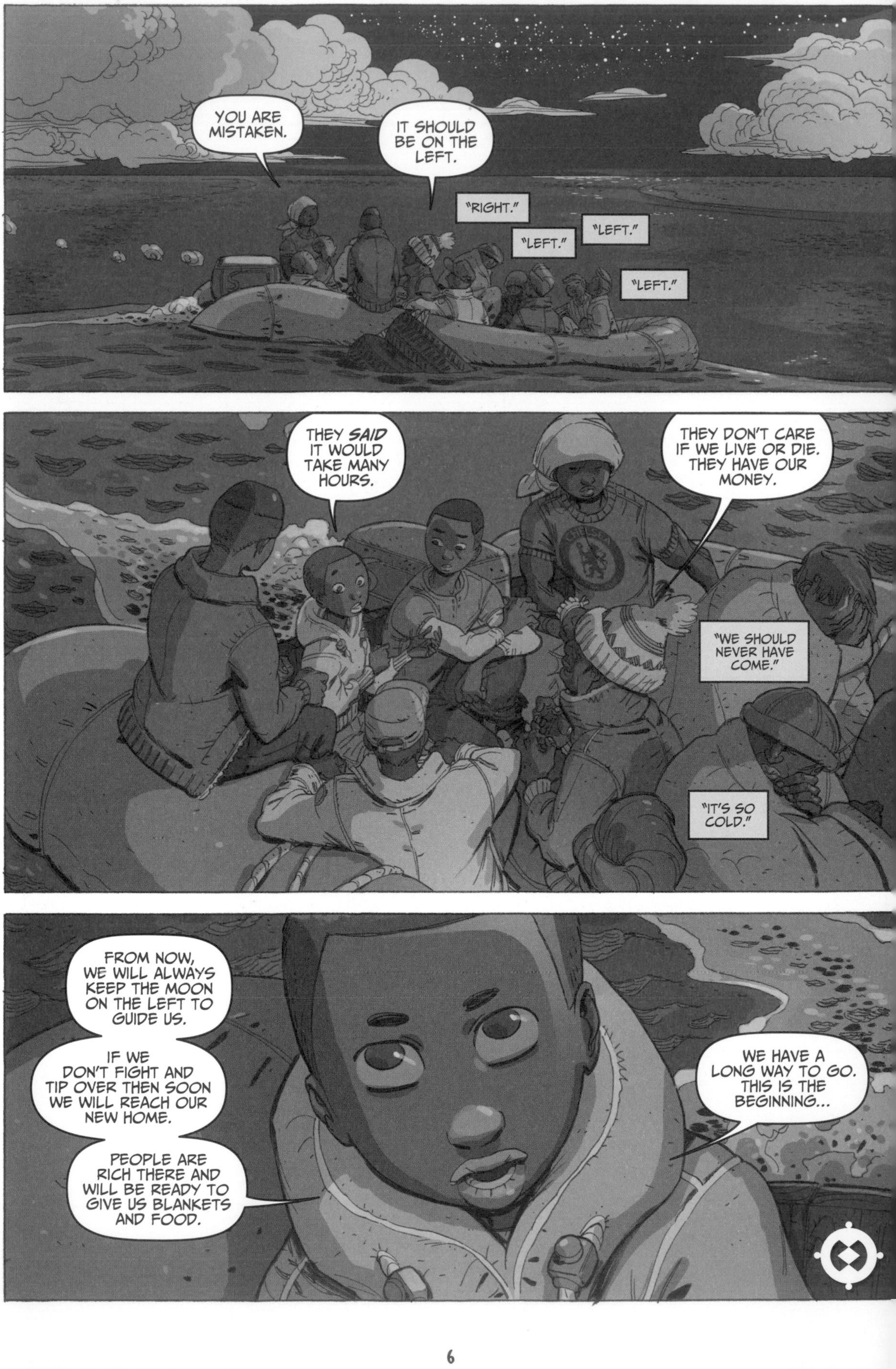
YOU ARE MISTAKEN.
IT SHOULD BE ON THE LEFT.
"RIGHT."
"LEFT."
"LEFT."
"LEFT."
THEY *SAID* IT WOULD TAKE MANY HOURS.
THEY DON'T CARE IF WE LIVE OR DIE. THEY HAVE OUR MONEY.
"WE SHOULD NEVER HAVE COME."
"IT'S SO COLD."
FROM NOW, WE WILL ALWAYS KEEP THE MOON ON THE LEFT TO GUIDE US.
IF WE DON'T FIGHT AND TIP OVER THEN SOON WE WILL REACH OUR NEW HOME.
PEOPLE ARE RICH THERE AND WILL BE READY TO GIVE US BLANKETS AND FOOD.
WE HAVE A LONG WAY TO GO. THIS IS THE BEGINNING...

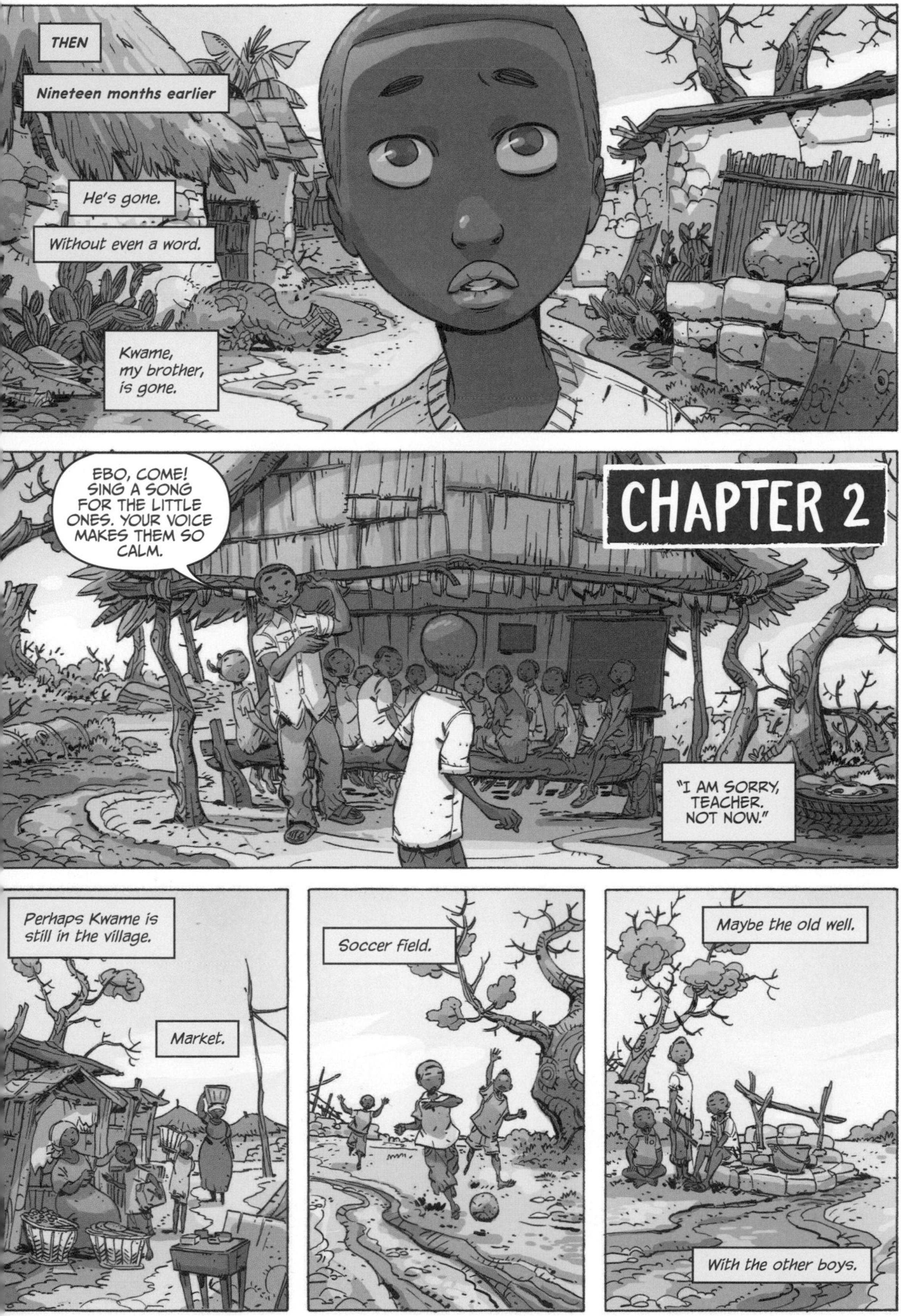
THEN
Nineteen months earlier
He's gone.
Without even a word.
Kwame, my brother, is gone.
CHAPTER 2
EBO, COME! SING A SONG FOR THE LITTLE ONES. YOUR VOICE MAKES THEM SO CALM.
"I AM SORRY, TEACHER. NOT NOW."
Perhaps Kwame is still in the village.
Market.
Soccer field.
Maybe the old well.
With the other boys.

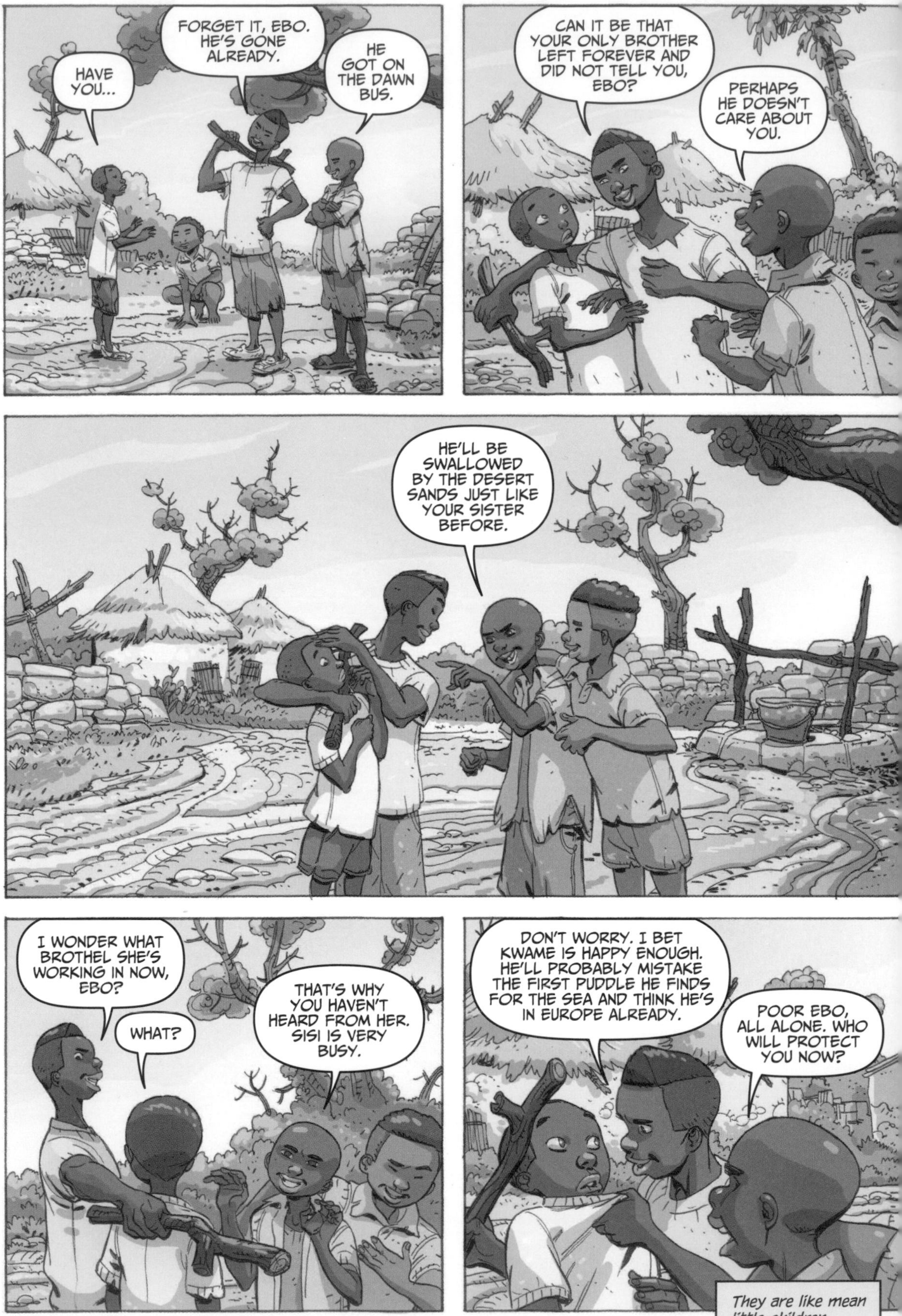
HAVE YOU...
FORGET IT, EBO. HE'S GONE ALREADY.
HE GOT ON THE DAWN BUS.
CAN IT BE THAT YOUR ONLY BROTHER LEFT FOREVER AND DID NOT TELL YOU, EBO?
PERHAPS HE DOESN'T CARE ABOUT YOU.
HE'LL BE SWALLOWED BY THE DESERT SANDS JUST LIKE YOUR SISTER BEFORE.
I WONDER WHAT BROTHEL SHE'S WORKING IN NOW, EBO?
WHAT?
THAT'S WHY YOU HAVEN'T HEARD FROM HER. SISI IS VERY BUSY.
DON'T WORRY. I BET KWAME IS HAPPY ENOUGH. HE'LL PROBABLY MISTAKE THE FIRST PUDDLE HE FINDS FOR THE SEA AND THINK HE'S IN EUROPE ALREADY.
POOR EBO, ALL ALONE. WHO WILL PROTECT YOU NOW?
They are like mean little children.

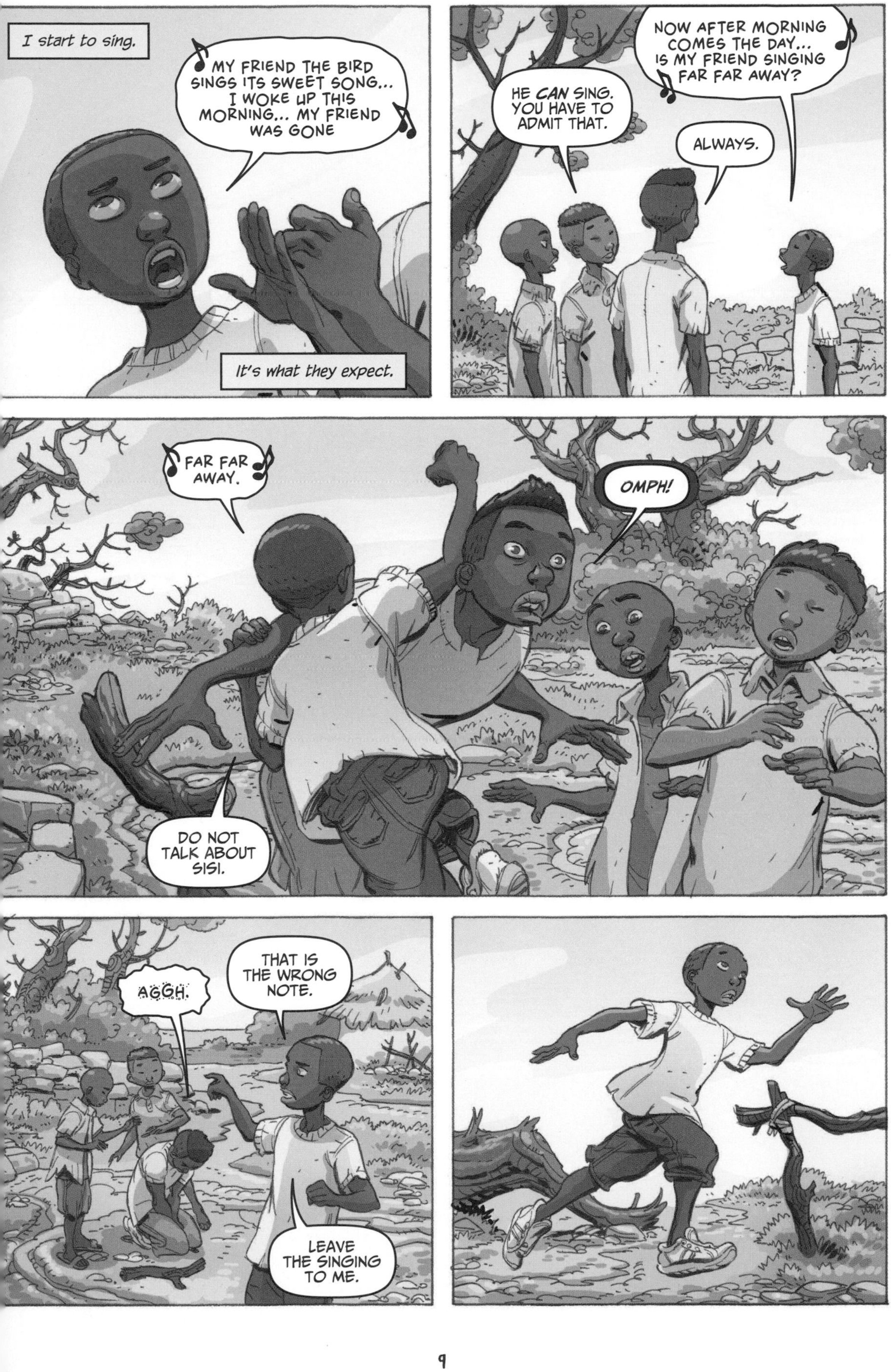
I start to sing.
MY FRIEND THE BIRD SINGS ITS SWEET SONG... I WOKE UP THIS MORNING... MY FRIEND WAS GONE
It's what they expect.
HE CAN SING. YOU HAVE TO ADMIT THAT.
NOW AFTER MORNING COMES THE DAY... IS MY FRIEND SINGING FAR FAR AWAY?
ALWAYS.
FAR FAR AWAY.
OMPH!
DO NOT TALK ABOUT SISI.
AGGH.
THAT IS THE WRONG NOTE.
LEAVE THE SINGING TO ME.

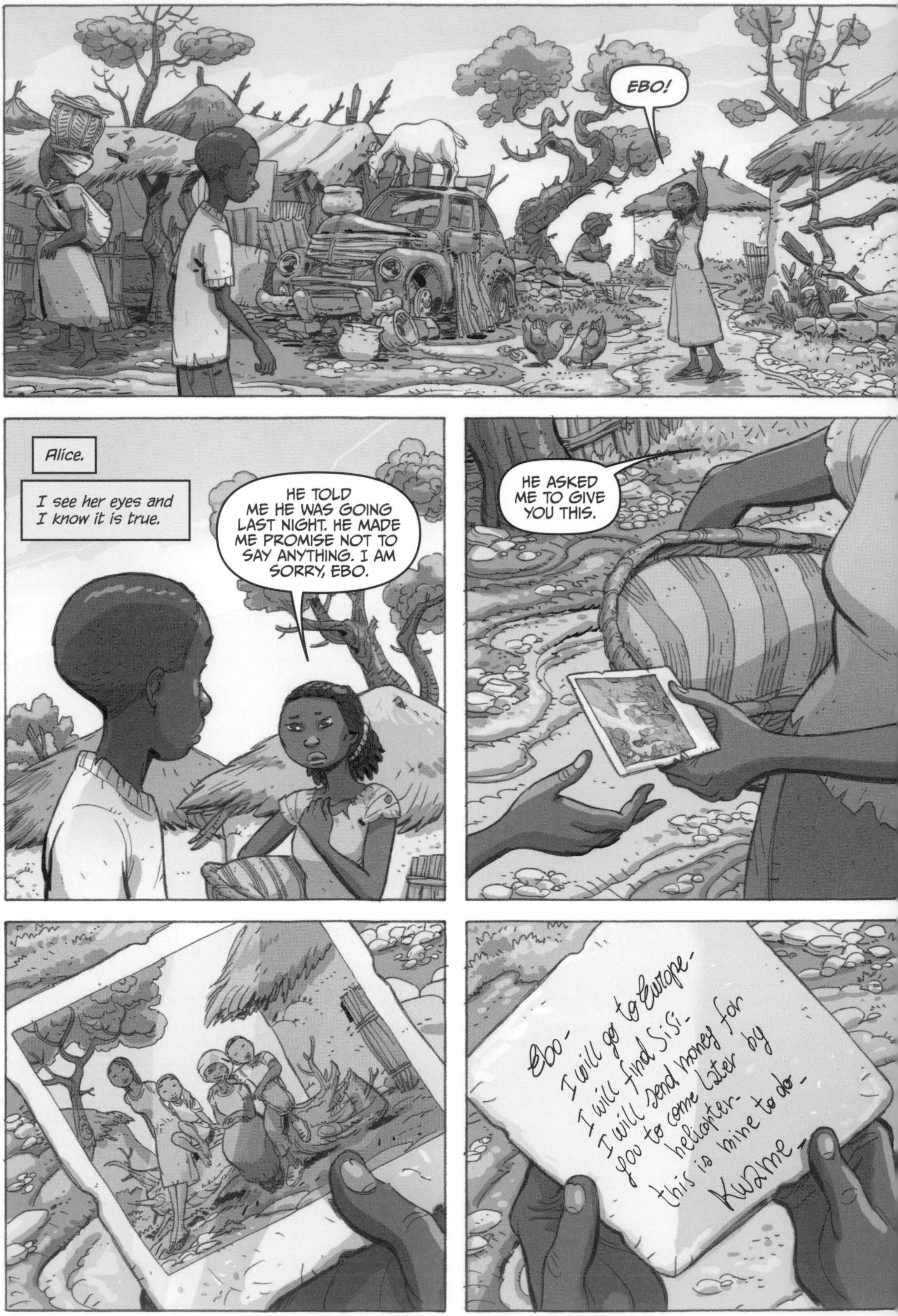
EBO!
Alice.
I see her eyes and I know it is true.
HE TOLD ME HE WAS GOING LAST NIGHT. HE MADE ME PROMISE NOT TO SAY ANYTHING. I AM SORRY, EBO.
HE ASKED ME TO GIVE YOU THIS.
Ebo-
I will go to Europe-
I will find Sisi-
I will send money for
you to come later by
helicopter-
this is mine to do-
Kwame-

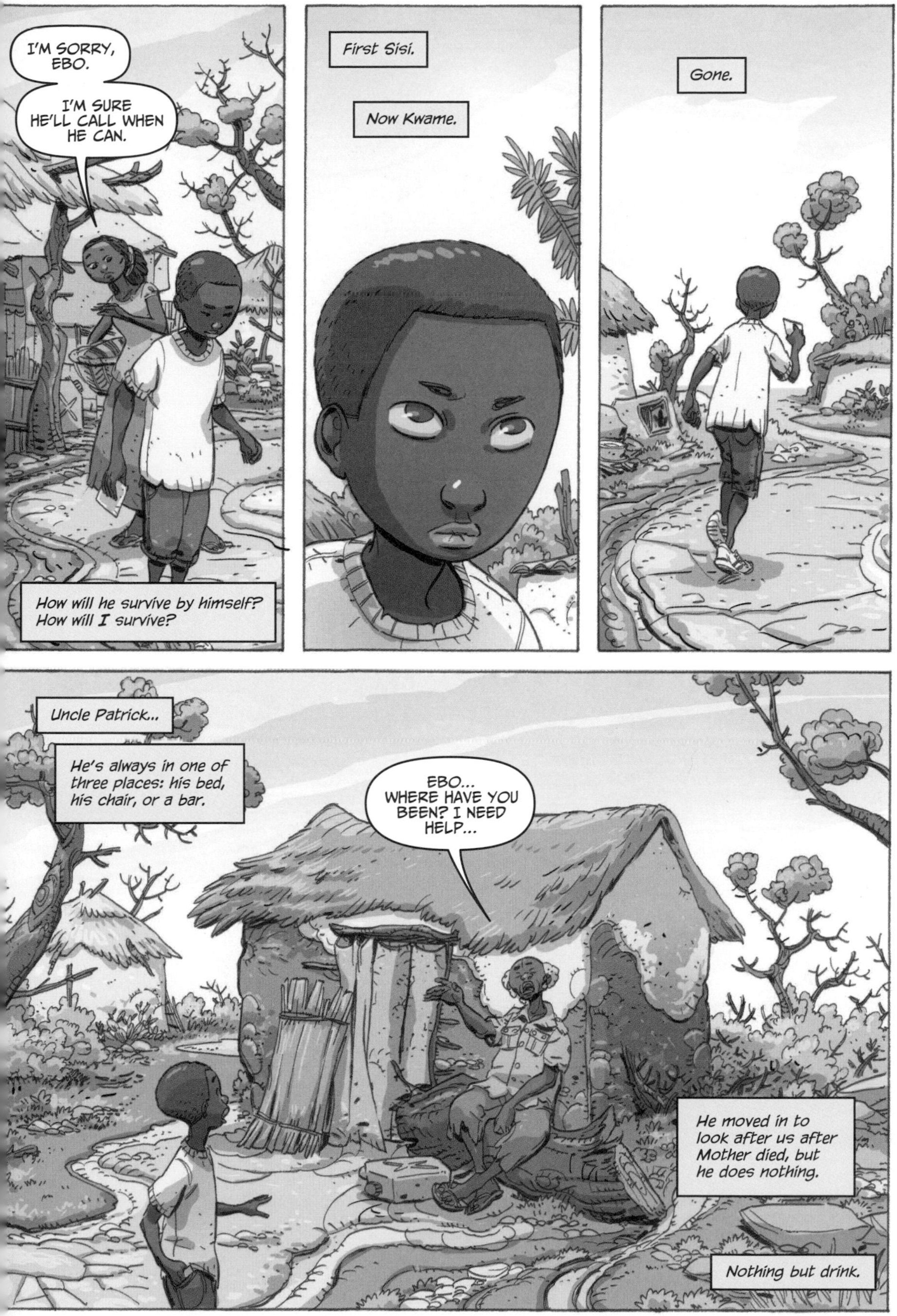
I'M SORRY, EBO.
I'M SURE HE'LL CALL WHEN HE CAN.
How will he survive by himself? How will I survive?
First Sisi.
Now Kwame.
Gone.
Uncle Patrick...
He's always in one of three places: his bed, his chair, or a bar.
EBO... WHERE HAVE YOU BEEN? I NEED HELP...
He moved in to look after us after Mother died, but he does nothing.
Nothing but drink.

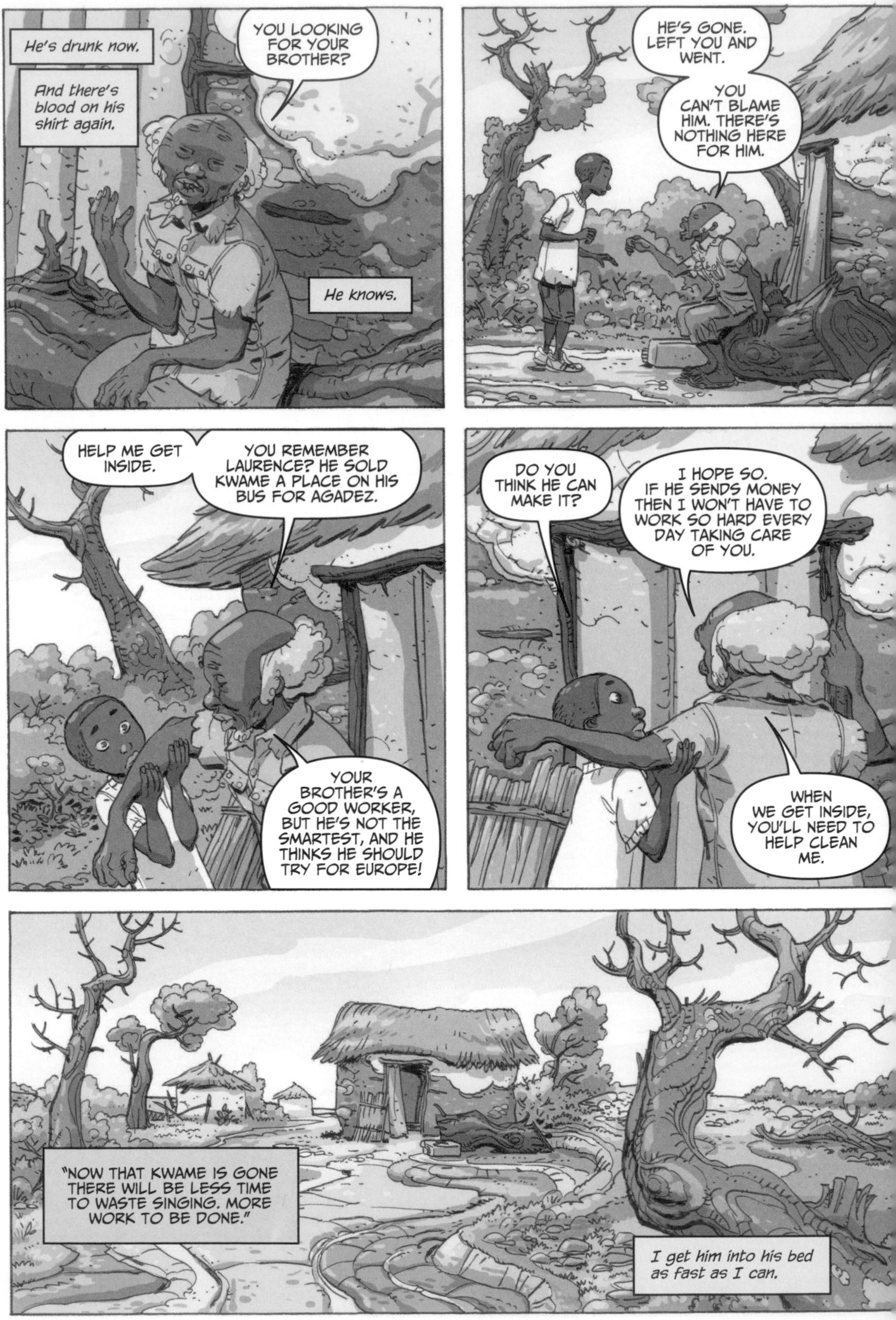
He's drunk now.
And there's blood on his shirt again.
YOU LOOKING FOR YOUR BROTHER?
He knows.
HE'S GONE. LEFT YOU AND WENT.
YOU CAN'T BLAME HIM. THERE'S NOTHING HERE FOR HIM.
HELP ME GET INSIDE.
YOU REMEMBER LAURENCE? HE SOLD KWAME A PLACE ON HIS BUS FOR AGADEZ.
YOUR BROTHER'S A GOOD WORKER, BUT HE'S NOT THE SMARTEST, AND HE THINKS HE SHOULD TRY FOR EUROPE!
DO YOU THINK HE CAN MAKE IT?
I HOPE SO. IF HE SENDS MONEY THEN I WON'T HAVE TO WORK SO HARD EVERY DAY TAKING CARE OF YOU.
WHEN WE GET INSIDE, YOU'LL NEED TO HELP CLEAN ME.
"NOW THAT KWAME IS GONE THERE WILL BE LESS TIME TO WASTE SINGING. MORE WORK TO BE DONE."
I get him into his bed as fast as I can.

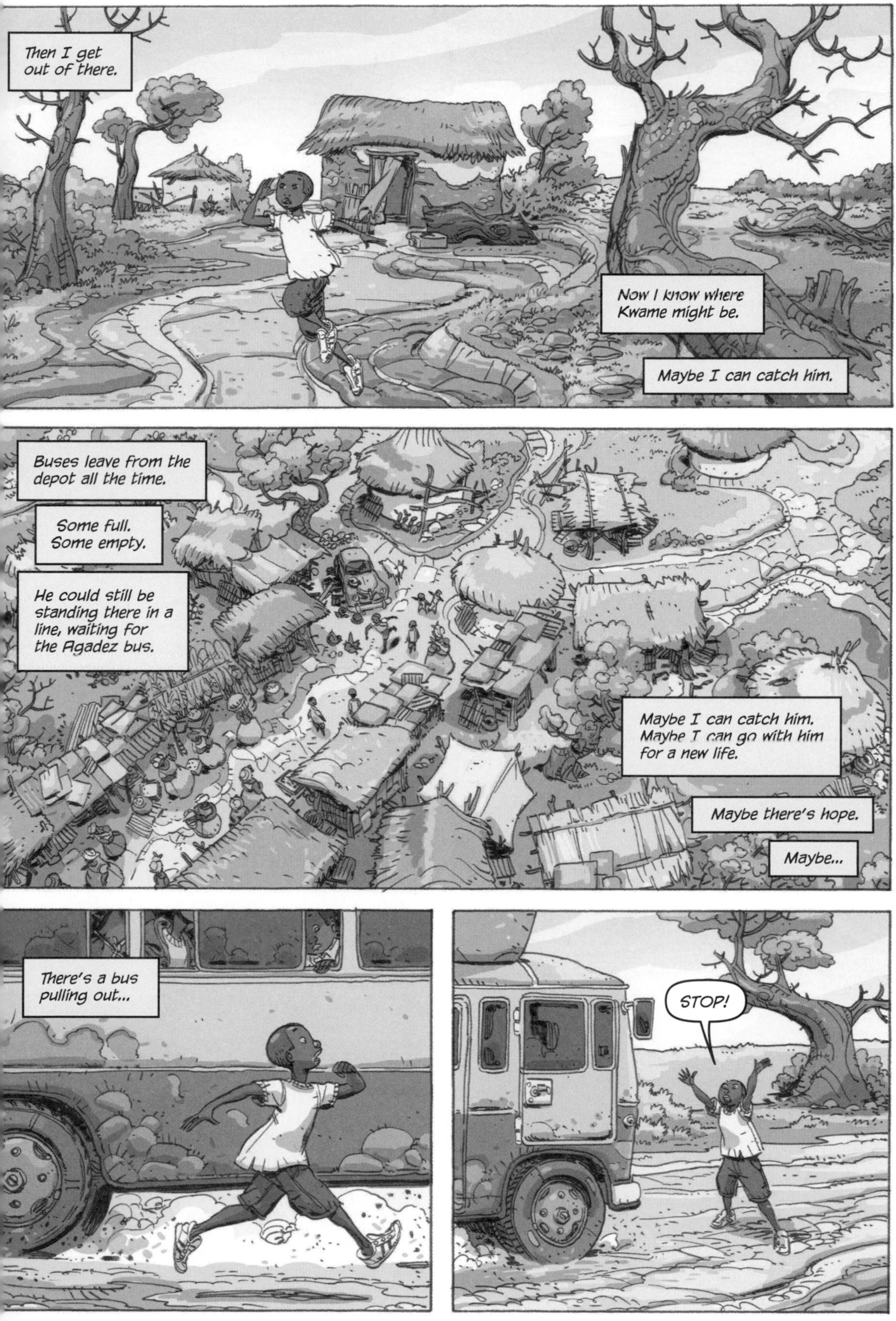
Then I get out of there.
Now I know where Kwame might be.
Maybe I can catch him.
Buses leave from the depot all the time.
Some full. Some empty.
He could still be standing there in a line, waiting for the Agadez bus.
Maybe I can catch him. Maybe I can go with him for a new life.
Maybe there's hope.
Maybe...
There's a bus pulling out...
STOP!

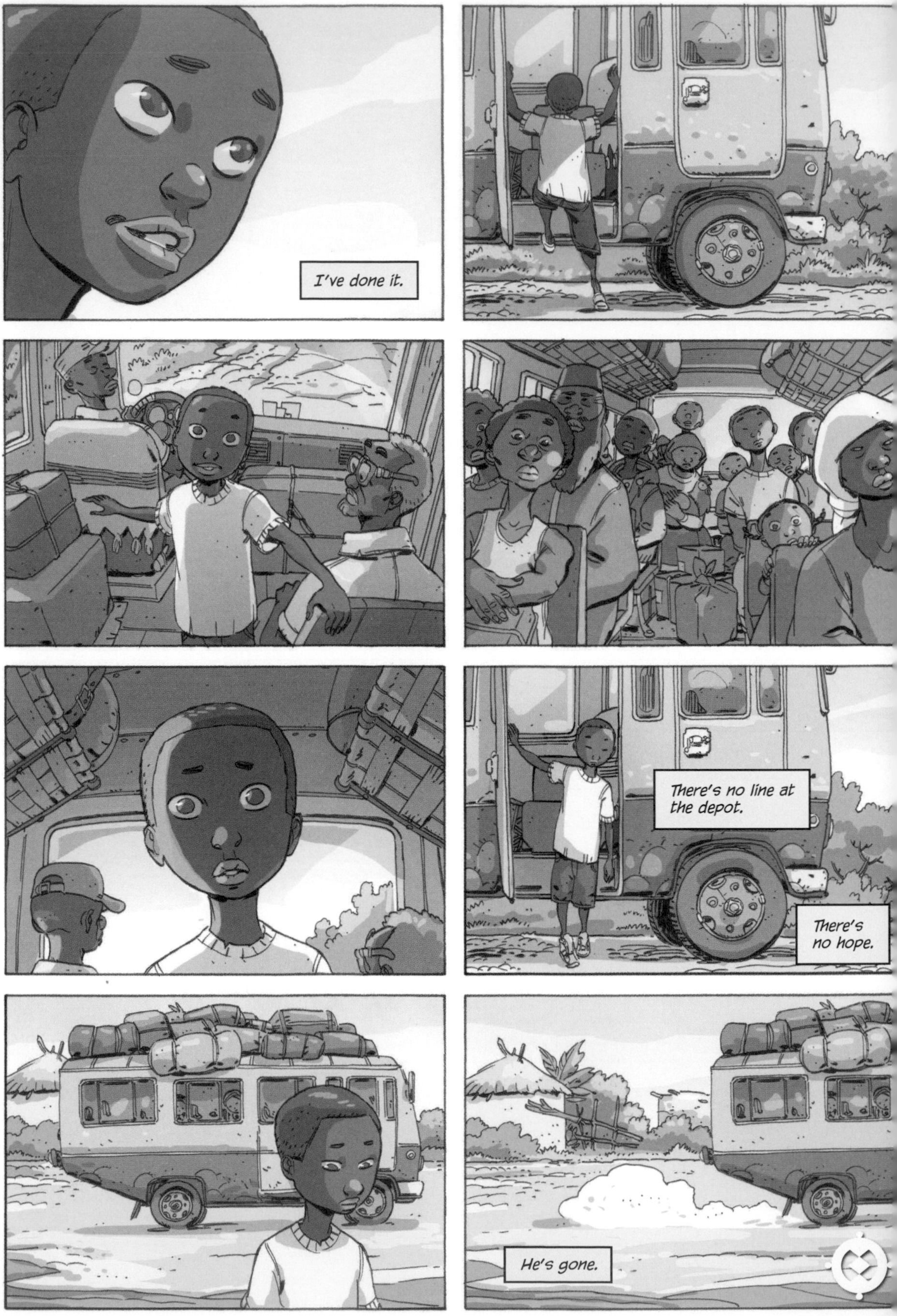
I've done it.
There's no line at the depot.
There's no hope.
He's gone.

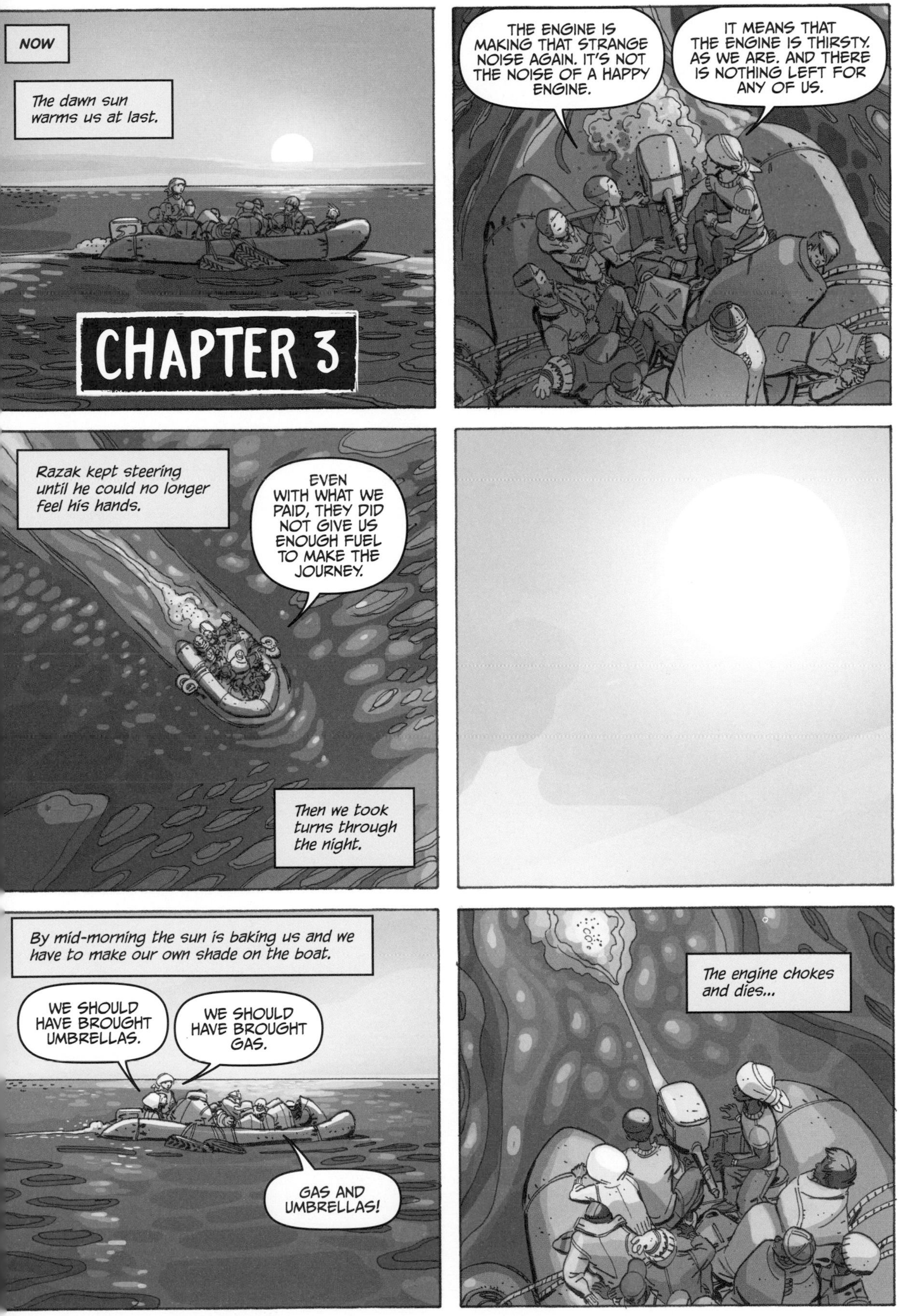
NOW
The dawn sun warms us at last.
CHAPTER 3
THE ENGINE IS MAKING THAT STRANGE NOISE AGAIN. IT'S NOT THE NOISE OF A HAPPY ENGINE.
IT MEANS THAT THE ENGINE IS THIRSTY. AS WE ARE. AND THERE IS NOTHING LEFT FOR ANY OF US.
Razak kept steering until he could no longer feel his hands.
EVEN WITH WHAT WE PAID, THEY DID NOT GIVE US ENOUGH FUEL TO MAKE THE JOURNEY.
Then we took turns through the night.
By mid-morning the sun is baking us and we have to make our own shade on the boat.
WE SHOULD HAVE BROUGHT UMBRELLAS.
WE SHOULD HAVE BROUGHT GAS.
GAS AND UMBRELLAS!
The engine chokes and dies...

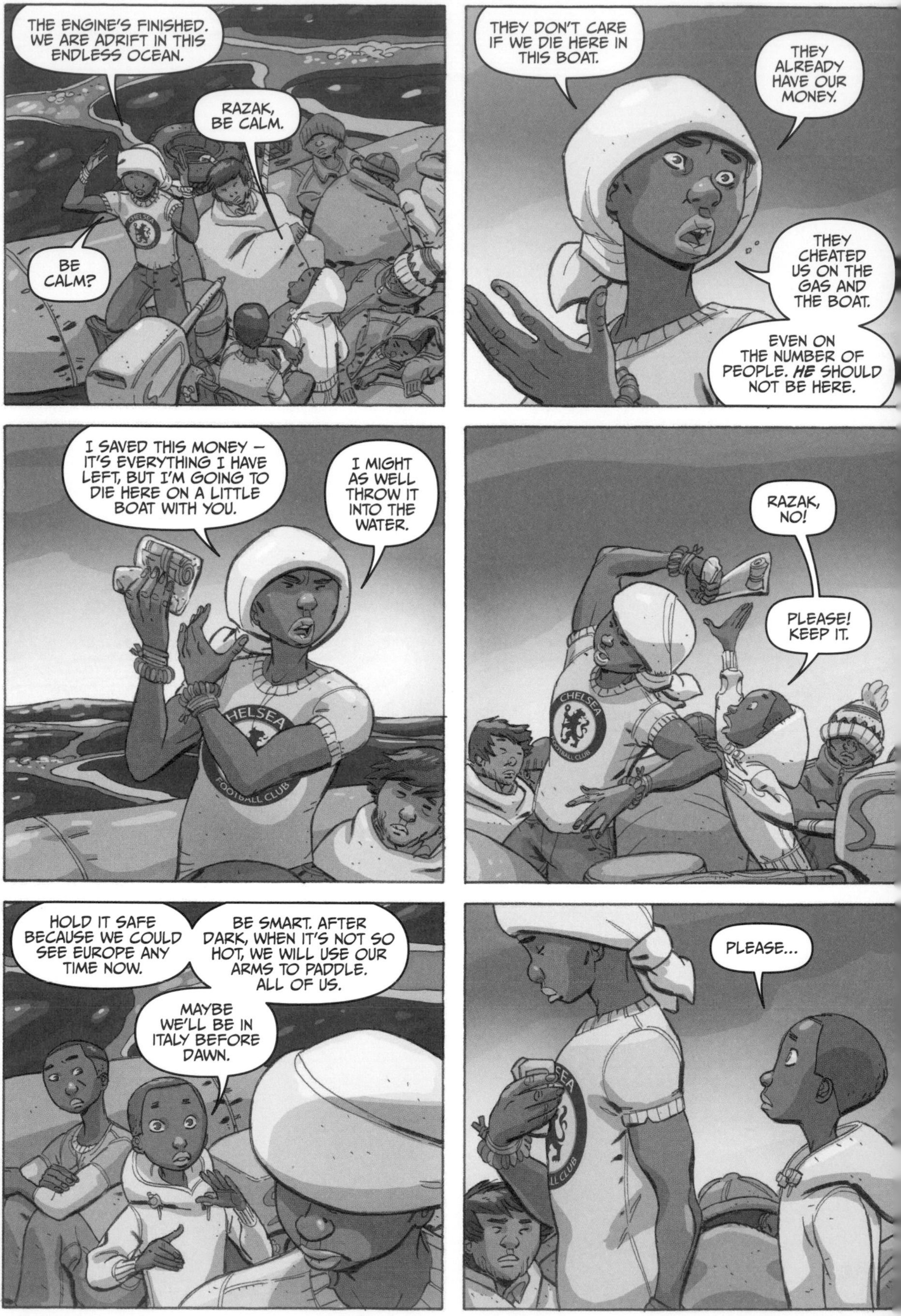
THE ENGINE'S FINISHED. WE ARE ADRIFT IN THIS ENDLESS OCEAN.
RAZAK, BE CALM.
BE CALM?
THEY DON'T CARE IF WE DIE HERE IN THIS BOAT.
THEY ALREADY HAVE OUR MONEY.
THEY CHEATED US ON THE GAS AND THE BOAT.
EVEN ON THE NUMBER OF PEOPLE. *HE* SHOULD NOT BE HERE.
I SAVED THIS MONEY – IT'S EVERYTHING I HAVE LEFT, BUT I'M GOING TO DIE HERE ON A LITTLE BOAT WITH YOU.
I MIGHT AS WELL THROW IT INTO THE WATER.
RAZAK, NO!
PLEASE! KEEP IT.
HOLD IT SAFE BECAUSE WE COULD SEE EUROPE ANY TIME NOW.
BE SMART. AFTER DARK, WHEN IT'S NOT SO HOT, WE WILL USE OUR ARMS TO PADDLE. ALL OF US.
MAYBE WE'LL BE IN ITALY BEFORE DAWN.
PLEASE...

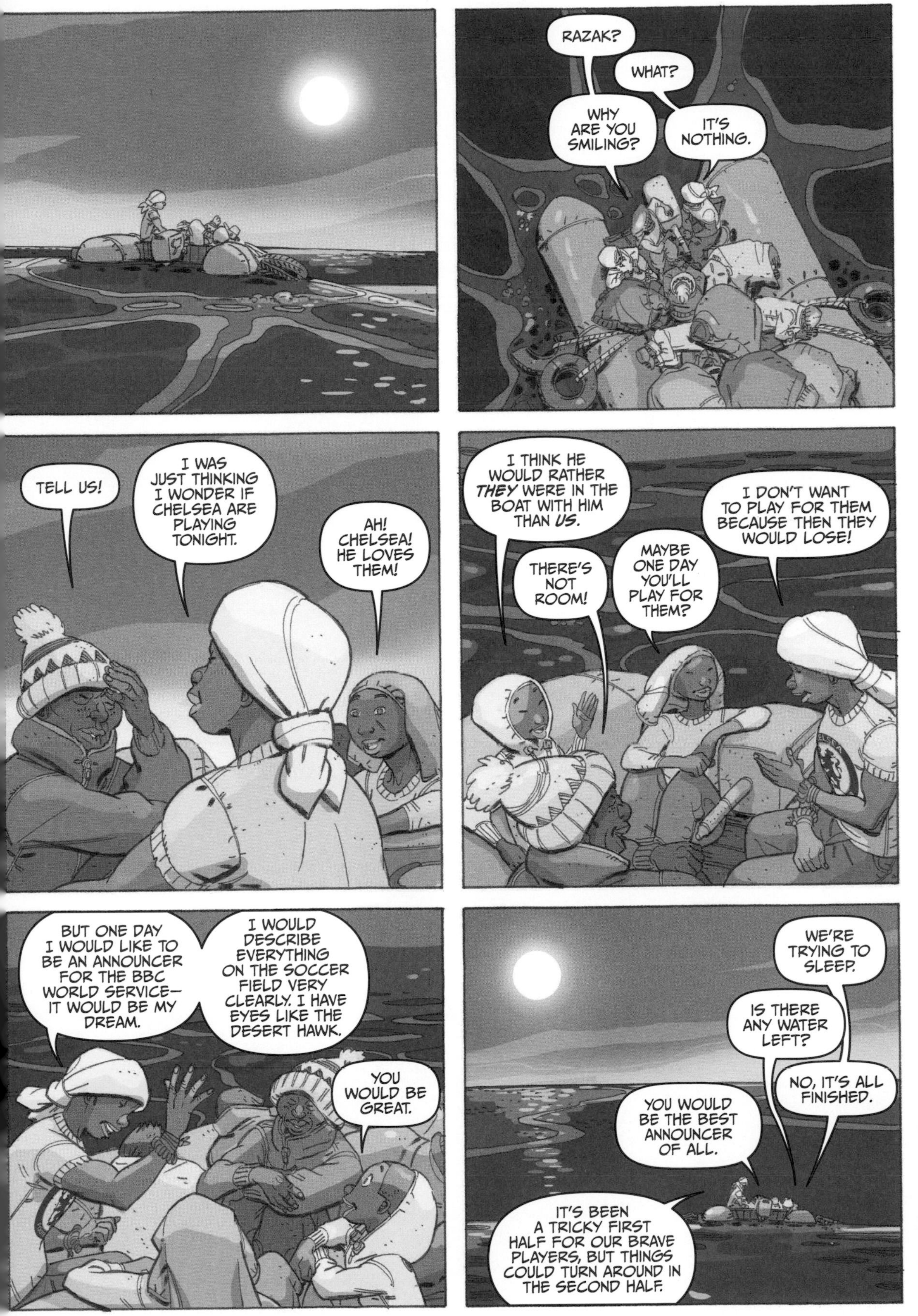
RAZAK?
WHAT?
WHY ARE YOU SMILING?
IT'S NOTHING.
TELL US!
I WAS JUST THINKING I WONDER IF CHELSEA ARE PLAYING TONIGHT.
AH! CHELSEA! HE LOVES THEM!
I THINK HE WOULD RATHER *THEY* WERE IN THE BOAT WITH HIM THAN *US*.
THERE'S NOT ROOM!
MAYBE ONE DAY YOU'LL PLAY FOR THEM?
I DON'T WANT TO PLAY FOR THEM BECAUSE THEN THEY WOULD LOSE!
BUT ONE DAY I WOULD LIKE TO BE AN ANNOUNCER FOR THE BBC WORLD SERVICE— IT WOULD BE MY DREAM.
I WOULD DESCRIBE EVERYTHING ON THE SOCCER FIELD VERY CLEARLY. I HAVE EYES LIKE THE DESERT HAWK.
YOU WOULD BE GREAT.
WE'RE TRYING TO SLEEP.
IS THERE ANY WATER LEFT?
NO, IT'S ALL FINISHED.
YOU WOULD BE THE BEST ANNOUNCER OF ALL.
IT'S BEEN A TRICKY FIRST HALF FOR OUR BRAVE PLAYERS, BUT THINGS COULD TURN AROUND IN THE SECOND HALF.

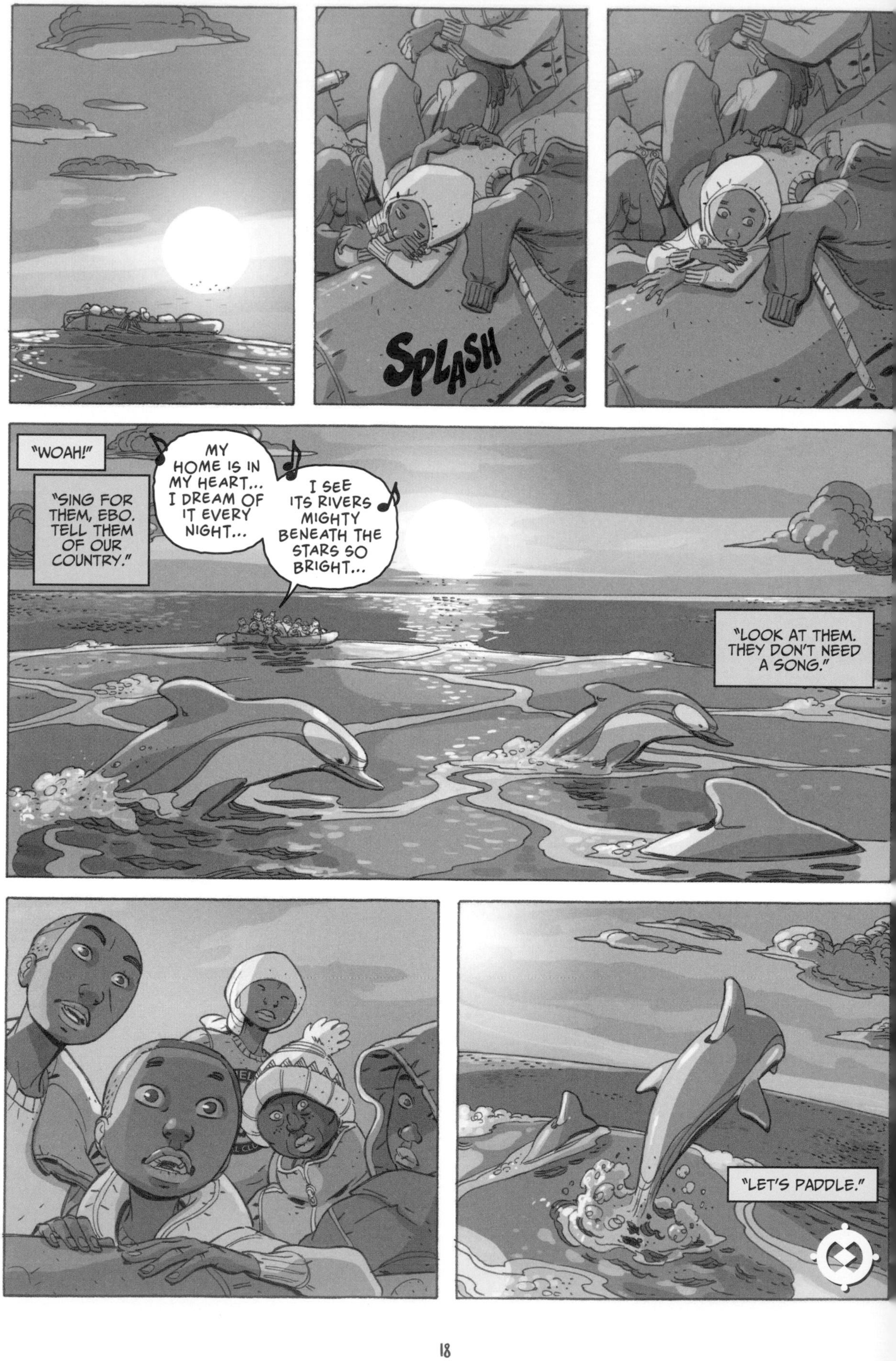
SPLASH
"WOAH!"
"SING FOR THEM, EBO. TELL THEM OF OUR COUNTRY."
MY HOME IS IN MY HEART... I DREAM OF IT EVERY NIGHT...
I SEE ITS RIVERS MIGHTY BENEATH THE STARS SO BRIGHT...
"LOOK AT THEM. THEY DON'T NEED A SONG."
"LET'S PADDLE."

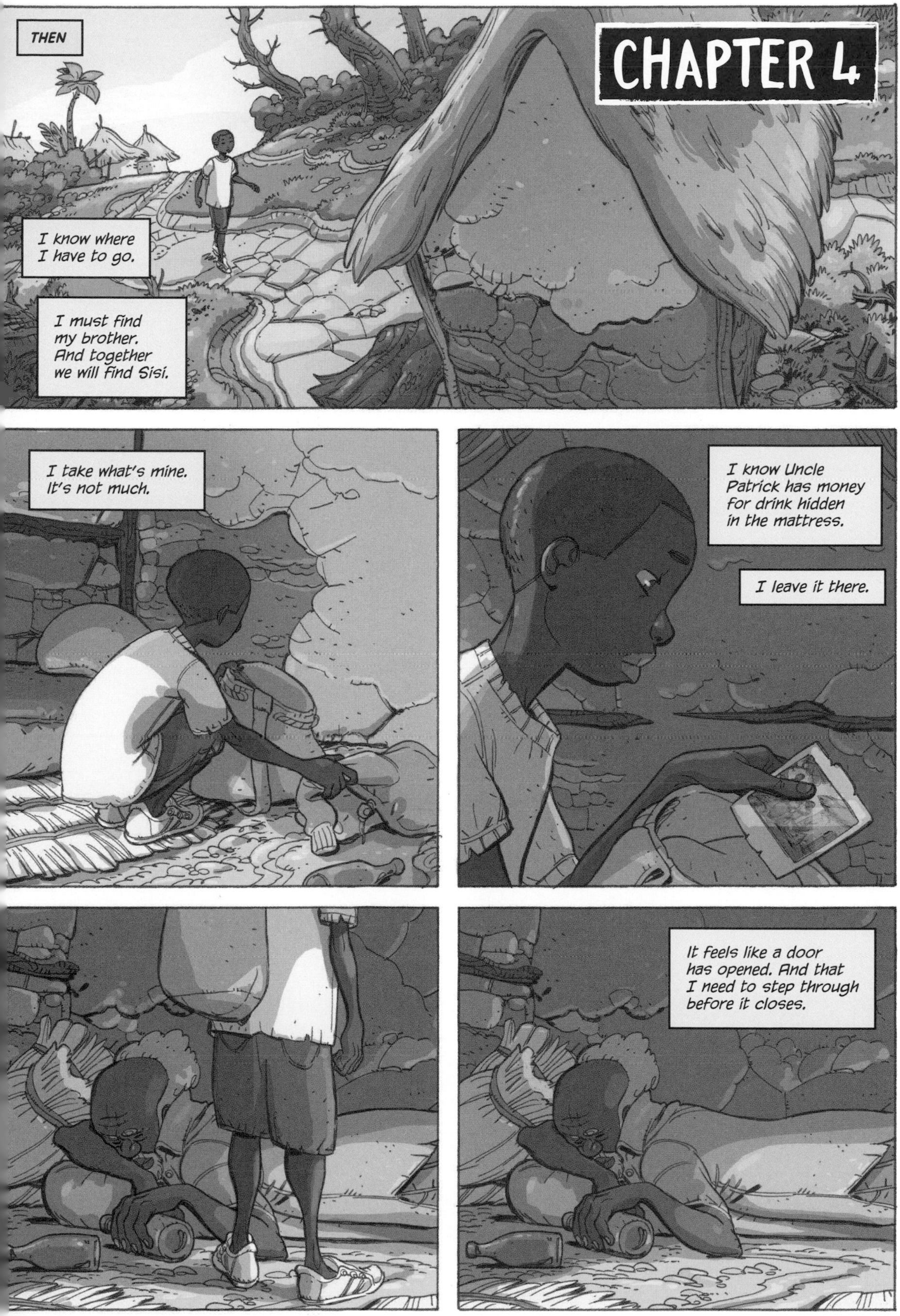

THEN
CHAPTER 4
I know where I have to go.
I must find my brother. And together we will find Sisi.
I take what's mine. It's not much.
I know Uncle Patrick has money for drink hidden in the mattress.
I leave it there.
It feels like a door has opened. And that I need to step through before it closes.

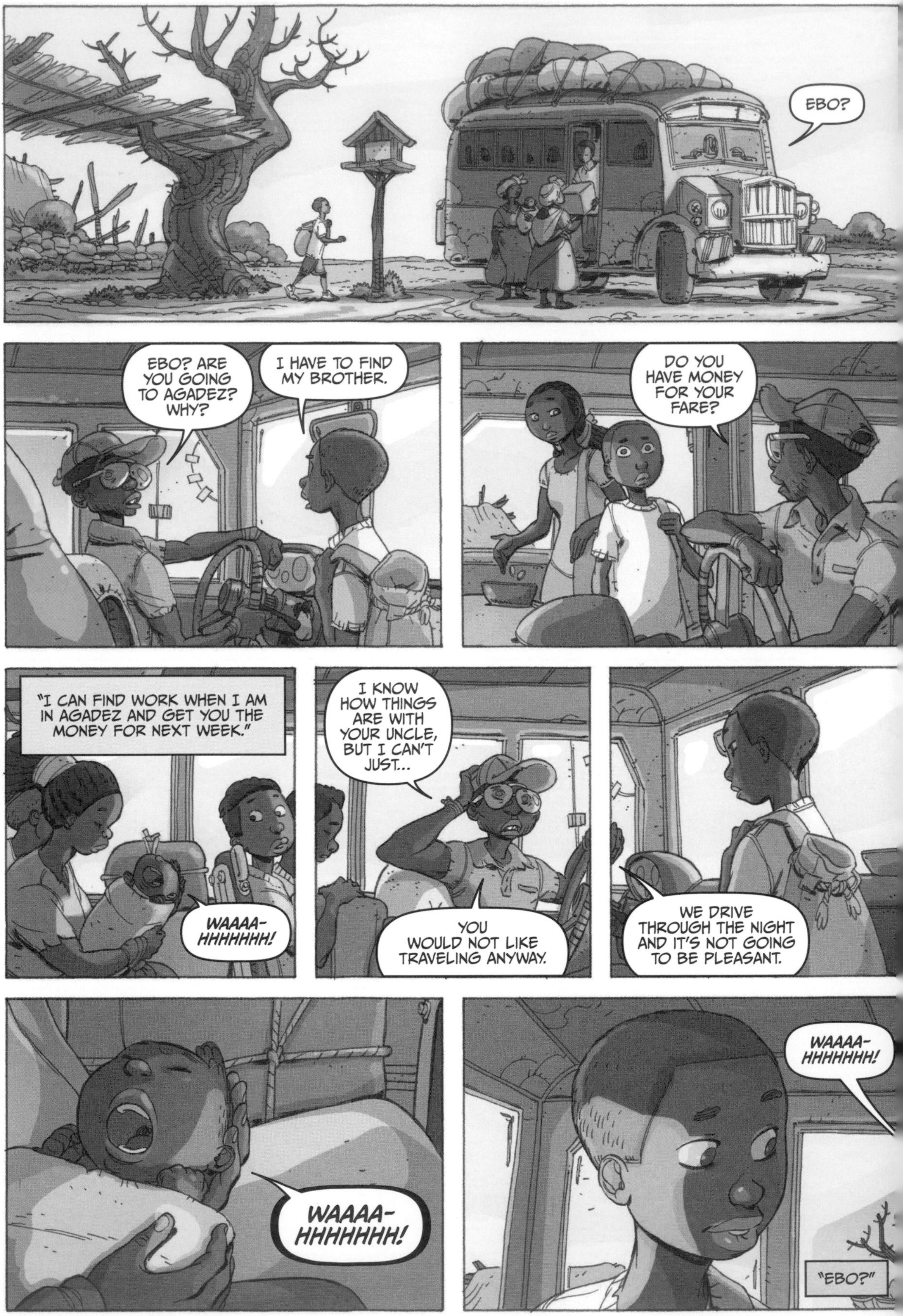
EBO?
EBO? ARE YOU GOING TO AGADEZ? WHY?
I HAVE TO FIND MY BROTHER.
DO YOU HAVE MONEY FOR YOUR FARE?
"I CAN FIND WORK WHEN I AM IN AGADEZ AND GET YOU THE MONEY FOR NEXT WEEK."
WAAAA-HHHHHHH!
I KNOW HOW THINGS ARE WITH YOUR UNCLE, BUT I CAN'T JUST...
YOU WOULD NOT LIKE TRAVELING ANYWAY.
WE DRIVE THROUGH THE NIGHT AND IT'S NOT GOING TO BE PLEASANT.
WAAAA-HHHHHHH!
WAAAA-HHHHHHH!
"EBO?"

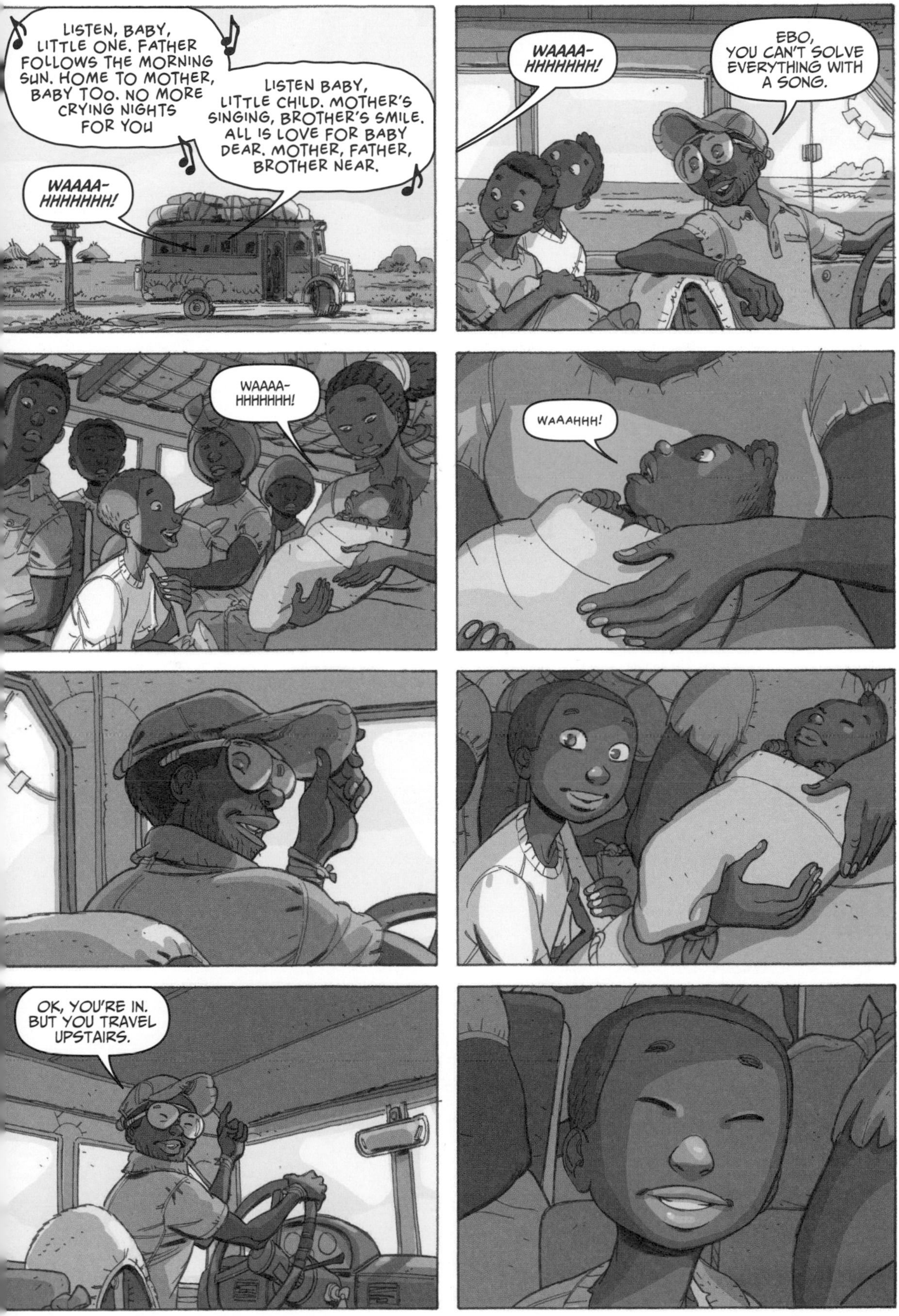
LISTEN, BABY, LITTLE ONE. FATHER FOLLOWS THE MORNING SUN. HOME TO MOTHER, BABY TOO. NO MORE CRYING NIGHTS FOR YOU
LISTEN BABY, LITTLE CHILD. MOTHER'S SINGING, BROTHER'S SMILE. ALL IS LOVE FOR BABY DEAR. MOTHER, FATHER, BROTHER NEAR.
WAAAA-HHHHHHH!
WAAAA-HHHHHHH!
EBO, YOU CAN'T SOLVE EVERYTHING WITH A SONG.
WAAAA-HHHHHHH!
WAAAHHH!
OK, YOU'RE IN. BUT YOU TRAVEL UPSTAIRS.

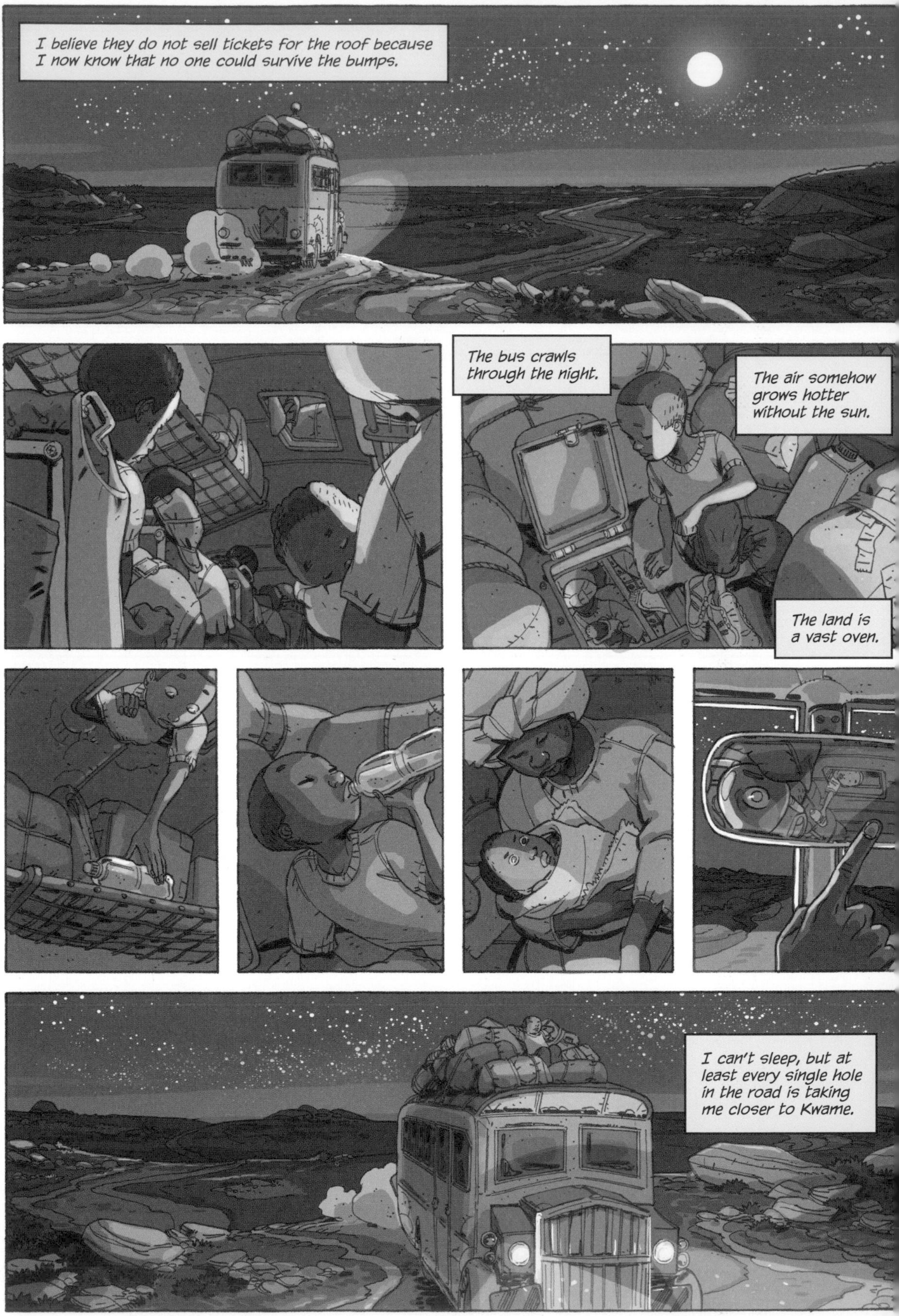

I believe they do not sell tickets for the roof because I now know that no one could survive the bumps.
The bus crawls through the night.
The air somehow grows hotter without the sun.
The land is a vast oven.
I can't sleep, but at least every single hole in the road is taking me closer to Kwame.

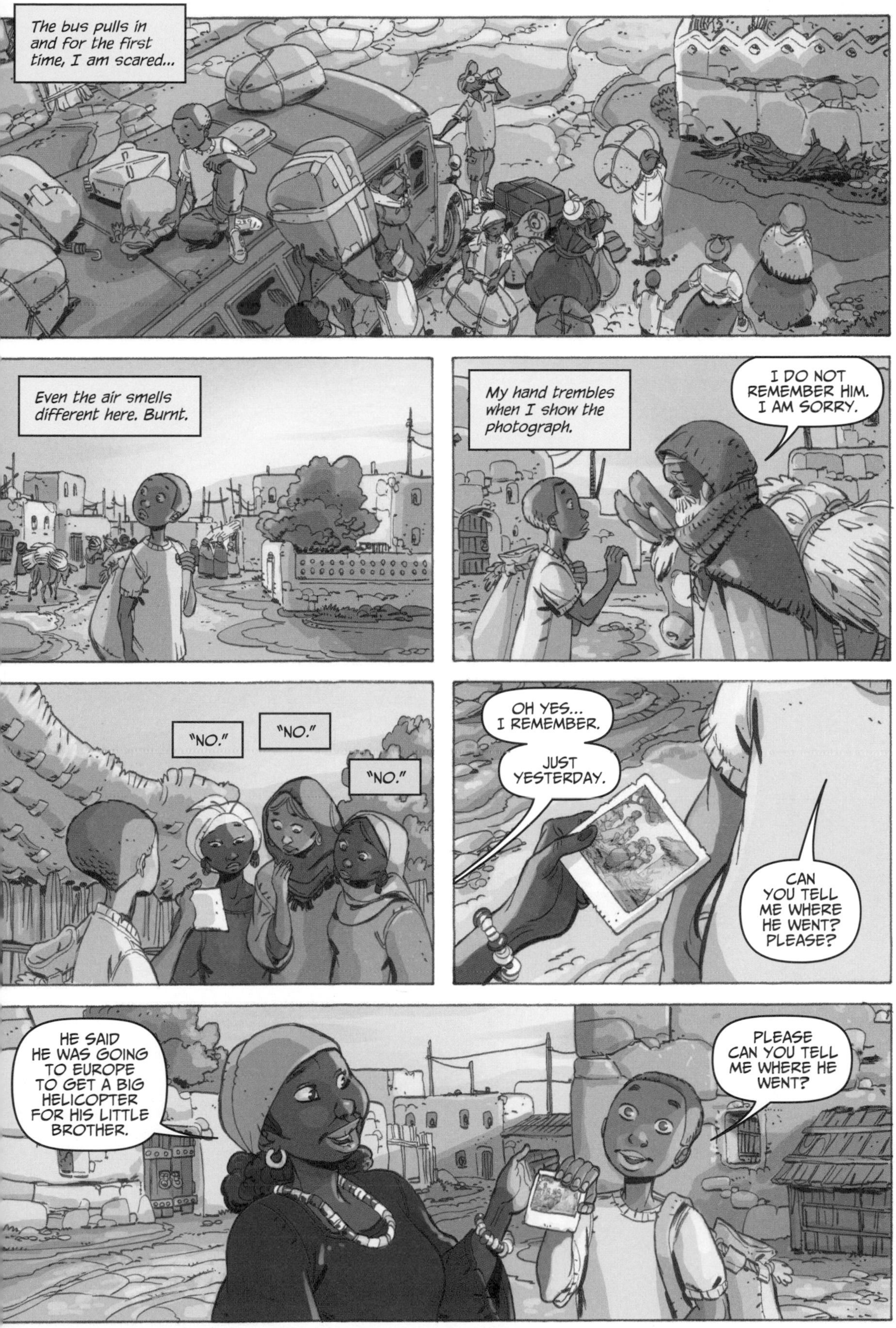
The bus pulls in and for the first time, I am scared...
Even the air smells different here. Burnt.
My hand trembles when I show the photograph.
I DO NOT REMEMBER HIM. I AM SORRY.
"NO."
"NO."
"NO."
OH YES... I REMEMBER.
JUST YESTERDAY.
CAN YOU TELL ME WHERE HE WENT? PLEASE?
HE SAID HE WAS GOING TO EUROPE TO GET A BIG HELICOPTER FOR HIS LITTLE BROTHER.
PLEASE CAN YOU TELL ME WHERE HE WENT?

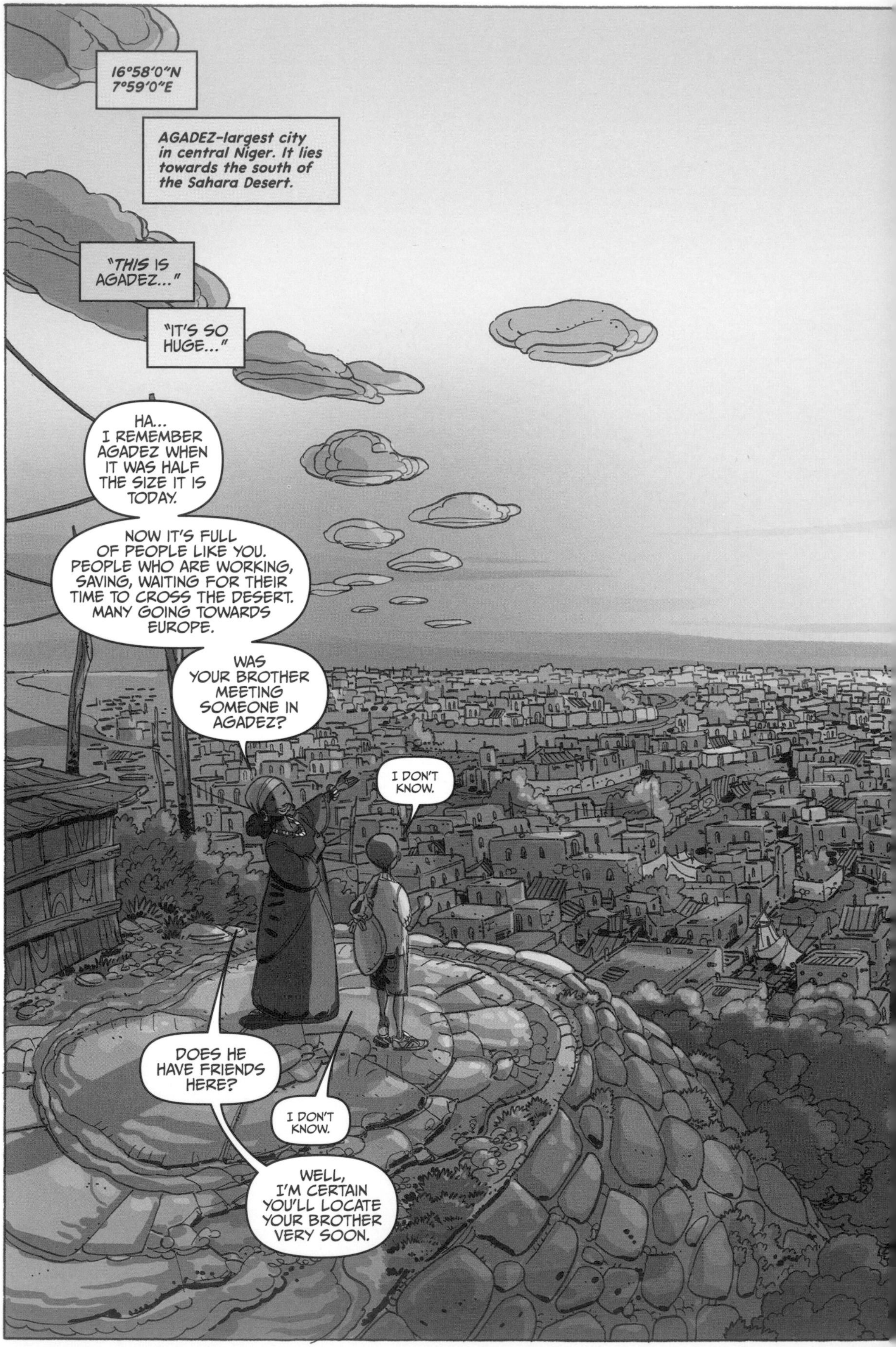
16°58'0"N 7°59'0"E
AGADEZ–largest city in central Niger. It lies towards the south of the Sahara Desert.
"THIS IS AGADEZ..."
"IT'S SO HUGE..."
HA... I REMEMBER AGADEZ WHEN IT WAS HALF THE SIZE IT IS TODAY.
NOW IT'S FULL OF PEOPLE LIKE YOU. PEOPLE WHO ARE WORKING, SAVING, WAITING FOR THEIR TIME TO CROSS THE DESERT. MANY GOING TOWARDS EUROPE.
WAS YOUR BROTHER MEETING SOMEONE IN AGADEZ?
I DON'T KNOW.
DOES HE HAVE FRIENDS HERE?
I DON'T KNOW.
WELL, I'M CERTAIN YOU'LL LOCATE YOUR BROTHER VERY SOON.

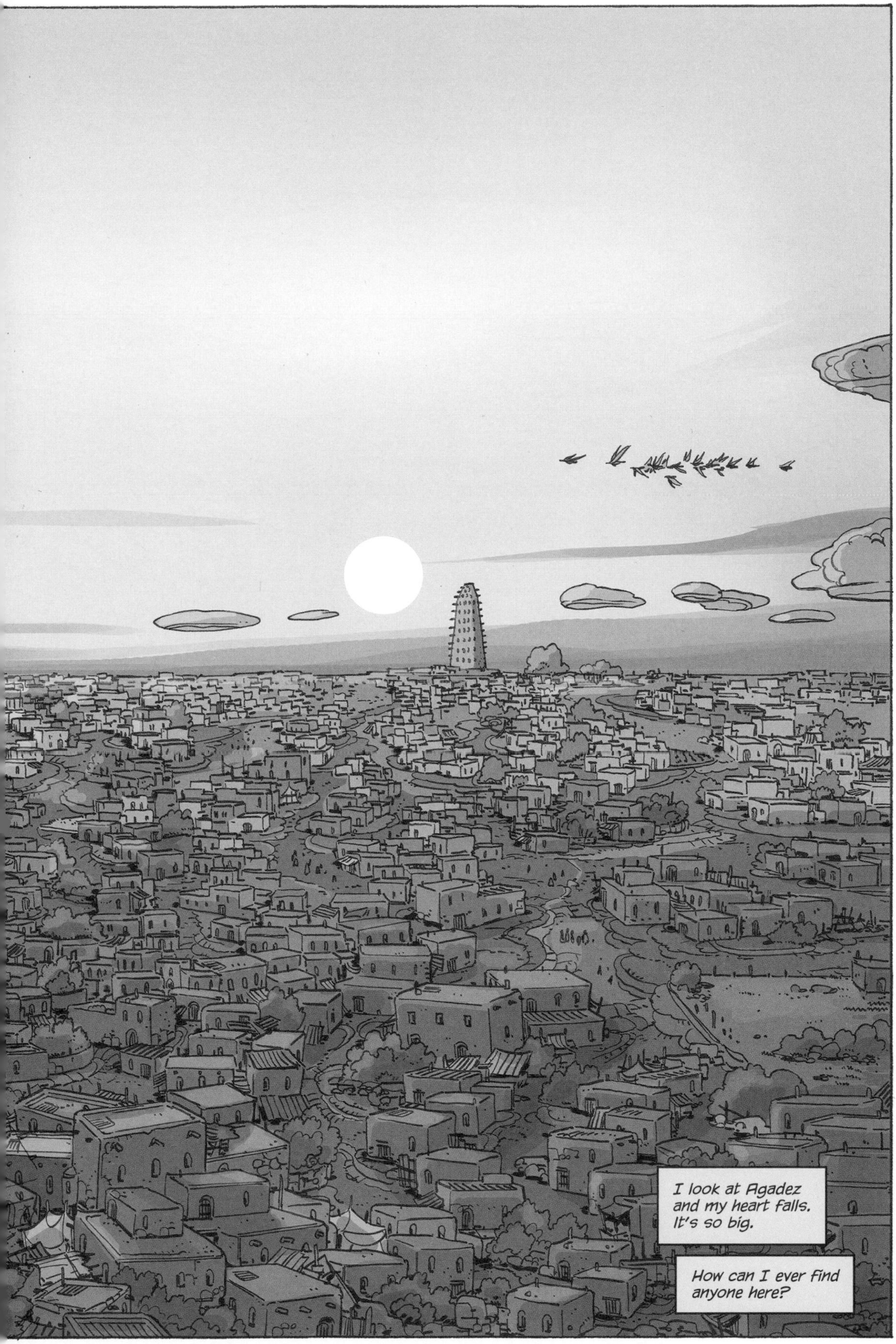
I look at Agadez and my heart falls. It's so big.
How can I ever find anyone here?

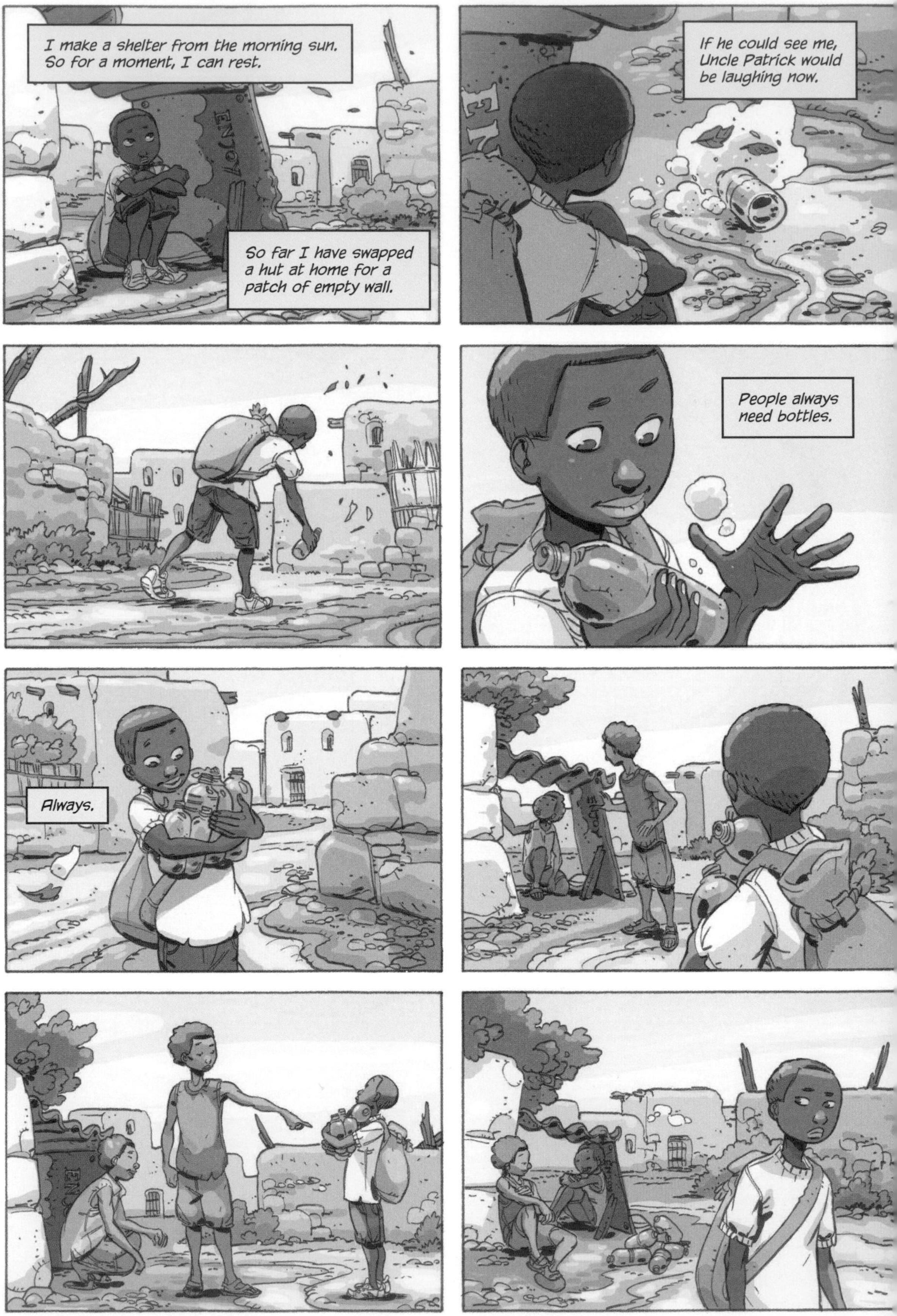
I make a shelter from the morning sun.
So for a moment, I can rest.
So far I have swapped a hut at home for a patch of empty wall.
If he could see me, Uncle Patrick would be laughing now.
People always need bottles.
Always.

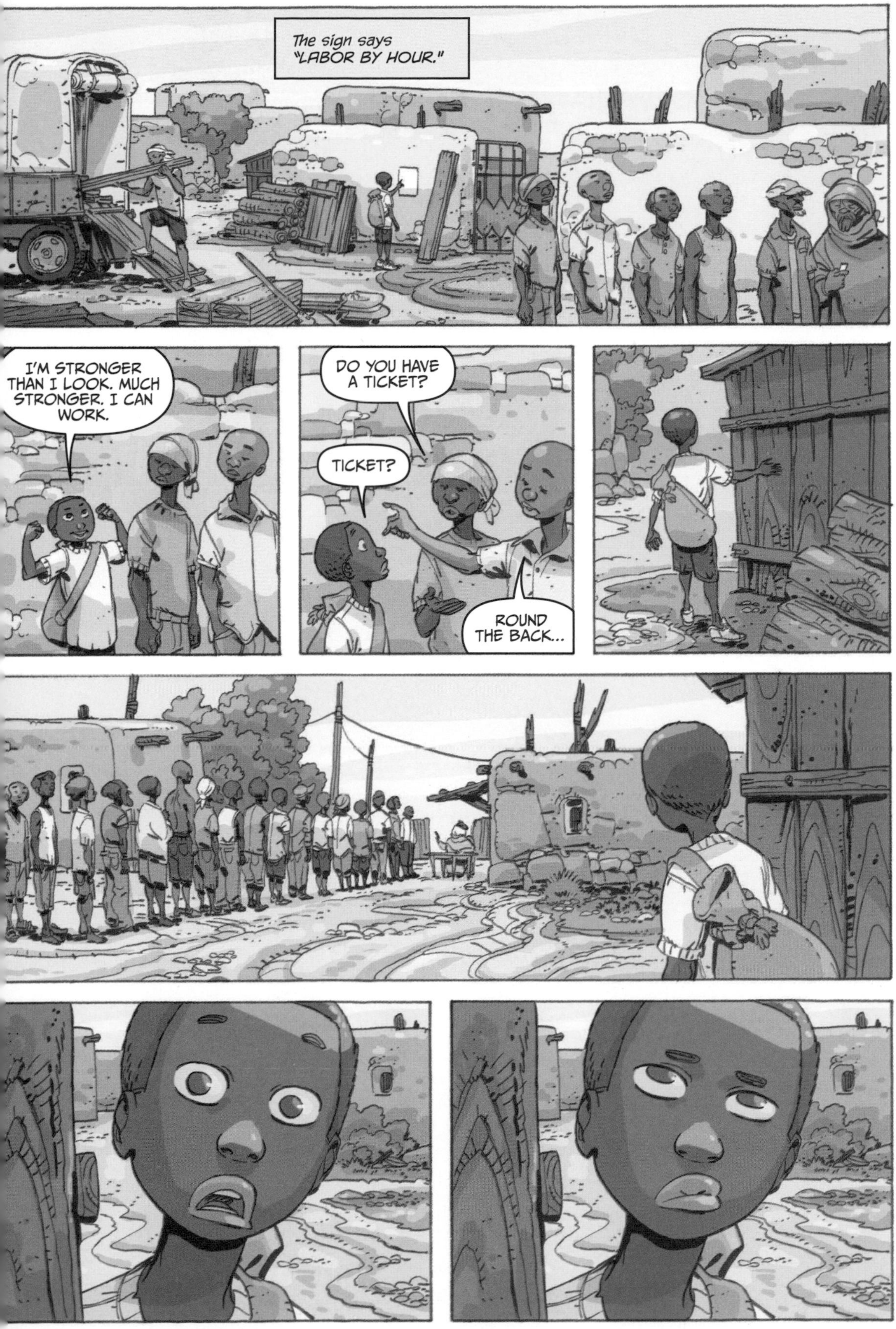
The sign says "LABOR BY HOUR."
I'M STRONGER THAN I LOOK. MUCH STRONGER. I CAN WORK.
DO YOU HAVE A TICKET?
TICKET?
ROUND THE BACK...

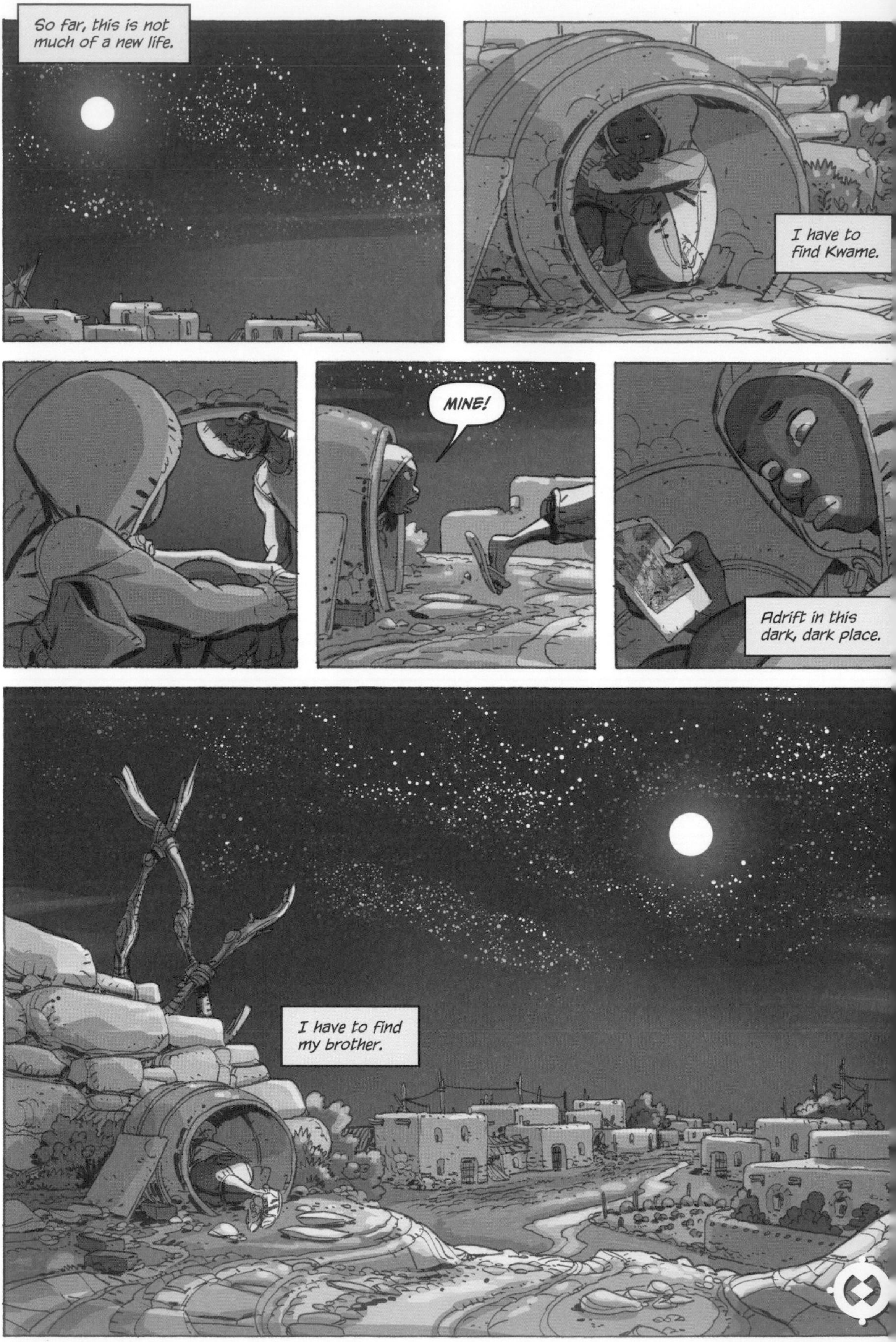
So far, this is not much of a new life.
I have to find Kwame.
MINE!
Adrift in this dark, dark place.
I have to find my brother.

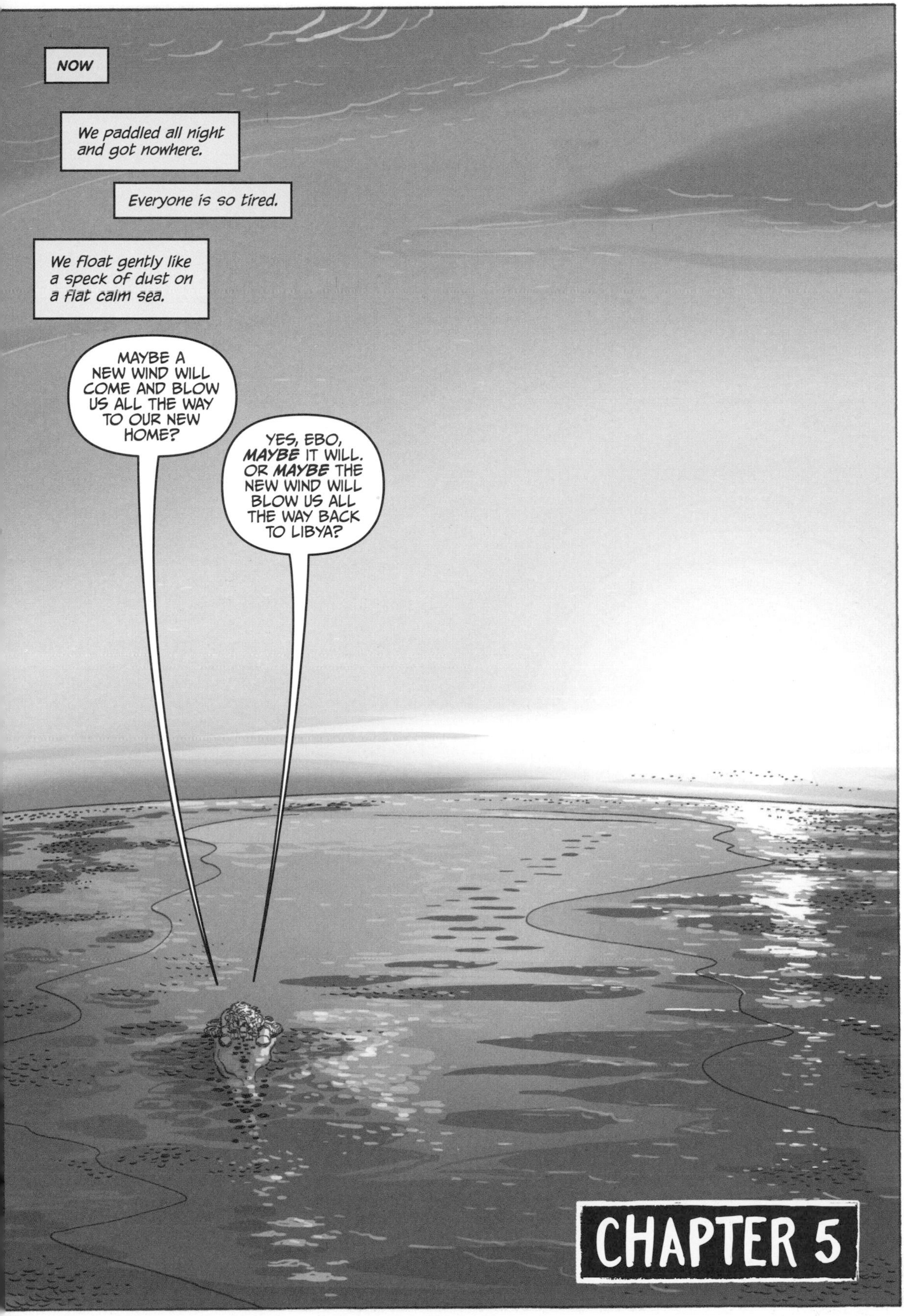
NOW
We paddled all night and got nowhere.
Everyone is so tired.
We float gently like a speck of dust on a flat calm sea.
MAYBE A NEW WIND WILL COME AND BLOW US ALL THE WAY TO OUR NEW HOME?
YES, EBO, *MAYBE* IT WILL. OR *MAYBE* THE NEW WIND WILL BLOW US ALL THE WAY BACK TO LIBYA?
CHAPTER 5

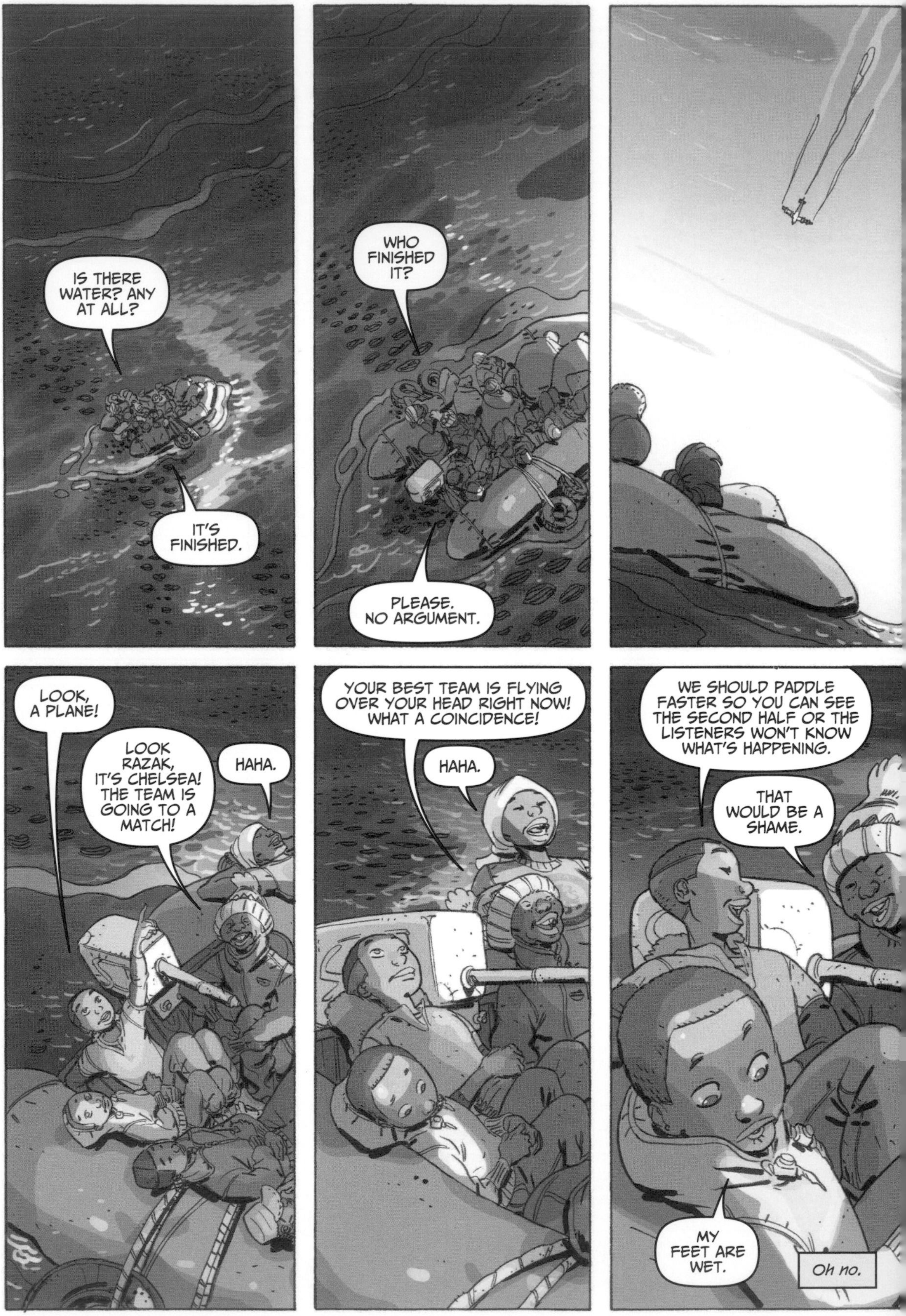
IS THERE WATER? ANY AT ALL?
IT'S FINISHED.
WHO FINISHED IT?
PLEASE. NO ARGUMENT.
LOOK, A PLANE!
LOOK RAZAK, IT'S CHELSEA! THE TEAM IS GOING TO A MATCH!
HAHA.
YOUR BEST TEAM IS FLYING OVER YOUR HEAD RIGHT NOW! WHAT A COINCIDENCE!
HAHA.
WE SHOULD PADDLE FASTER SO YOU CAN SEE THE SECOND HALF OR THE LISTENERS WON'T KNOW WHAT'S HAPPENING.
THAT WOULD BE A SHAME.
MY FEET ARE WET.
Oh no.

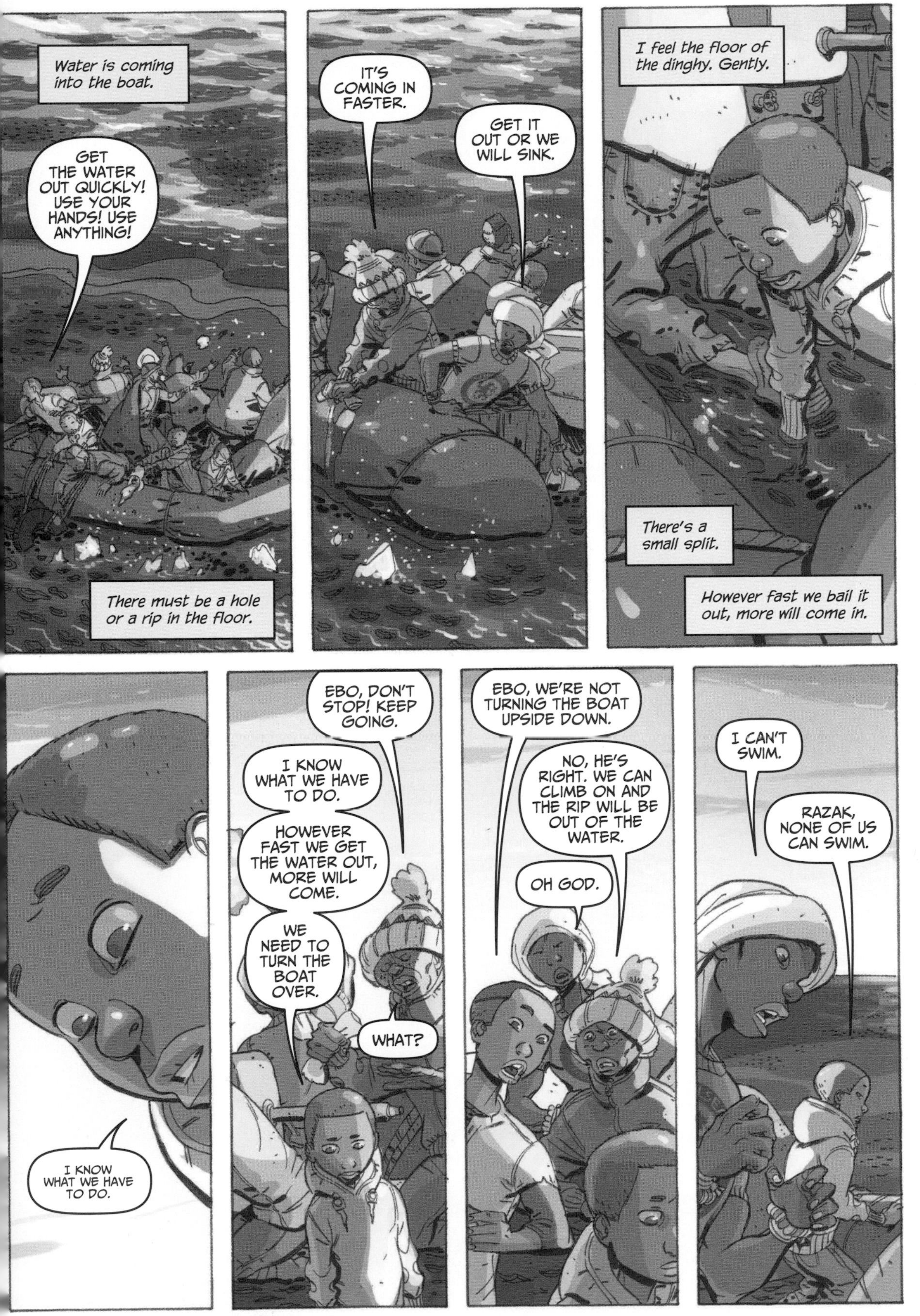
Water is coming into the boat.
GET THE WATER OUT QUICKLY! USE YOUR HANDS! USE ANYTHING!
There must be a hole or a rip in the floor.
IT'S COMING IN FASTER.
GET IT OUT OR WE WILL SINK.
I feel the floor of the dinghy. Gently.
There's a small split.
However fast we bail it out, more will come in.
I KNOW WHAT WE HAVE TO DO.
EBO, DON'T STOP! KEEP GOING.
I KNOW WHAT WE HAVE TO DO.
HOWEVER FAST WE GET THE WATER OUT, MORE WILL COME.
WE NEED TO TURN THE BOAT OVER.
WHAT?
EBO, WE'RE NOT TURNING THE BOAT UPSIDE DOWN.
NO, HE'S RIGHT. WE CAN CLIMB ON AND THE RIP WILL BE OUT OF THE WATER.
OH GOD.
I CAN'T SWIM.
RAZAK, NONE OF US CAN SWIM.

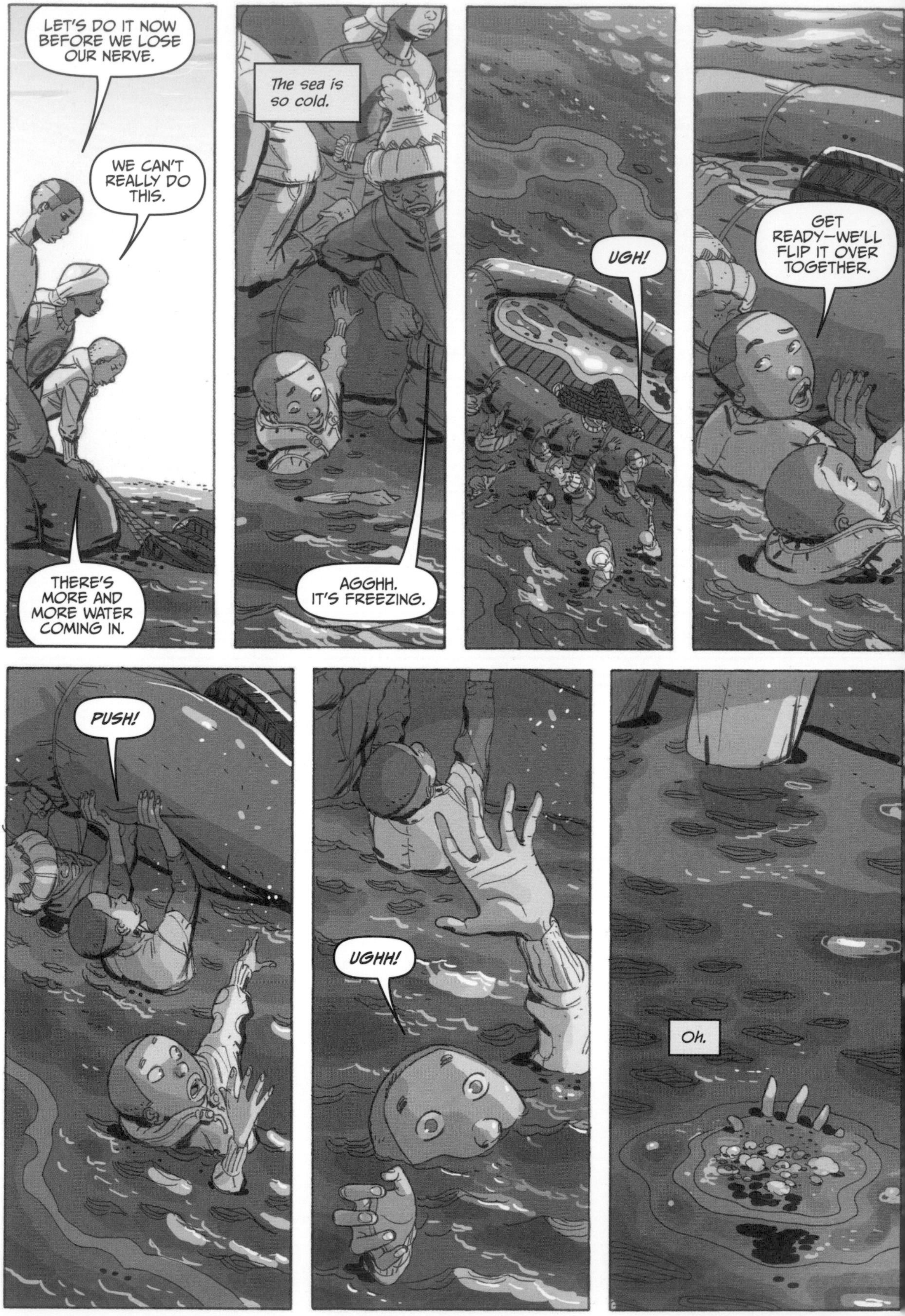
LET'S DO IT NOW BEFORE WE LOSE OUR NERVE.
WE CAN'T REALLY DO THIS.
THERE'S MORE AND MORE WATER COMING IN.
The sea is so cold.
AGGHH. IT'S FREEZING.
UGH!
GET READY—WE'LL FLIP IT OVER TOGETHER.
PUSH!
UGHH!
Oh.

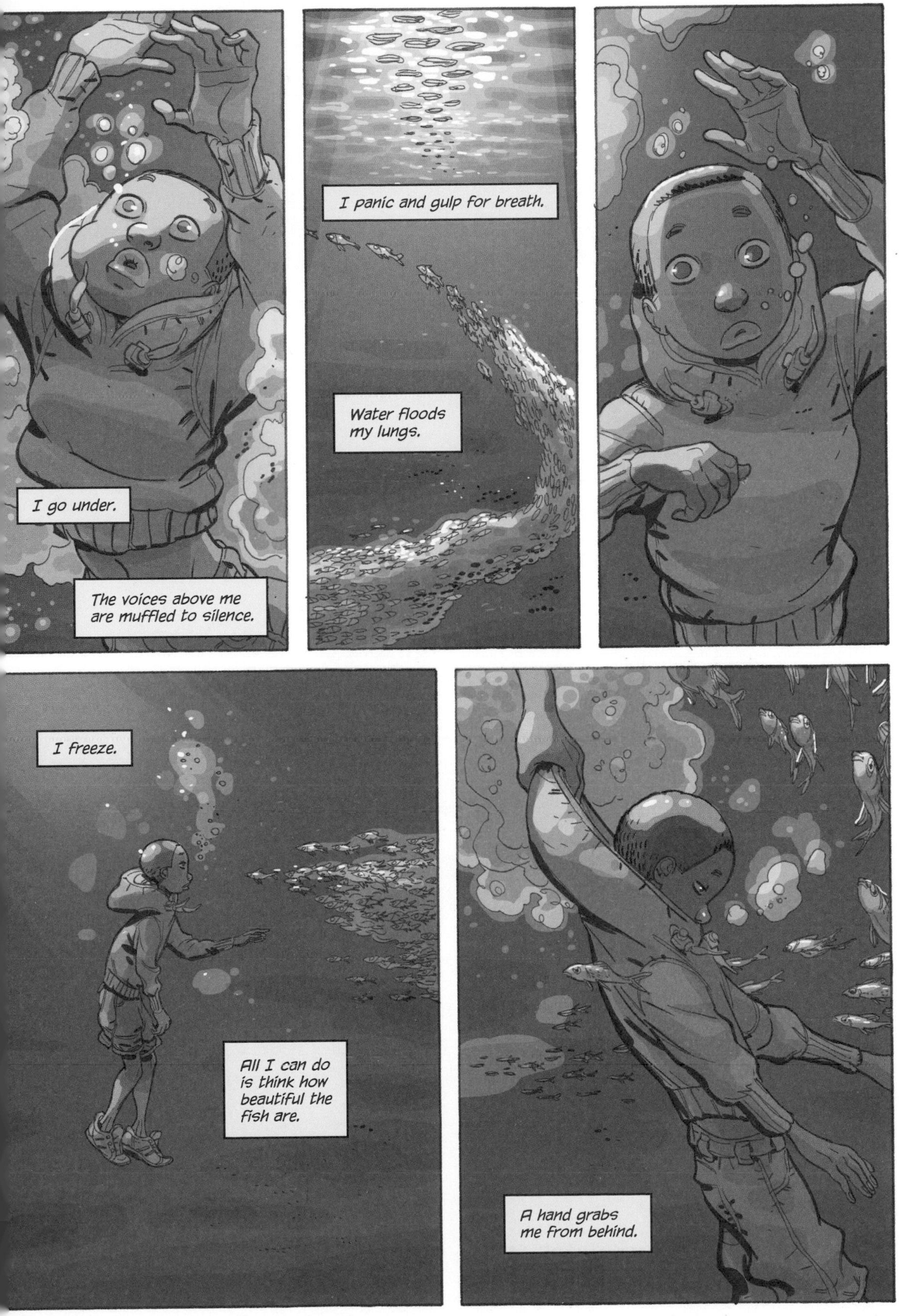
I go under.
The voices above me are muffled to silence.
I panic and gulp for breath.
Water floods my lungs.
I freeze.
All I can do is think how beautiful the fish are.
A hand grabs me from behind.

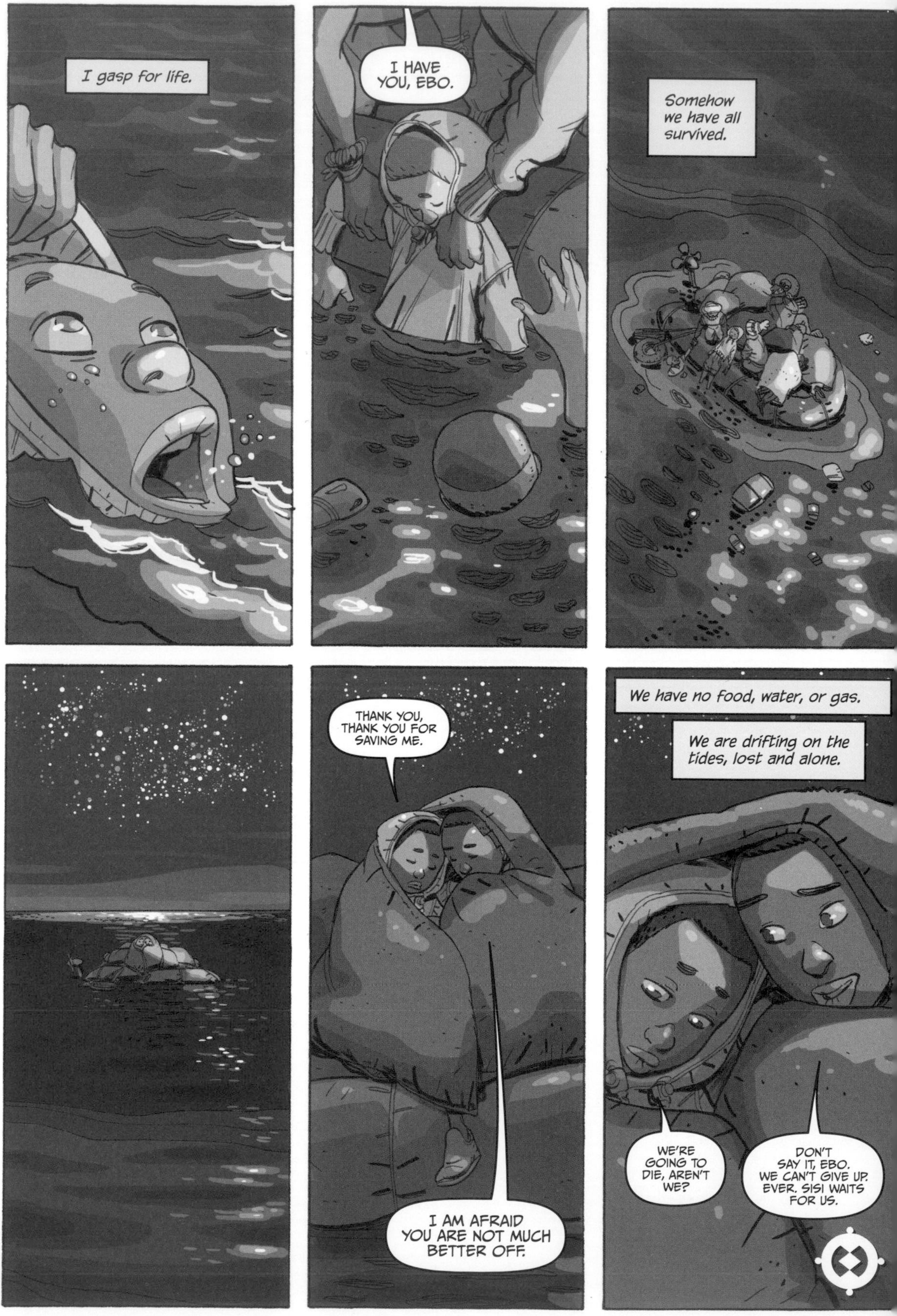
I gasp for life.
I HAVE YOU, EBO.
Somehow we have all survived.
THANK YOU, THANK YOU FOR SAVING ME.
I AM AFRAID YOU ARE NOT MUCH BETTER OFF.
We have no food, water, or gas.
We are drifting on the tides, lost and alone.
WE'RE GOING TO DIE, AREN'T WE?
DON'T SAY IT, EBO. WE CAN'T GIVE UP. EVER. SISI WAITS FOR US.

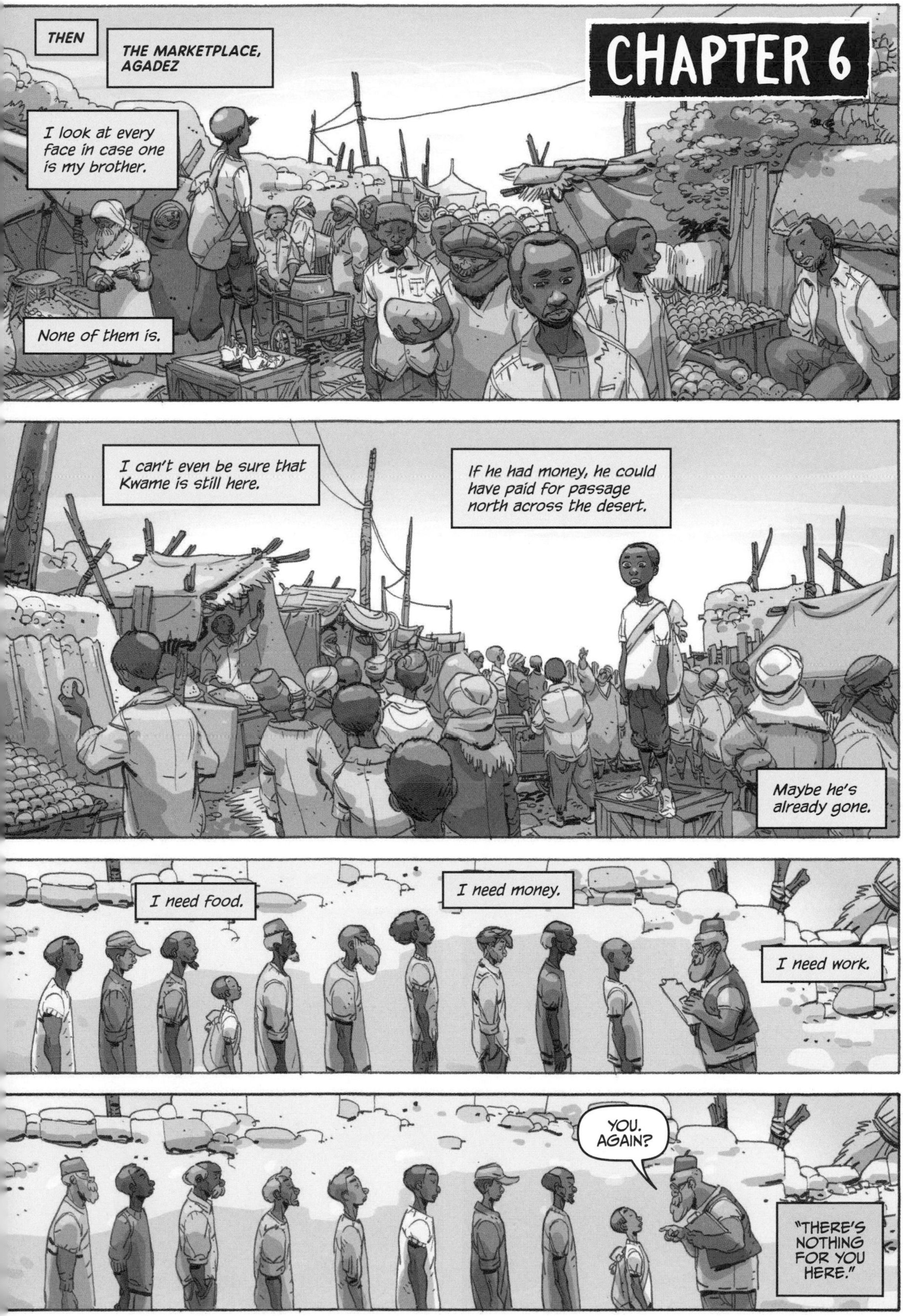
THEN
THE MARKETPLACE, AGADEZ
CHAPTER 6
I look at every face in case one is my brother.
None of them is.
I can't even be sure that Kwame is still here.
If he had money, he could have paid for passage north across the desert.
Maybe he's already gone.
I need food.
I need money.
I need work.
YOU. AGAIN?
"THERE'S NOTHING FOR YOU HERE."

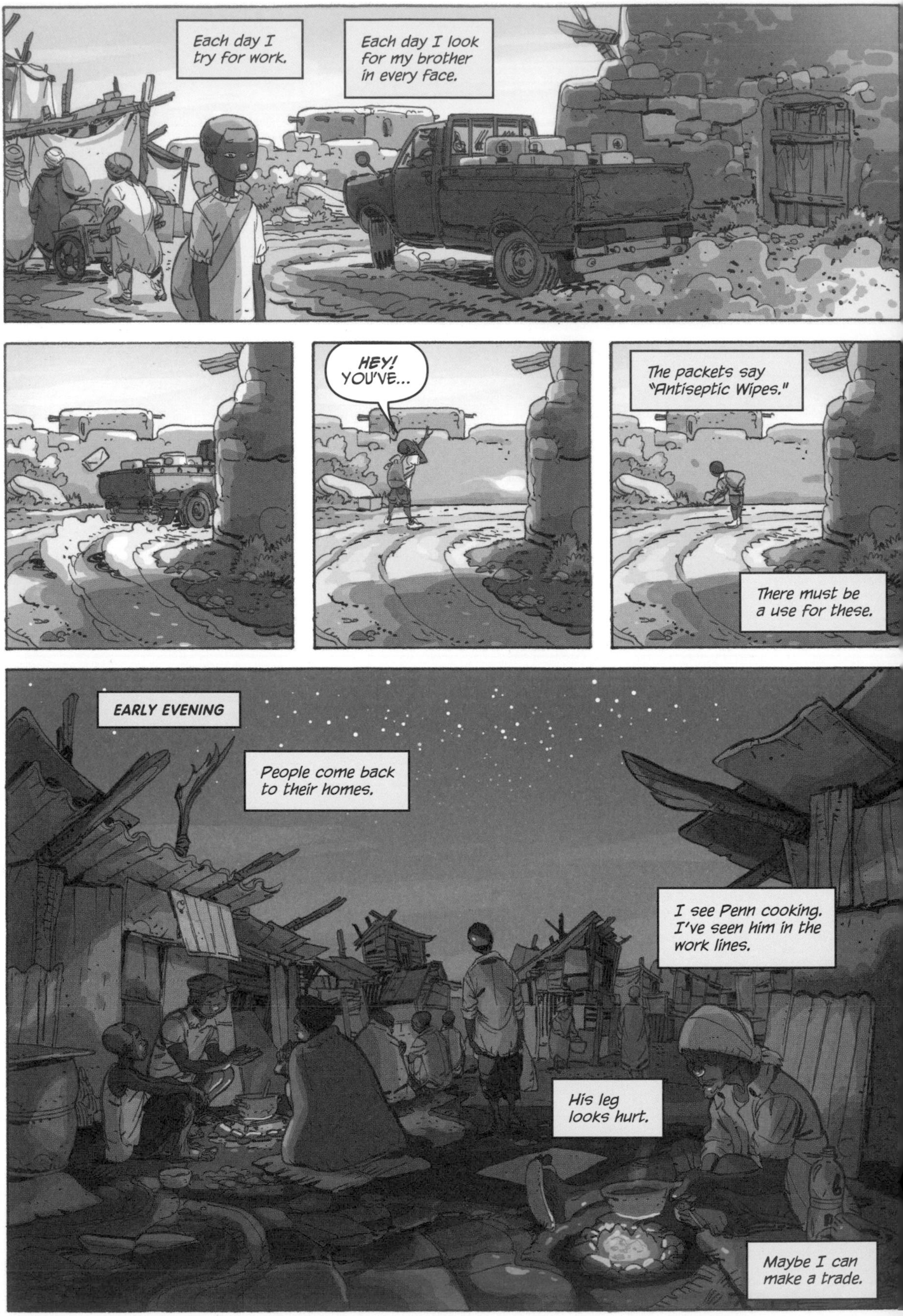
Each day I try for work.
Each day I look for my brother in every face.
HEY! YOU'VE...
The packets say "Antiseptic Wipes."
There must be a use for these.
EARLY EVENING
People come back to their homes.
I see Penn cooking. I've seen him in the work lines.
His leg looks hurt.
Maybe I can make a trade.

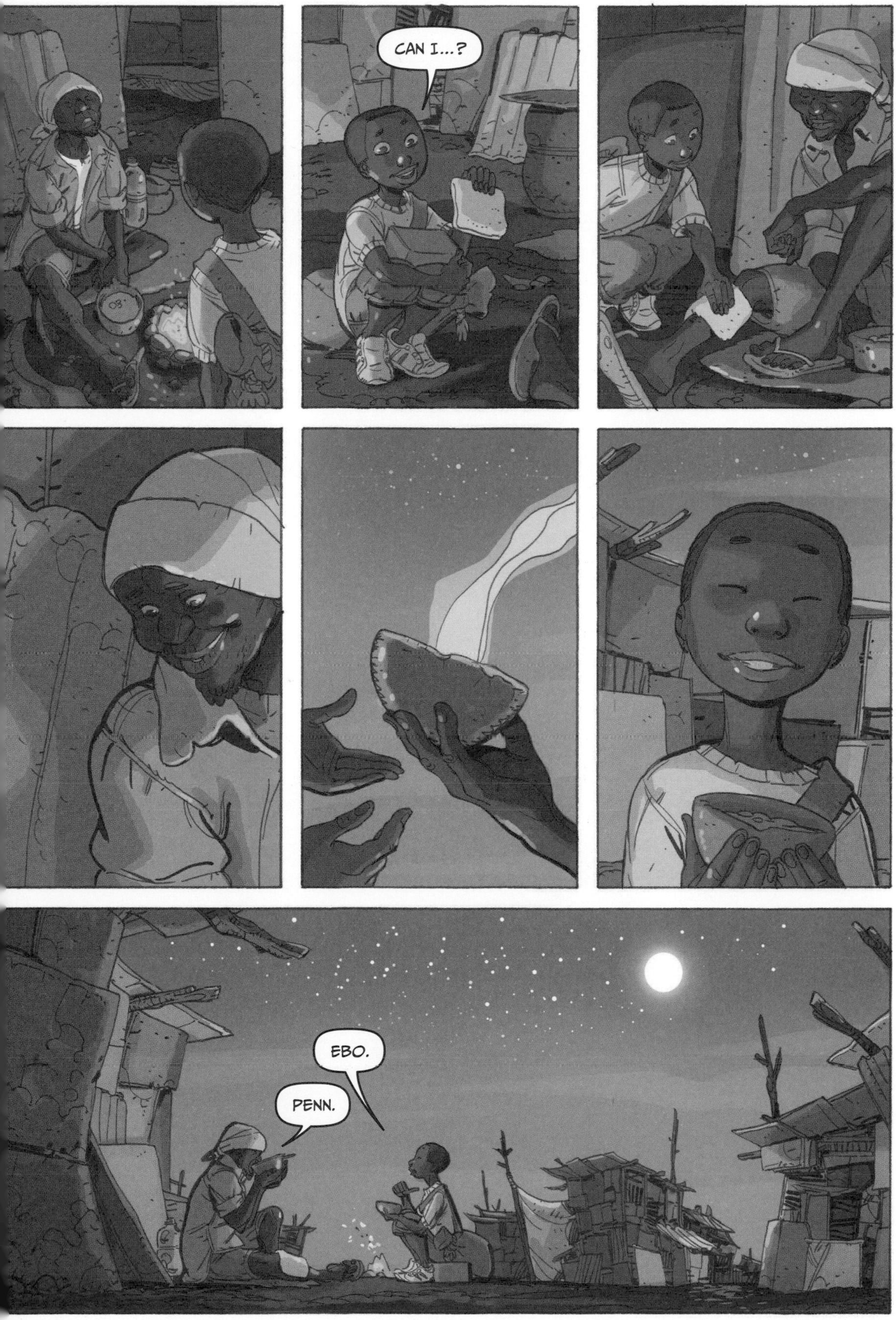
CAN I...?
EBO.
PENN.

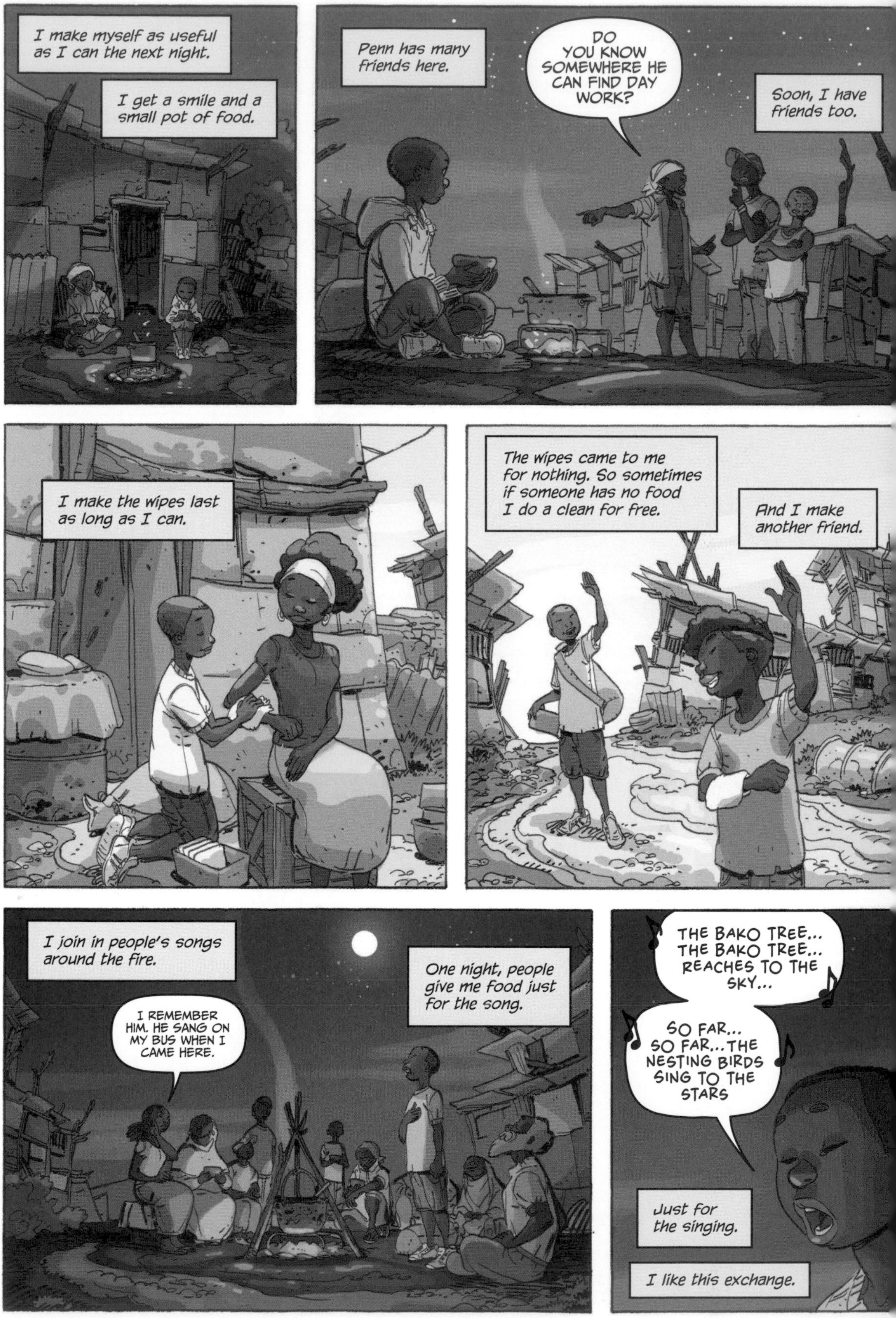
I make myself as useful as I can the next night.
I get a smile and a small pot of food.
Penn has many friends here.
DO YOU KNOW SOMEWHERE HE CAN FIND DAY WORK?
Soon, I have friends too.
I make the wipes last as long as I can.
The wipes came to me for nothing. So sometimes if someone has no food I do a clean for free.
And I make another friend.
I join in people's songs around the fire.
I REMEMBER HIM. HE SANG ON MY BUS WHEN I CAME HERE.
One night, people give me food just for the song.
THE BAKO TREE... THE BAKO TREE... REACHES TO THE SKY...
SO FAR... SO FAR... THE NESTING BIRDS SING TO THE STARS
Just for the singing.
I like this exchange.

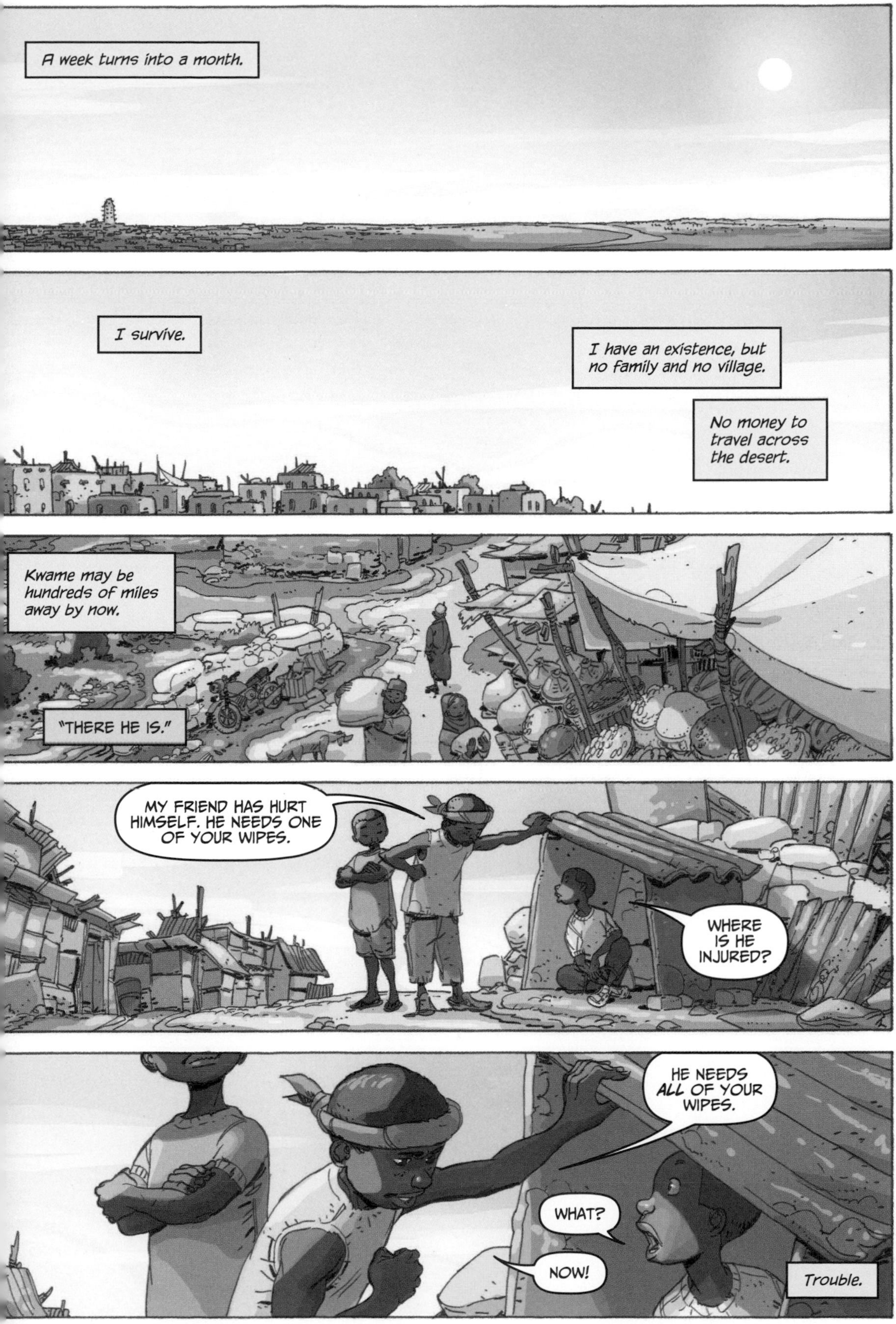
A week turns into a month.
I survive.
I have an existence, but no family and no village.
No money to travel across the desert.
Kwame may be hundreds of miles away by now.
"THERE HE IS."
MY FRIEND HAS HURT HIMSELF. HE NEEDS ONE OF YOUR WIPES.
WHERE IS HE INJURED?
HE NEEDS ALL OF YOUR WIPES.
WHAT?
NOW!
Trouble.

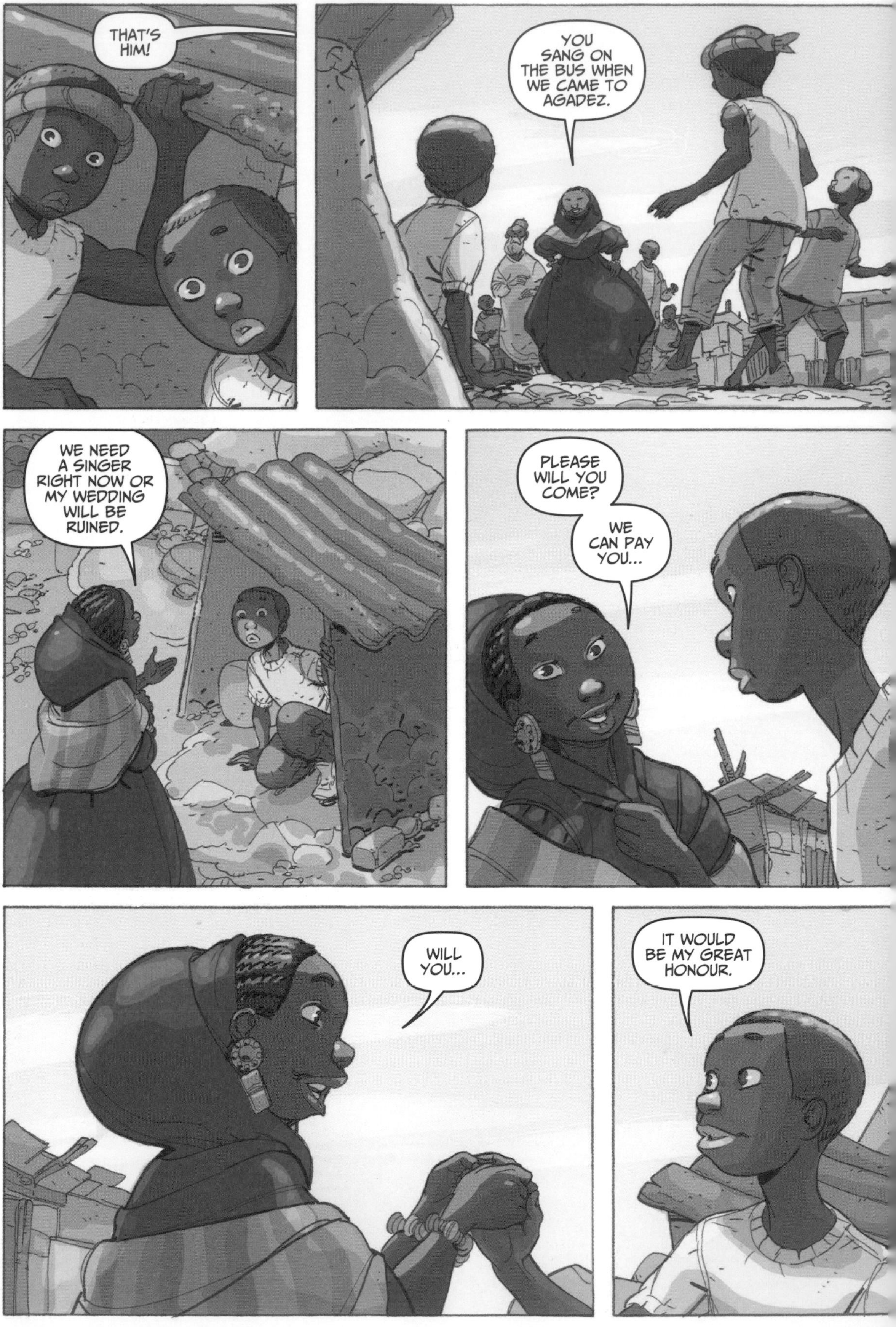
THAT'S HIM!
YOU SANG ON THE BUS WHEN WE CAME TO AGADEZ.
WE NEED A SINGER RIGHT NOW OR MY WEDDING WILL BE RUINED.
PLEASE WILL YOU COME?
WE CAN PAY YOU...
WILL YOU...
IT WOULD BE MY GREAT HONOUR.

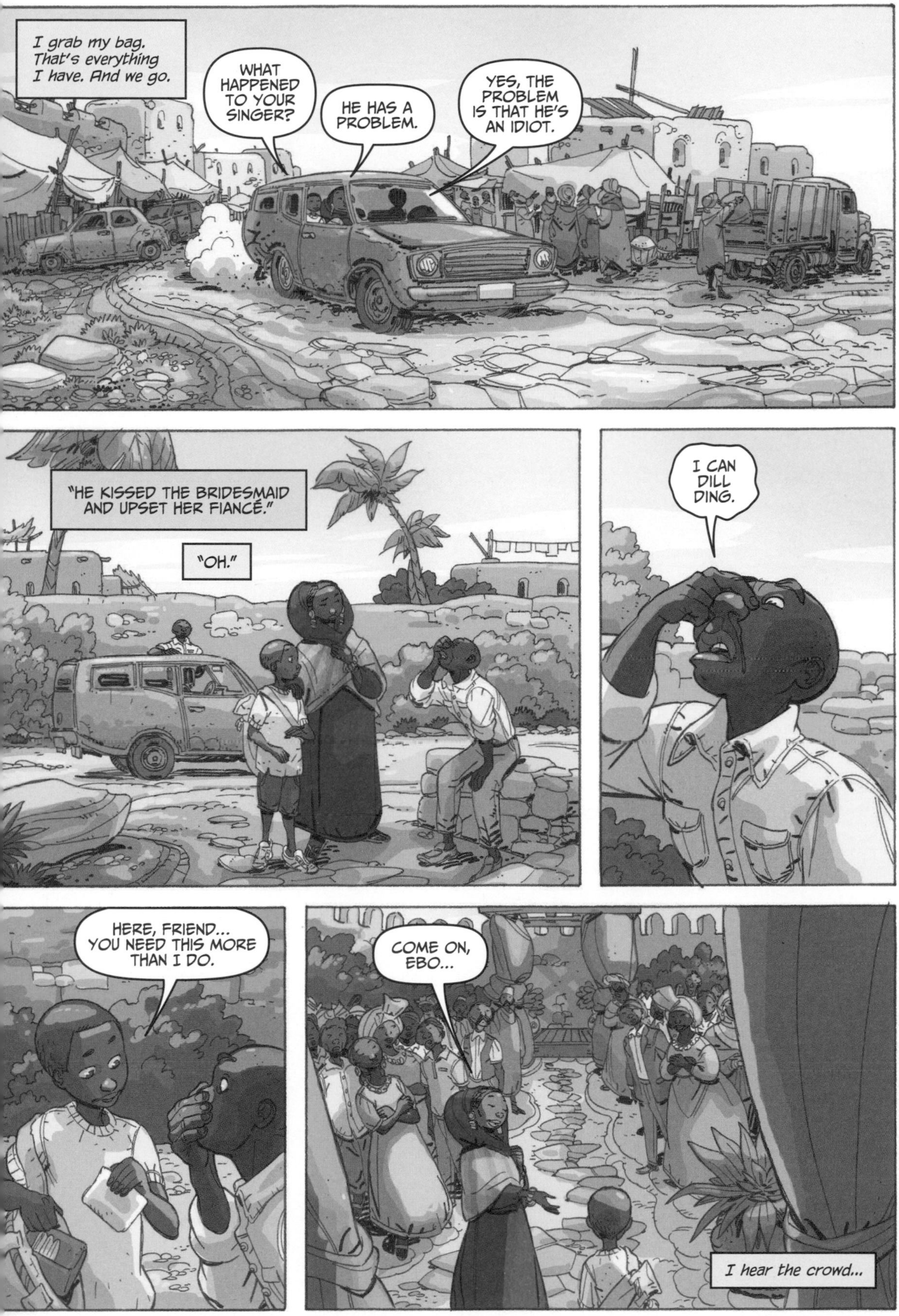
I grab my bag. That's everything I have. And we go.
WHAT HAPPENED TO YOUR SINGER?
HE HAS A PROBLEM.
YES, THE PROBLEM IS THAT HE'S AN IDIOT.
"HE KISSED THE BRIDESMAID AND UPSET HER FIANCÉ."
"OH."
I CAN DILL DING.
HERE, FRIEND... YOU NEED THIS MORE THAN I DO.
COME ON, EBO...
I hear the crowd...

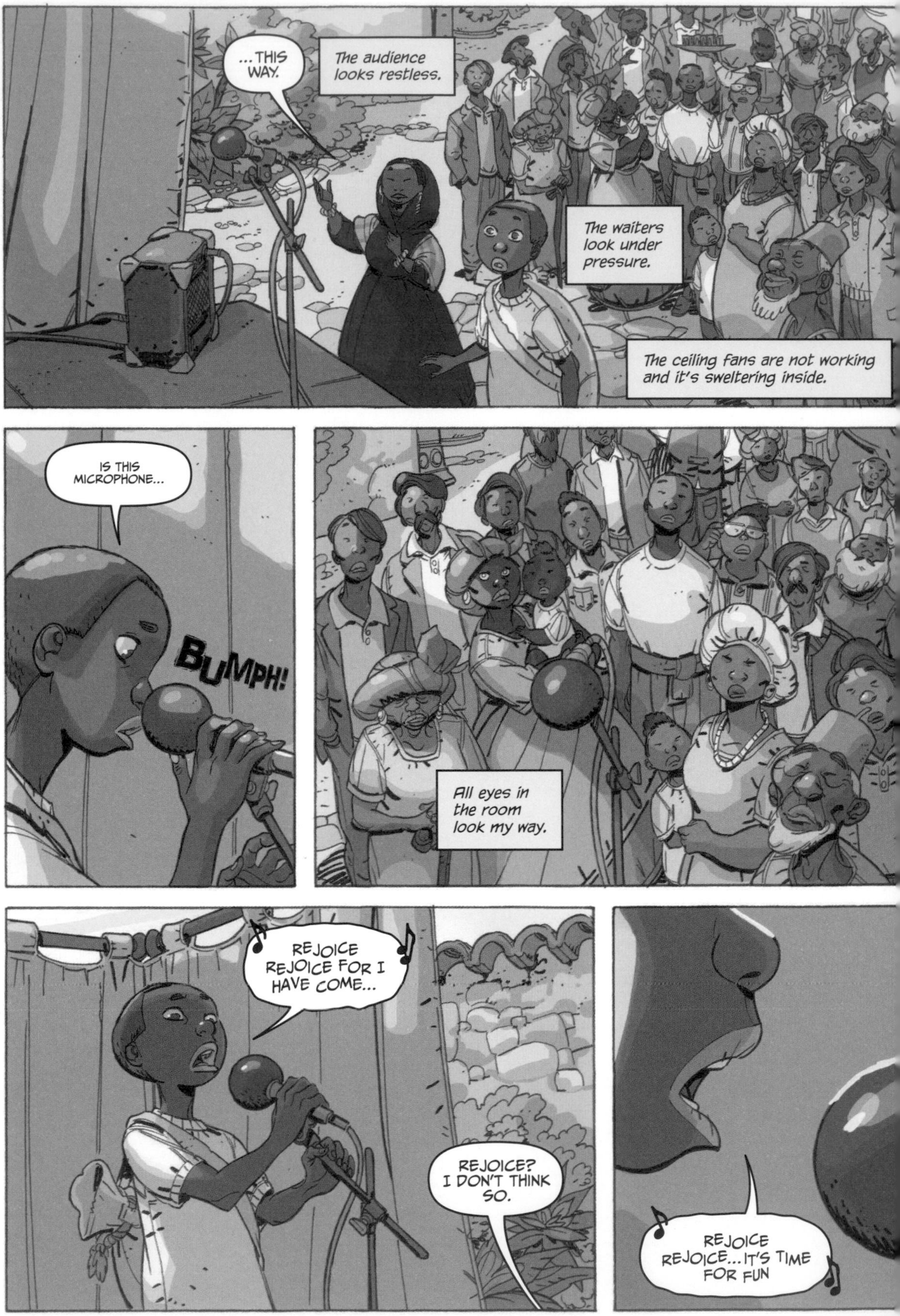
...THIS WAY.
The audience looks restless.
The waiters look under pressure.
The ceiling fans are not working and it's sweltering inside.
IS THIS MICROPHONE...
BUMPH!
All eyes in the room look my way.
REJOICE REJOICE FOR I HAVE COME...
REJOICE? I DON'T THINK SO.
REJOICE REJOICE... IT'S TIME FOR FUN

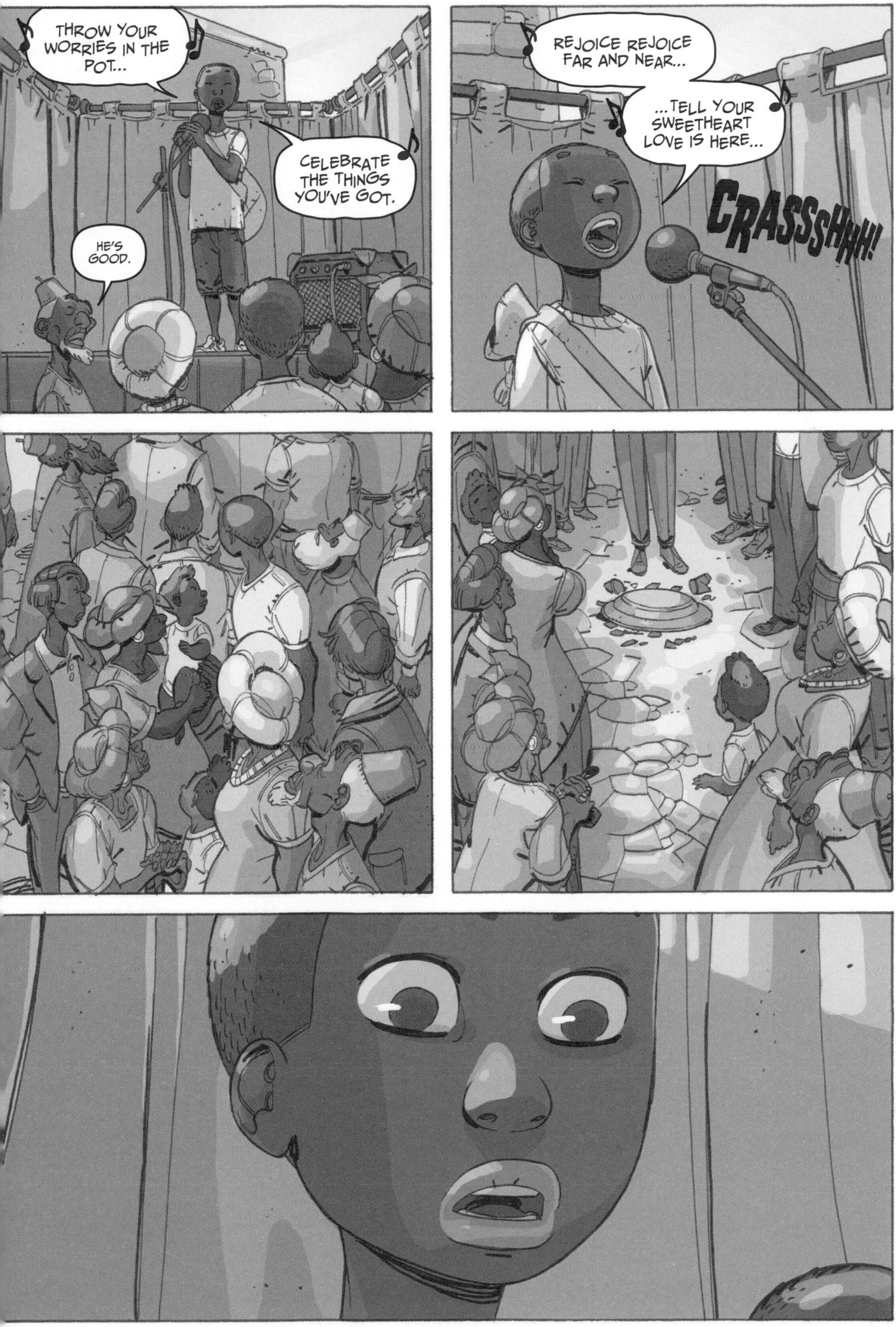
THROW YOUR WORRIES IN THE POT...
CELEBRATE THE THINGS YOU'VE GOT.
HE'S GOOD.
REJOICE REJOICE FAR AND NEAR...
...TELL YOUR SWEETHEART LOVE IS HERE...
CRASSSHHH!

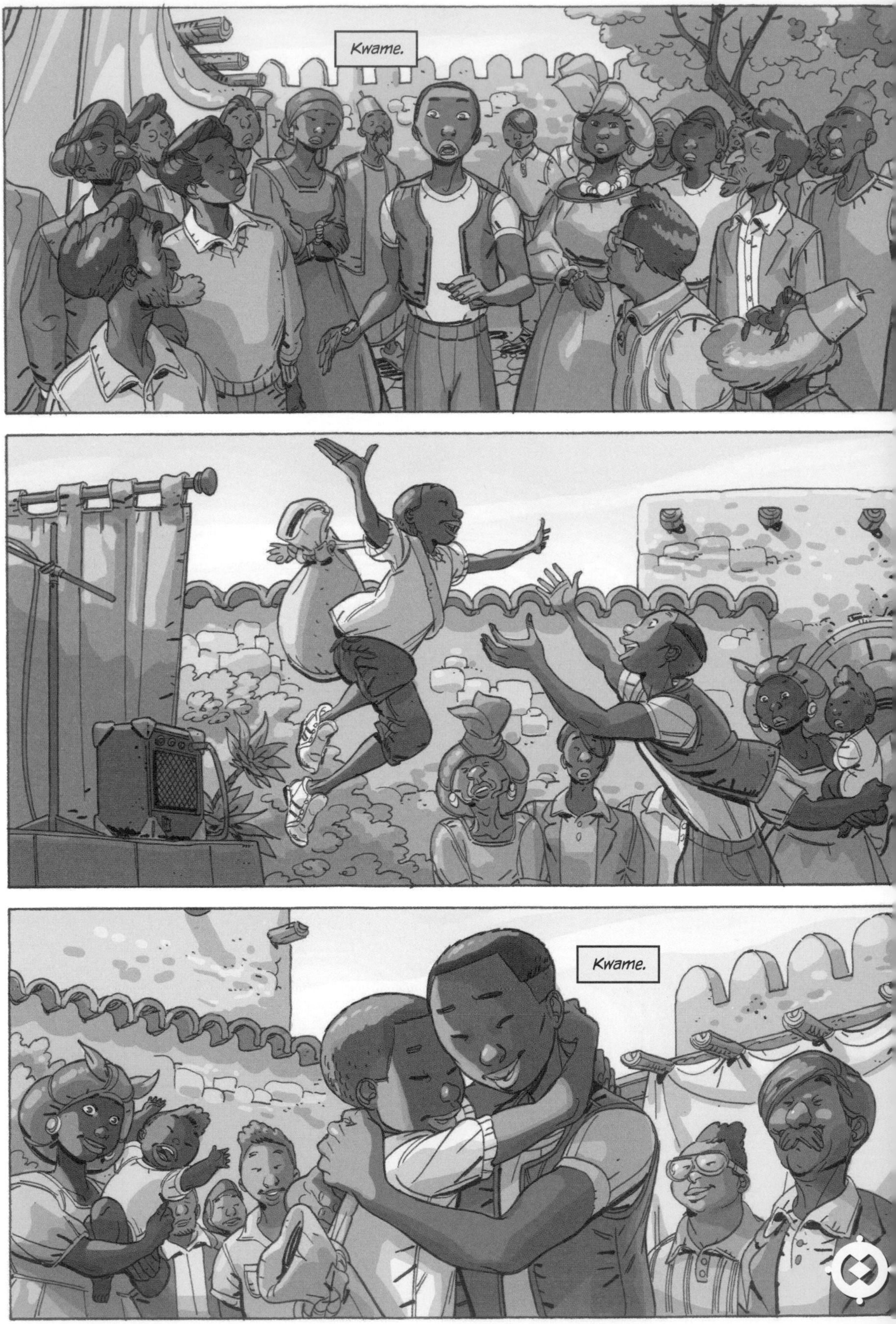
Kwame.
Kwame.

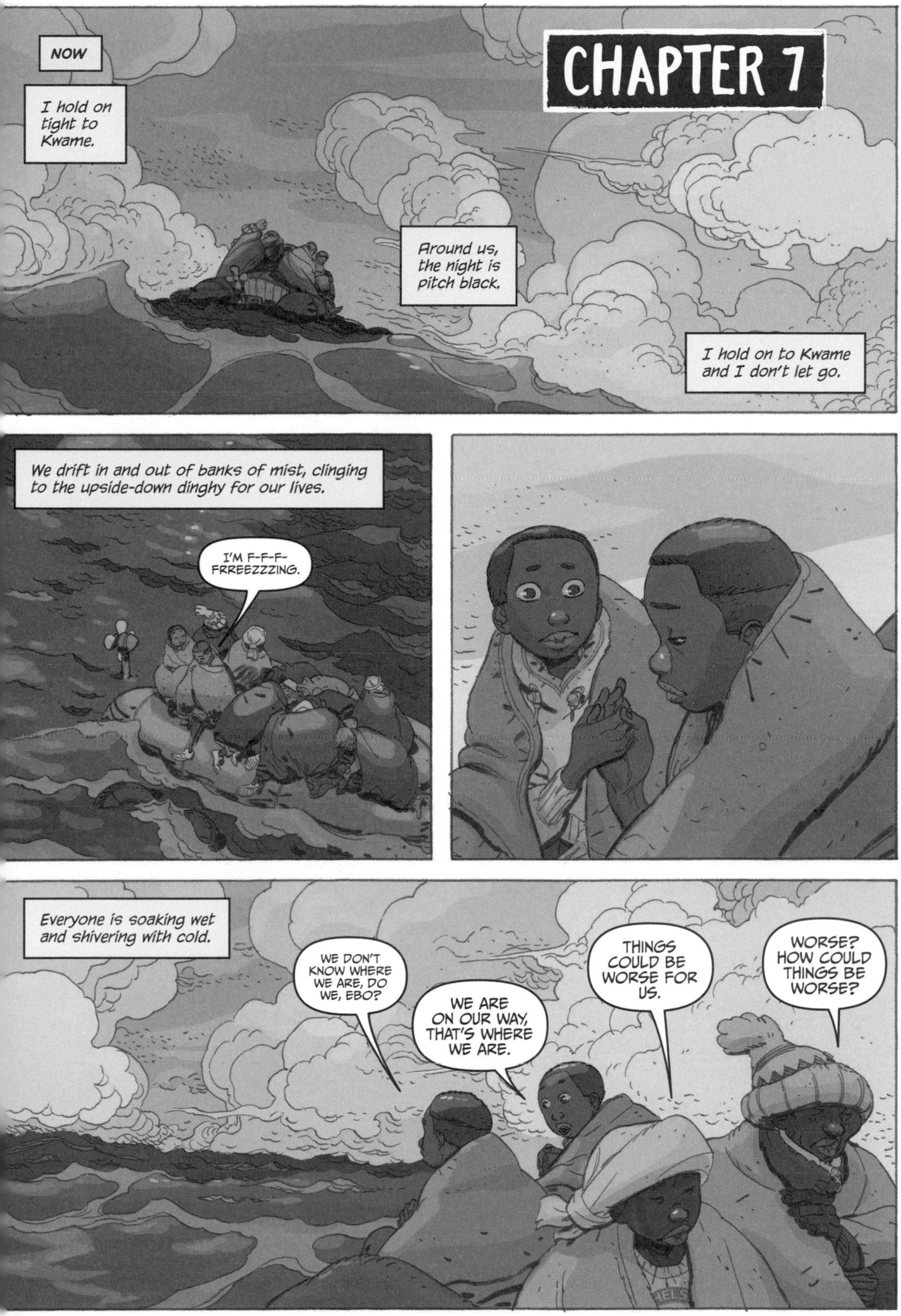
NOW
CHAPTER 7
I hold on tight to Kwame.
Around us, the night is pitch black.
I hold on to Kwame and I don't let go.
We drift in and out of banks of mist, clinging to the upside-down dinghy for our lives.
I'M F-F-F-FRREEZZZING.
Everyone is soaking wet and shivering with cold.
WE DON'T KNOW WHERE WE ARE, DO WE, EBO?
WE ARE ON OUR WAY, THAT'S WHERE WE ARE.
THINGS COULD BE WORSE FOR US.
WORSE? HOW COULD THINGS BE WORSE?

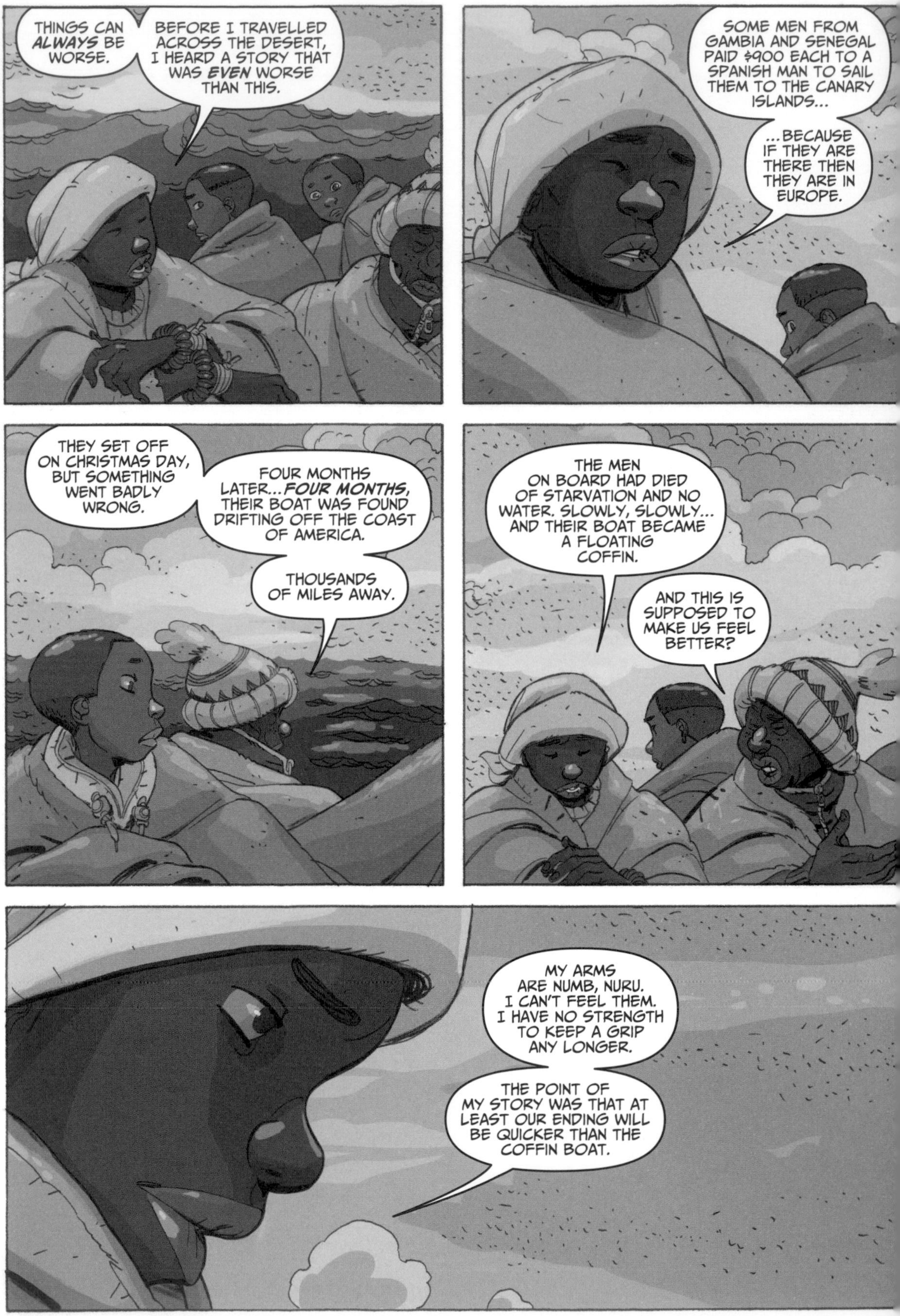
THINGS CAN ALWAYS BE WORSE.
BEFORE I TRAVELLED ACROSS THE DESERT, I HEARD A STORY THAT WAS EVEN WORSE THAN THIS.
SOME MEN FROM GAMBIA AND SENEGAL PAID $900 EACH TO A SPANISH MAN TO SAIL THEM TO THE CANARY ISLANDS...
...BECAUSE IF THEY ARE THERE THEN THEY ARE IN EUROPE.
THEY SET OFF ON CHRISTMAS DAY, BUT SOMETHING WENT BADLY WRONG.
FOUR MONTHS LATER...FOUR MONTHS, THEIR BOAT WAS FOUND DRIFTING OFF THE COAST OF AMERICA.
THOUSANDS OF MILES AWAY.
THE MEN ON BOARD HAD DIED OF STARVATION AND NO WATER. SLOWLY, SLOWLY... AND THEIR BOAT BECAME A FLOATING COFFIN.
AND THIS IS SUPPOSED TO MAKE US FEEL BETTER?
MY ARMS ARE NUMB, NURU. I CAN'T FEEL THEM. I HAVE NO STRENGTH TO KEEP A GRIP ANY LONGER.
THE POINT OF MY STORY WAS THAT AT LEAST OUR ENDING WILL BE QUICKER THAN THE COFFIN BOAT.

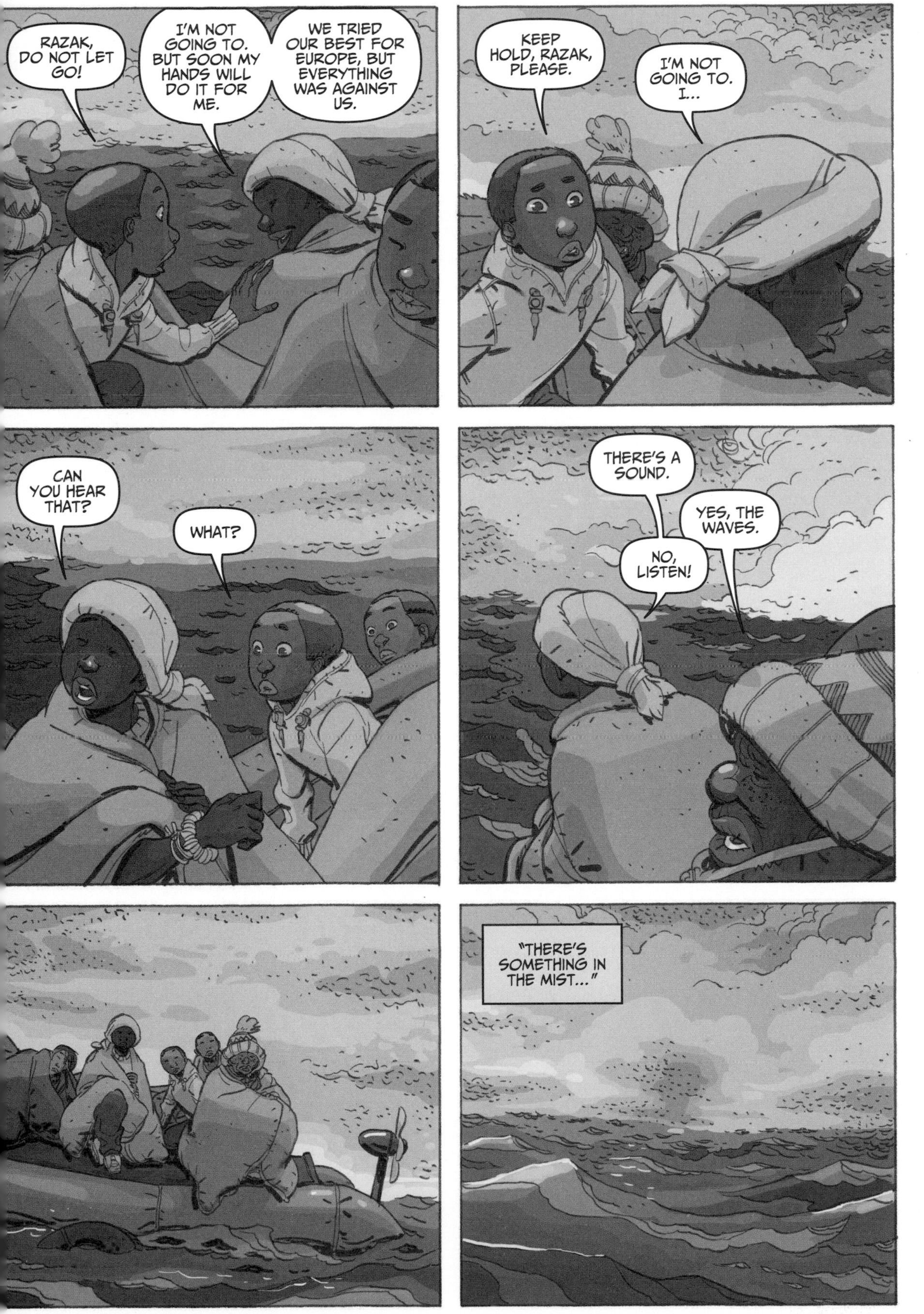
RAZAK, DO NOT LET GO!
I'M NOT GOING TO. BUT SOON MY HANDS WILL DO IT FOR ME.
WE TRIED OUR BEST FOR EUROPE, BUT EVERYTHING WAS AGAINST US.
KEEP HOLD, RAZAK, PLEASE.
I'M NOT GOING TO. I...
CAN YOU HEAR THAT?
WHAT?
THERE'S A SOUND.
YES, THE WAVES.
NO, LISTEN!
"THERE'S SOMETHING IN THE MIST..."

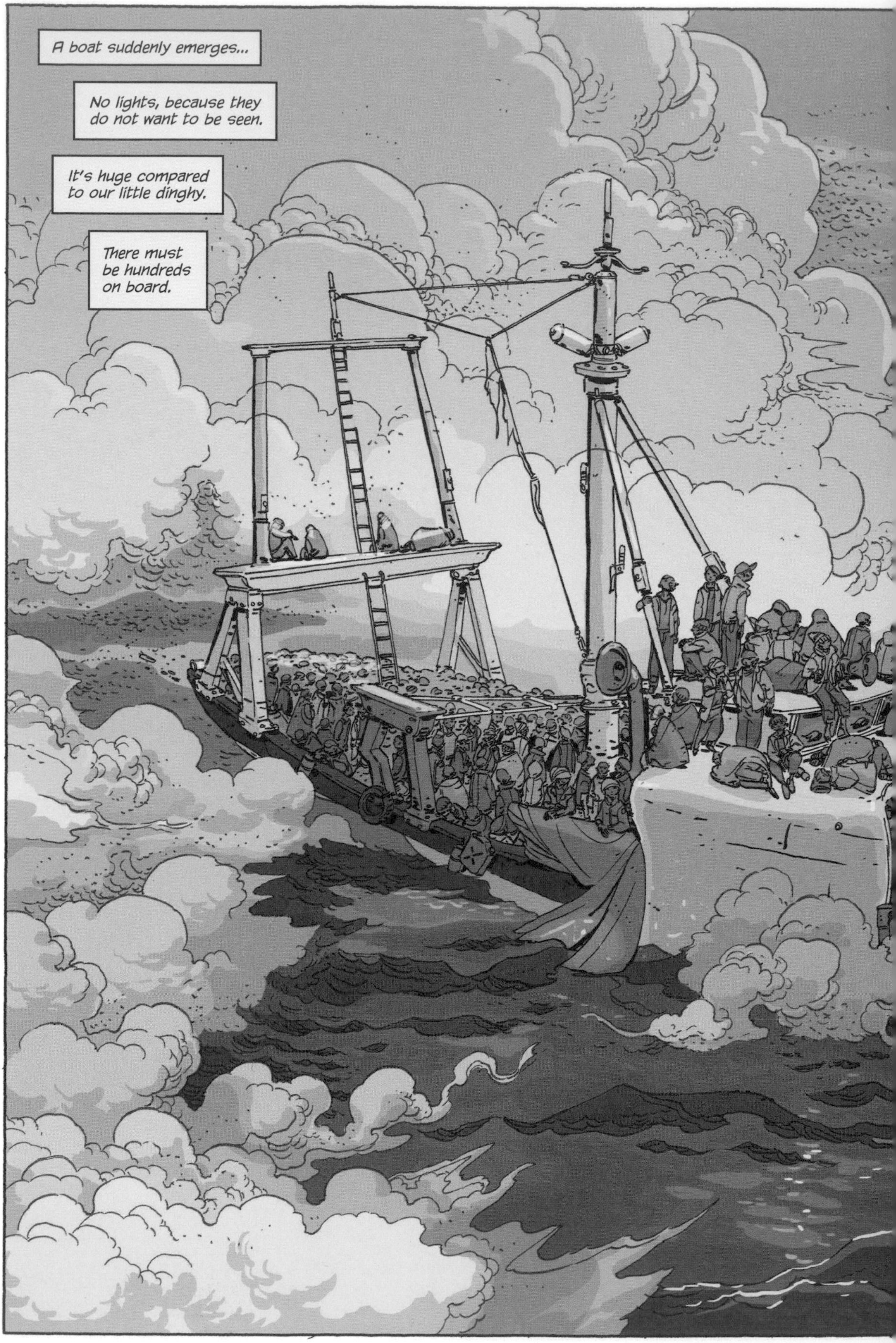
A boat suddenly emerges...
No lights, because they do not want to be seen.
It's huge compared to our little dinghy.
There must be hundreds on board.

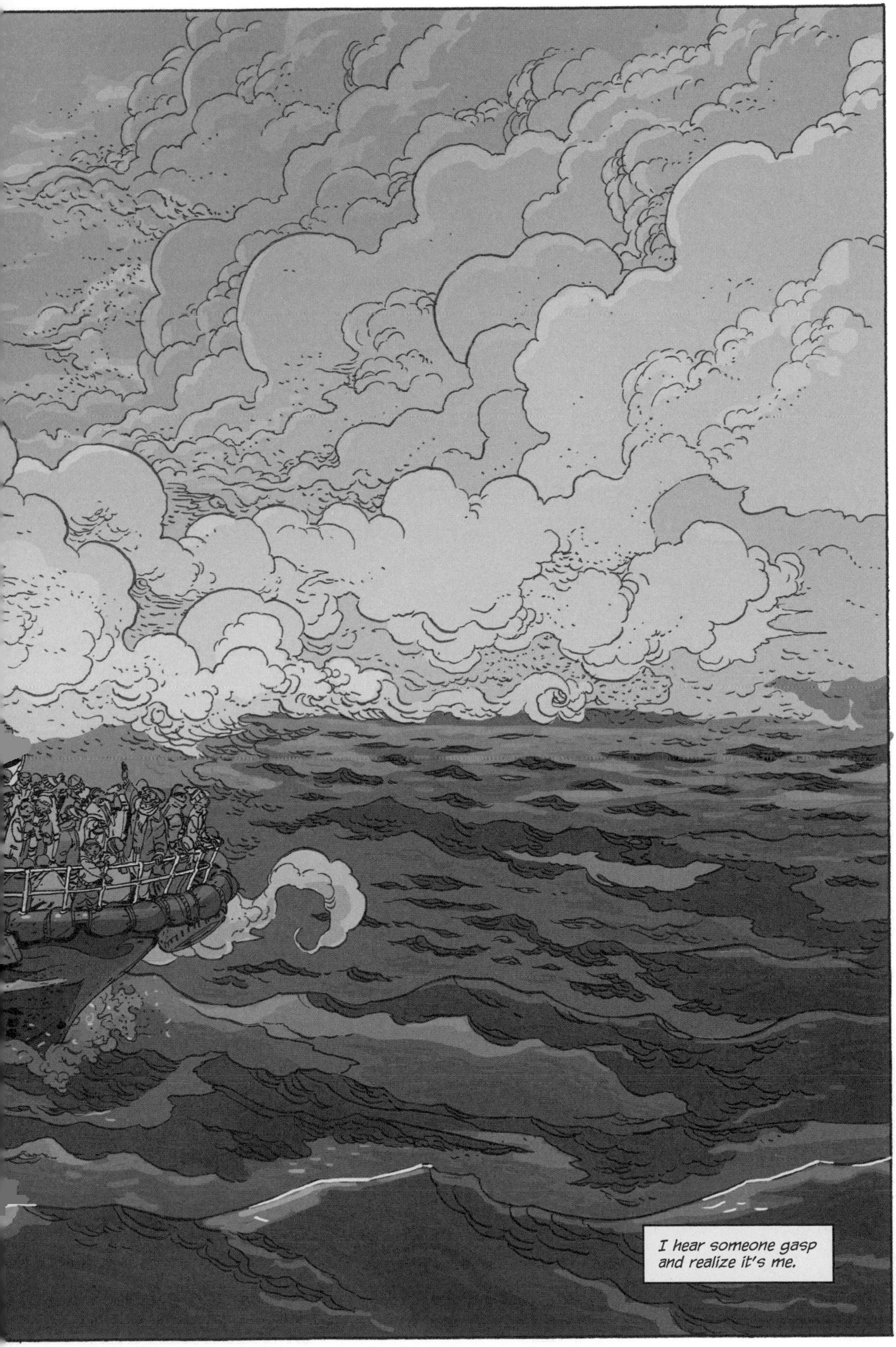
I hear someone gasp
and realize it's me.

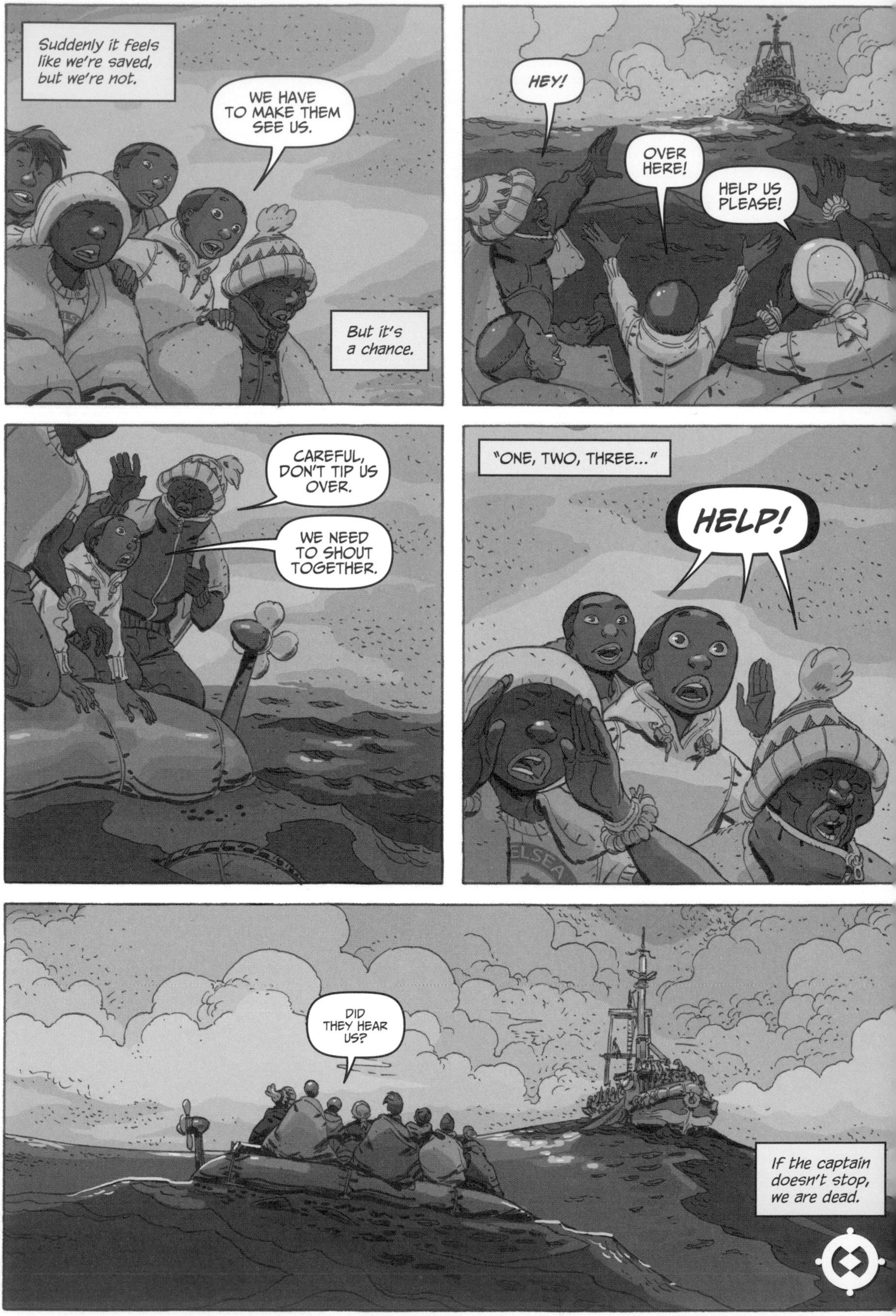
Suddenly it feels like we're saved, but we're not.
WE HAVE TO MAKE THEM SEE US.
But it's a chance.
HEY!
OVER HERE!
HELP US PLEASE!
CAREFUL, DON'T TIP US OVER.
WE NEED TO SHOUT TOGETHER.
"ONE, TWO, THREE..."
HELP!
DID THEY HEAR US?
If the captain doesn't stop, we are dead.

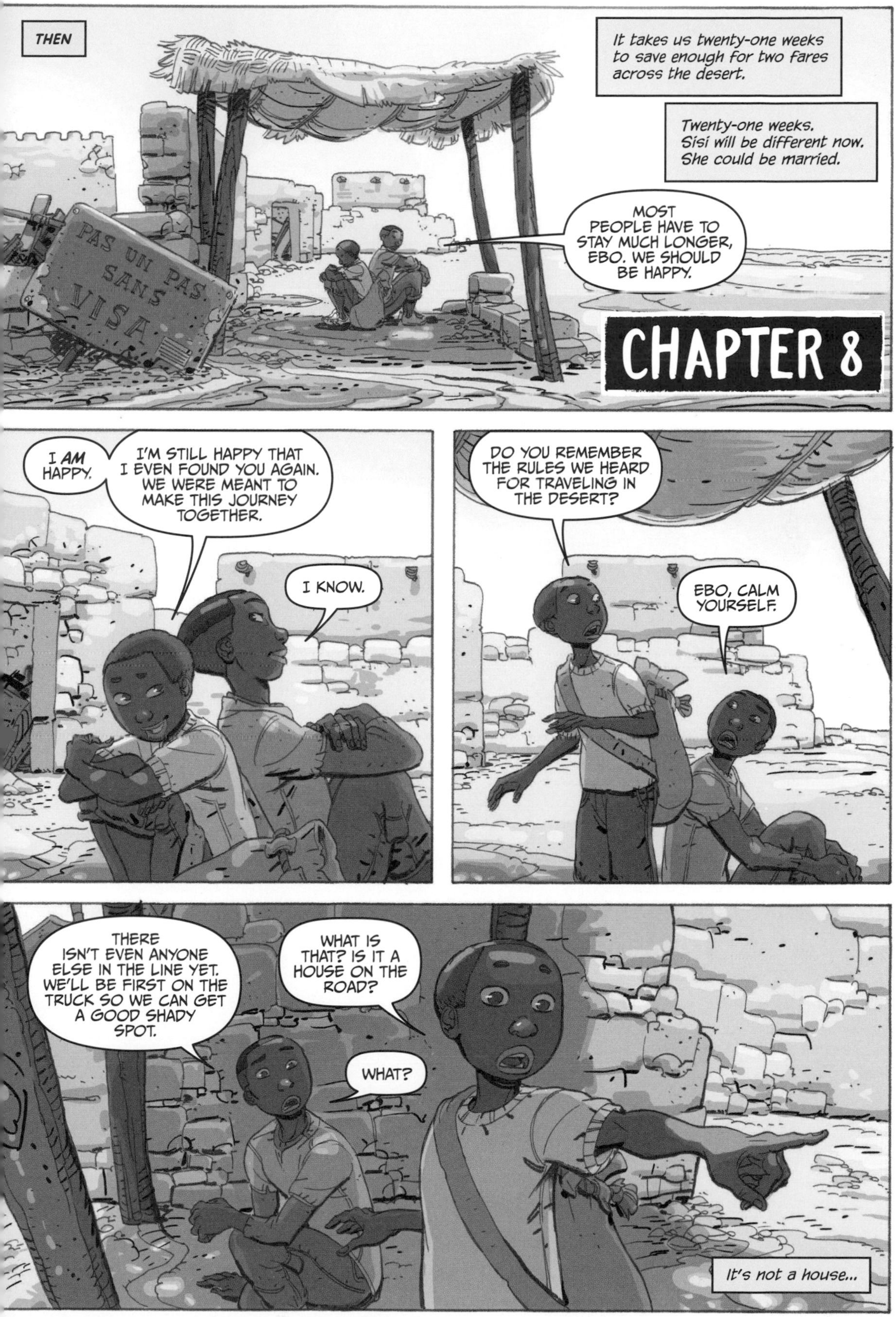
THEN
It takes us twenty-one weeks to save enough for two fares across the desert.
Twenty-one weeks. Sisi will be different now. She could be married.
PAS UN PAS SANS VISA
MOST PEOPLE HAVE TO STAY MUCH LONGER, EBO. WE SHOULD BE HAPPY.
CHAPTER 8
I *AM* HAPPY.
I'M STILL HAPPY THAT I EVEN FOUND YOU AGAIN. WE WERE MEANT TO MAKE THIS JOURNEY TOGETHER.
I KNOW.
DO YOU REMEMBER THE RULES WE HEARD FOR TRAVELING IN THE DESERT?
EBO, CALM YOURSELF.
THERE ISN'T EVEN ANYONE ELSE IN THE LINE YET. WE'LL BE FIRST ON THE TRUCK SO WE CAN GET A GOOD SHADY SPOT.
WHAT IS THAT? IS IT A HOUSE ON THE ROAD?
WHAT?
It's not a house...

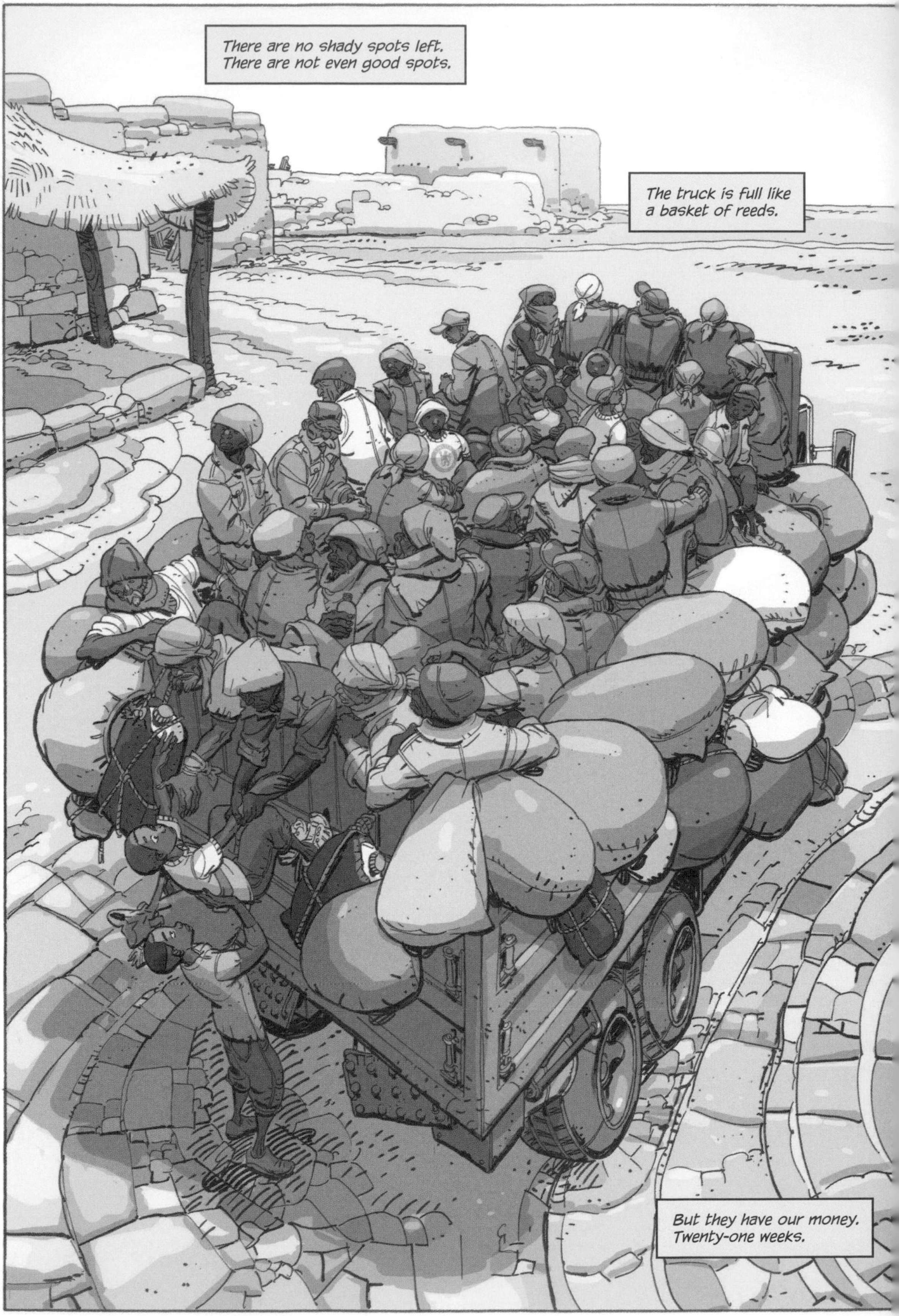
There are no shady spots left. There are not even good spots.
The truck is full like a basket of reeds.
But they have our money. Twenty-one weeks.

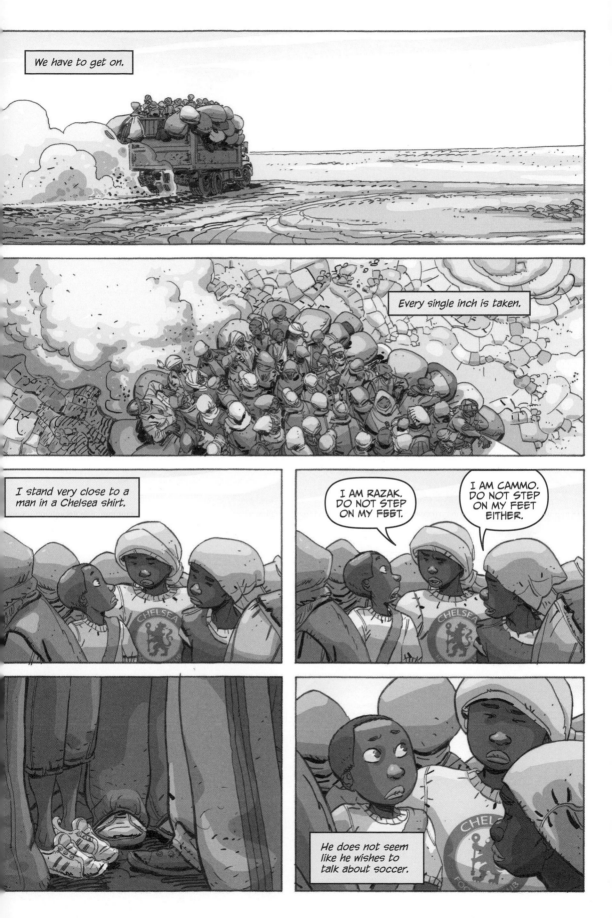

We have to get on.

Every single inch is taken.

I stand very close to a man in a Chelsea shirt.

I AM RAZAK. DO NOT STEP ON MY FEET.

I AM CAMMO. DO NOT STEP ON MY FEET EITHER.

He does not seem like he wishes to talk about soccer.

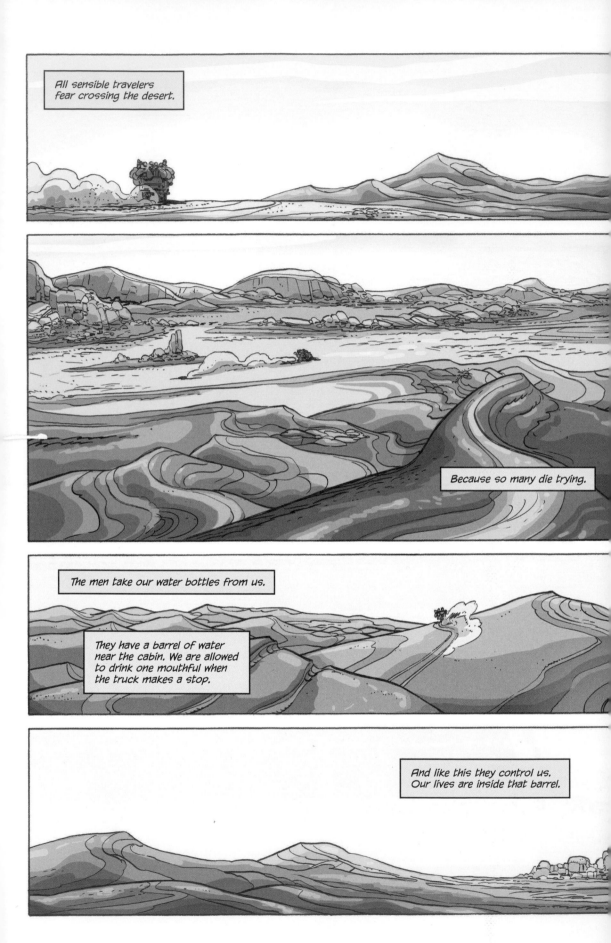

All sensible travelers fear crossing the desert.

Because so many die trying.

The men take our water bottles from us.

They have a barrel of water near the cabin. We are allowed to drink one mouthful when the truck makes a stop.

And like this they control us. Our lives are inside that barrel.

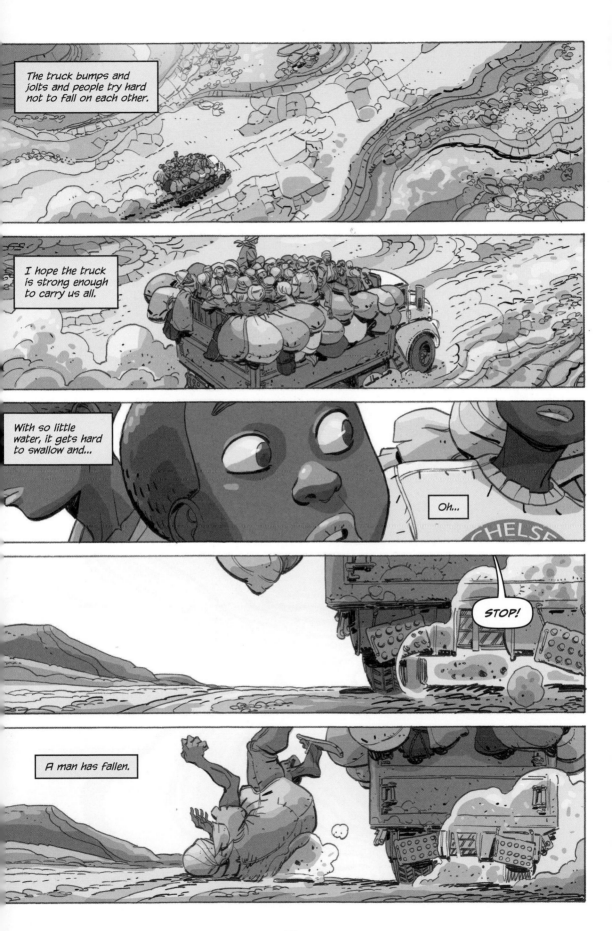

The truck bumps and jolts and people try hard not to fall on each other.

I hope the truck is strong enough to carry us all.

With so little water, it gets hard to swallow and...

Oh...

STOP!

A man has fallen.

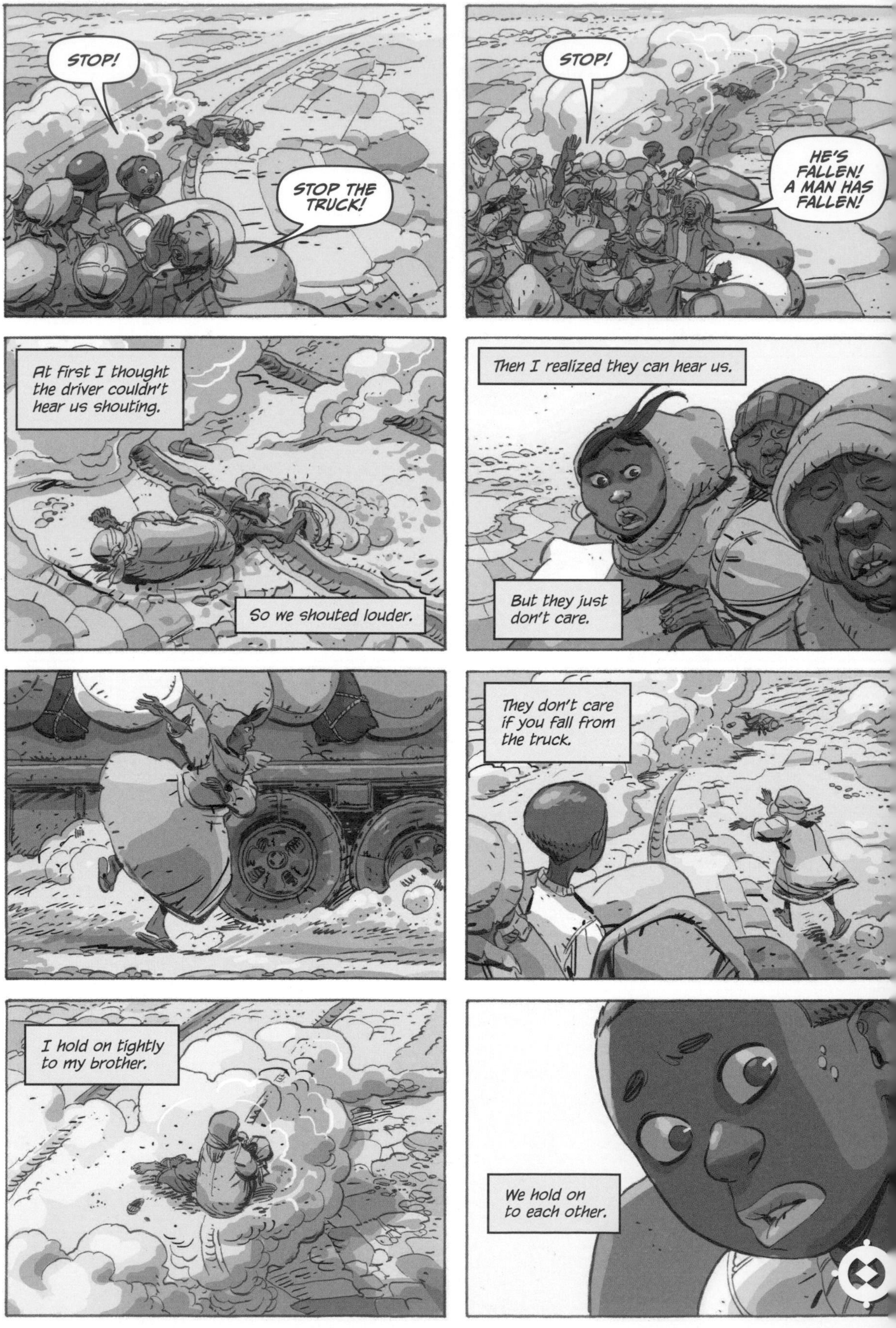
STOP!
STOP THE TRUCK!
STOP!
HE'S FALLEN! A MAN HAS FALLEN!
At first I thought the driver couldn't hear us shouting.
So we shouted louder.
Then I realized they can hear us.
But they just don't care.
They don't care if you fall from the truck.
I hold on tightly to my brother.
We hold on to each other.

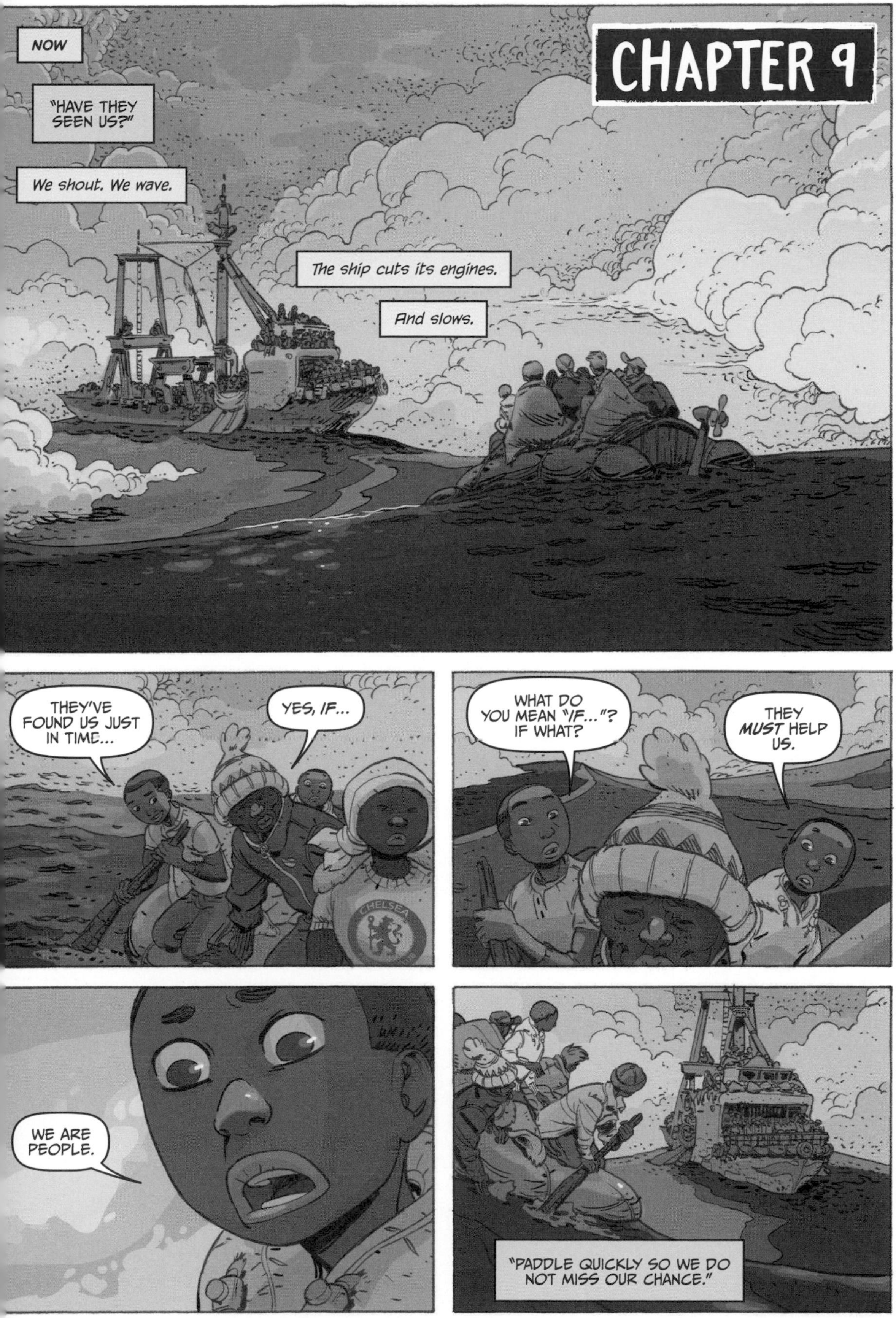
CHAPTER 9
NOW
"HAVE THEY SEEN US?"
We shout. We wave.
The ship cuts its engines.
And slows.
THEY'VE FOUND US JUST IN TIME...
YES, IF...
WHAT DO YOU MEAN "IF..."? IF WHAT?
THEY MUST HELP US.
WE ARE PEOPLE.
"PADDLE QUICKLY SO WE DO NOT MISS OUR CHANCE."

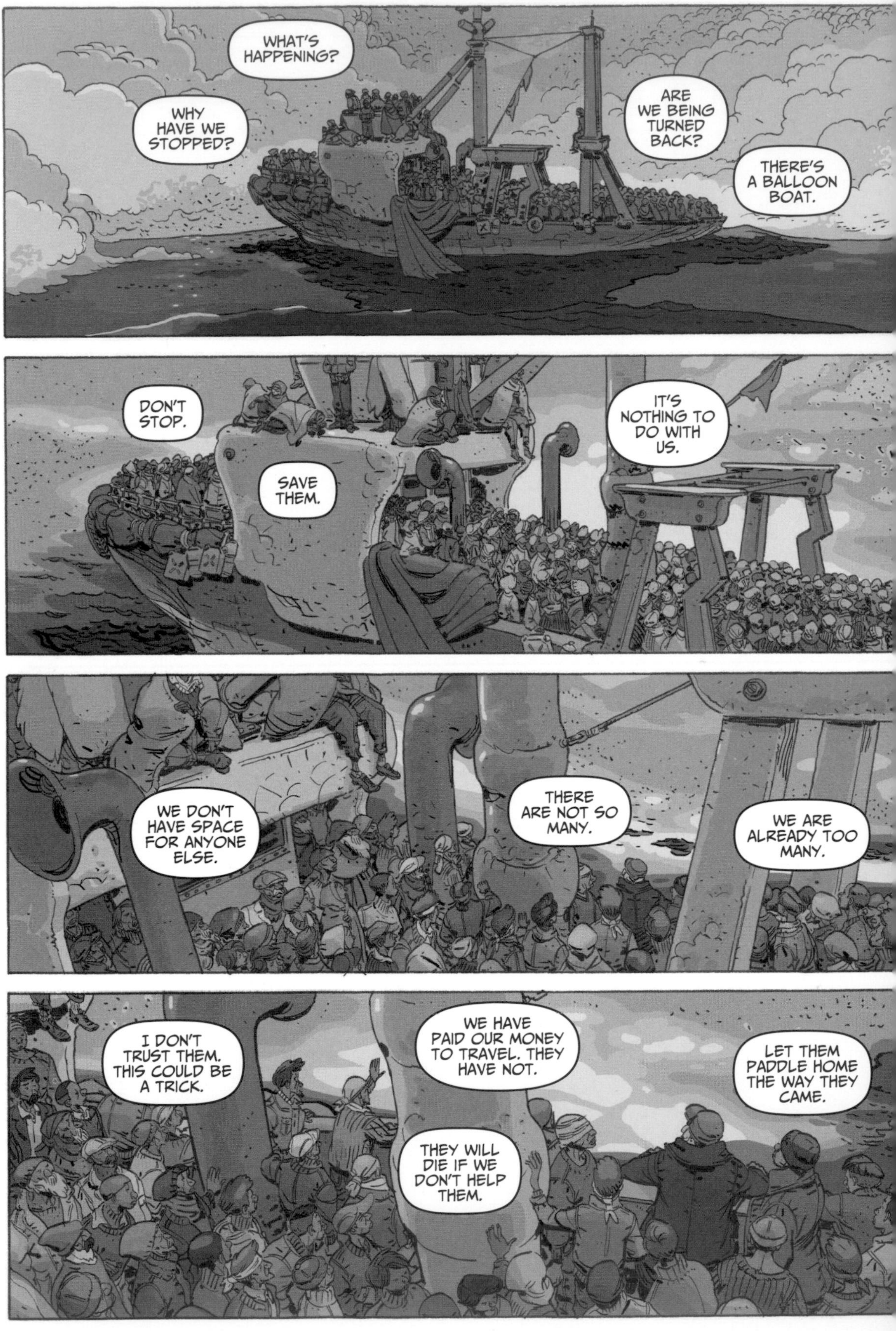
WHY HAVE WE STOPPED?
WHAT'S HAPPENING?
ARE WE BEING TURNED BACK?
THERE'S A BALLOON BOAT.
DON'T STOP.
SAVE THEM.
IT'S NOTHING TO DO WITH US.
WE DON'T HAVE SPACE FOR ANYONE ELSE.
THERE ARE NOT SO MANY.
WE ARE ALREADY TOO MANY.
I DON'T TRUST THEM. THIS COULD BE A TRICK.
WE HAVE PAID OUR MONEY TO TRAVEL. THEY HAVE NOT.
THEY WILL DIE IF WE DON'T HELP THEM.
LET THEM PADDLE HOME THE WAY THEY CAME.

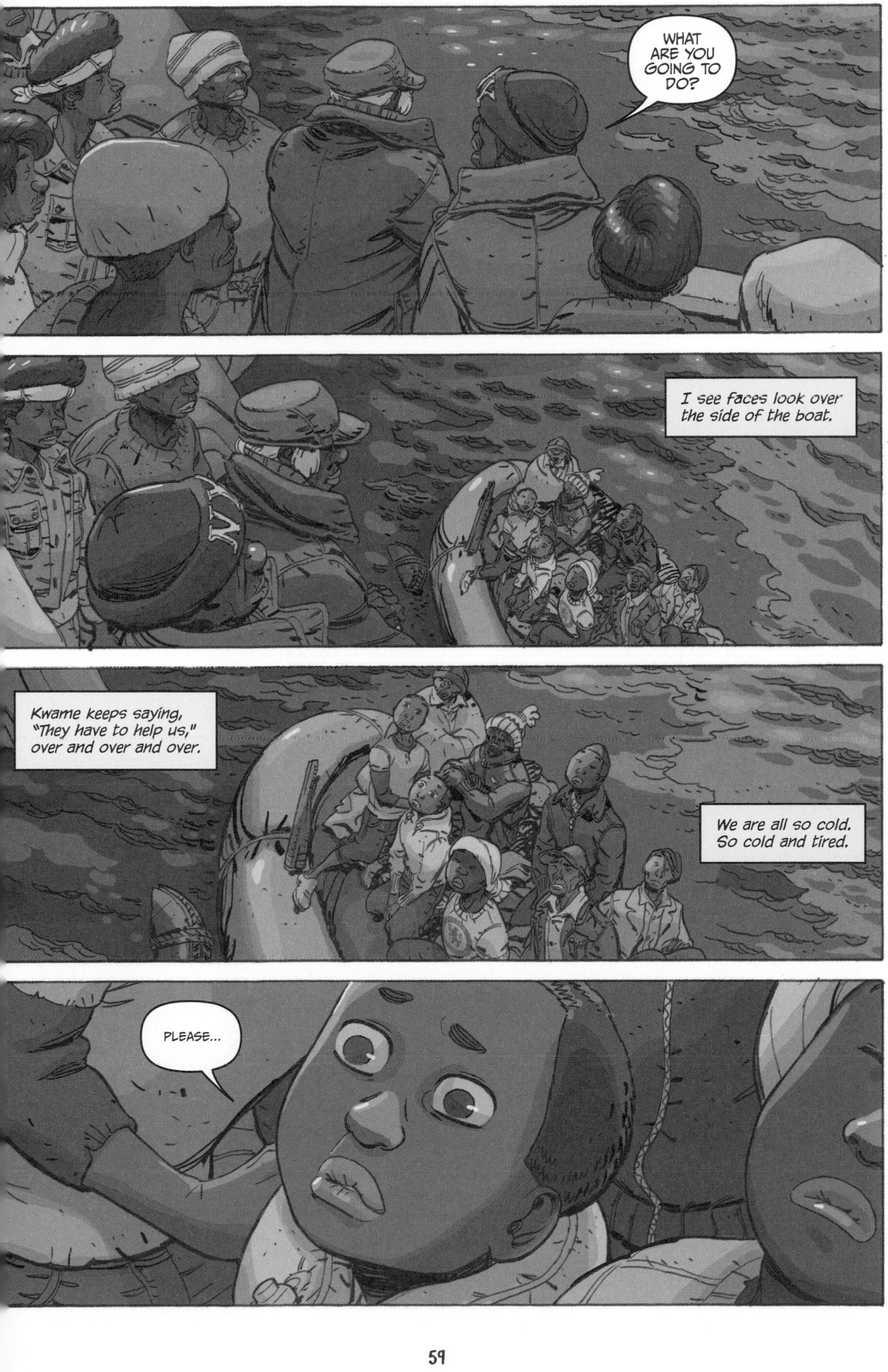
WHAT ARE YOU GOING TO DO?
I see faces look over the side of the boat.
Kwame keeps saying, "They have to help us," over and over and over.
We are all so cold. So cold and tired.
PLEASE...

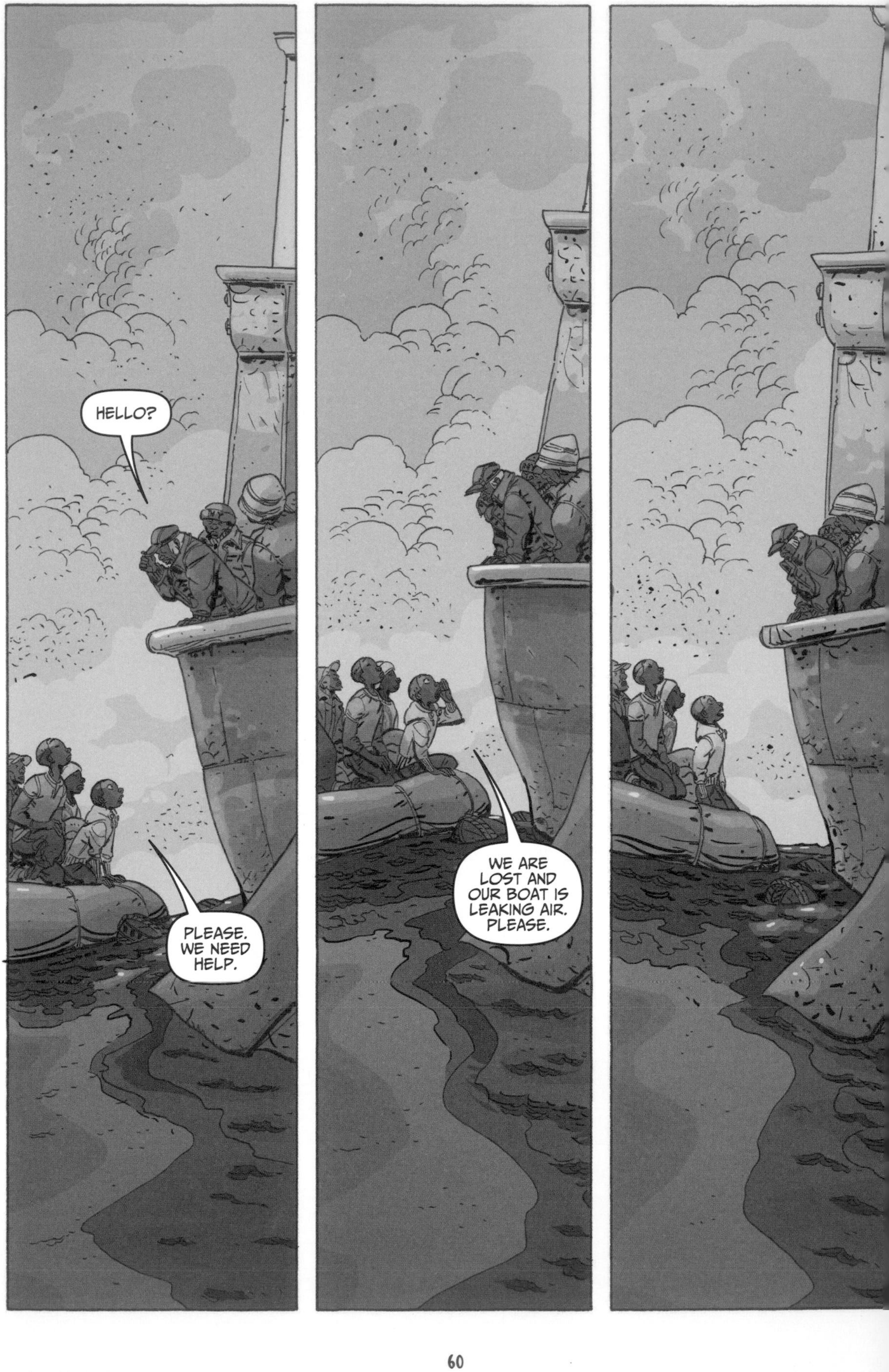
HELLO?
PLEASE. WE NEED HELP.
WE ARE LOST AND OUR BOAT IS LEAKING AIR. PLEASE.

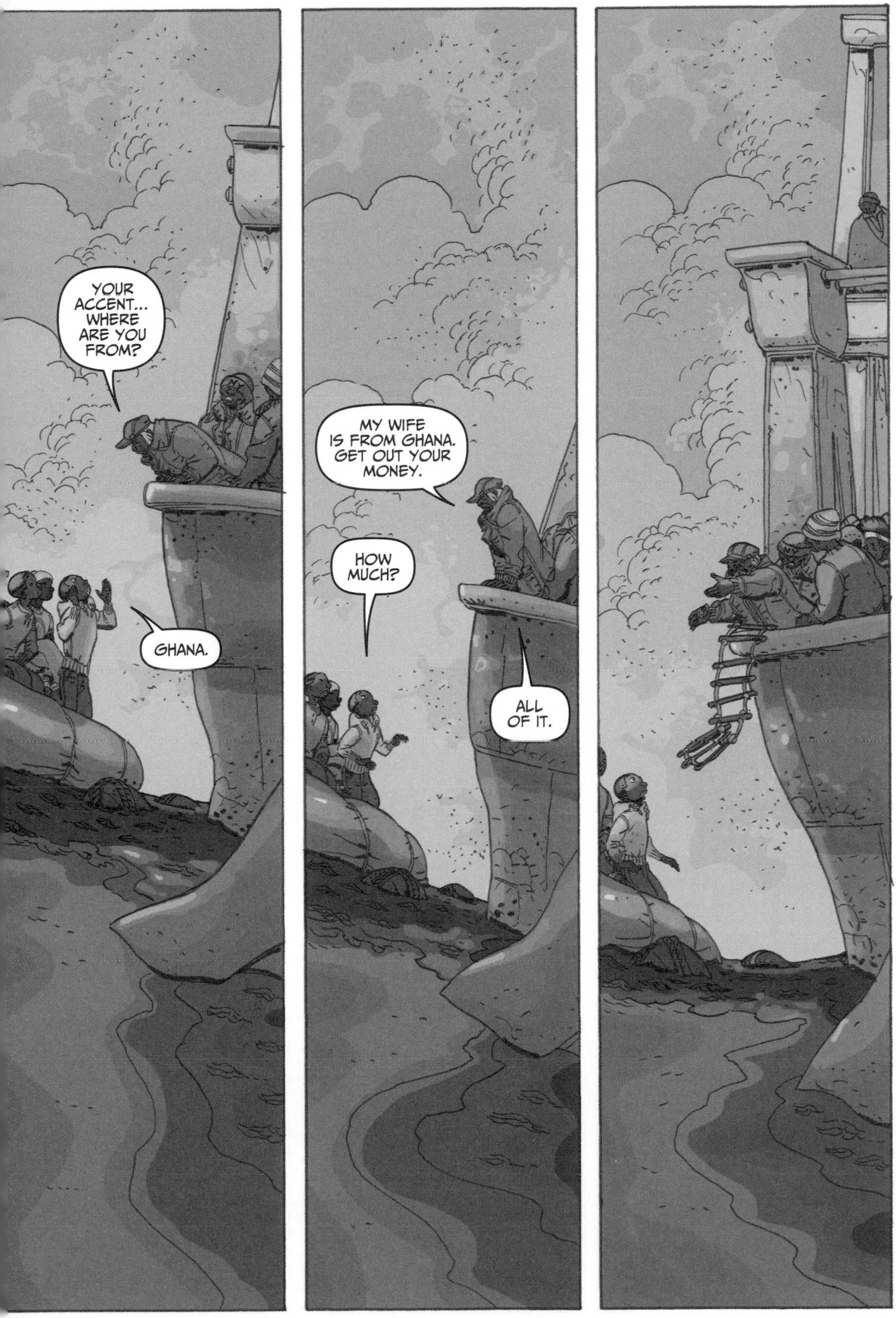
YOUR ACCENT... WHERE ARE YOU FROM?
GHANA.
MY WIFE IS FROM GHANA. GET OUT YOUR MONEY.
HOW MUCH?
ALL OF IT.

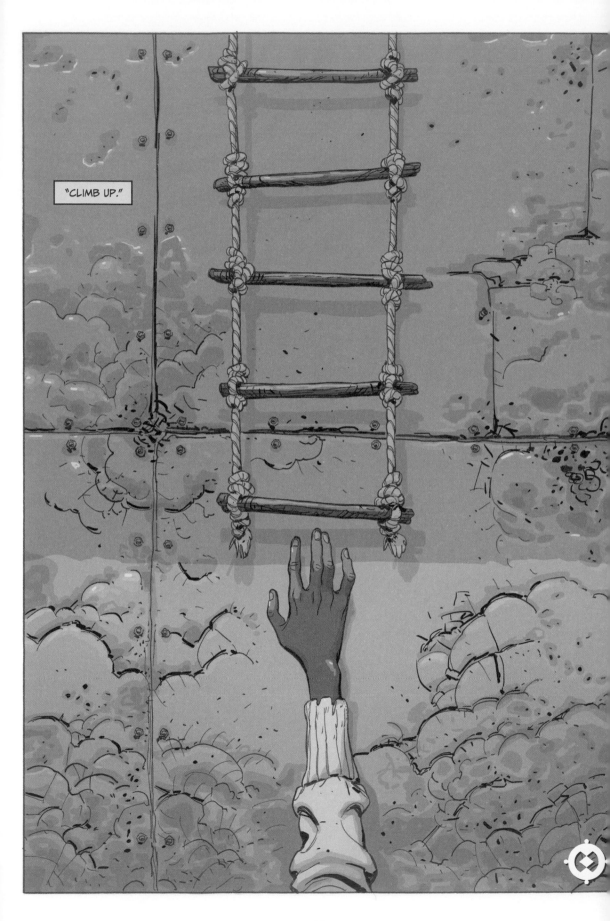

"CLIMB UP."

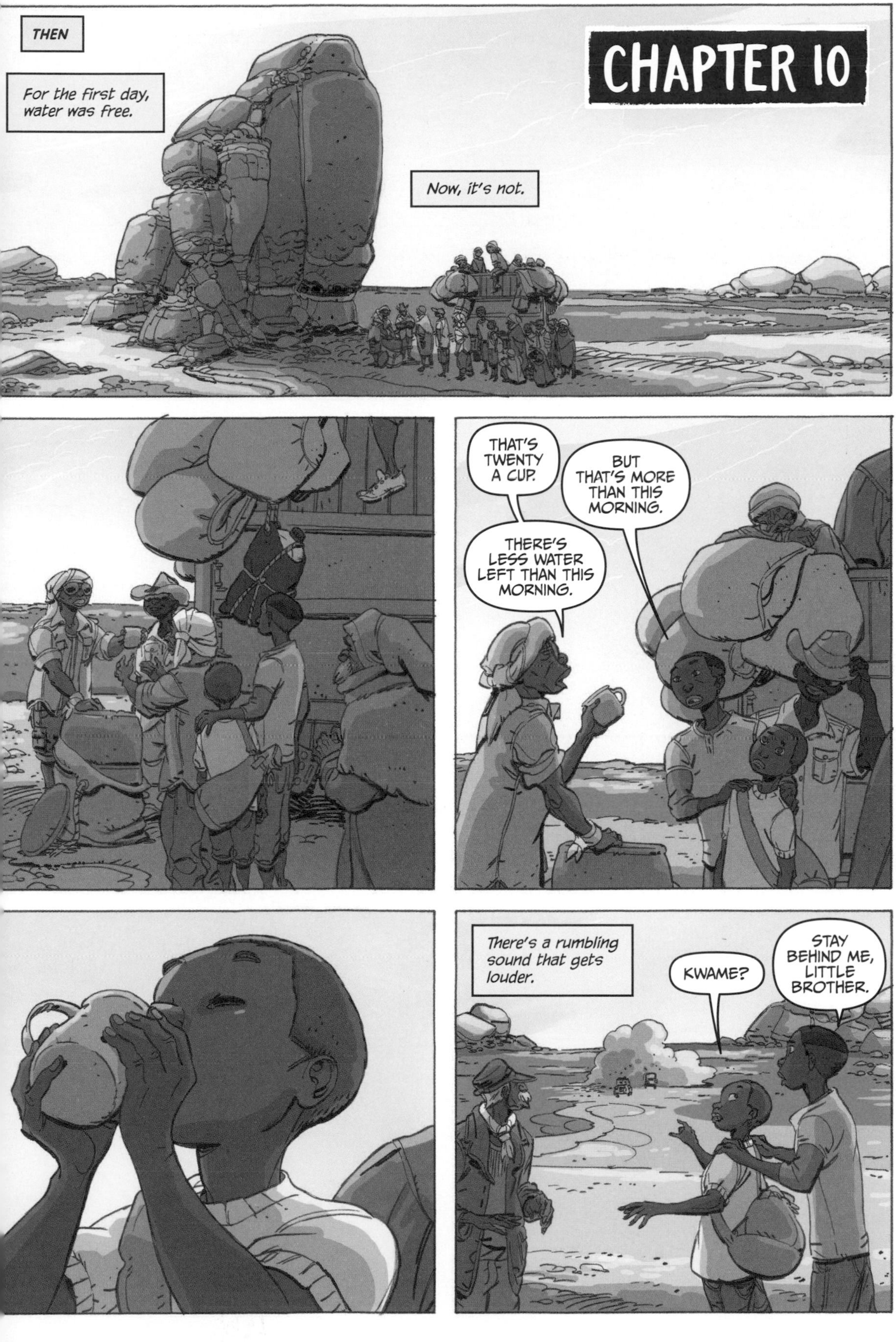
THEN
CHAPTER 10
For the first day, water was free.
Now, it's not.
THAT'S TWENTY A CUP.
THERE'S LESS WATER LEFT THAN THIS MORNING.
BUT THAT'S MORE THAN THIS MORNING.
There's a rumbling sound that gets louder.
KWAME?
STAY BEHIND ME, LITTLE BROTHER.

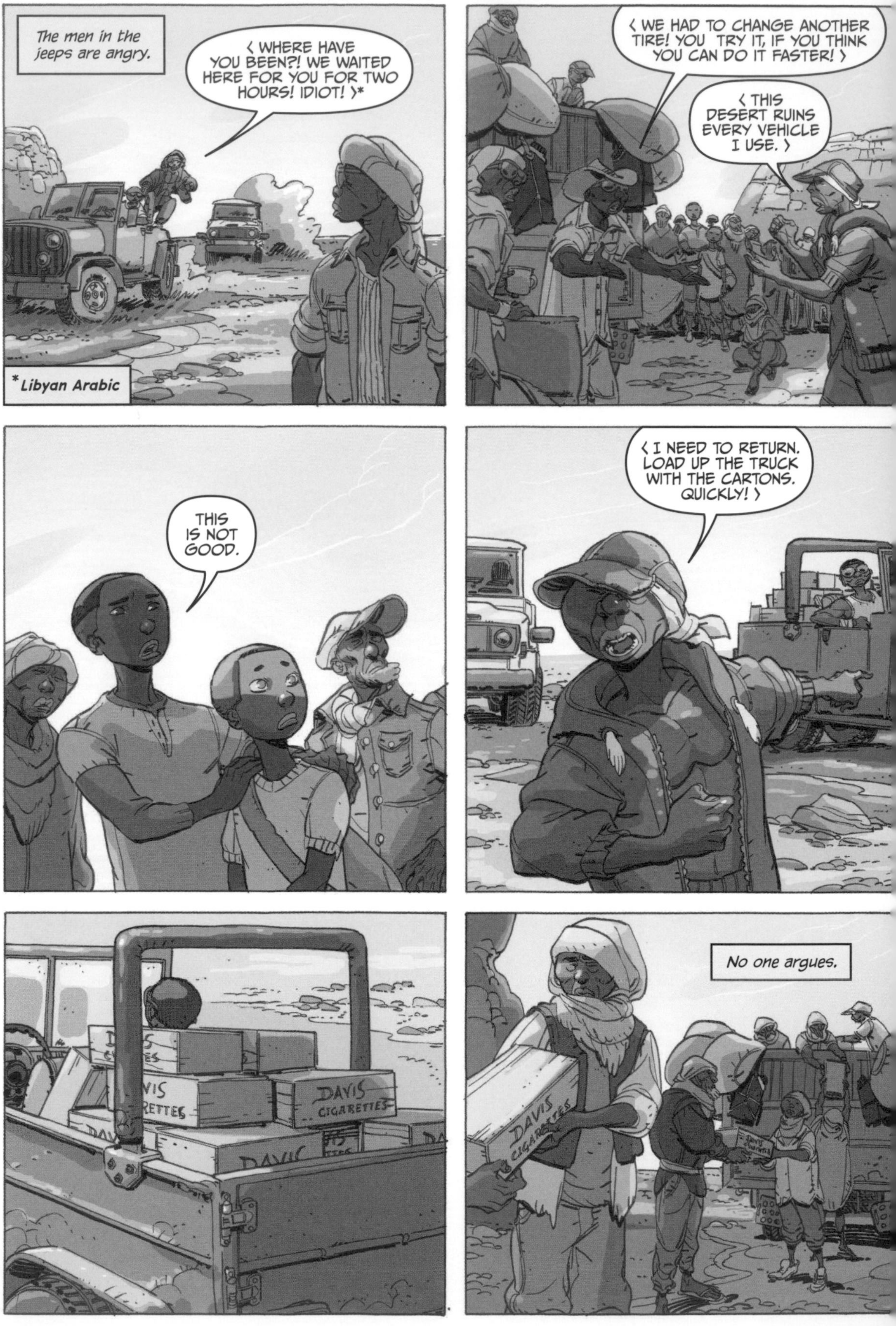
The men in the jeeps are angry.
‹ WHERE HAVE YOU BEEN?! WE WAITED HERE FOR YOU FOR TWO HOURS! IDIOT! ›*
*Libyan Arabic
‹ WE HAD TO CHANGE ANOTHER TIRE! YOU TRY IT, IF YOU THINK YOU CAN DO IT FASTER! ›
‹ THIS DESERT RUINS EVERY VEHICLE I USE. ›
THIS IS NOT GOOD.
‹ I NEED TO RETURN. LOAD UP THE TRUCK WITH THE CARTONS. QUICKLY! ›
DAVIS CIGARETTES
No one argues.
DAVIS CIGARETTES

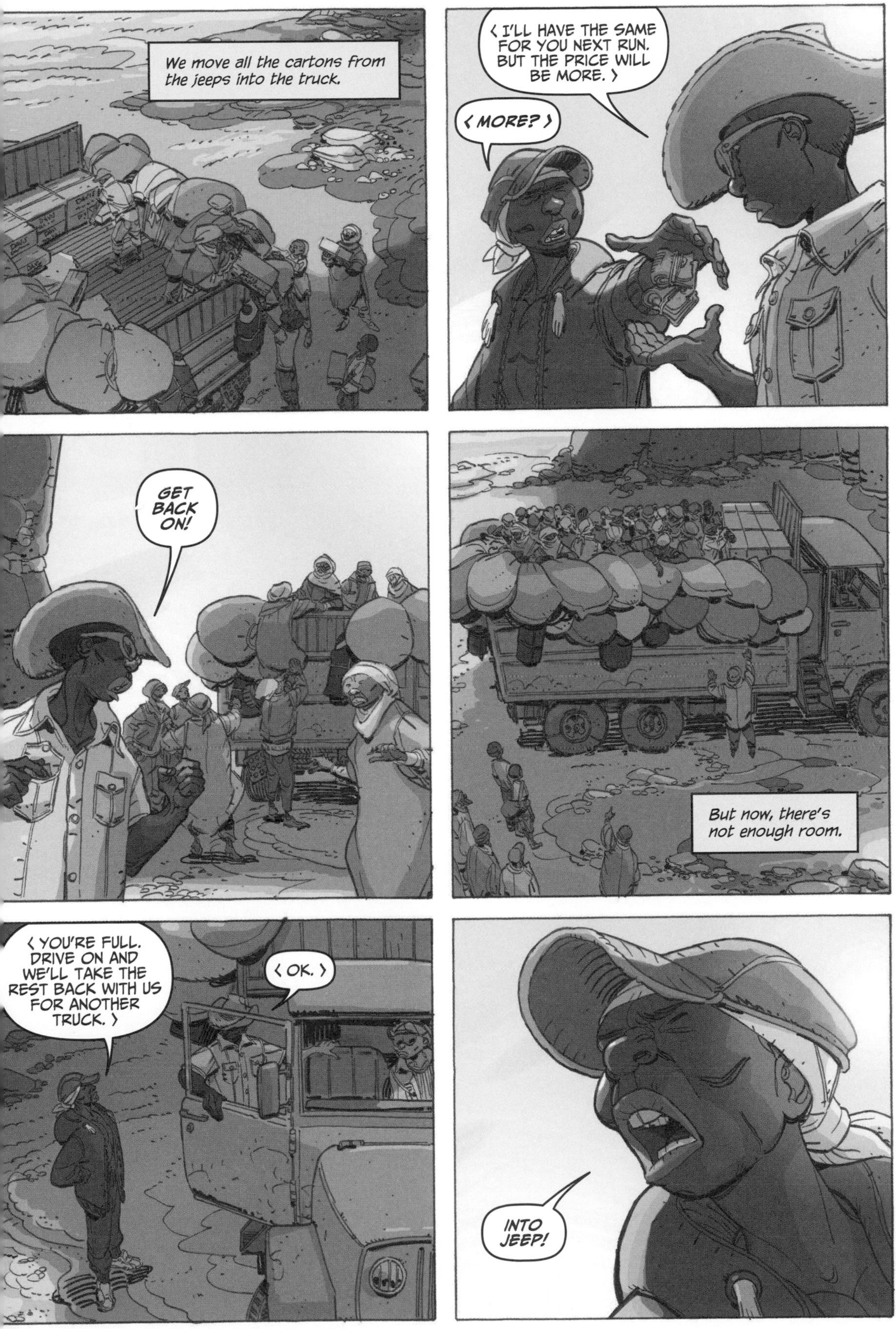
We move all the cartons from the jeeps into the truck.
‹ I'LL HAVE THE SAME FOR YOU NEXT RUN. BUT THE PRICE WILL BE MORE. ›
‹ MORE? ›
GET BACK ON!
But now, there's not enough room.
‹ YOU'RE FULL. DRIVE ON AND WE'LL TAKE THE REST BACK WITH US FOR ANOTHER TRUCK. ›
‹ OK. ›
INTO JEEP!

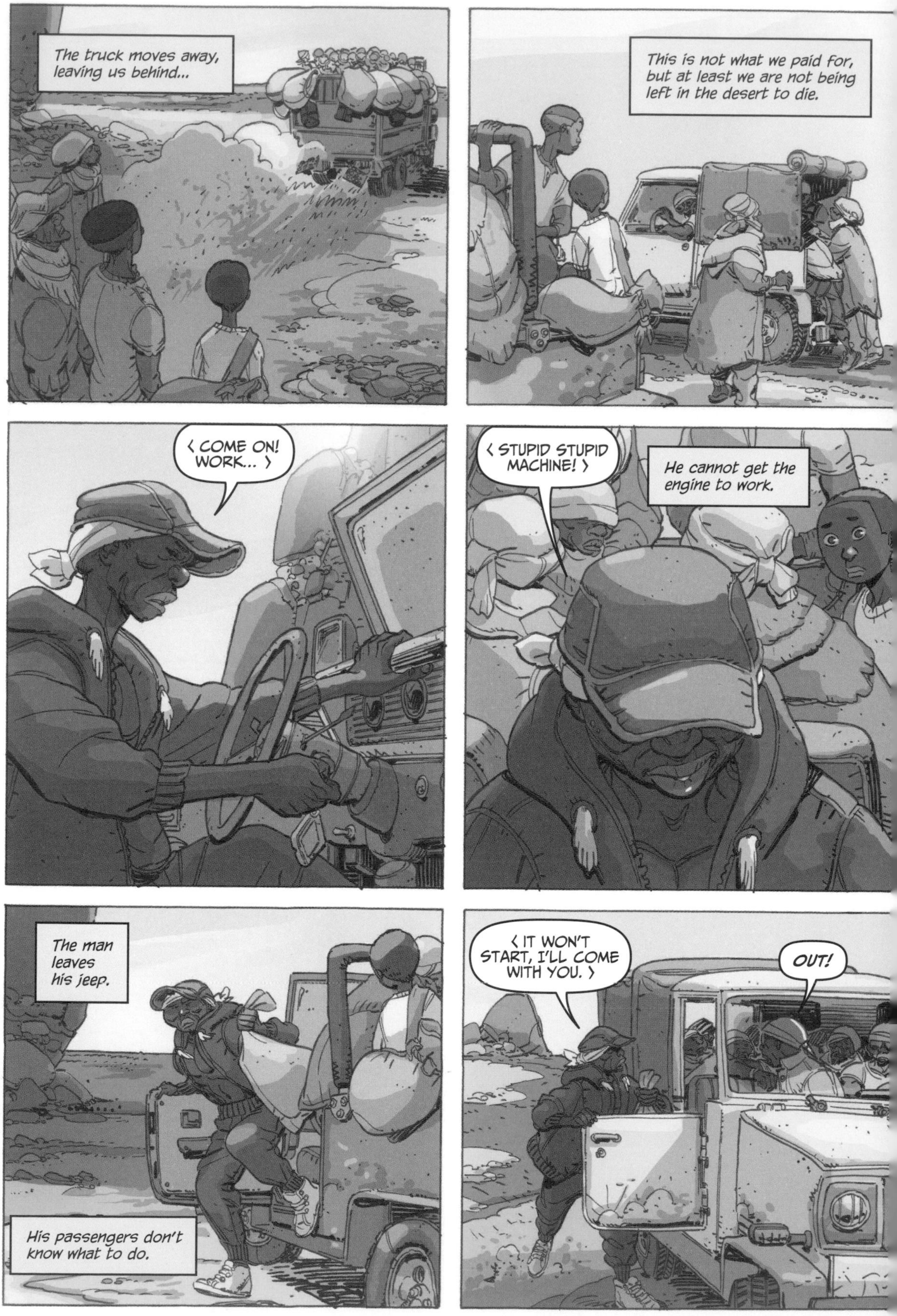
The truck moves away, leaving us behind...
This is not what we paid for, but at least we are not being left in the desert to die.
‹ COME ON! WORK... ›
‹ STUPID STUPID MACHINE! ›
He cannot get the engine to work.
The man leaves his jeep.
His passengers don't know what to do.
‹ IT WON'T START, I'LL COME WITH YOU. ›
OUT!

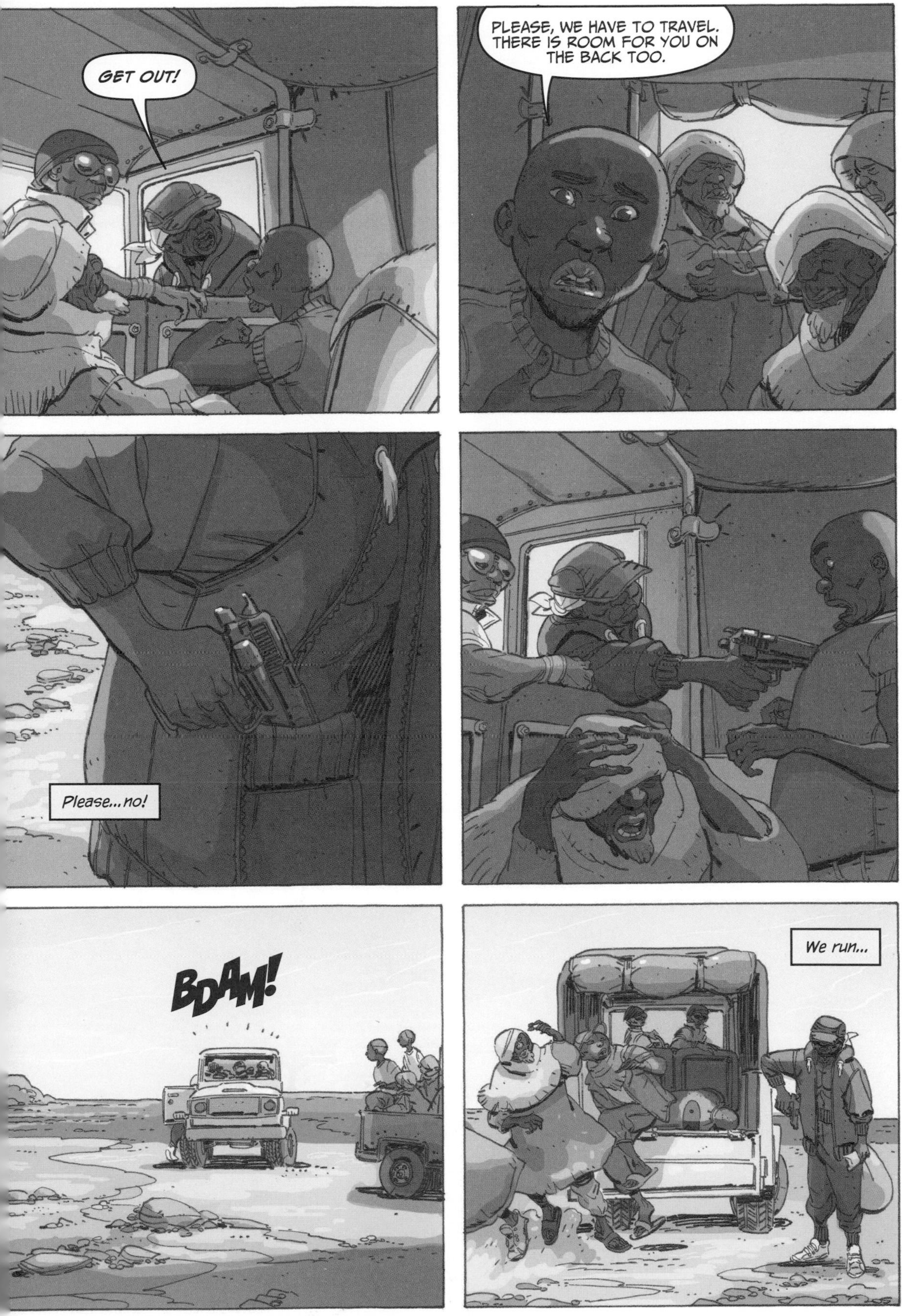
GET OUT!
PLEASE, WE HAVE TO TRAVEL. THERE IS ROOM FOR YOU ON THE BACK TOO.
Please...no!
BDAM!
We run...

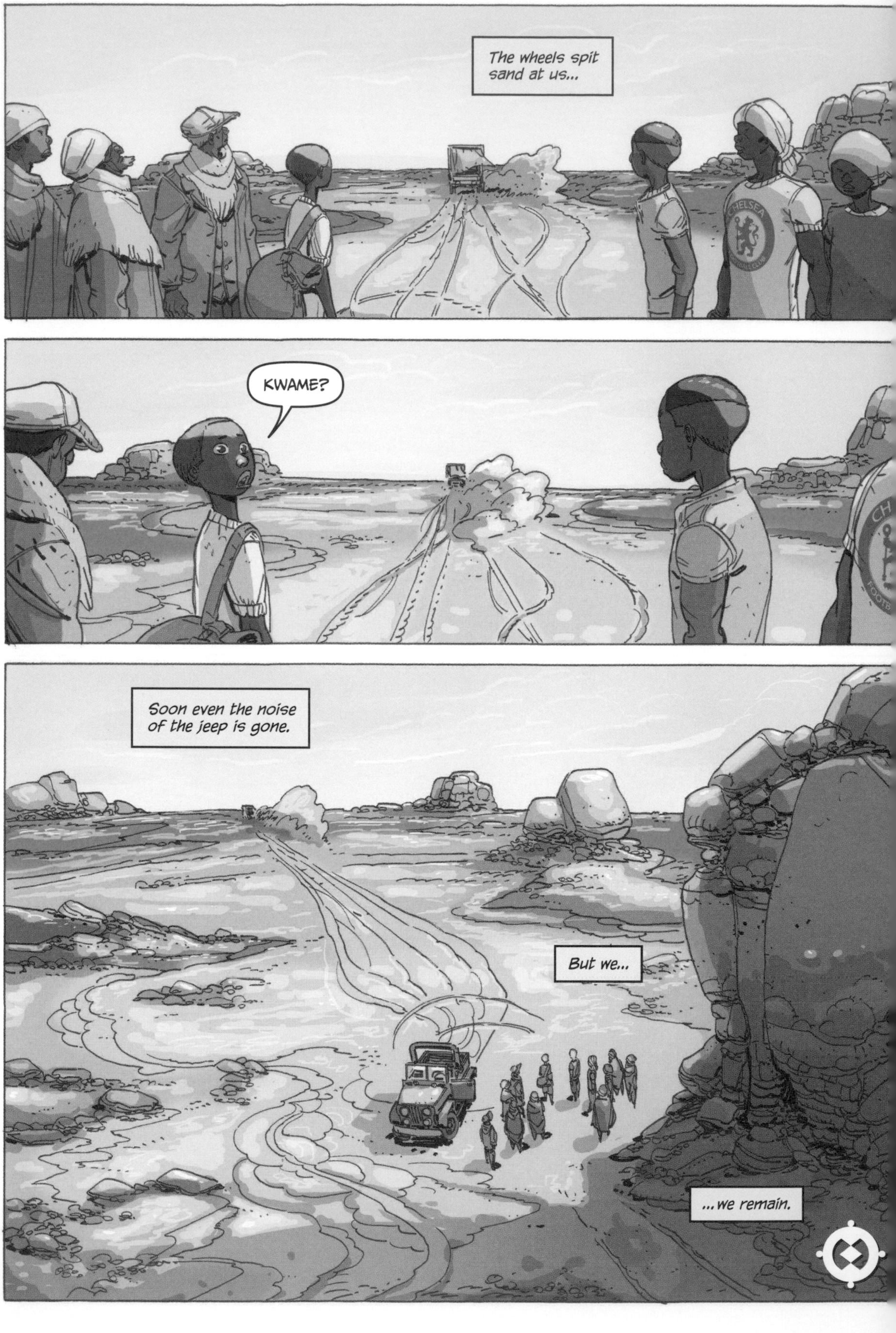
The wheels spit sand at us...
CHELSEA
KWAME?
Soon even the noise of the jeep is gone.
But we...
...we remain.

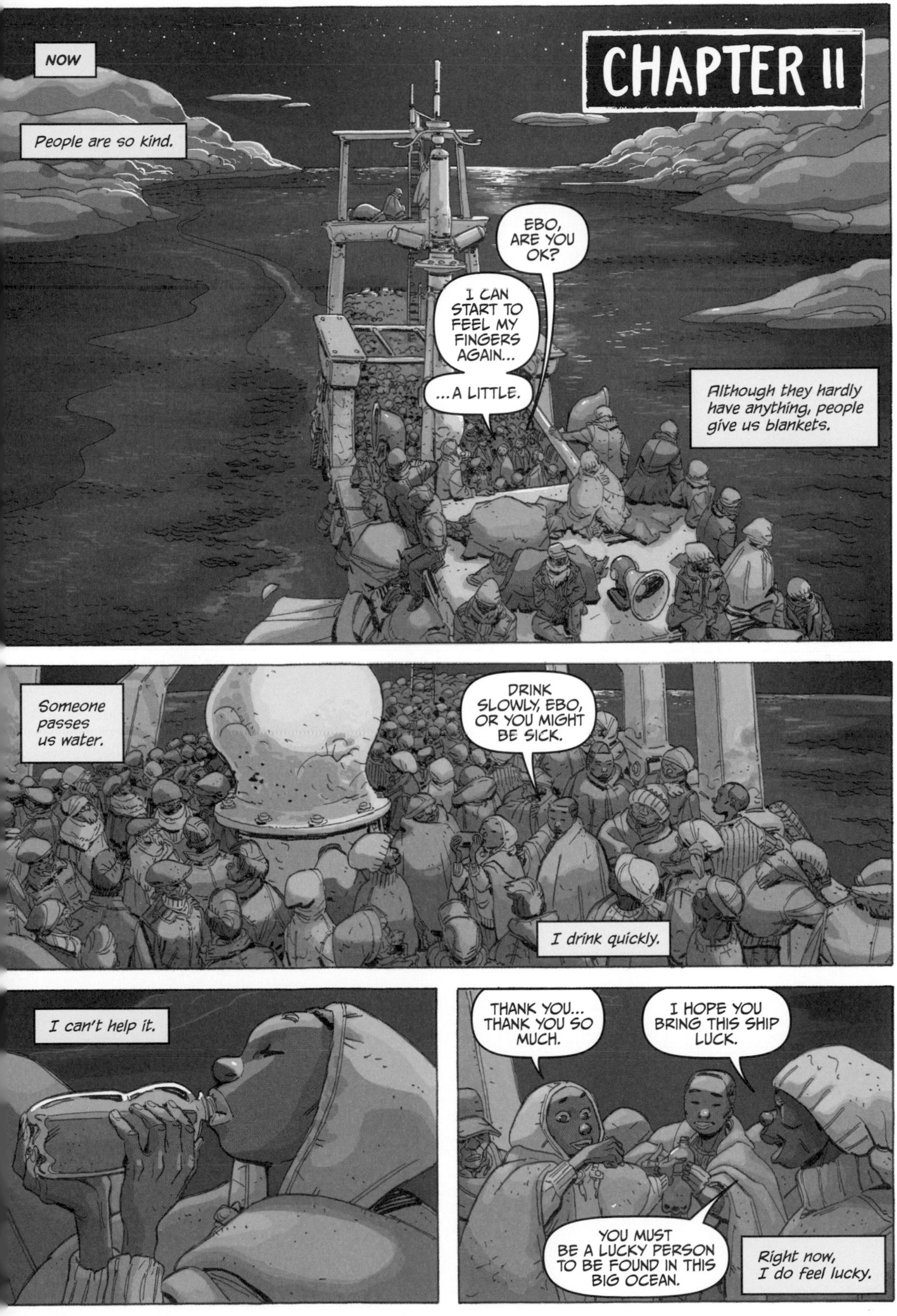
NOW
CHAPTER II
People are so kind.
EBO, ARE YOU OK?
I CAN START TO FEEL MY FINGERS AGAIN...
...A LITTLE.
Although they hardly have anything, people give us blankets.
Someone passes us water.
DRINK SLOWLY, EBO, OR YOU MIGHT BE SICK.
I drink quickly.
I can't help it.
THANK YOU... THANK YOU SO MUCH.
I HOPE YOU BRING THIS SHIP LUCK.
YOU MUST BE A LUCKY PERSON TO BE FOUND IN THIS BIG OCEAN.
Right now, I do feel lucky.

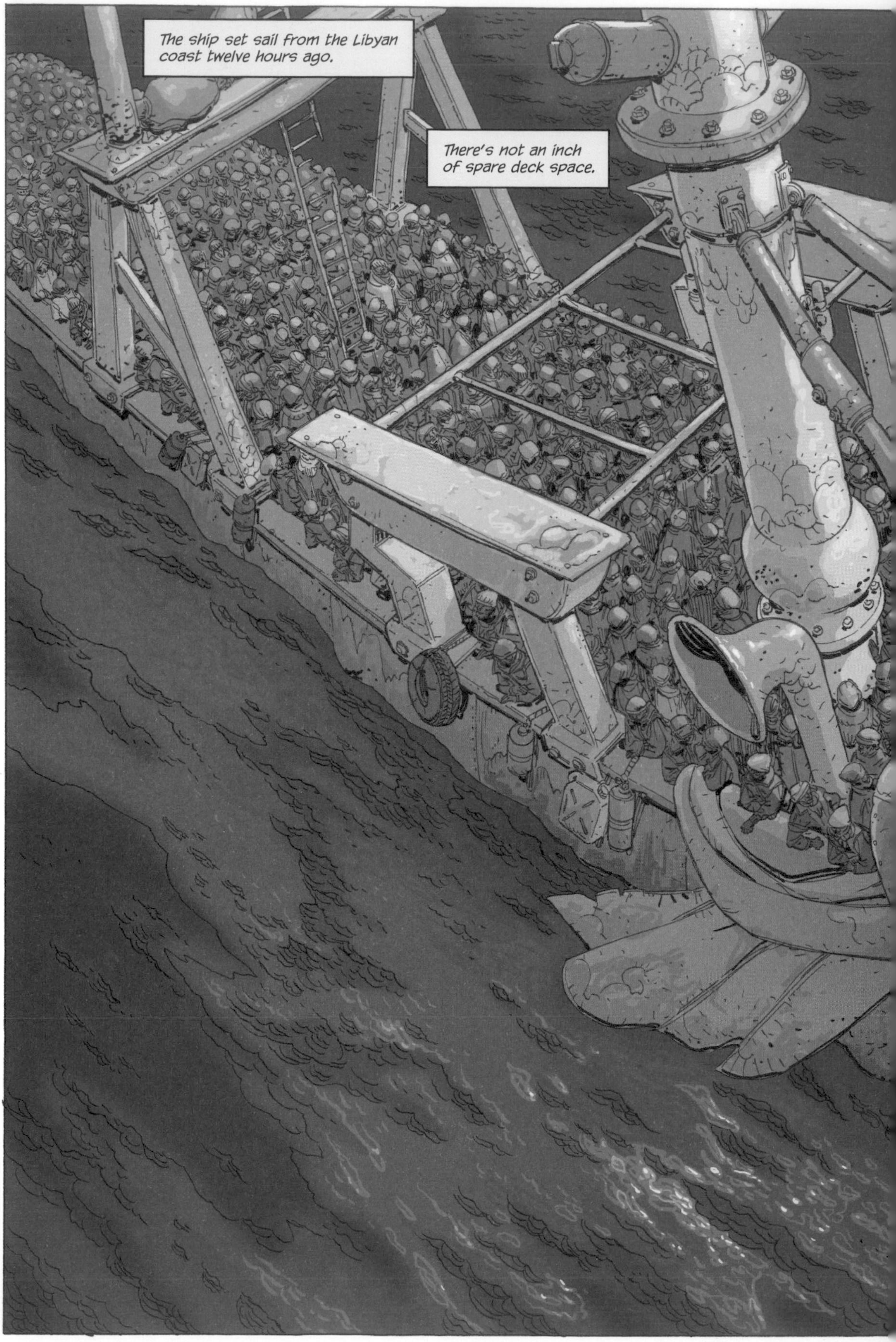
The ship set sail from the Libyan coast twelve hours ago.
There's not an inch of spare deck space.

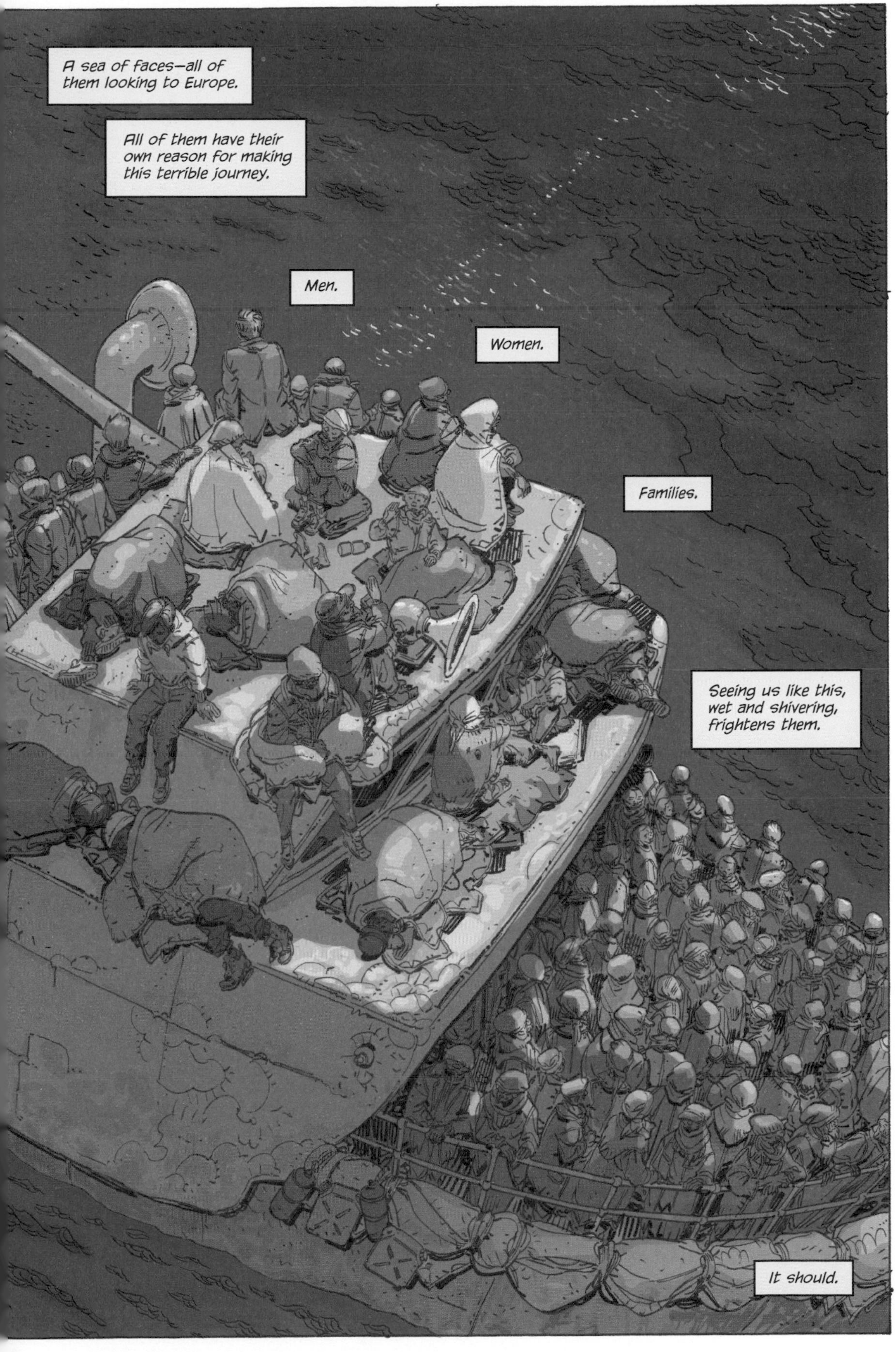
A sea of faces—all of them looking to Europe.
All of them have their own reason for making this terrible journey.
Men.
Women.
Families.
Seeing us like this, wet and shivering, frightens them.
It should.

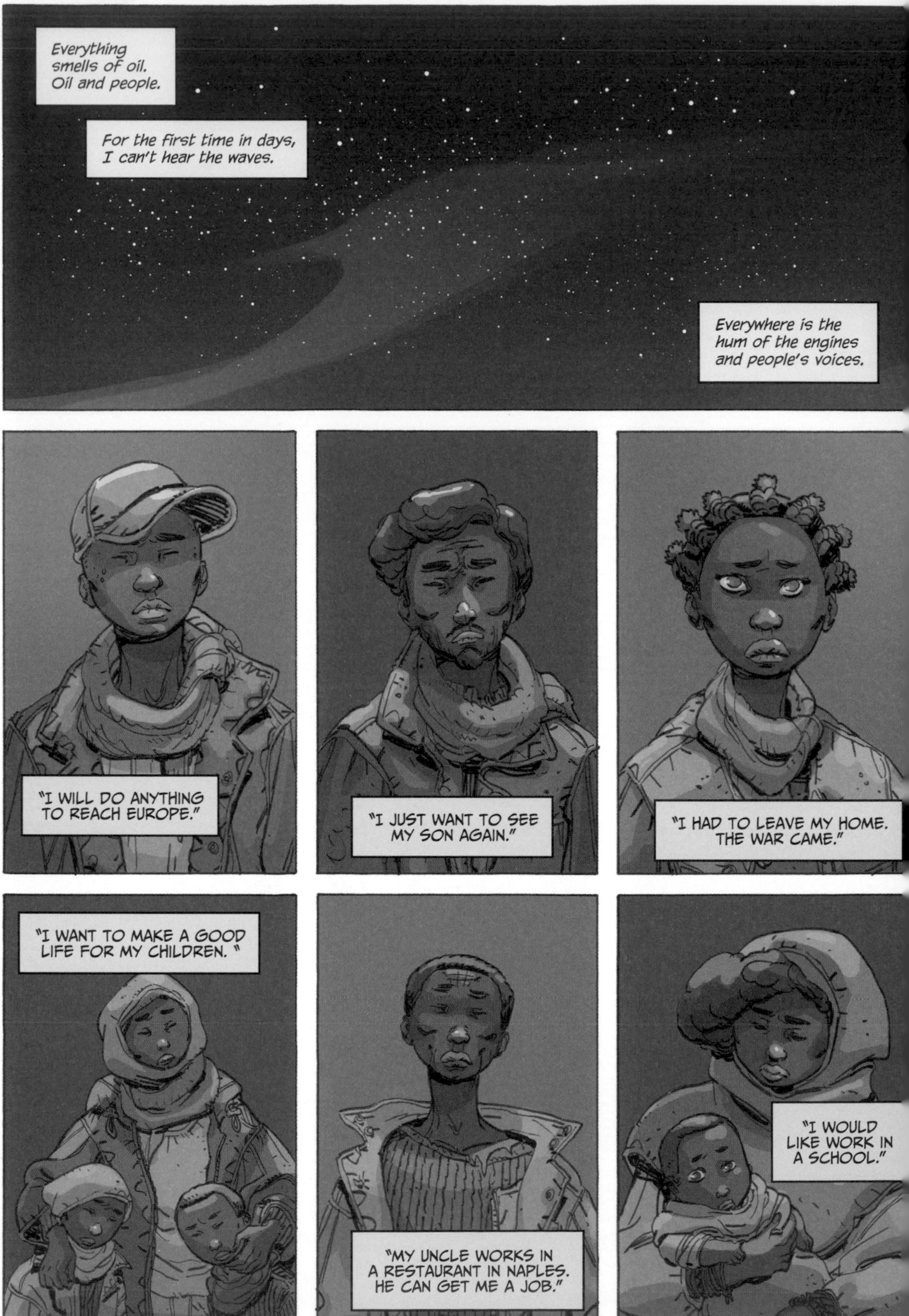
Everything smells of oil. Oil and people.
For the first time in days, I can't hear the waves.
Everywhere is the hum of the engines and people's voices.
"I WILL DO ANYTHING TO REACH EUROPE."
"I JUST WANT TO SEE MY SON AGAIN."
"I HAD TO LEAVE MY HOME. THE WAR CAME."
"I WANT TO MAKE A GOOD LIFE FOR MY CHILDREN. "
"MY UNCLE WORKS IN A RESTAURANT IN NAPLES. HE CAN GET ME A JOB."
"I WOULD LIKE WORK IN A SCHOOL."

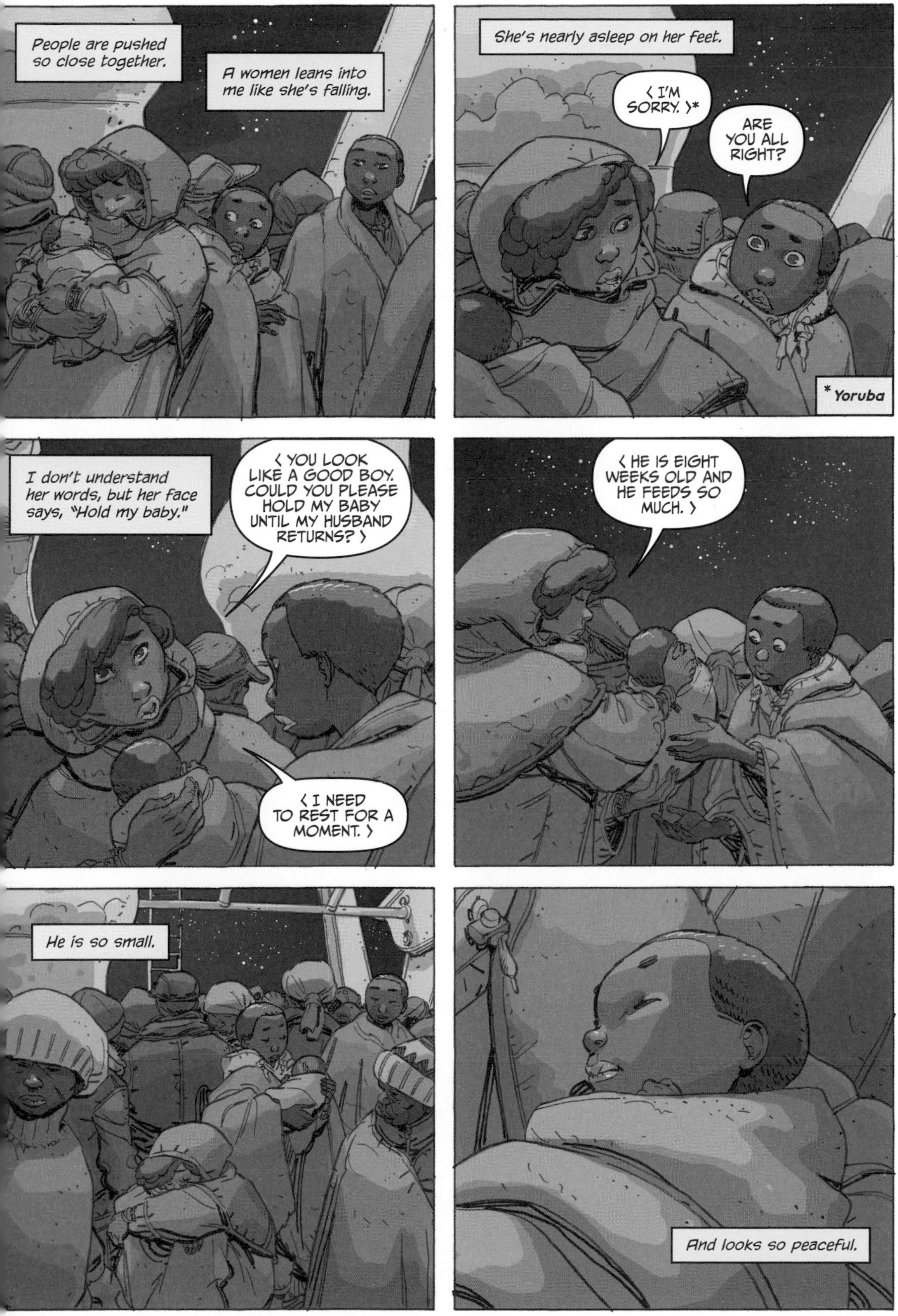
People are pushed so close together.
A women leans into me like she's falling.
She's nearly asleep on her feet.
‹ I'M SORRY. ›*
ARE YOU ALL RIGHT?
* Yoruba
I don't understand her words, but her face says, "Hold my baby."
‹ YOU LOOK LIKE A GOOD BOY. COULD YOU PLEASE HOLD MY BABY UNTIL MY HUSBAND RETURNS? ›
‹ I NEED TO REST FOR A MOMENT. ›
‹ HE IS EIGHT WEEKS OLD AND HE FEEDS SO MUCH. ›
He is so small.
And looks so peaceful.

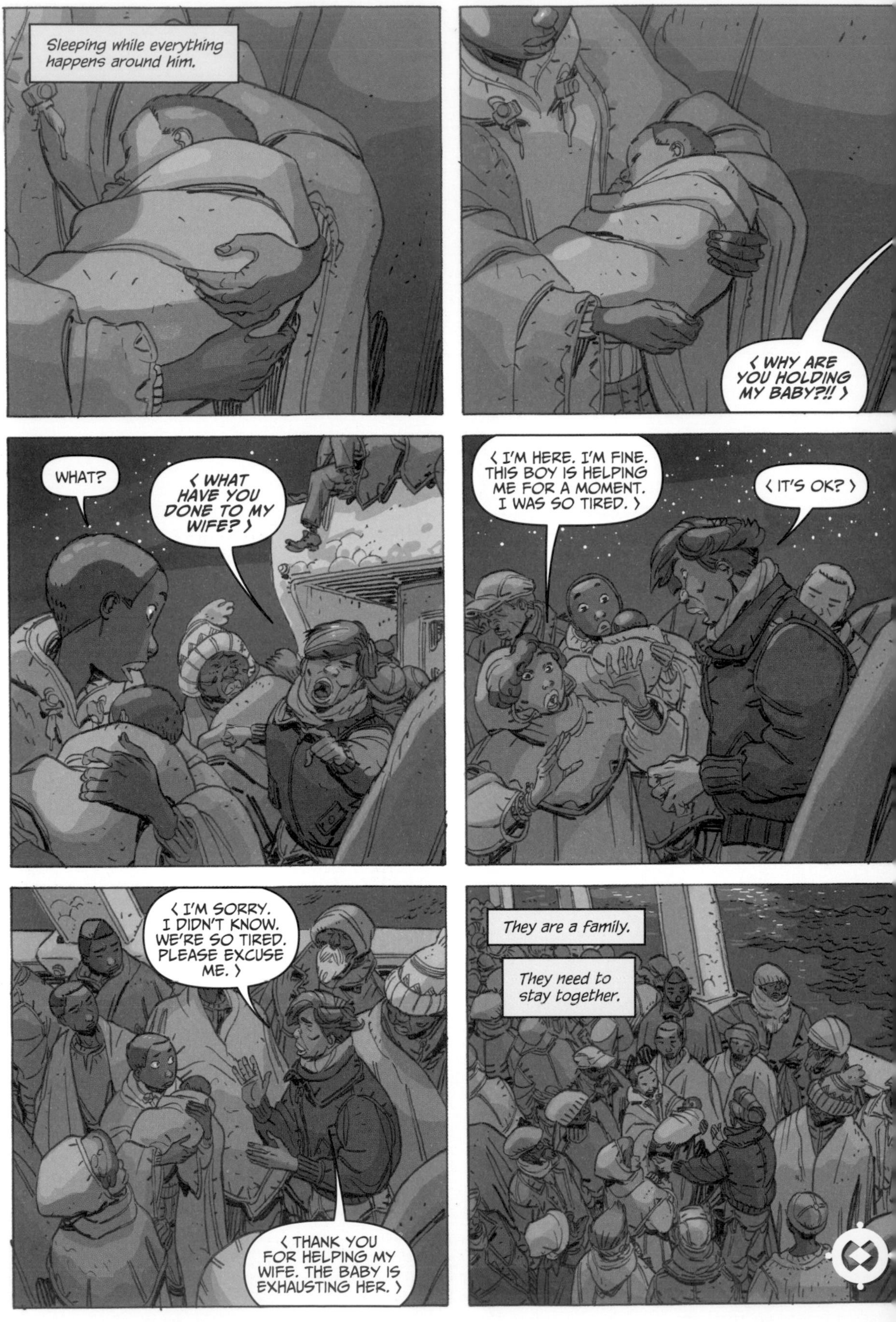
Sleeping while everything happens around him.
‹ WHY ARE YOU HOLDING MY BABY?!! ›
WHAT?
‹ WHAT HAVE YOU DONE TO MY WIFE? ›
‹ I'M HERE. I'M FINE. THIS BOY IS HELPING ME FOR A MOMENT. I WAS SO TIRED. ›
‹ IT'S OK? ›
‹ I'M SORRY. I DIDN'T KNOW. WE'RE SO TIRED. PLEASE EXCUSE ME. ›
‹ THANK YOU FOR HELPING MY WIFE. THE BABY IS EXHAUSTING HER. ›
They are a family.
They need to stay together.

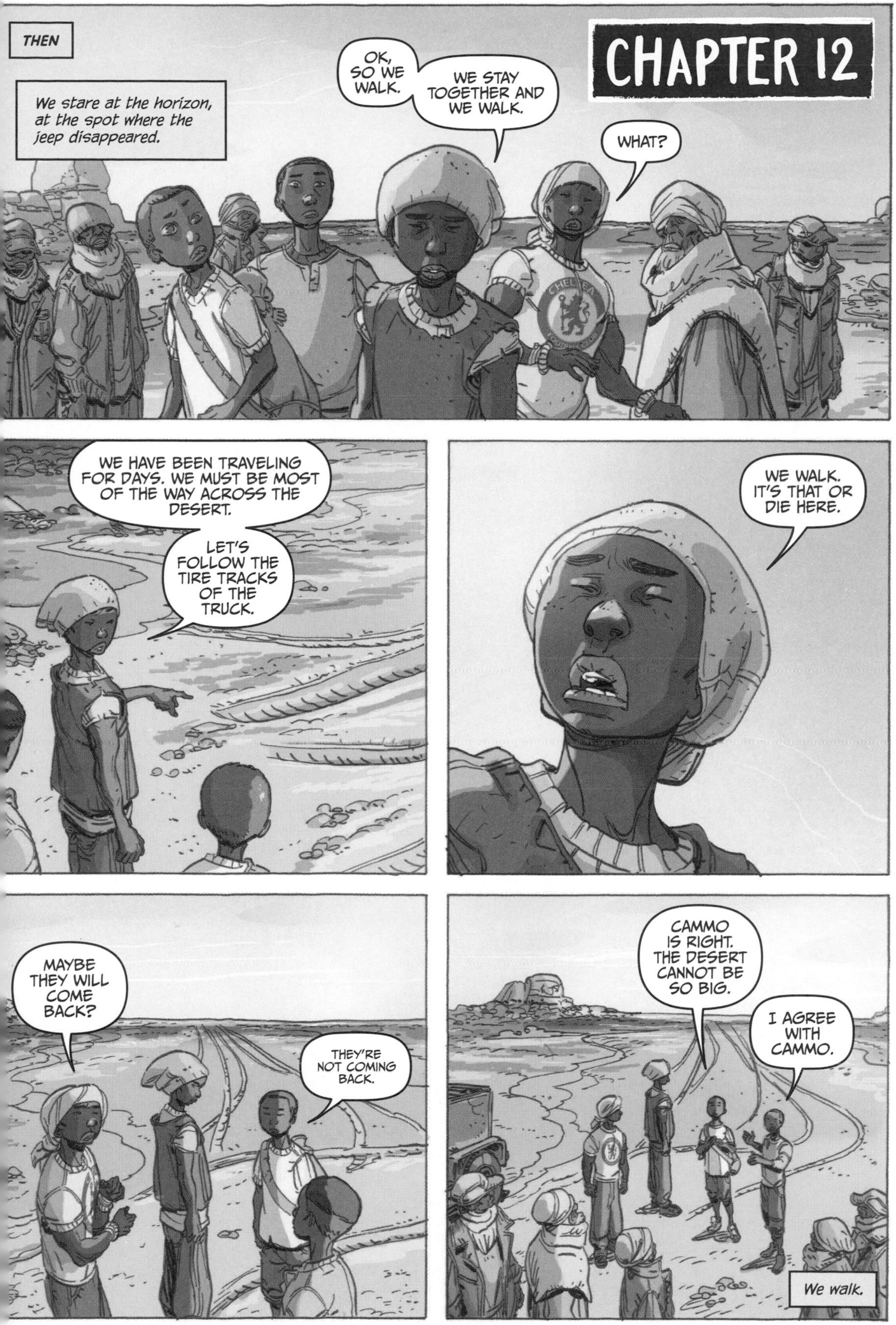
THEN
CHAPTER 12
We stare at the horizon, at the spot where the jeep disappeared.
OK, SO WE WALK.
WE STAY TOGETHER AND WE WALK.
WHAT?
WE HAVE BEEN TRAVELING FOR DAYS. WE MUST BE MOST OF THE WAY ACROSS THE DESERT.
LET'S FOLLOW THE TIRE TRACKS OF THE TRUCK.
WE WALK. IT'S THAT OR DIE HERE.
MAYBE THEY WILL COME BACK?
THEY'RE NOT COMING BACK.
CAMMO IS RIGHT. THE DESERT CANNOT BE SO BIG.
I AGREE WITH CAMMO.
We walk.

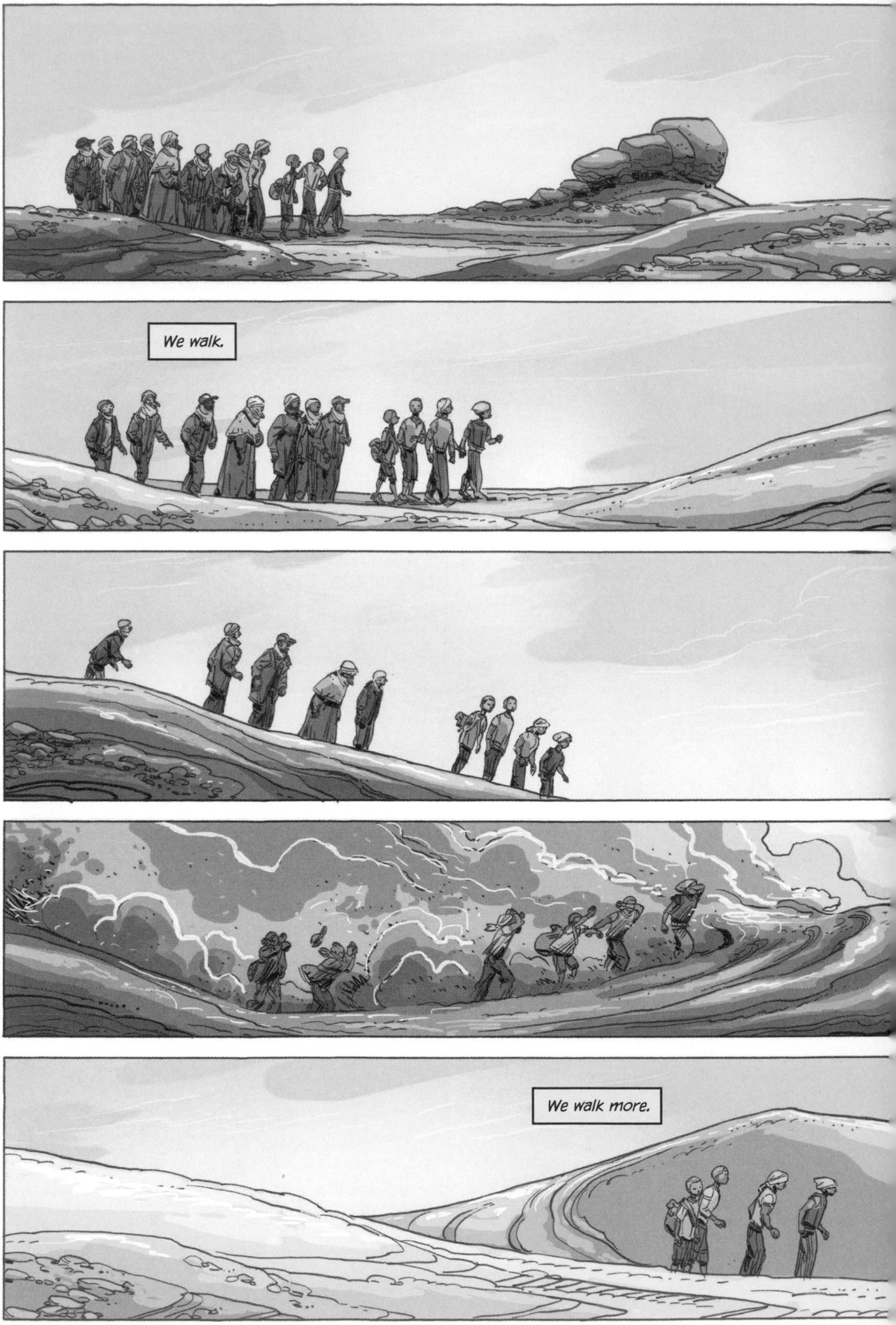
We walk.
We walk more.

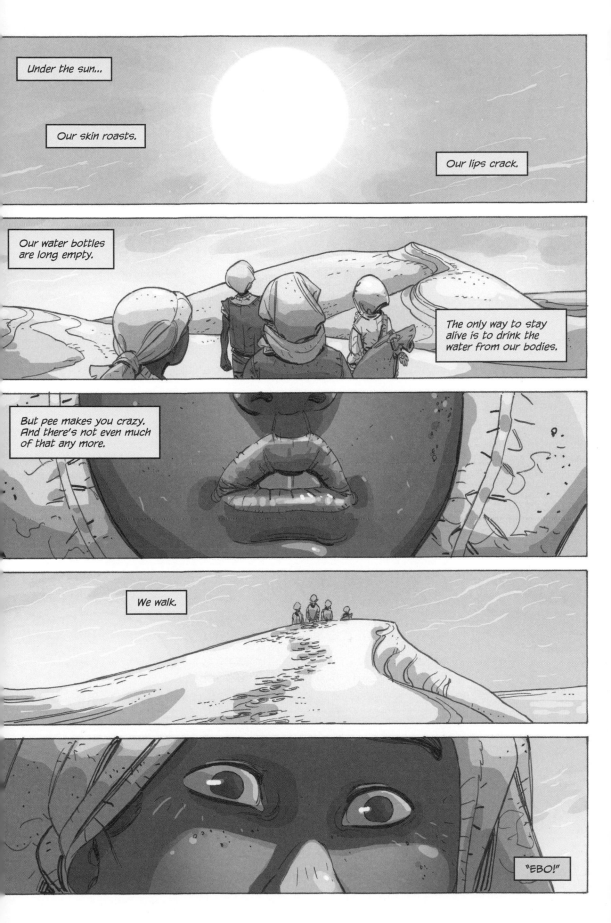

Under the sun...

Our skin roasts.

Our lips crack.

Our water bottles are long empty.

The only way to stay alive is to drink the water from our bodies.

But pee makes you crazy. And there's not even much of that any more.

We walk.

"EBO!"

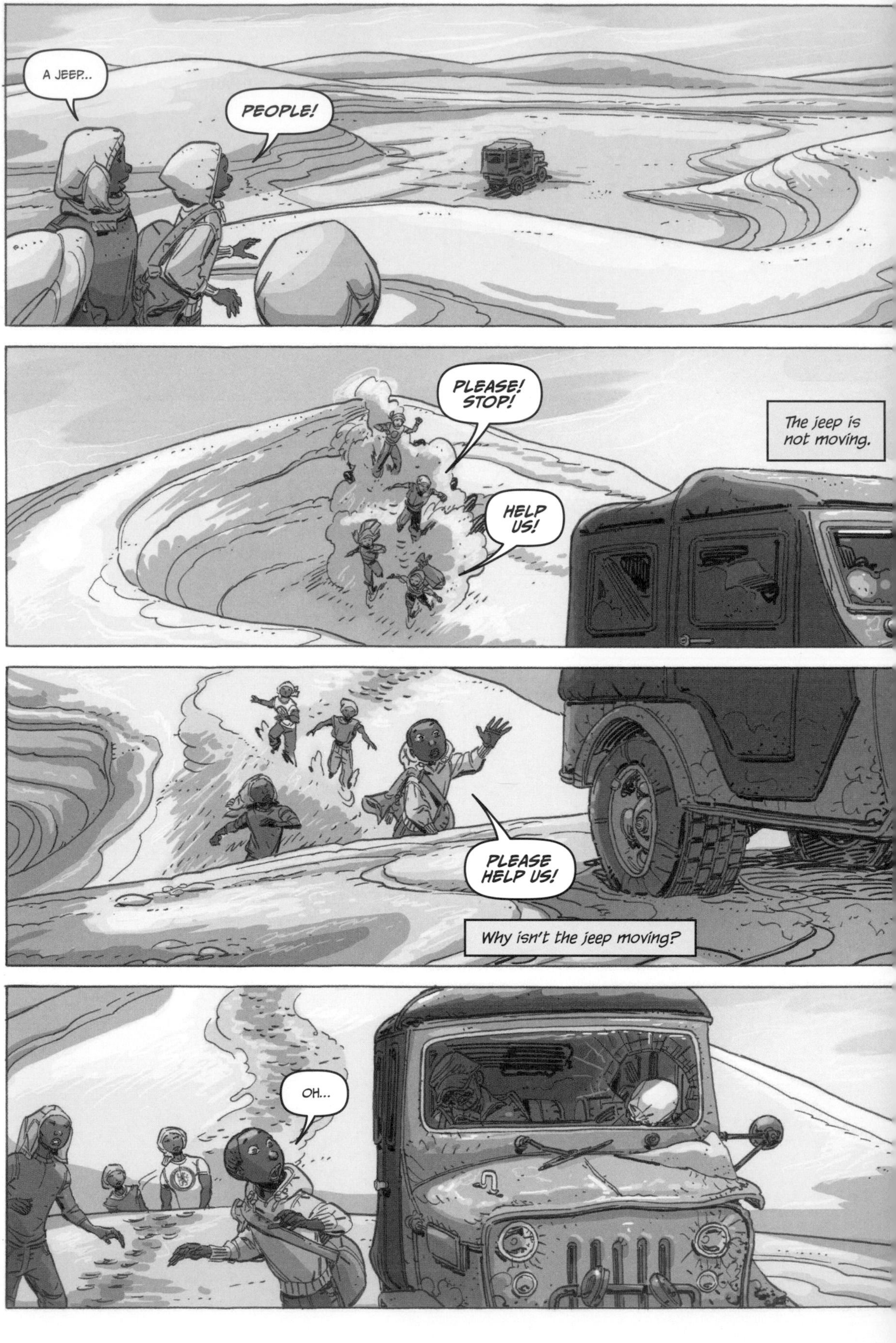
A JEEP...
PEOPLE!
PLEASE! STOP!
The jeep is not moving.
HELP US!
PLEASE HELP US!
Why isn't the jeep moving?
OH...

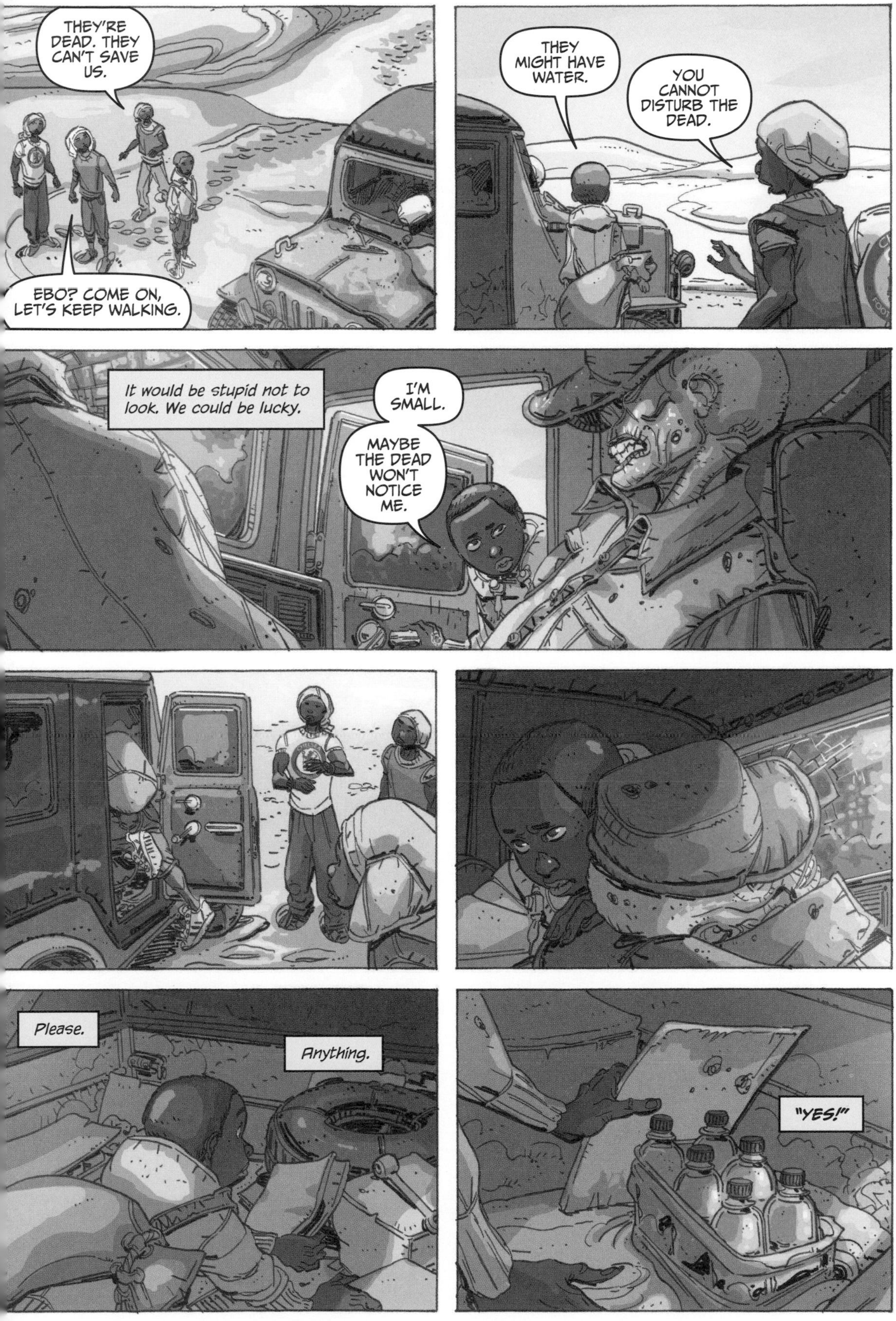
THEY'RE DEAD. THEY CAN'T SAVE US.
EBO? COME ON, LET'S KEEP WALKING.
THEY MIGHT HAVE WATER.
YOU CANNOT DISTURB THE DEAD.
It would be stupid not to look. We could be lucky.
I'M SMALL.
MAYBE THE DEAD WON'T NOTICE ME.
Please.
Anything.
"YES!"

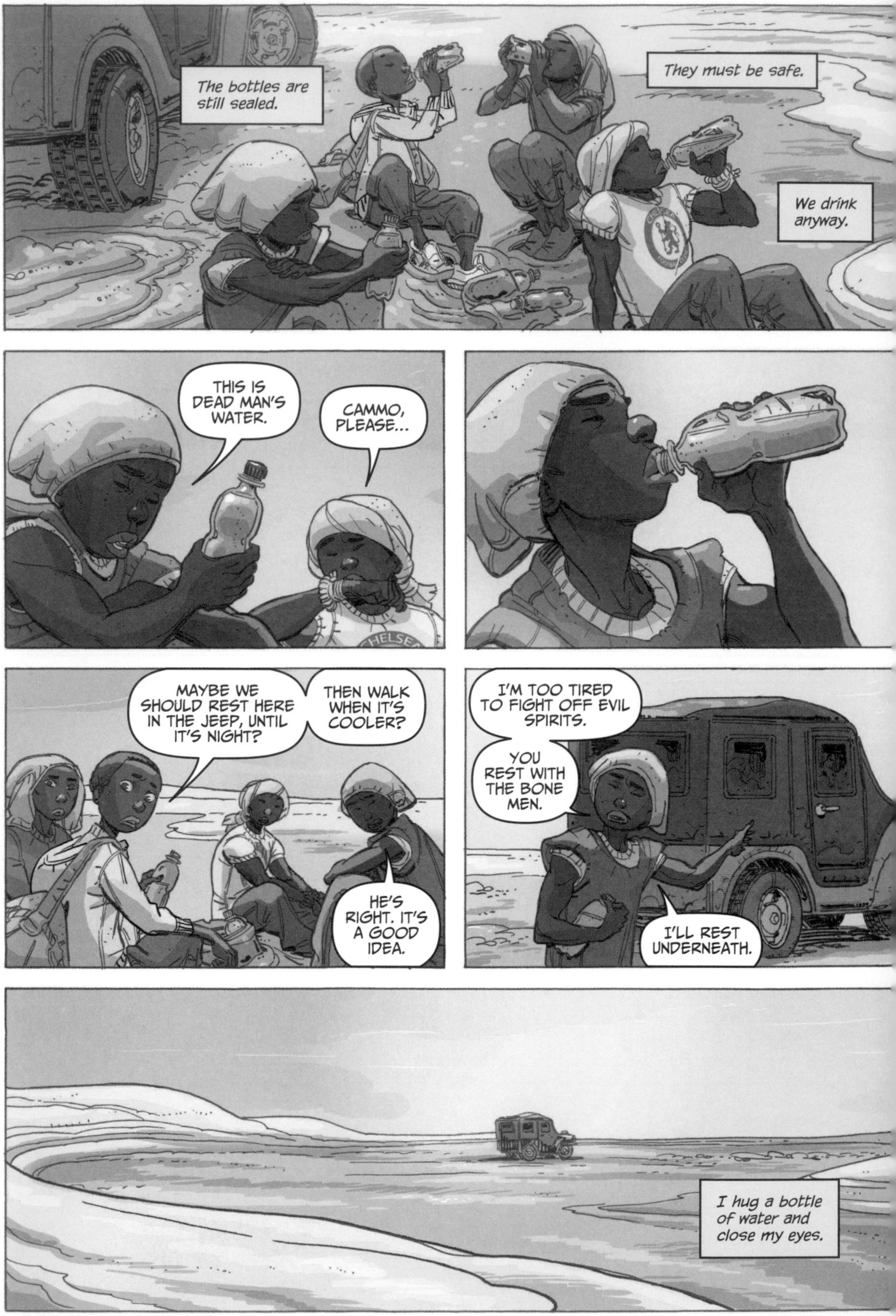

The bottles are still sealed.
They must be safe.
We drink anyway.
THIS IS DEAD MAN'S WATER.
CAMMO, PLEASE...
MAYBE WE SHOULD REST HERE IN THE JEEP, UNTIL IT'S NIGHT?
THEN WALK WHEN IT'S COOLER?
HE'S RIGHT. IT'S A GOOD IDEA.
I'M TOO TIRED TO FIGHT OFF EVIL SPIRITS.
YOU REST WITH THE BONE MEN.
I'LL REST UNDERNEATH.
I hug a bottle of water and close my eyes.

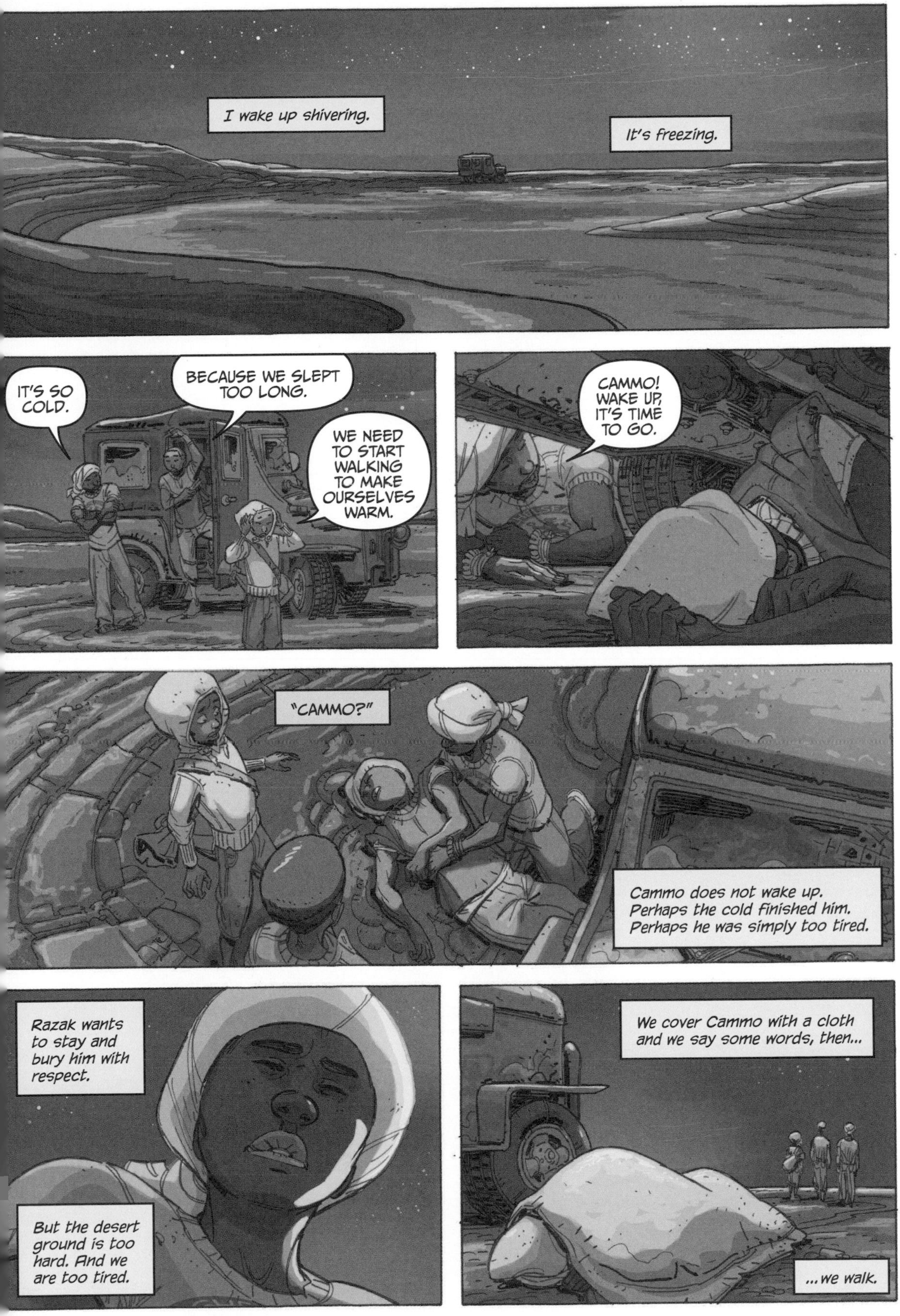
I wake up shivering.
It's freezing.
IT'S SO COLD.
BECAUSE WE SLEPT TOO LONG.
WE NEED TO START WALKING TO MAKE OURSELVES WARM.
CAMMO! WAKE UP, IT'S TIME TO GO.
"CAMMO?"
Cammo does not wake up. Perhaps the cold finished him. Perhaps he was simply too tired.
Razak wants to stay and bury him with respect.
But the desert ground is too hard. And we are too tired.
We cover Cammo with a cloth and we say some words, then...
...we walk.

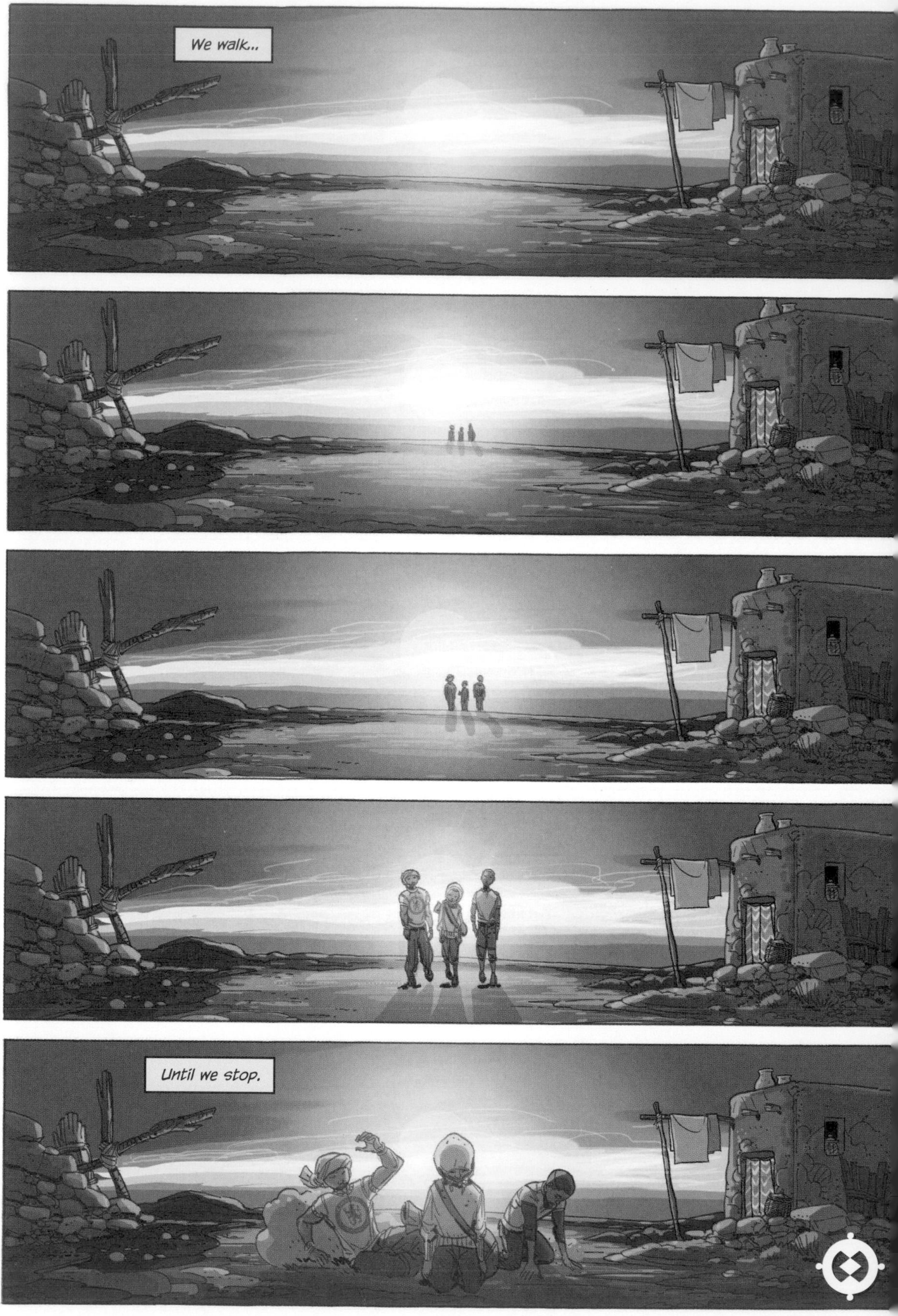
We walk...
Until we stop.

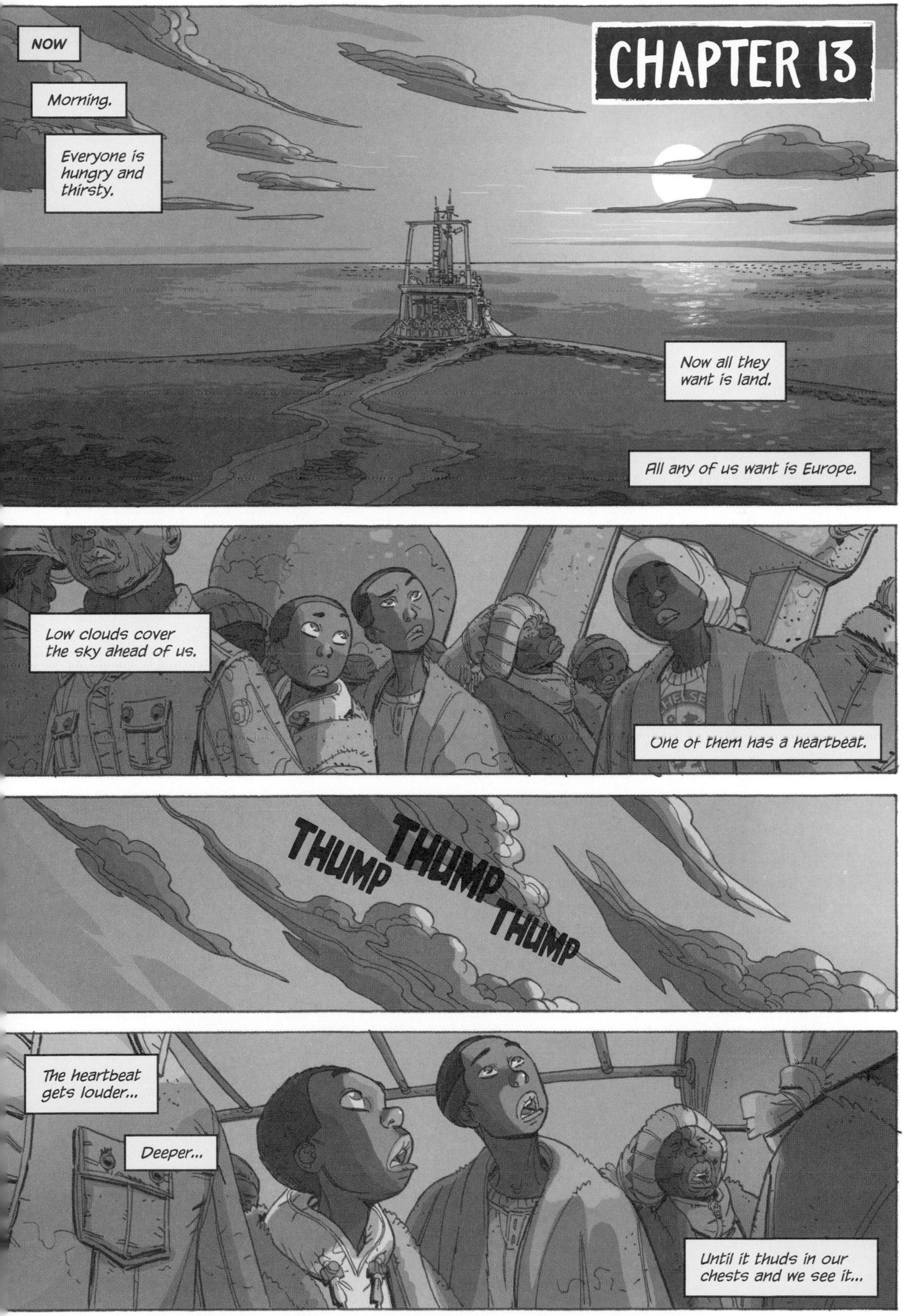
CHAPTER 13
NOW
Morning.
Everyone is hungry and thirsty.
Now all they want is land.
All any of us want is Europe.
Low clouds cover the sky ahead of us.
One of them has a heartbeat.
THUMP
THUMP
THUMP
The heartbeat gets louder...
Deeper...
Until it thuds in our chests and we see it...

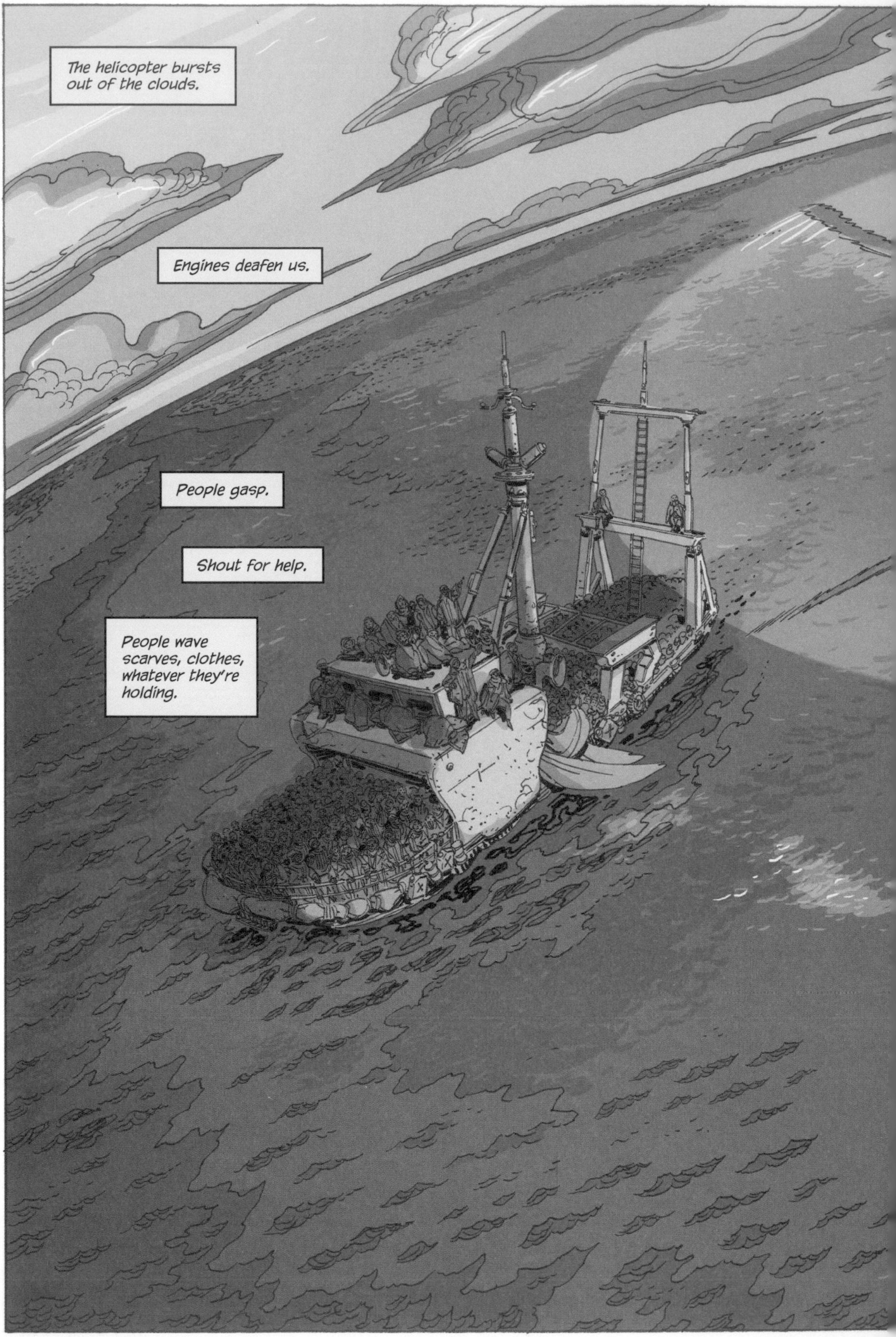
The helicopter bursts out of the clouds.
Engines deafen us.
People gasp.
Shout for help.
People wave scarves, clothes, whatever they're holding.

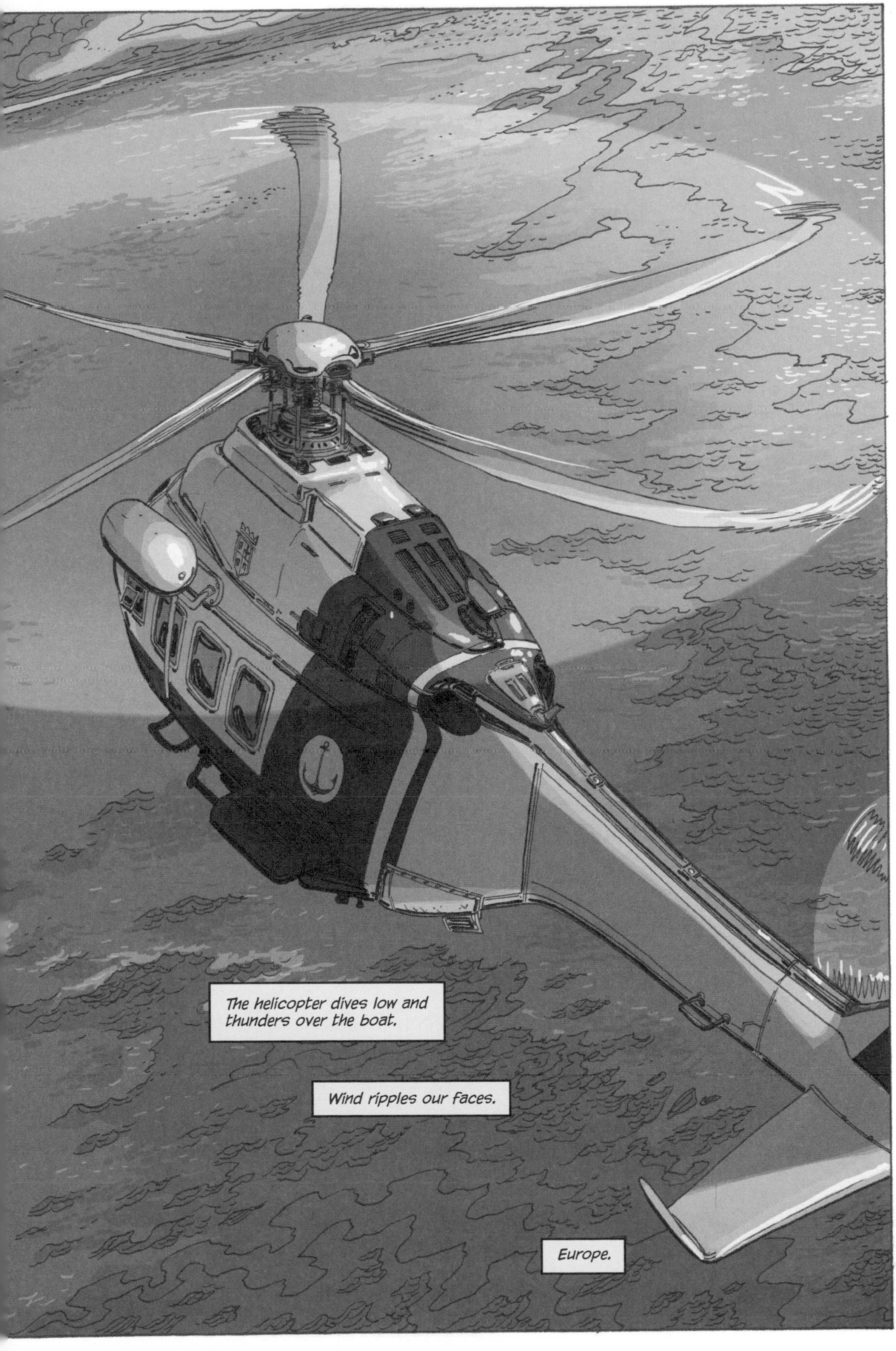
The helicopter dives low and thunders over the boat.
Wind ripples our faces.
Europe.

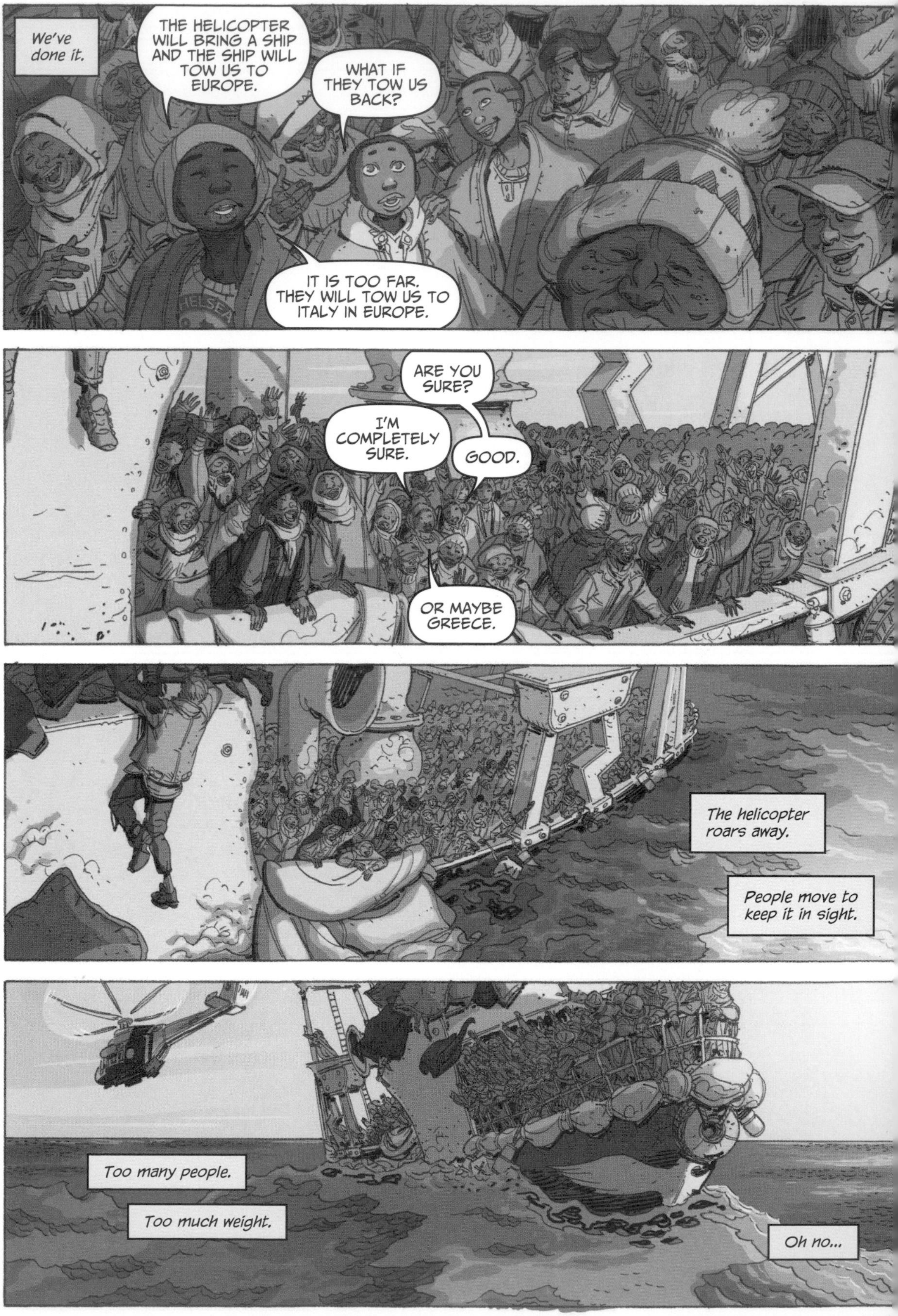
We've done it.
THE HELICOPTER WILL BRING A SHIP AND THE SHIP WILL TOW US TO EUROPE.
WHAT IF THEY TOW US BACK?
IT IS TOO FAR. THEY WILL TOW US TO ITALY IN EUROPE.
ARE YOU SURE?
I'M COMPLETELY SURE.
GOOD.
OR MAYBE GREECE.
The helicopter roars away.
People move to keep it in sight.
Too many people.
Too much weight.
Oh no...

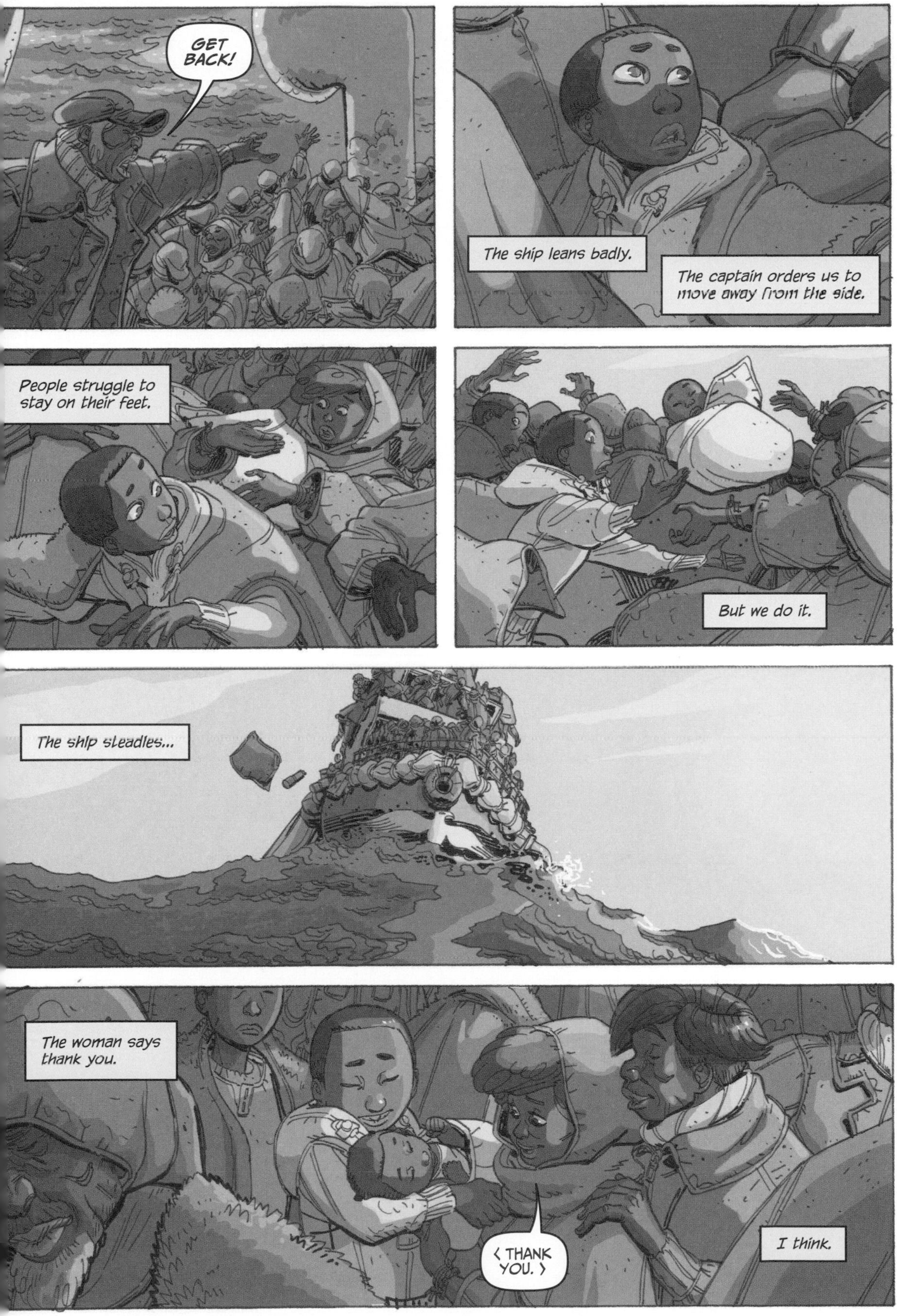
GET BACK!
The ship leans badly.
The captain orders us to move away from the side.
People struggle to stay on their feet.
But we do it.
The ship steadies...
The woman says thank you.
‹ THANK YOU. ›
I think.

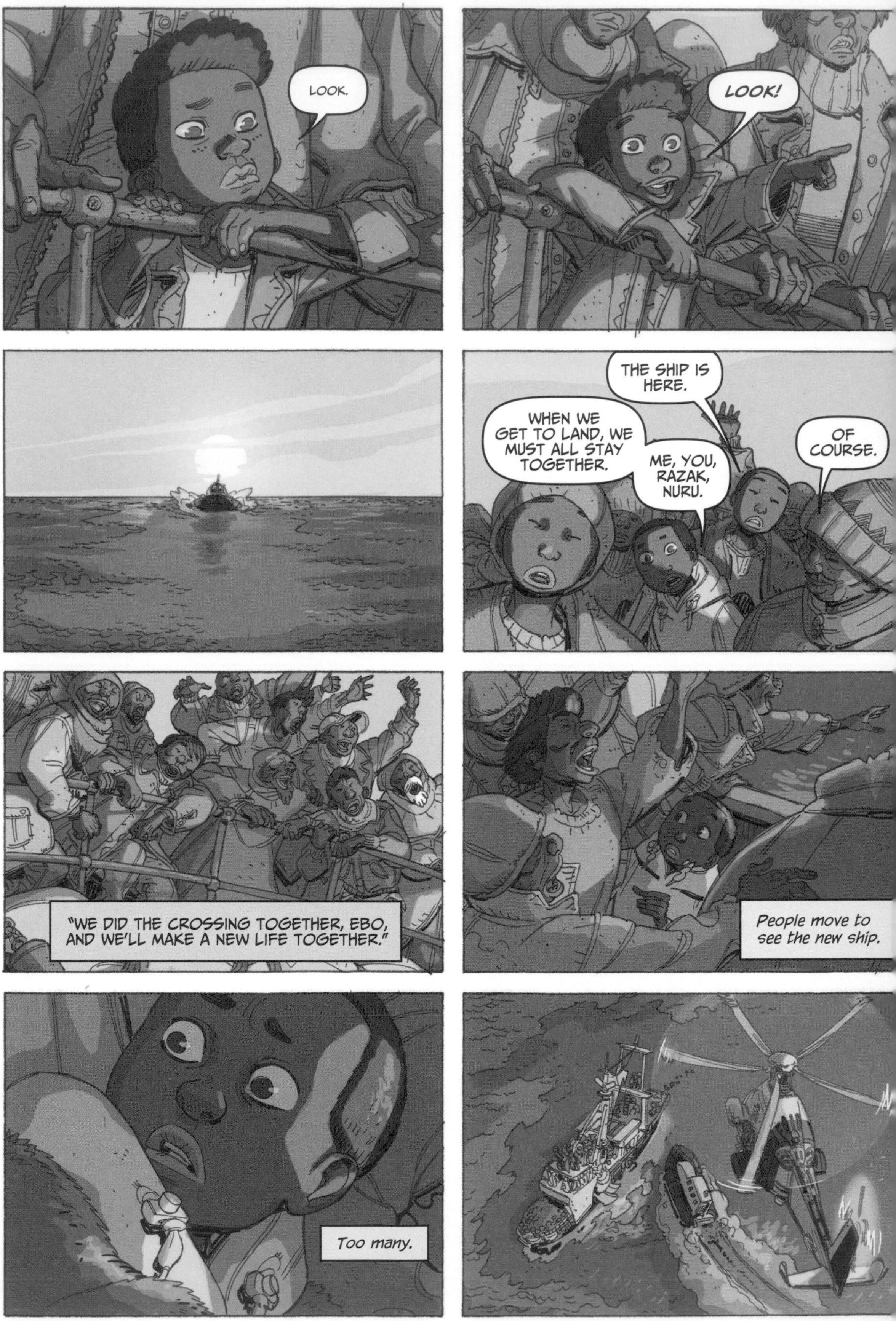
LOOK.
LOOK!
THE SHIP IS HERE.
WHEN WE GET TO LAND, WE MUST ALL STAY TOGETHER.
ME, YOU, RAZAK, NURU.
OF COURSE.
"WE DID THE CROSSING TOGETHER, EBO, AND WE'LL MAKE A NEW LIFE TOGETHER."
People move to see the new ship.
Too many.

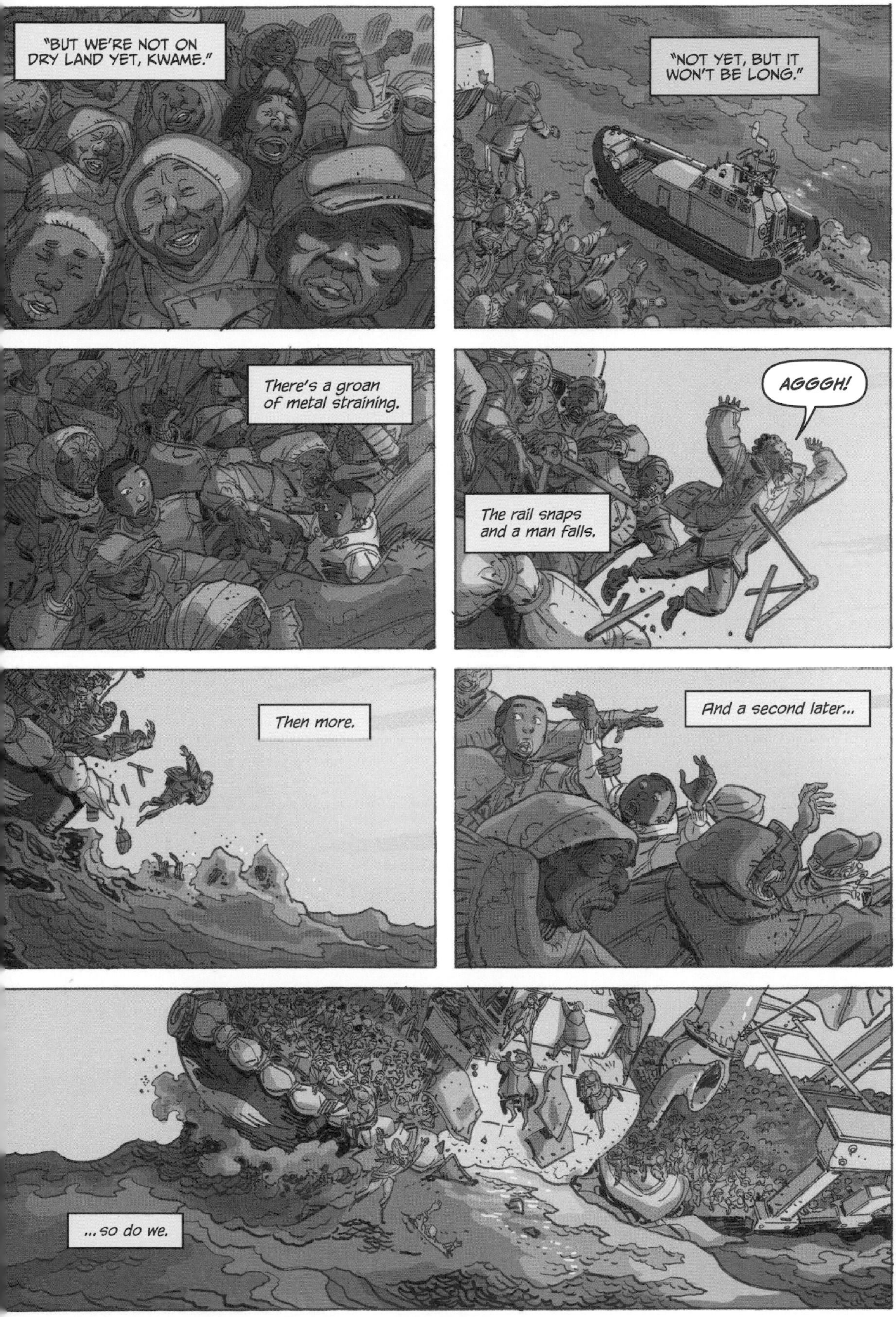
"BUT WE'RE NOT ON DRY LAND YET, KWAME."
"NOT YET, BUT IT WON'T BE LONG."
There's a groan of metal straining.
AGGGH!
The rail snaps and a man falls.
Then more.
And a second later...
...so do we.

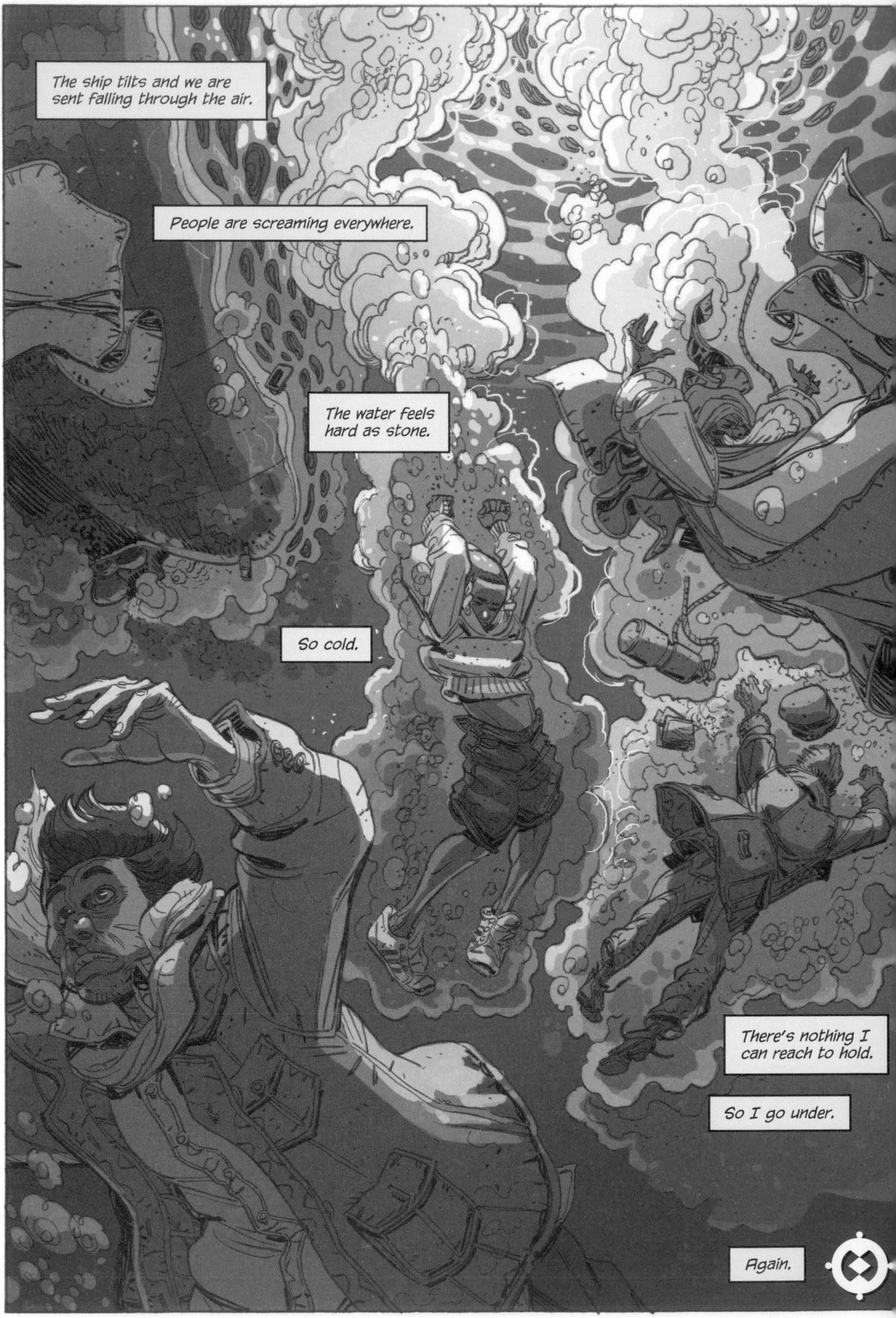
The ship tilts and we are sent falling through the air.
People are screaming everywhere.
The water feels hard as stone.
So cold.
There's nothing I can reach to hold.
So I go under.
Again.

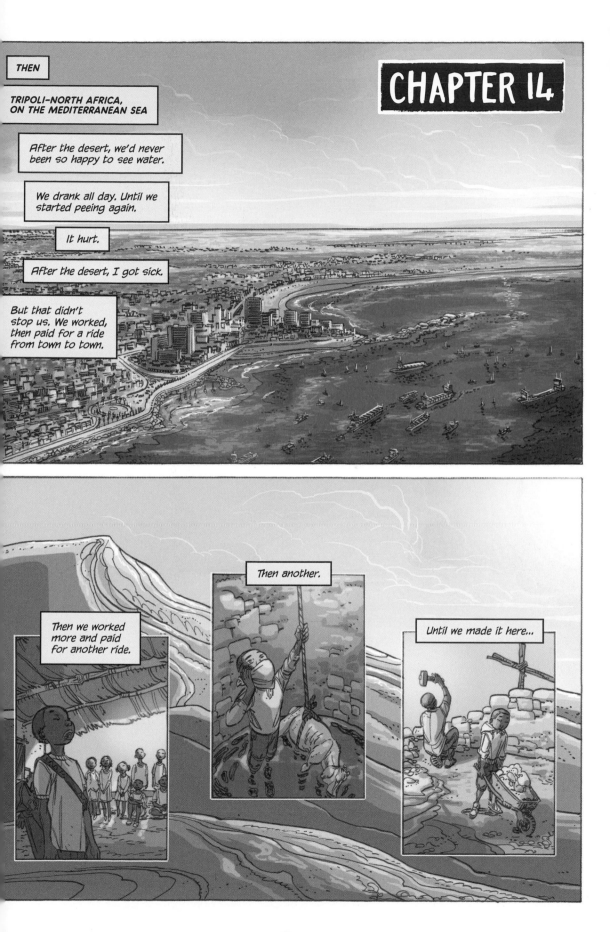

THEN

TRIPOLI—NORTH AFRICA,
ON THE MEDITERRANEAN SEA

CHAPTER 14

After the desert, we'd never been so happy to see water.

We drank all day. Until we started peeing again.

It hurt.

After the desert, I got sick.

But that didn't stop us. We worked, then paid for a ride from town to town.

Then we worked more and paid for another ride.

Then another.

Until we made it here...

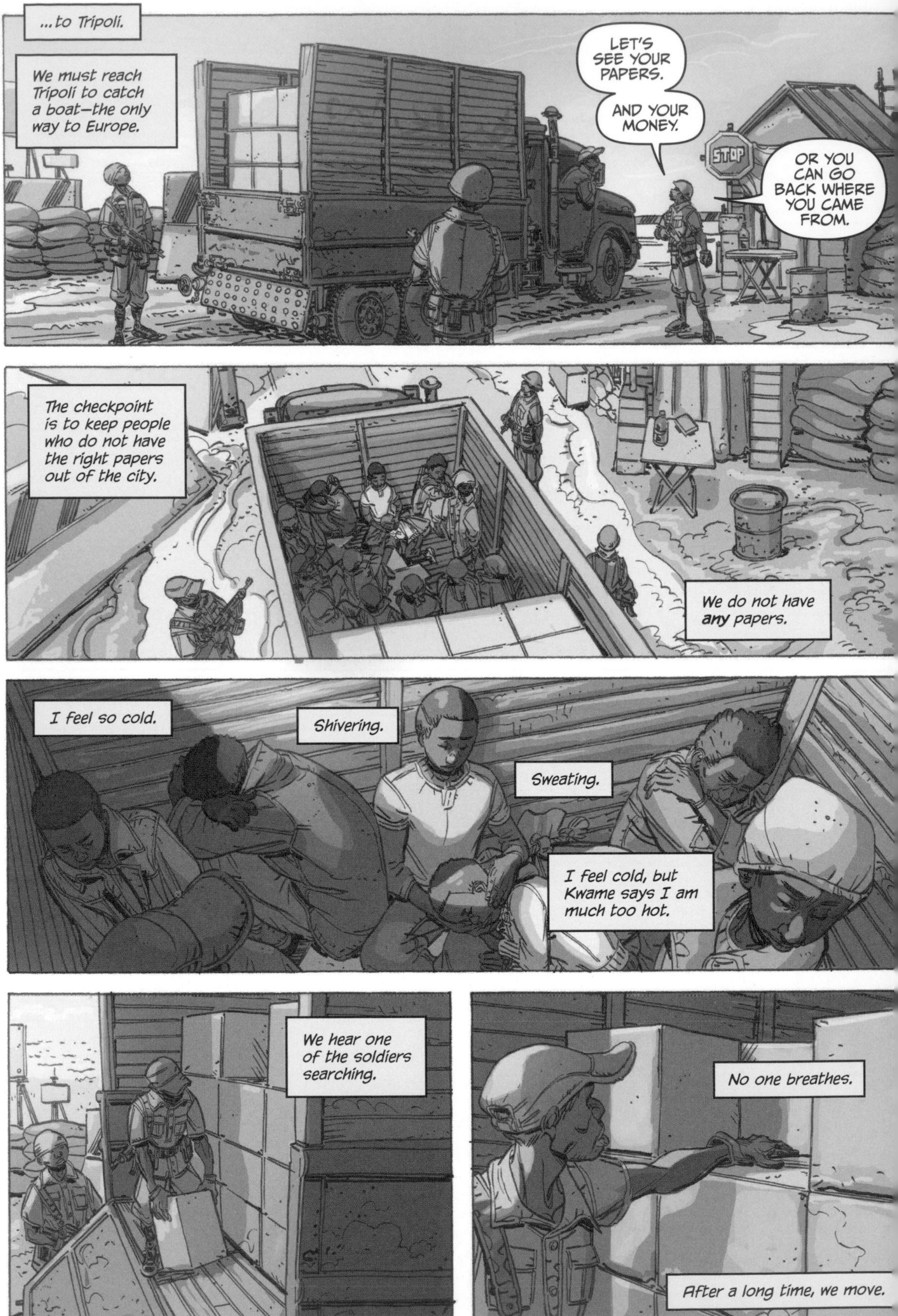
...to Tripoli.
We must reach Tripoli to catch a boat—the only way to Europe.
LET'S SEE YOUR PAPERS.
AND YOUR MONEY.
STOP
OR YOU CAN GO BACK WHERE YOU CAME FROM.
The checkpoint is to keep people who do not have the right papers out of the city.
We do not have **any** papers.
I feel so cold.
Shivering.
Sweating.
I feel cold, but Kwame says I am much too hot.
We hear one of the soldiers searching.
No one breathes.
After a long time, we move.

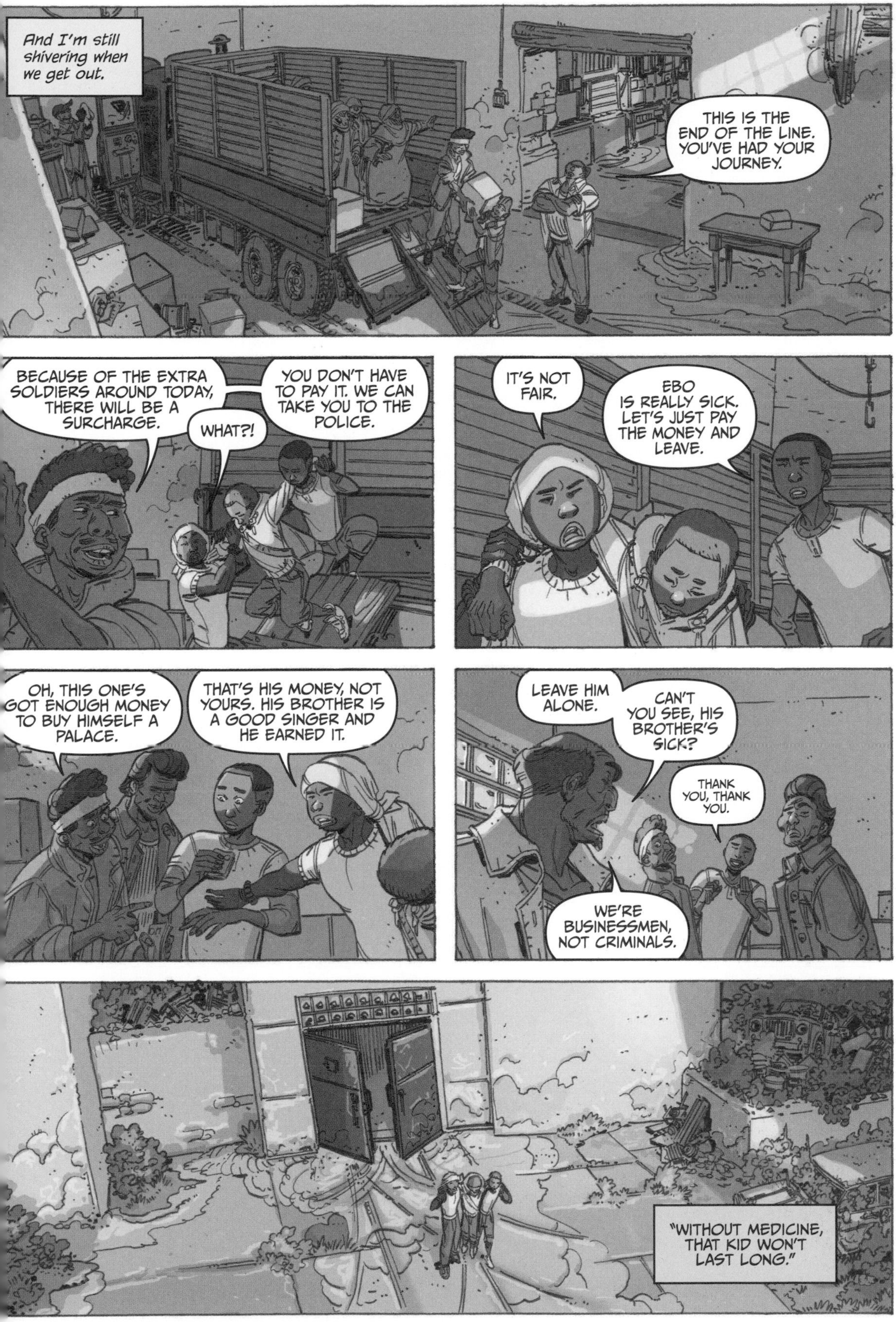

And I'm still shivering when we get out.
THIS IS THE END OF THE LINE. YOU'VE HAD YOUR JOURNEY.
BECAUSE OF THE EXTRA SOLDIERS AROUND TODAY, THERE WILL BE A SURCHARGE.
WHAT?!
YOU DON'T HAVE TO PAY IT. WE CAN TAKE YOU TO THE POLICE.
IT'S NOT FAIR.
EBO IS REALLY SICK. LET'S JUST PAY THE MONEY AND LEAVE.
OH, THIS ONE'S GOT ENOUGH MONEY TO BUY HIMSELF A PALACE.
THAT'S HIS MONEY, NOT YOURS. HIS BROTHER IS A GOOD SINGER AND HE EARNED IT.
LEAVE HIM ALONE.
CAN'T YOU SEE, HIS BROTHER'S SICK?
THANK YOU, THANK YOU.
WE'RE BUSINESSMEN, NOT CRIMINALS.
"WITHOUT MEDICINE, THAT KID WON'T LAST LONG."

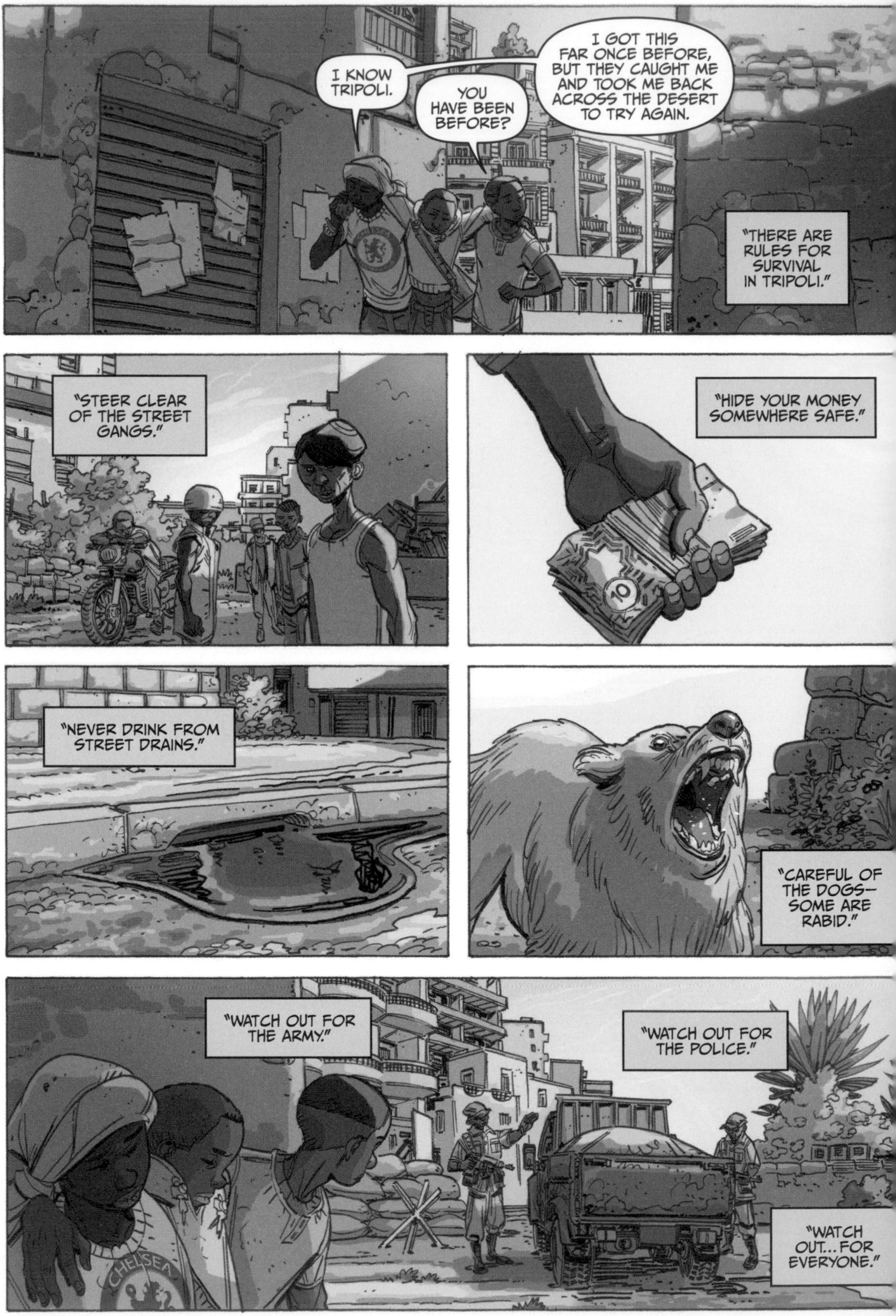
I KNOW TRIPOLI.
YOU HAVE BEEN BEFORE?
I GOT THIS FAR ONCE BEFORE, BUT THEY CAUGHT ME AND TOOK ME BACK ACROSS THE DESERT TO TRY AGAIN.
"THERE ARE RULES FOR SURVIVAL IN TRIPOLI."
"STEER CLEAR OF THE STREET GANGS."
"HIDE YOUR MONEY SOMEWHERE SAFE."
"NEVER DRINK FROM STREET DRAINS."
"CAREFUL OF THE DOGS— SOME ARE RABID."
"WATCH OUT FOR THE ARMY."
"WATCH OUT FOR THE POLICE."
"WATCH OUT... FOR EVERYONE."

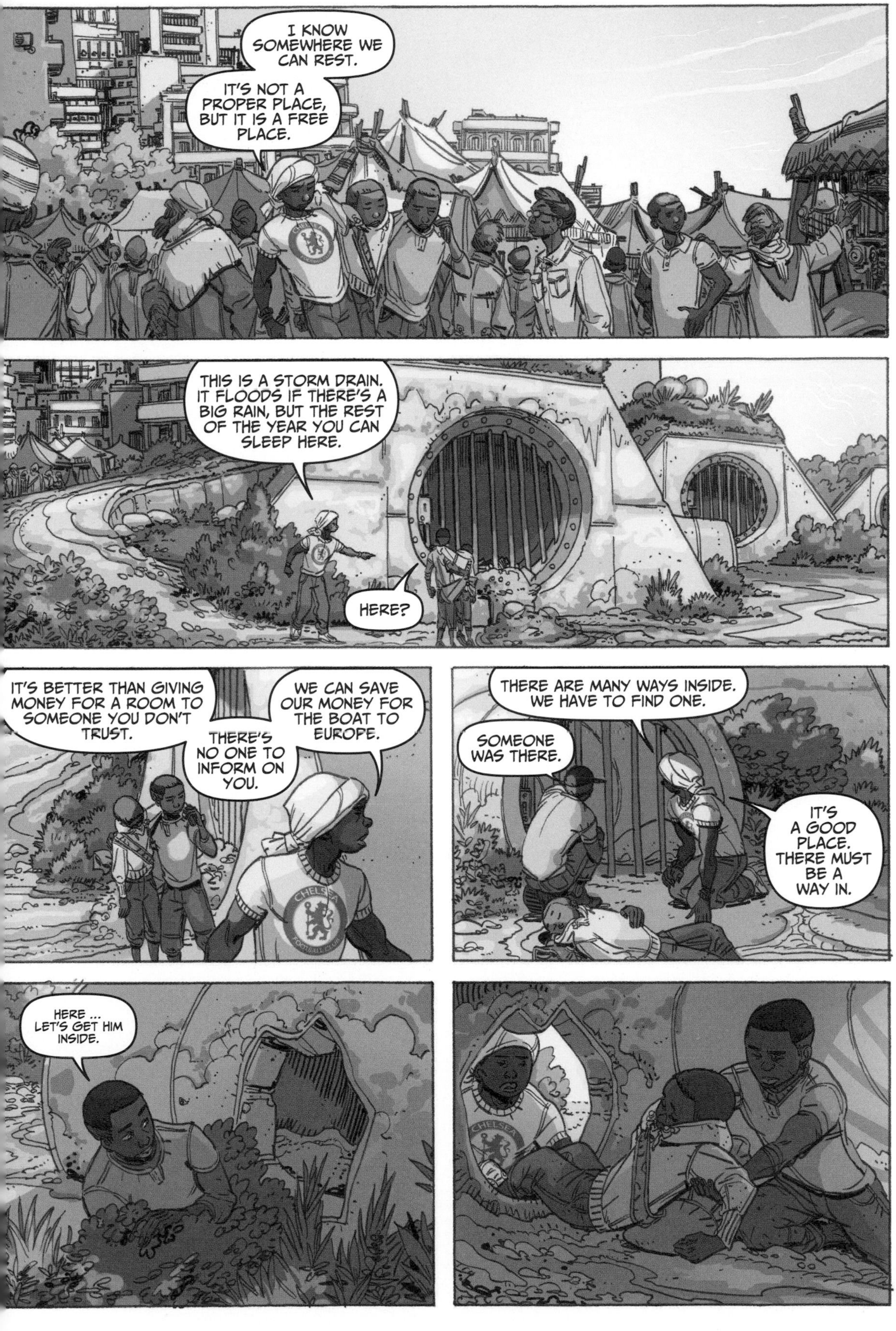
I KNOW SOMEWHERE WE CAN REST.
IT'S NOT A PROPER PLACE, BUT IT IS A FREE PLACE.
THIS IS A STORM DRAIN. IT FLOODS IF THERE'S A BIG RAIN, BUT THE REST OF THE YEAR YOU CAN SLEEP HERE.
HERE?
IT'S BETTER THAN GIVING MONEY FOR A ROOM TO SOMEONE YOU DON'T TRUST.
THERE'S NO ONE TO INFORM ON YOU.
WE CAN SAVE OUR MONEY FOR THE BOAT TO EUROPE.
THERE ARE MANY WAYS INSIDE. WE HAVE TO FIND ONE.
SOMEONE WAS THERE.
IT'S A GOOD PLACE. THERE MUST BE A WAY IN.
HERE ... LET'S GET HIM INSIDE.

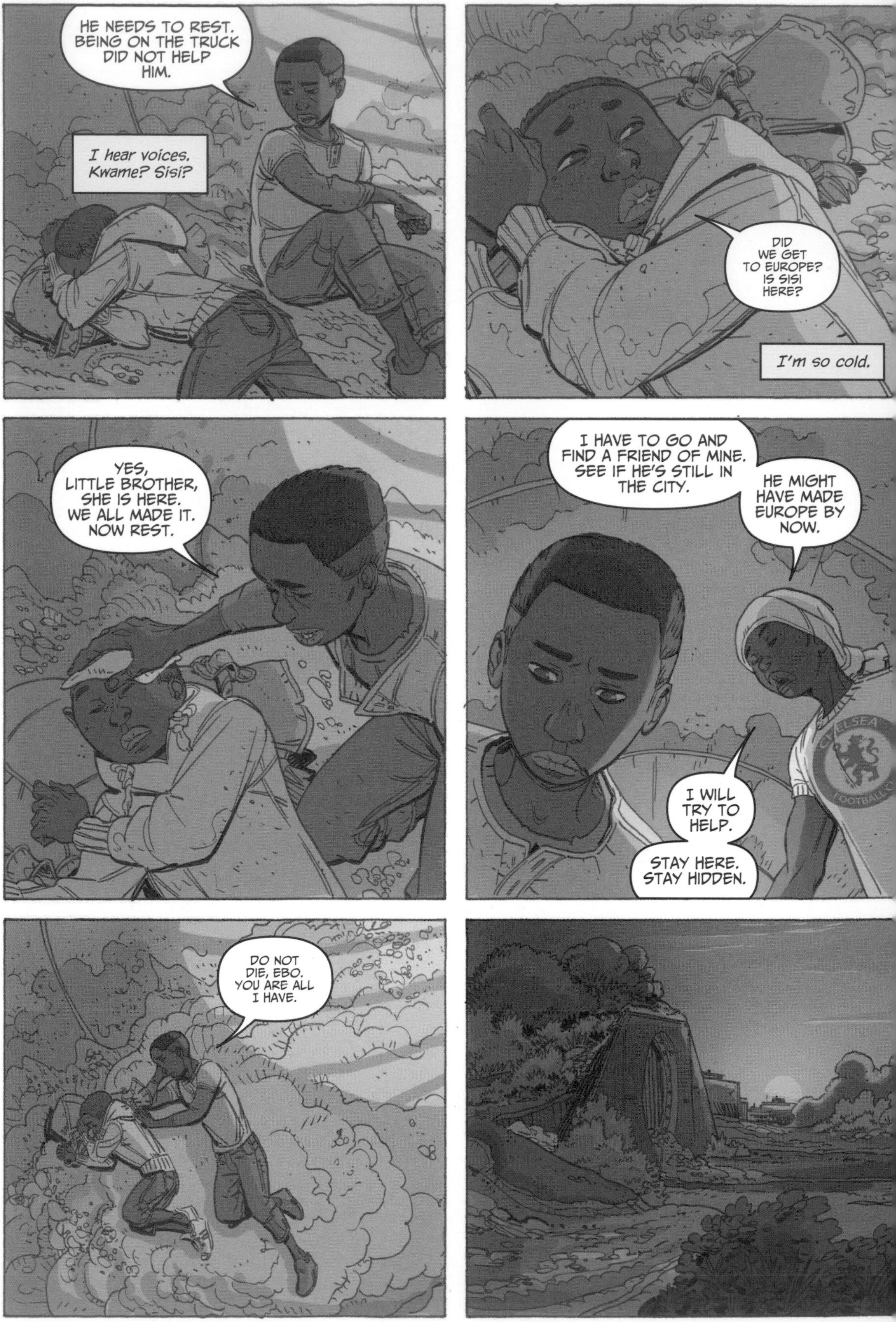
HE NEEDS TO REST. BEING ON THE TRUCK DID NOT HELP HIM.
I hear voices. Kwame? Sisi?
DID WE GET TO EUROPE? IS SISI HERE?
I'm so cold.
YES, LITTLE BROTHER, SHE IS HERE. WE ALL MADE IT. NOW REST.
I HAVE TO GO AND FIND A FRIEND OF MINE. SEE IF HE'S STILL IN THE CITY.
HE MIGHT HAVE MADE EUROPE BY NOW.
I WILL TRY TO HELP.
STAY HERE. STAY HIDDEN.
DO NOT DIE, EBO. YOU ARE ALL I HAVE.

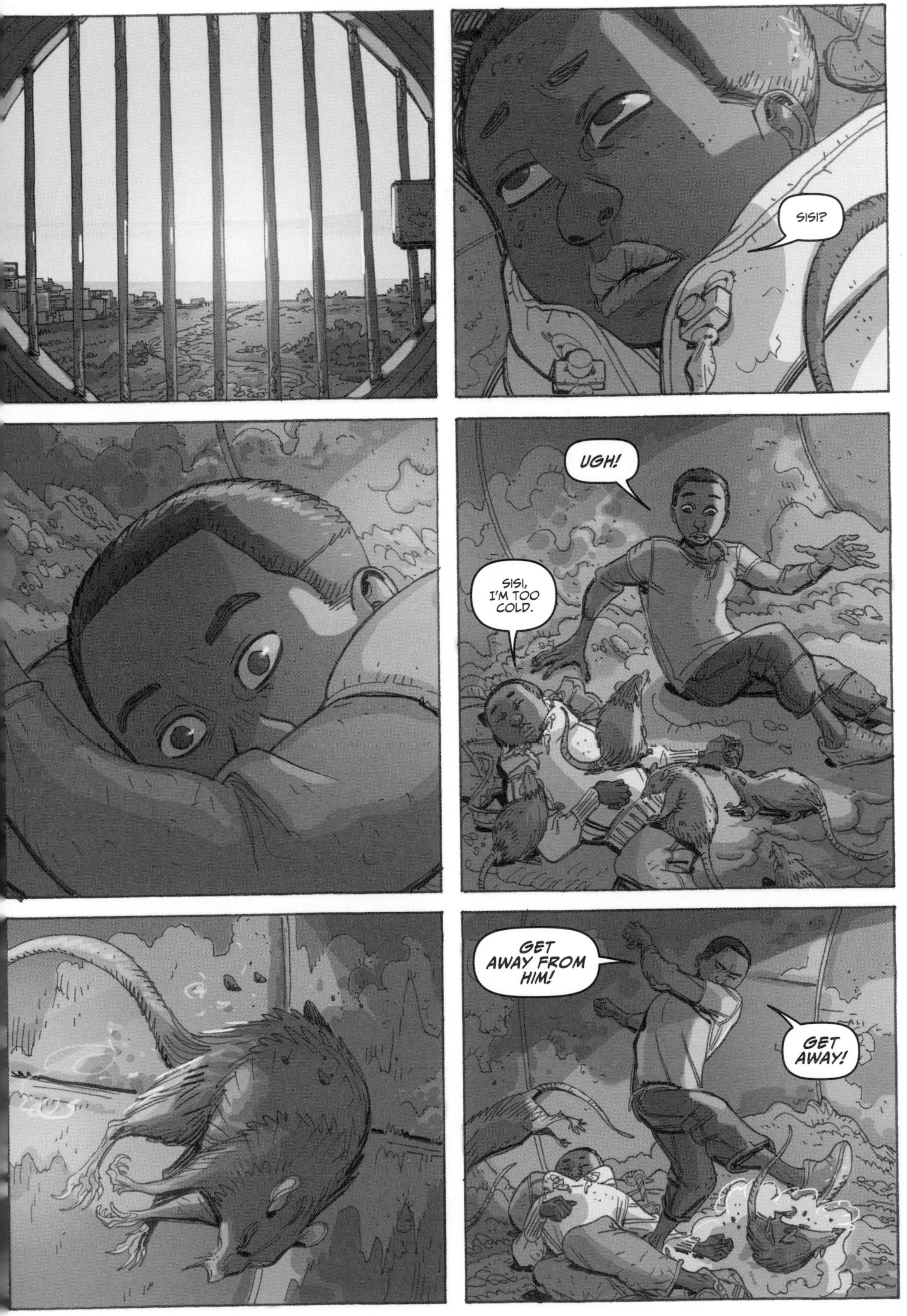
SISI?
UGH!
SISI, I'M TOO COLD.
GET AWAY FROM HIM!
GET AWAY!

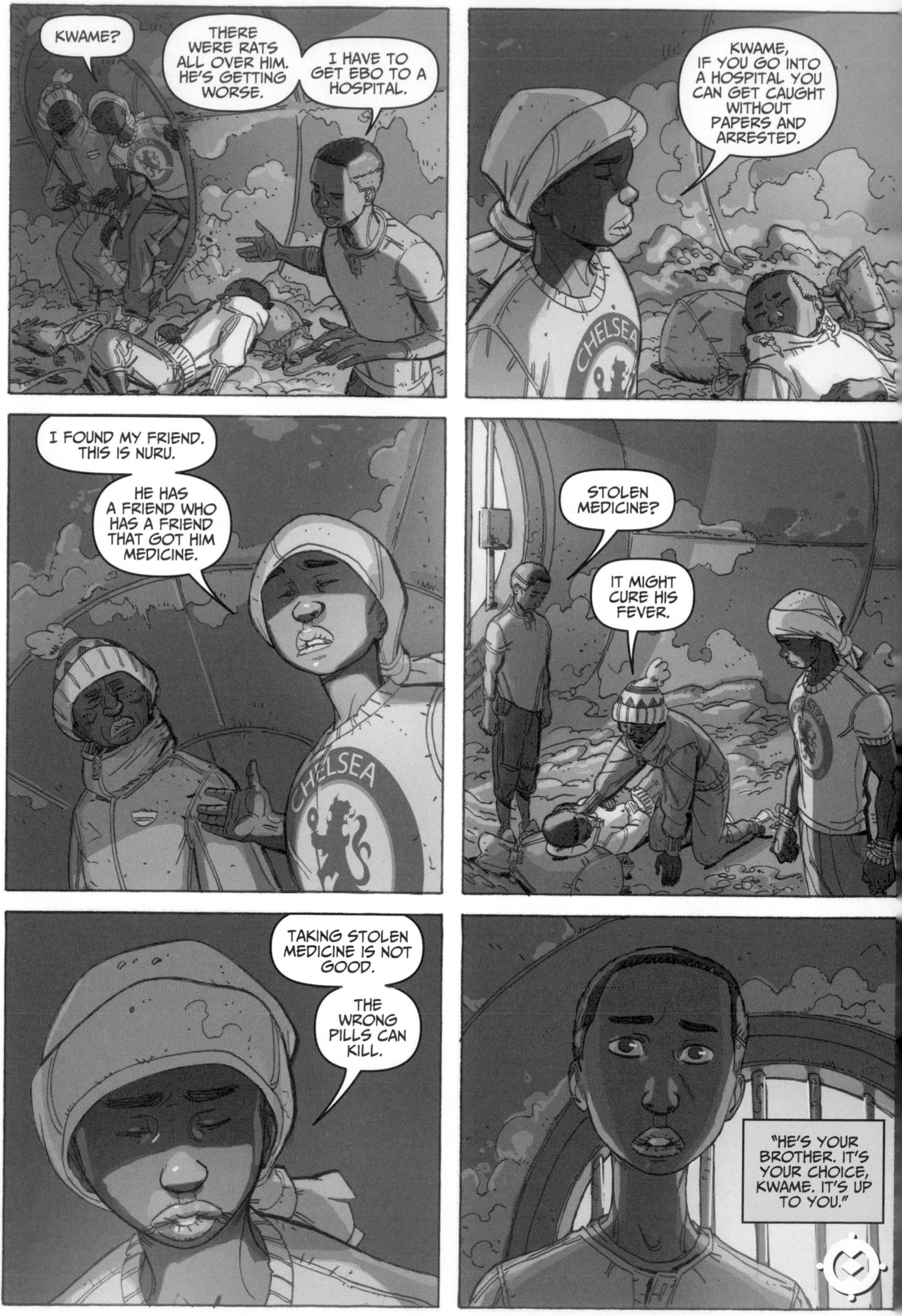
KWAME?
THERE WERE RATS ALL OVER HIM. HE'S GETTING WORSE.
I HAVE TO GET EBO TO A HOSPITAL.
CHELSEA
KWAME, IF YOU GO INTO A HOSPITAL YOU CAN GET CAUGHT WITHOUT PAPERS AND ARRESTED.
CHELSEA
I FOUND MY FRIEND. THIS IS NURU.
HE HAS A FRIEND WHO HAS A FRIEND THAT GOT HIM MEDICINE.
CHELSEA
STOLEN MEDICINE?
IT MIGHT CURE HIS FEVER.
CHELSEA
TAKING STOLEN MEDICINE IS NOT GOOD.
THE WRONG PILLS CAN KILL.
"HE'S YOUR BROTHER. IT'S YOUR CHOICE, KWAME. IT'S UP TO YOU."

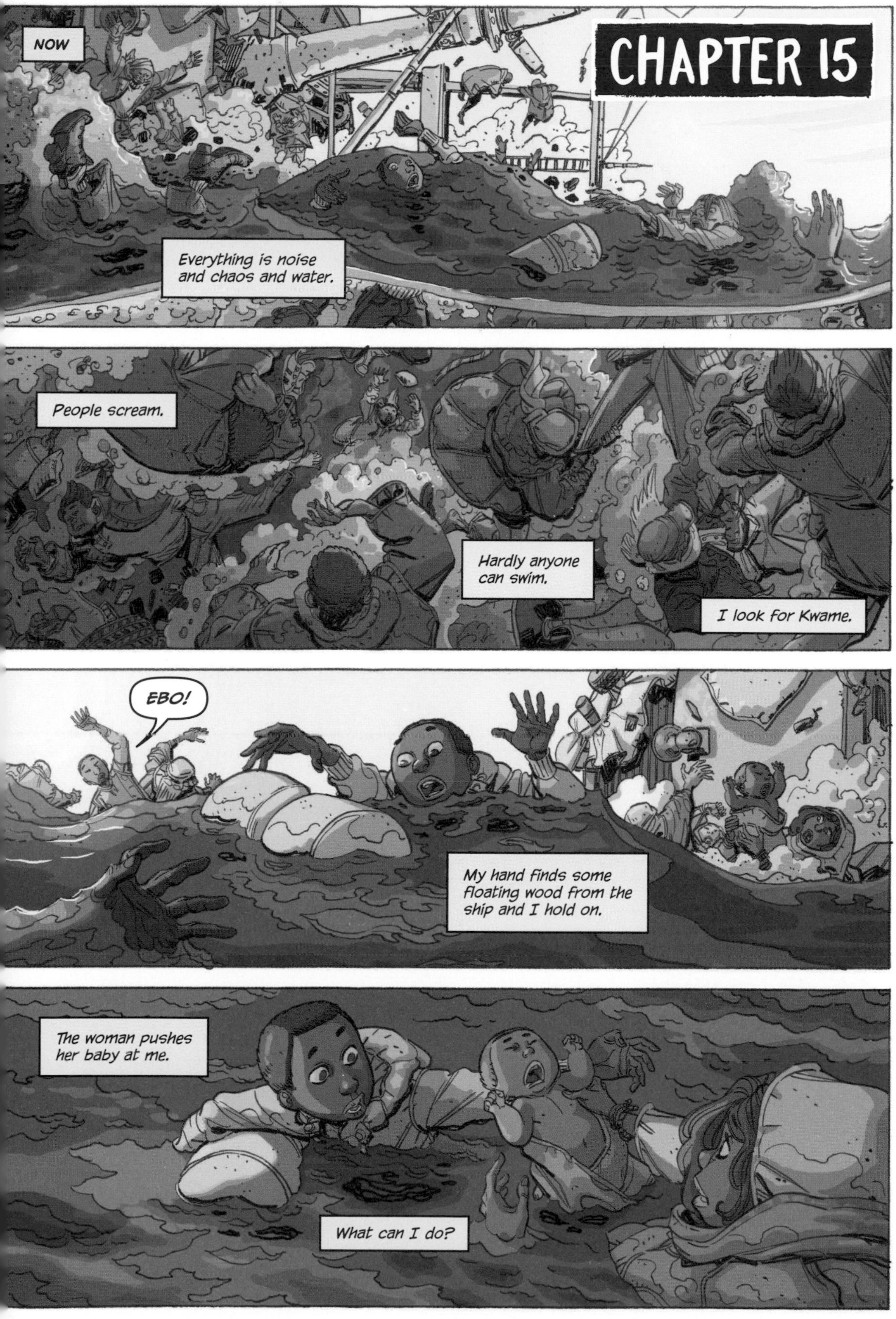
NOW
CHAPTER 15
Everything is noise and chaos and water.
People scream.
Hardly anyone can swim.
I look for Kwame.
EBO!
My hand finds some floating wood from the ship and I hold on.
The woman pushes her baby at me.
What can I do?

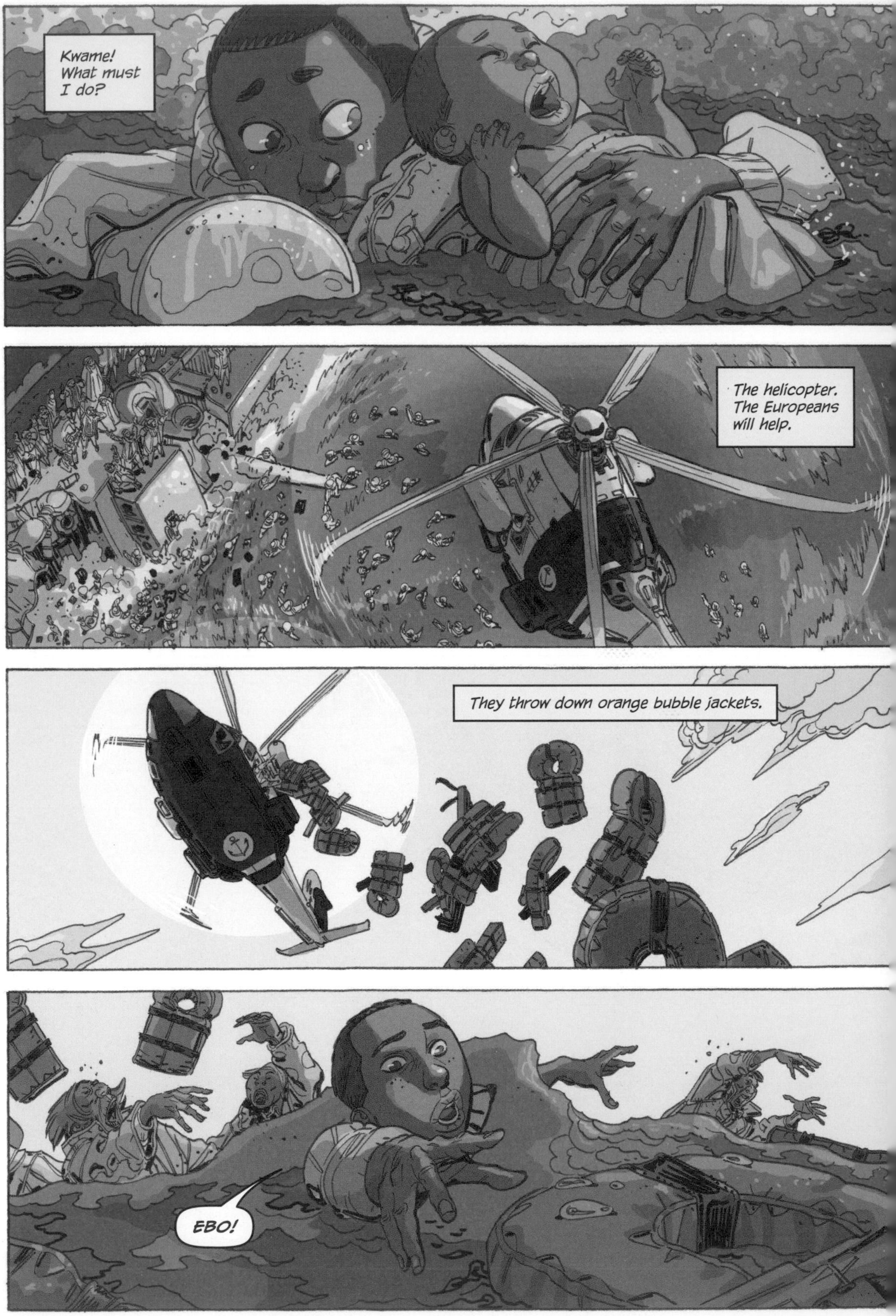
Kwame! What must I do?
The helicopter. The Europeans will help.
They throw down orange bubble jackets.
EBO!

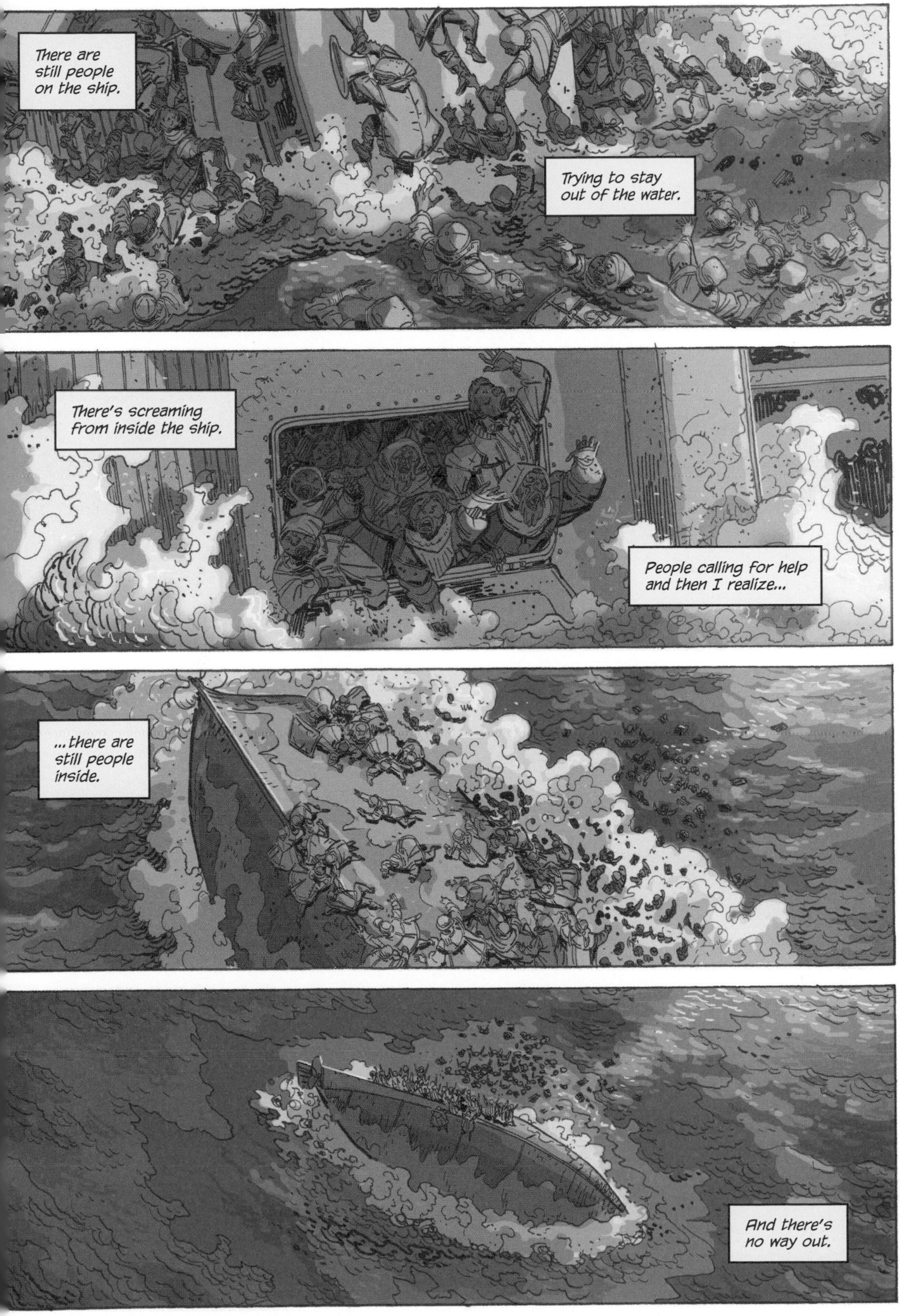
There are still people on the ship.
Trying to stay out of the water.
There's screaming from inside the ship.
People calling for help and then I realize...
...there are still people inside.
And there's no way out.

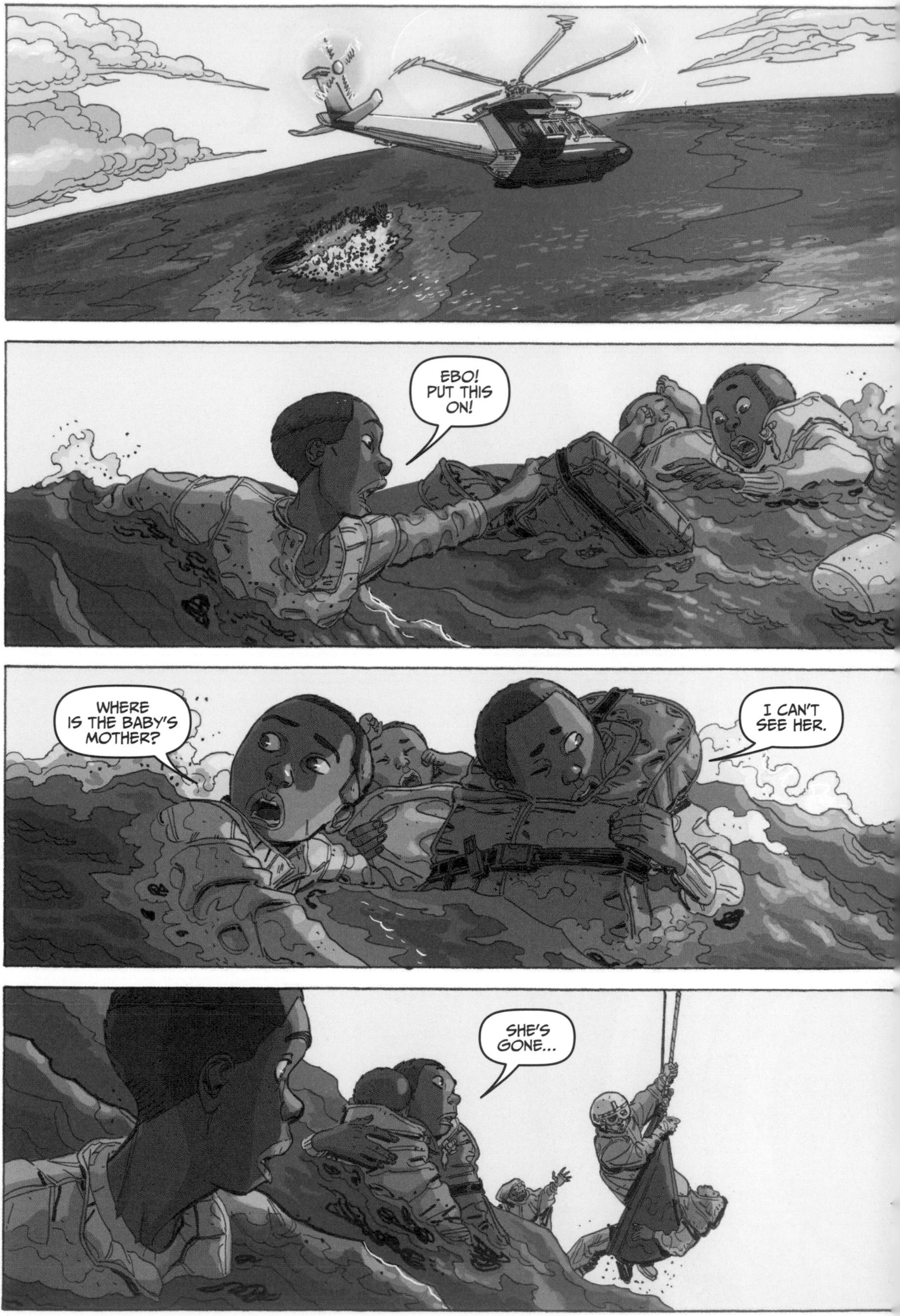
EBO! PUT THIS ON!
WHERE IS THE BABY'S MOTHER?
I CAN'T SEE HER.
SHE'S GONE...

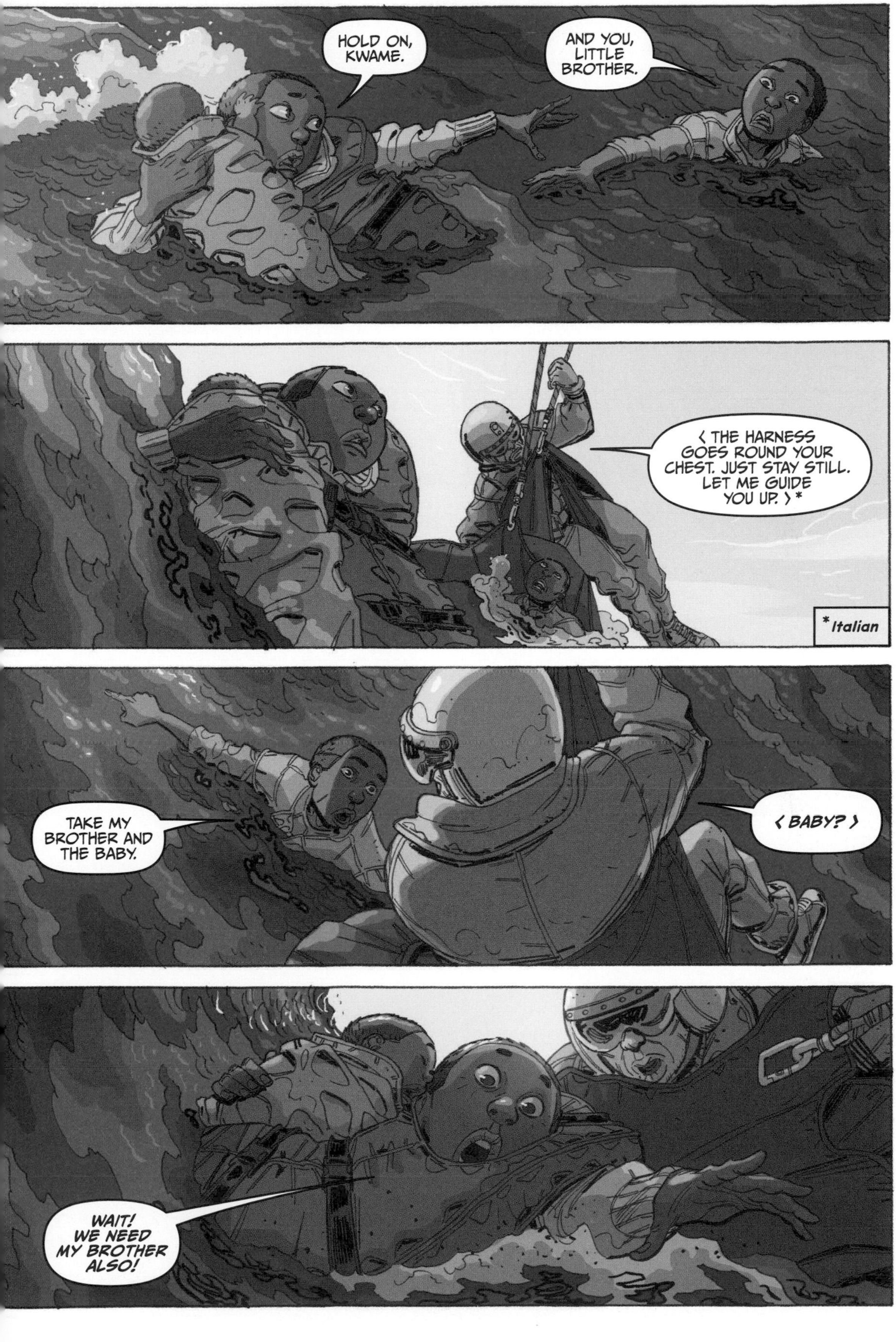
HOLD ON, KWAME.
AND YOU, LITTLE BROTHER.
‹ THE HARNESS GOES ROUND YOUR CHEST. JUST STAY STILL. LET ME GUIDE YOU UP. › *
* Italian
TAKE MY BROTHER AND THE BABY.
‹ BABY? ›
WAIT! WE NEED MY BROTHER ALSO!

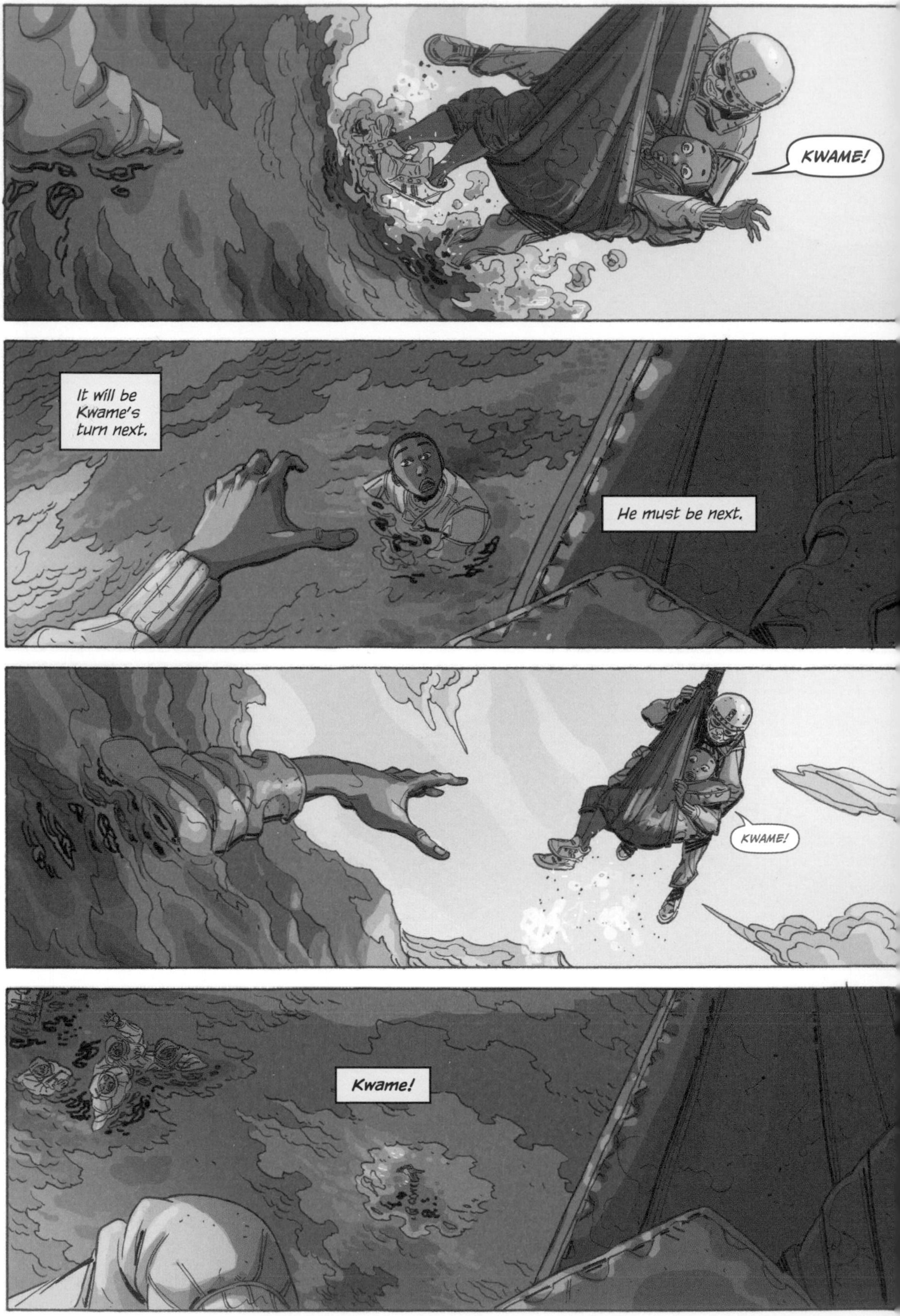
KWAME!
It will be Kwame's turn next.
He must be next.
KWAME!
Kwame!

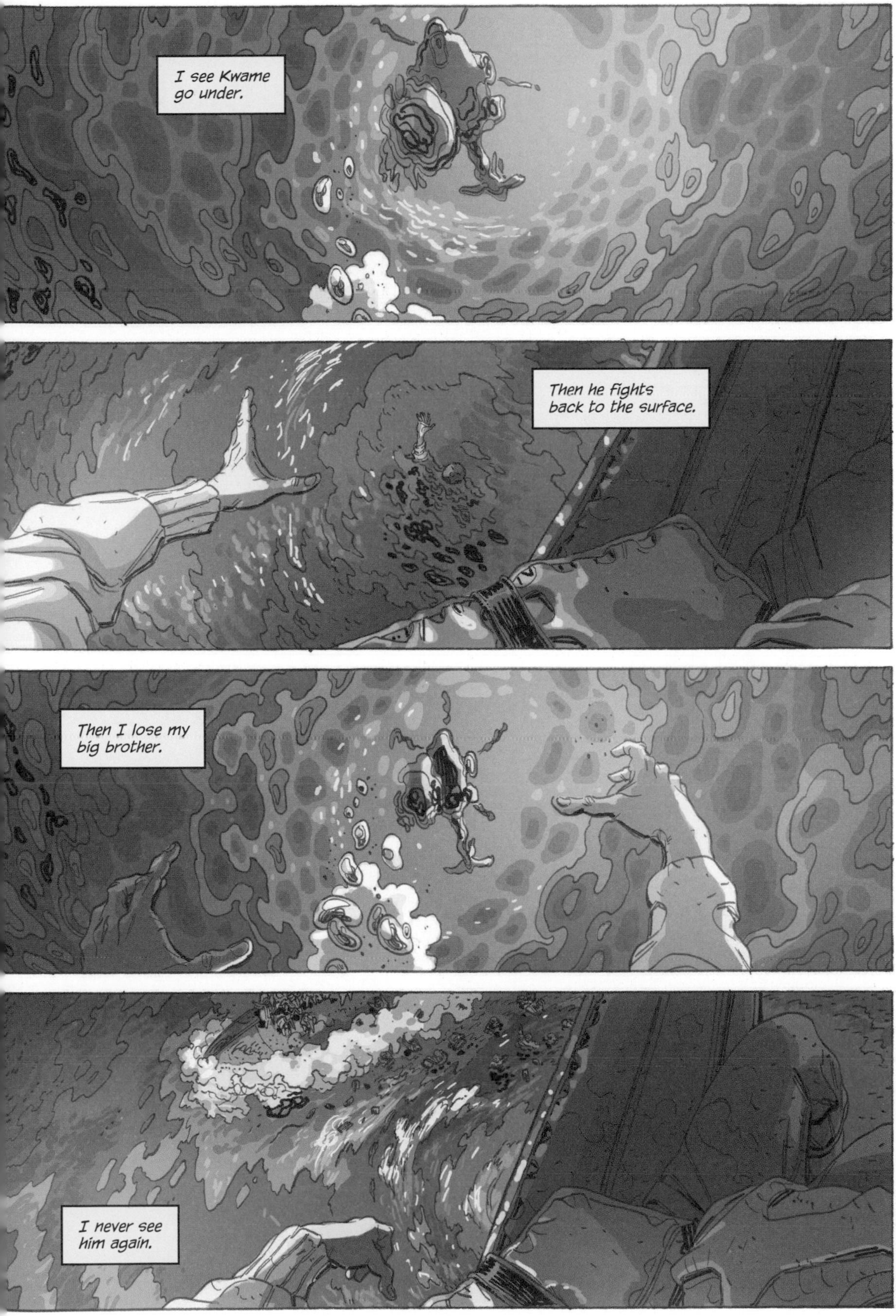
I see Kwame go under.
Then he fights back to the surface.
Then I lose my big brother.
I never see him again.

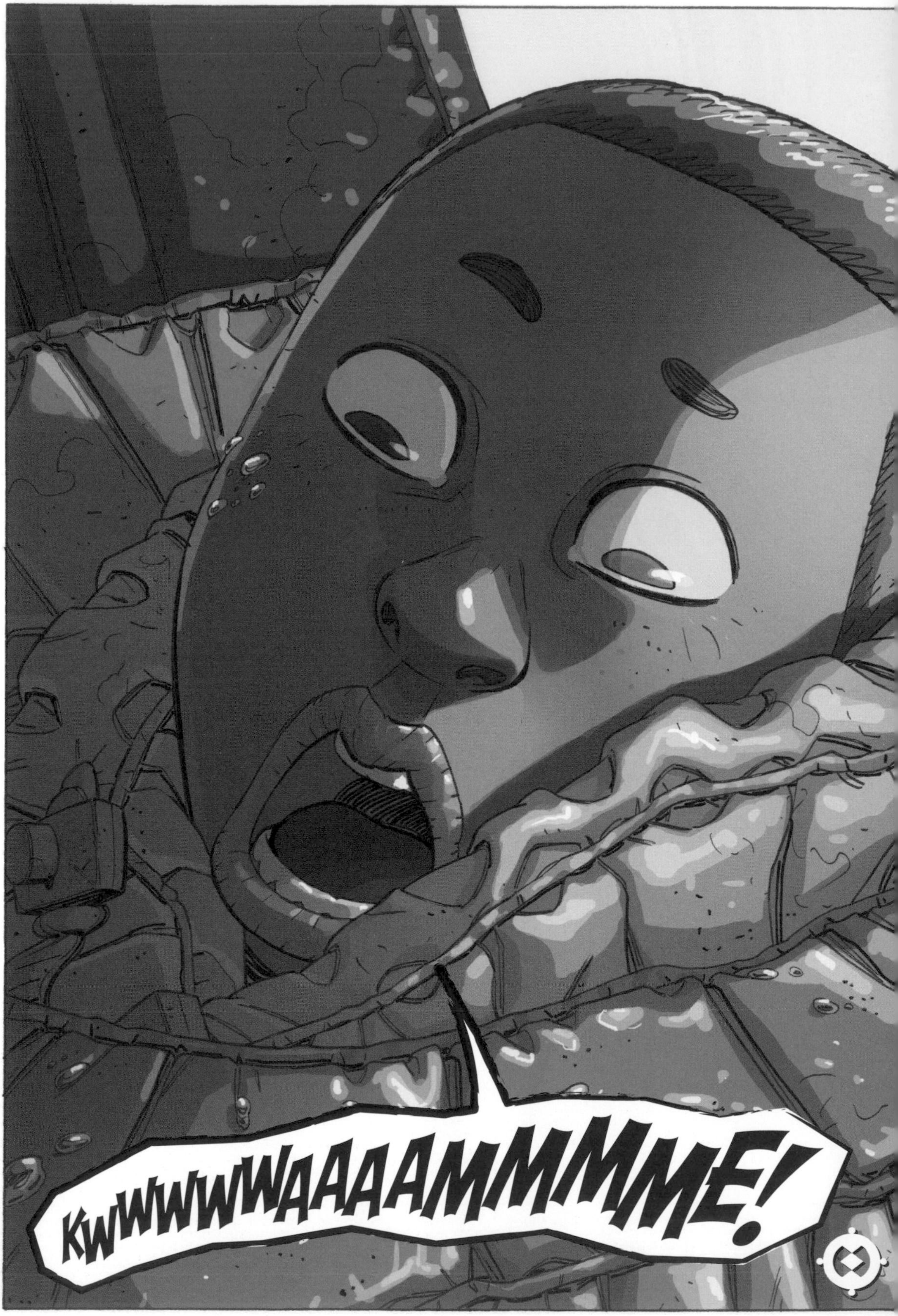
KWWWWWAAAAAMMMMME!

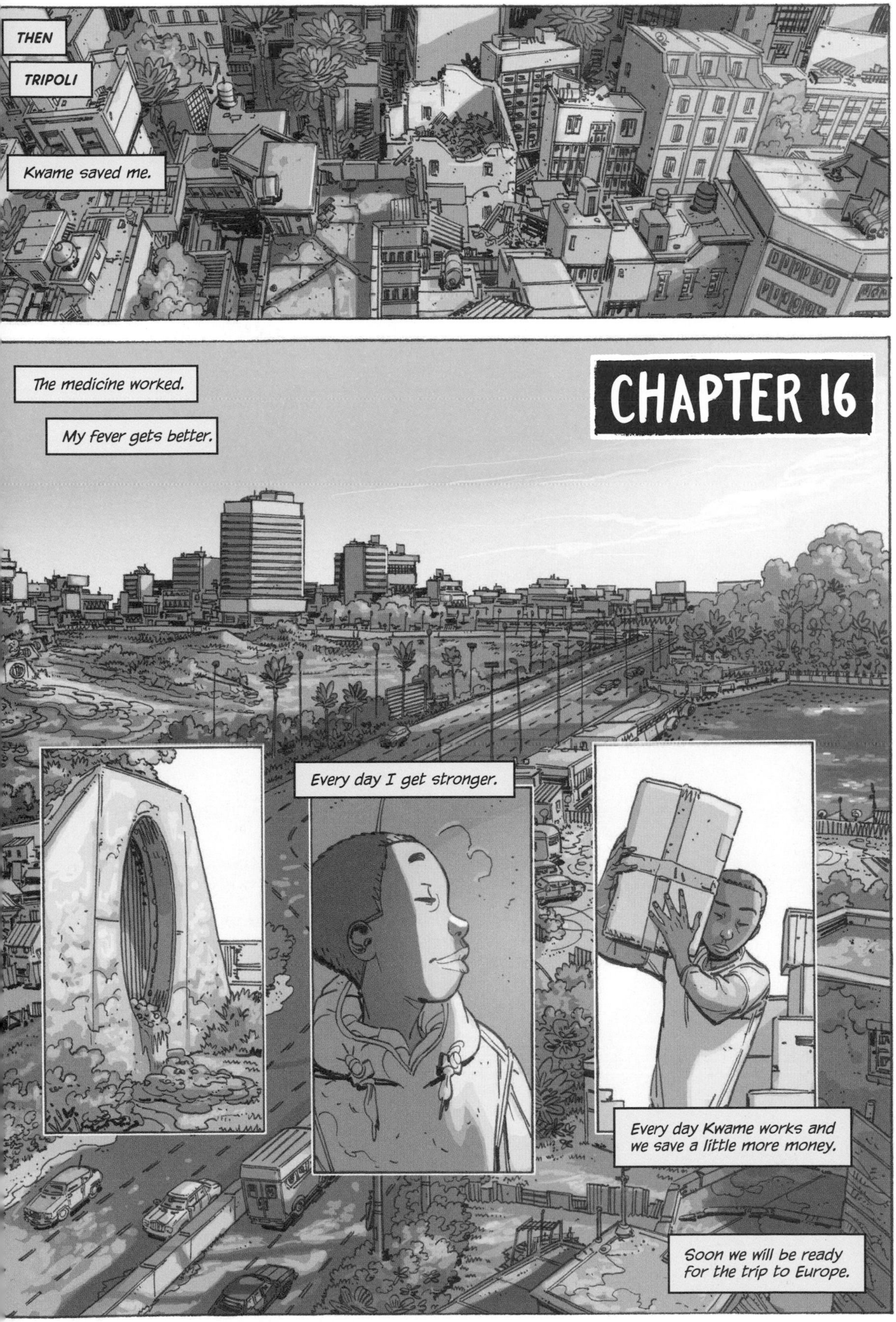
THEN
TRIPOLI
Kwame saved me.
The medicine worked.
My fever gets better.
CHAPTER 16
Every day I get stronger.
Every day Kwame works and we save a little more money.
Soon we will be ready for the trip to Europe.

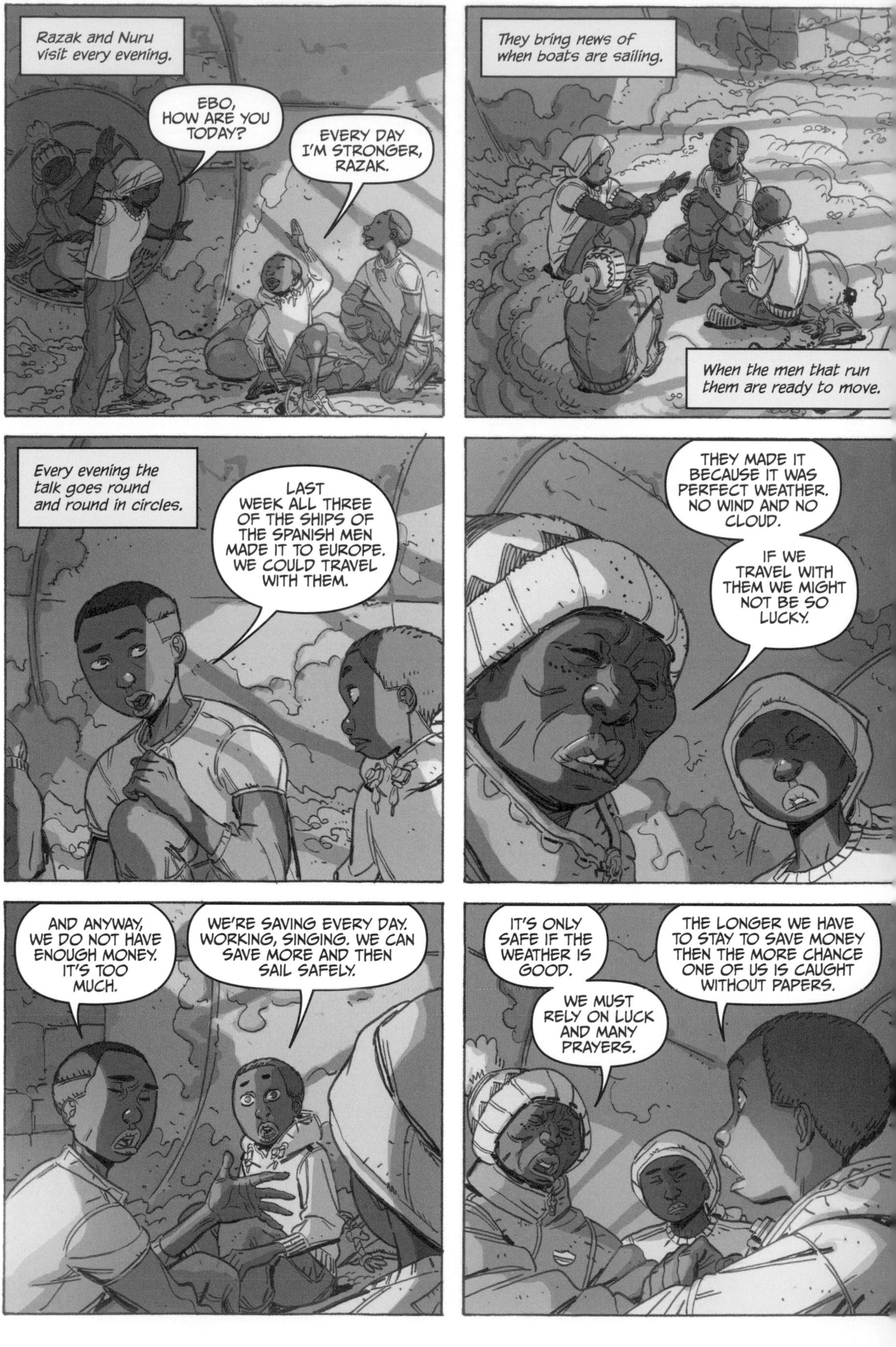

Razak and Nuru visit every evening.
EBO, HOW ARE YOU TODAY?
EVERY DAY I'M STRONGER, RAZAK.
They bring news of when boats are sailing.
When the men that run them are ready to move.
Every evening the talk goes round and round in circles.
LAST WEEK ALL THREE OF THE SHIPS OF THE SPANISH MEN MADE IT TO EUROPE. WE COULD TRAVEL WITH THEM.
THEY MADE IT BECAUSE IT WAS PERFECT WEATHER. NO WIND AND NO CLOUD.
IF WE TRAVEL WITH THEM WE MIGHT NOT BE SO LUCKY.
AND ANYWAY, WE DO NOT HAVE ENOUGH MONEY. IT'S TOO MUCH.
WE'RE SAVING EVERY DAY. WORKING, SINGING. WE CAN SAVE MORE AND THEN SAIL SAFELY.
IT'S ONLY SAFE IF THE WEATHER IS GOOD.
WE MUST RELY ON LUCK AND MANY PRAYERS.
THE LONGER WE HAVE TO STAY TO SAVE MONEY THEN THE MORE CHANCE ONE OF US IS CAUGHT WITHOUT PAPERS.

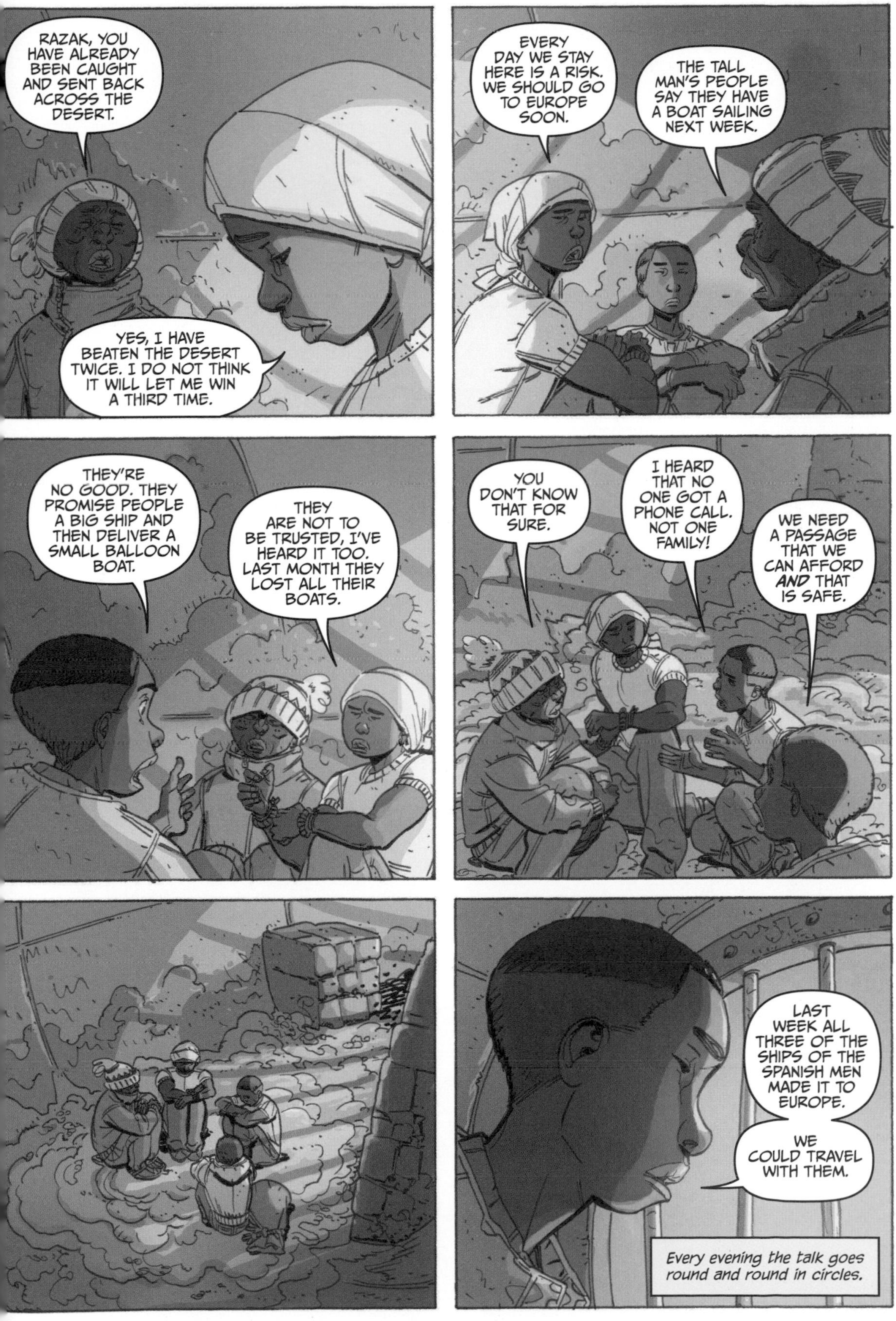
RAZAK, YOU HAVE ALREADY BEEN CAUGHT AND SENT BACK ACROSS THE DESERT.
YES, I HAVE BEATEN THE DESERT TWICE. I DO NOT THINK IT WILL LET ME WIN A THIRD TIME.
EVERY DAY WE STAY HERE IS A RISK. WE SHOULD GO TO EUROPE SOON.
THE TALL MAN'S PEOPLE SAY THEY HAVE A BOAT SAILING NEXT WEEK.
THEY'RE NO GOOD. THEY PROMISE PEOPLE A BIG SHIP AND THEN DELIVER A SMALL BALLOON BOAT.
THEY ARE NOT TO BE TRUSTED, I'VE HEARD IT TOO. LAST MONTH THEY LOST ALL THEIR BOATS.
YOU DON'T KNOW THAT FOR SURE.
I HEARD THAT NO ONE GOT A PHONE CALL. NOT ONE FAMILY!
WE NEED A PASSAGE THAT WE CAN AFFORD ***AND*** THAT IS SAFE.
LAST WEEK ALL THREE OF THE SHIPS OF THE SPANISH MEN MADE IT TO EUROPE.
WE COULD TRAVEL WITH THEM.
Every evening the talk goes round and round in circles.

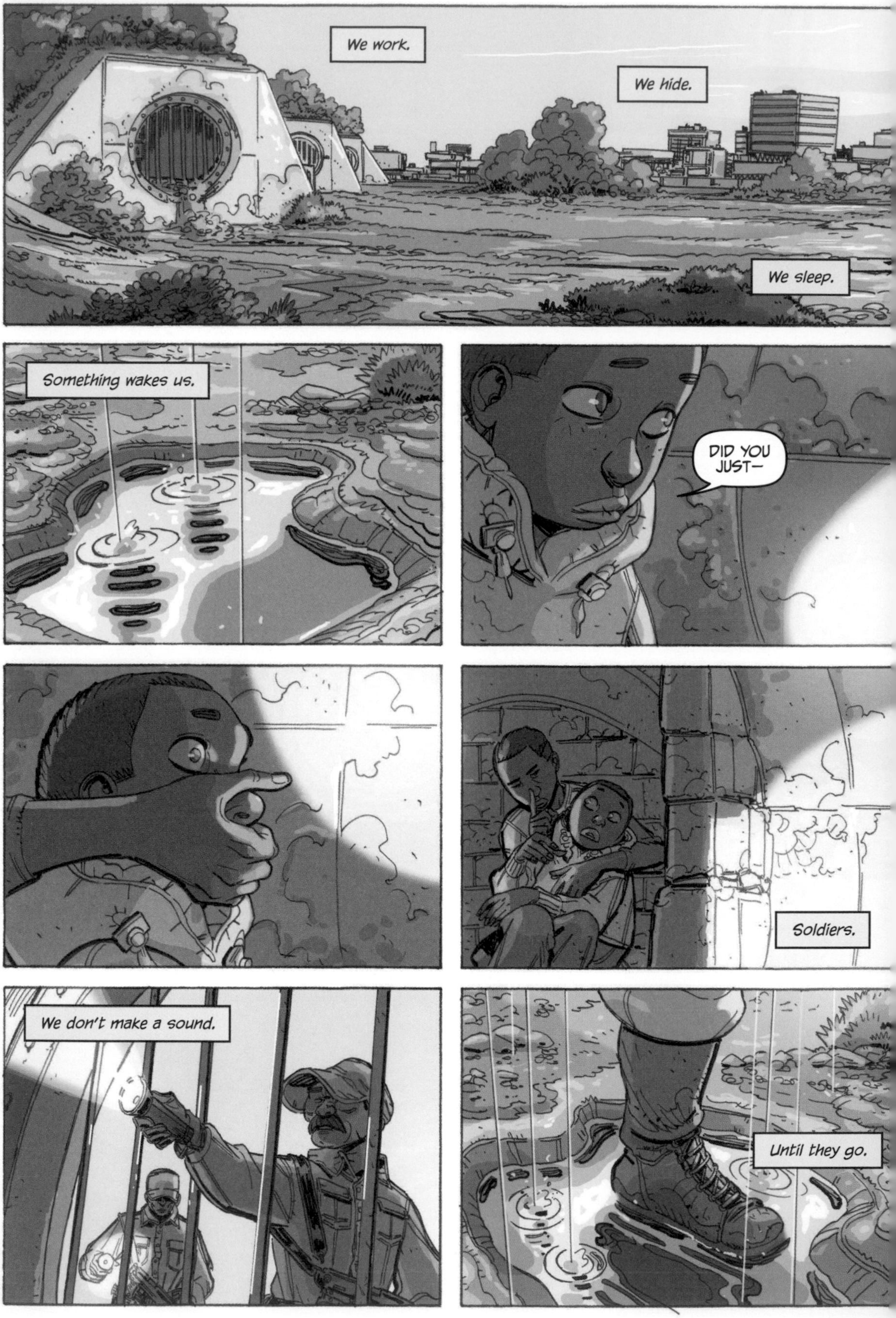
We work.
We hide.
We sleep.
Something wakes us.
DID YOU JUST—
Soldiers.
We don't make a sound.
Until they go.

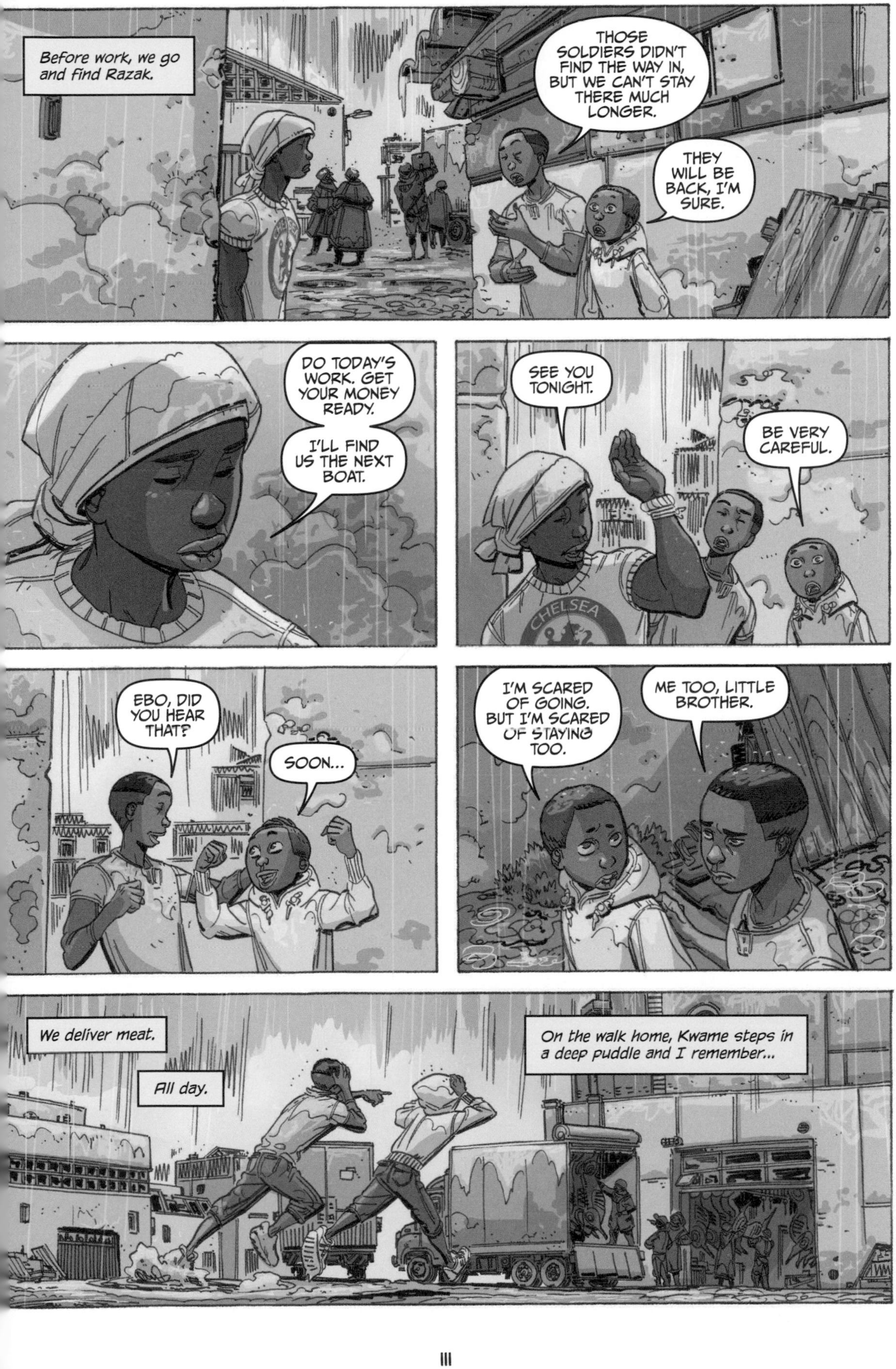
Before work, we go and find Razak.
THOSE SOLDIERS DIDN'T FIND THE WAY IN, BUT WE CAN'T STAY THERE MUCH LONGER.
THEY WILL BE BACK, I'M SURE.
DO TODAY'S WORK. GET YOUR MONEY READY.
I'LL FIND US THE NEXT BOAT.
SEE YOU TONIGHT.
BE VERY CAREFUL.
CHELSEA
EBO, DID YOU HEAR THAT?
SOON...
I'M SCARED OF GOING. BUT I'M SCARED OF STAYING TOO.
ME TOO, LITTLE BROTHER.
We deliver meat.
All day.
On the walk home, Kwame steps in a deep puddle and I remember...

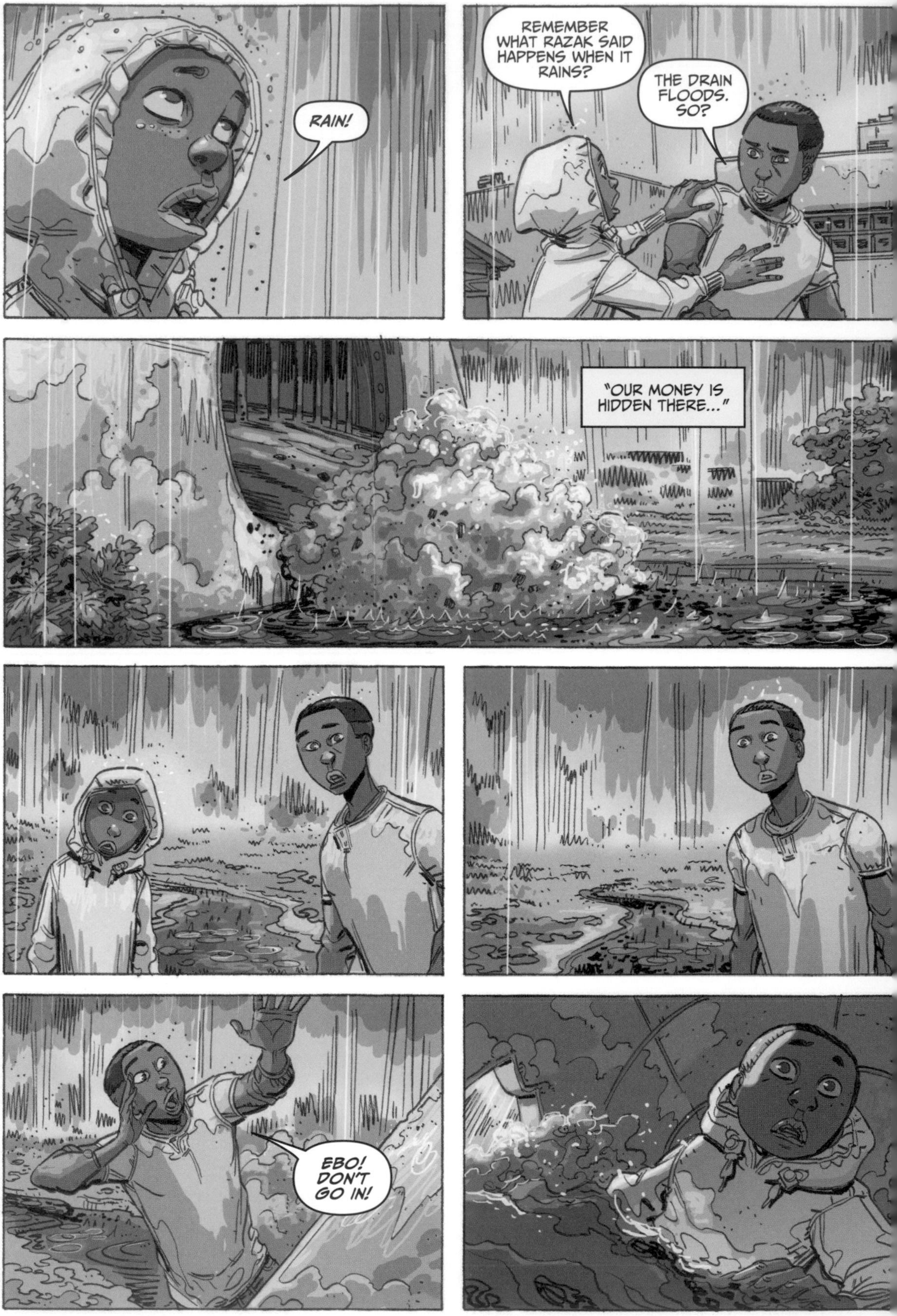
RAIN!
REMEMBER WHAT RAZAK SAID HAPPENS WHEN IT RAINS?
THE DRAIN FLOODS. SO?
"OUR MONEY IS HIDDEN THERE..."
EBO! DON'T GO IN!

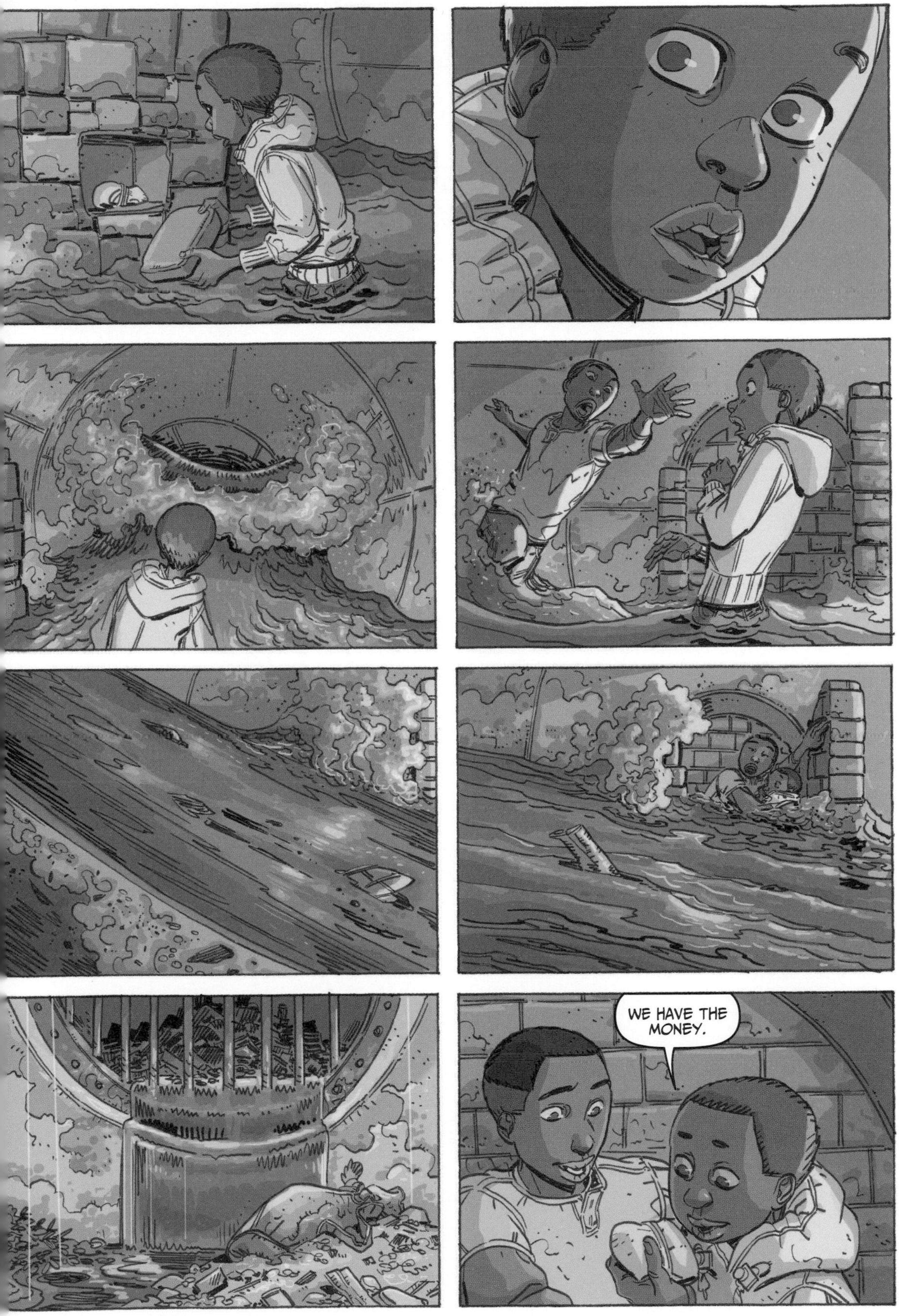
WE HAVE THE MONEY.

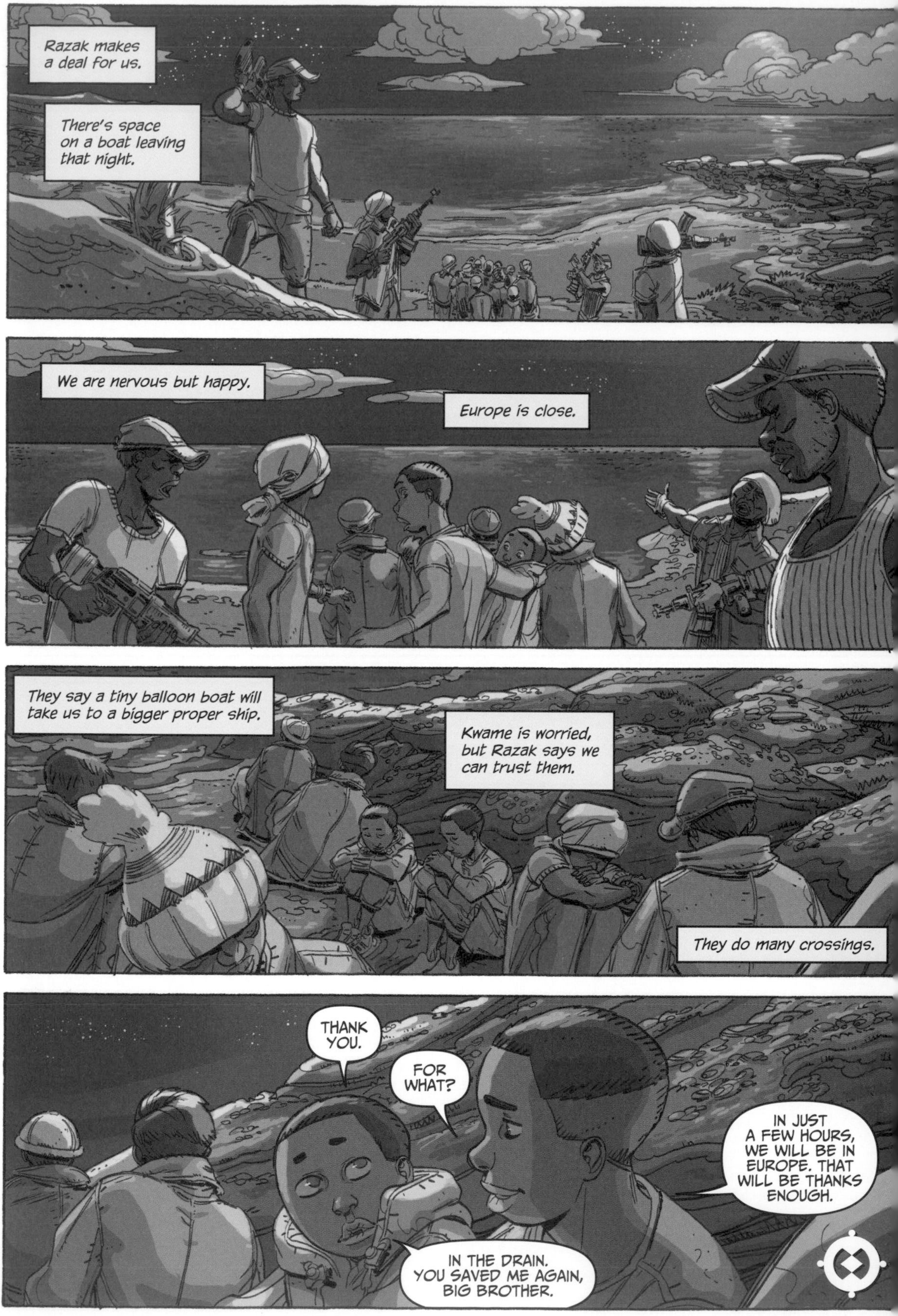
Razak makes a deal for us.
There's space on a boat leaving that night.
We are nervous but happy.
Europe is close.
They say a tiny balloon boat will take us to a bigger proper ship.
Kwame is worried, but Razak says we can trust them.
They do many crossings.
THANK YOU.
FOR WHAT?
IN THE DRAIN. YOU SAVED ME AGAIN, BIG BROTHER.
IN JUST A FEW HOURS, WE WILL BE IN EUROPE. THAT WILL BE THANKS ENOUGH.

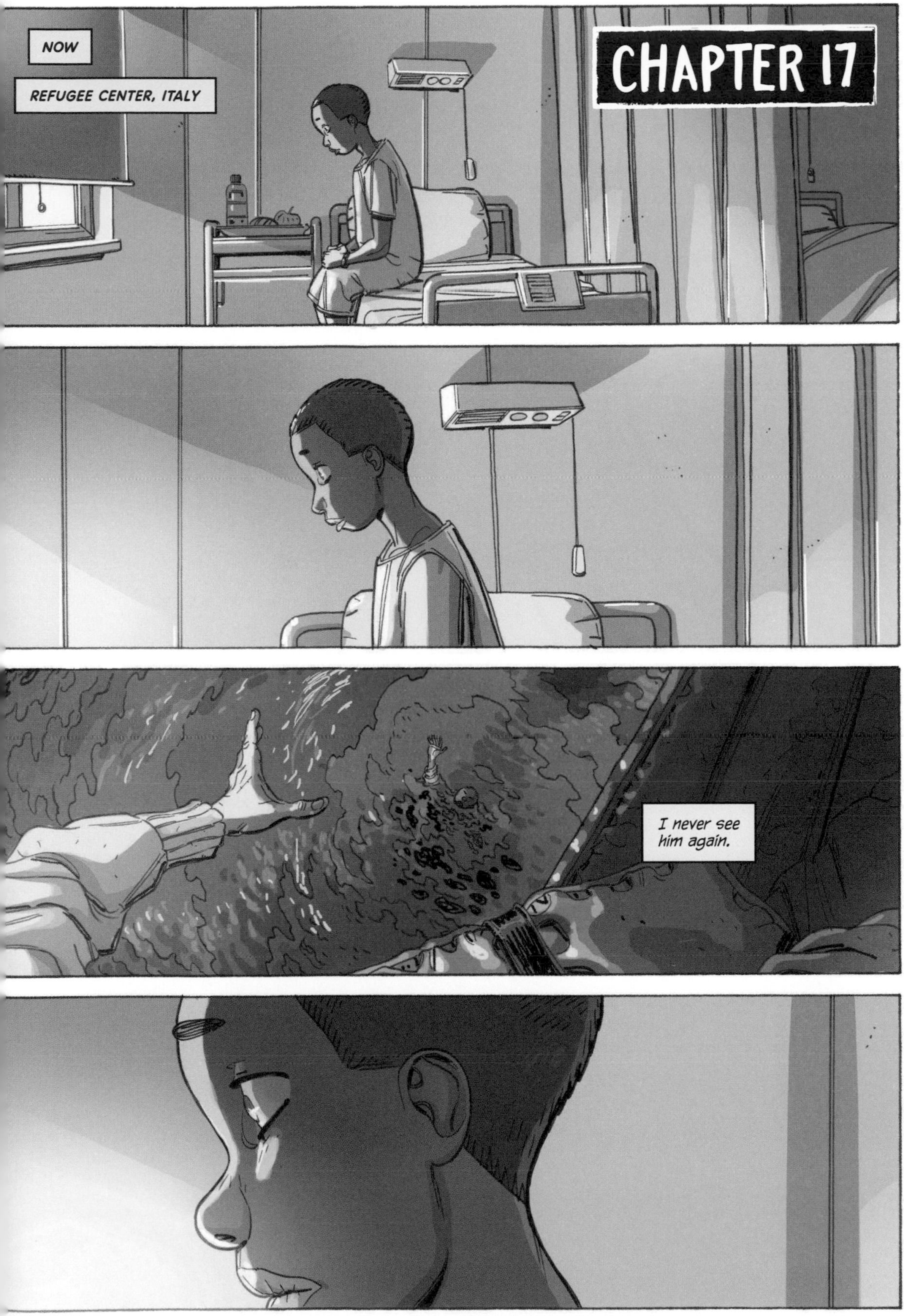
NOW
REFUGEE CENTER, ITALY
CHAPTER 17
I never see him again.

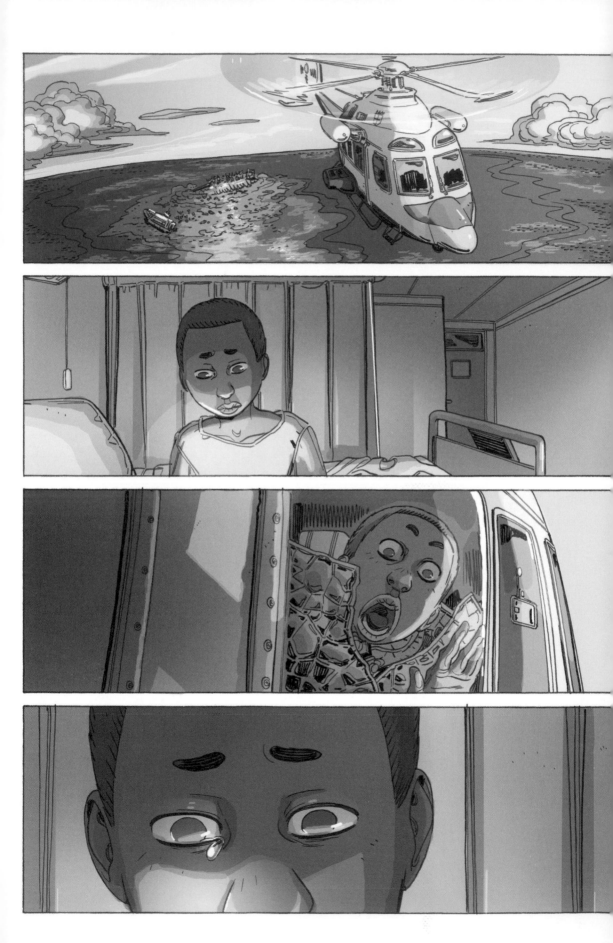

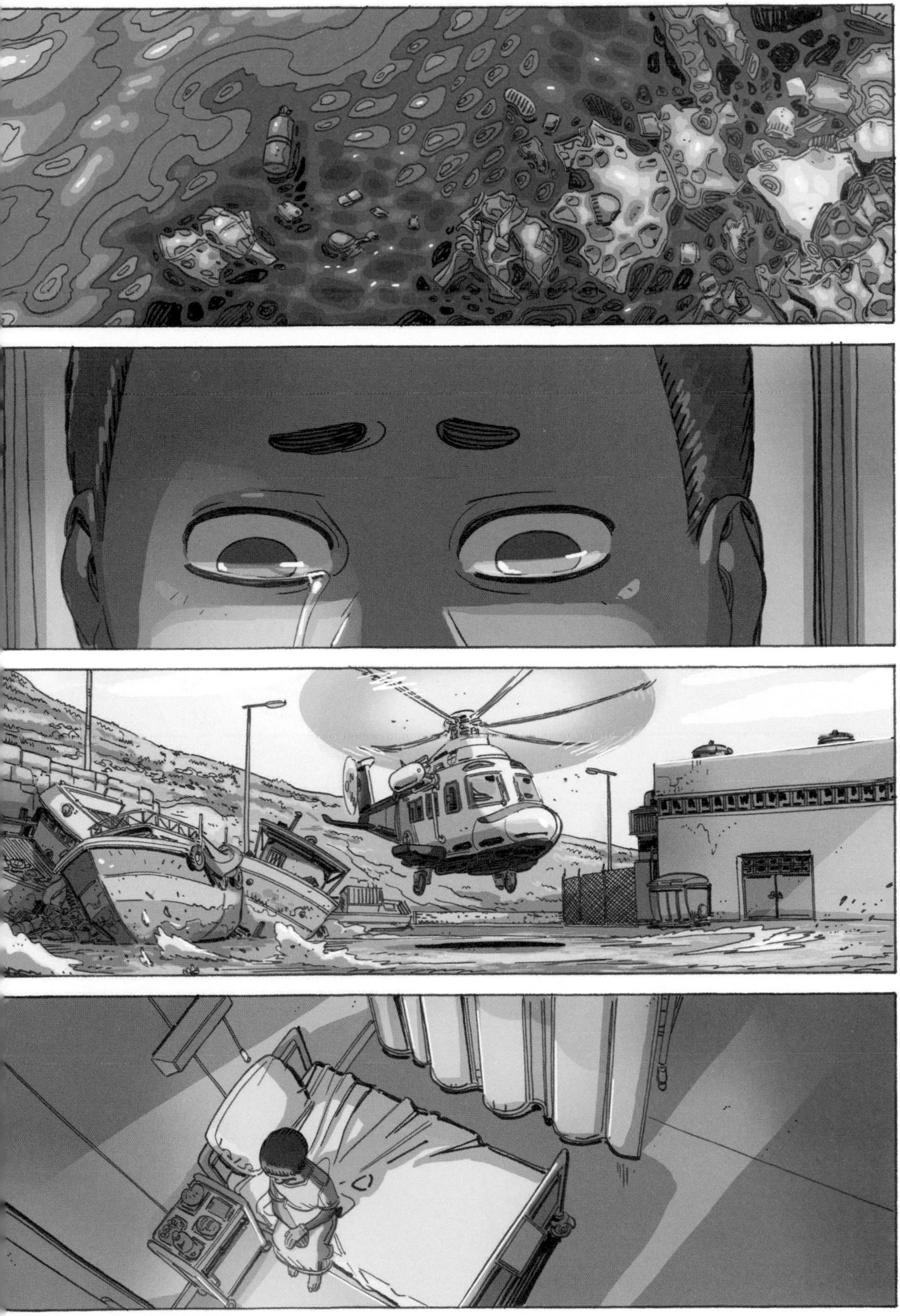

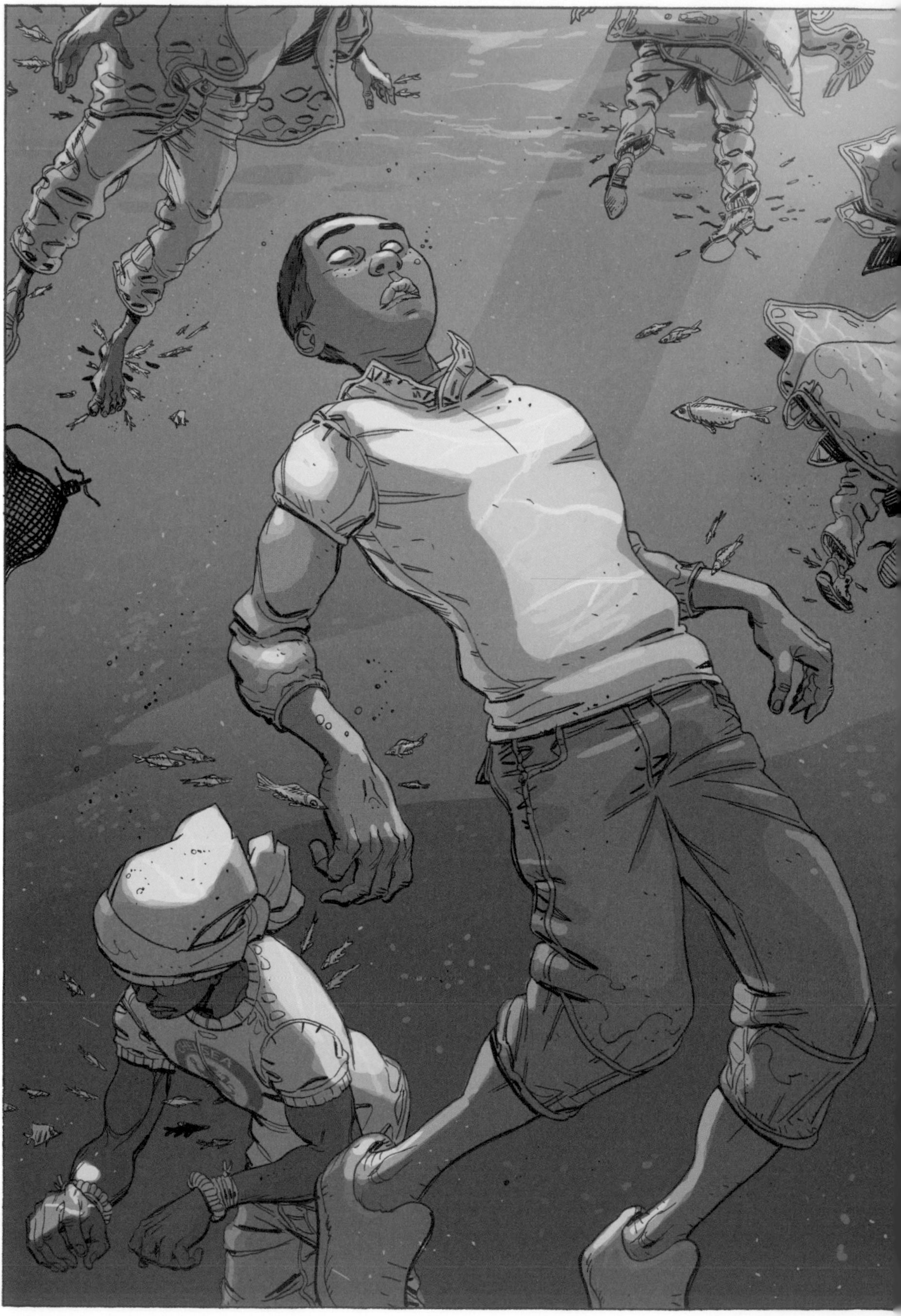

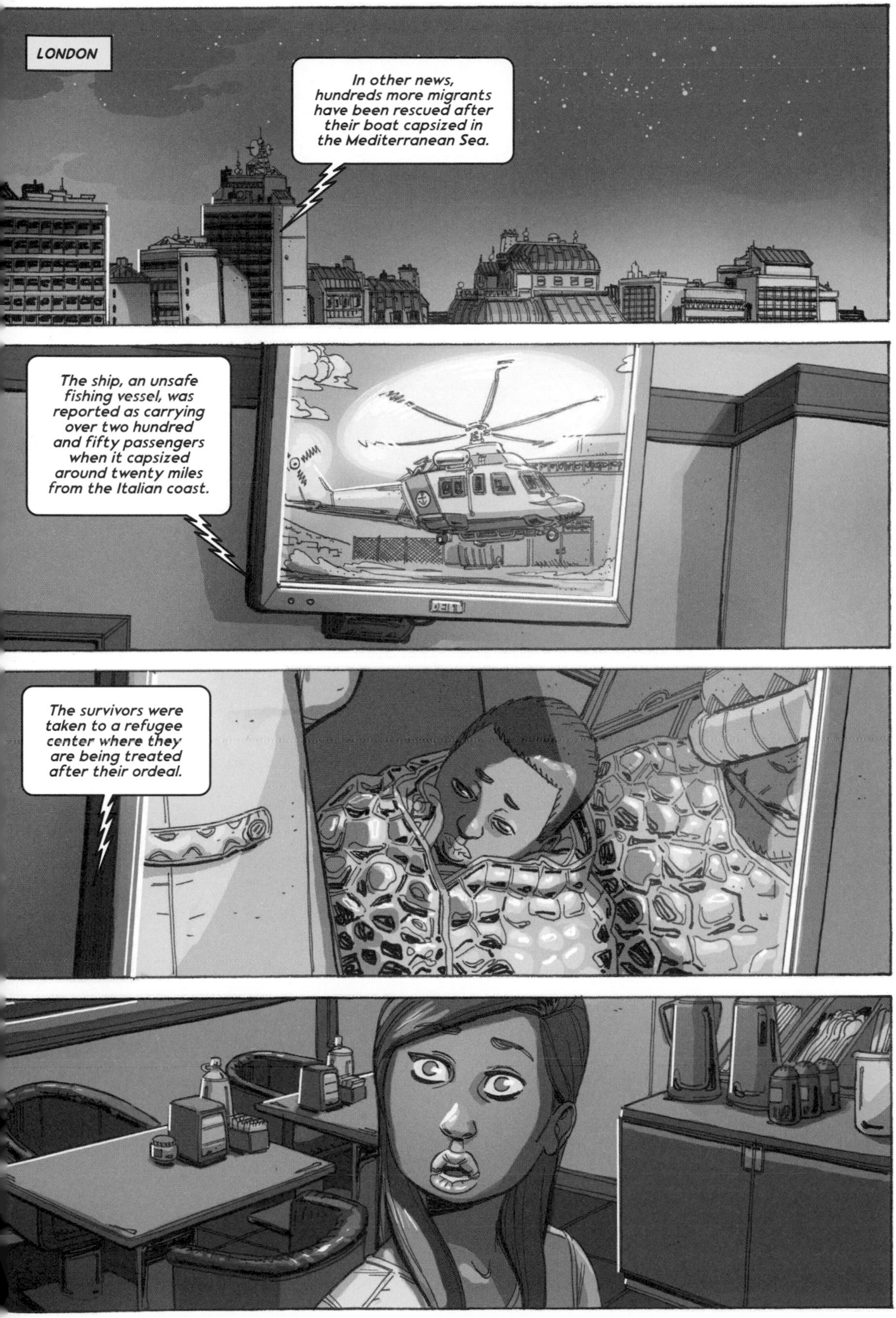
LONDON
In other news, hundreds more migrants have been rescued after their boat capsized in the Mediterranean Sea.
The ship, an unsafe fishing vessel, was reported as carrying over two hundred and fifty passengers when it capsized around twenty miles from the Italian coast.
The survivors were taken to a refugee center where they are being treated after their ordeal.

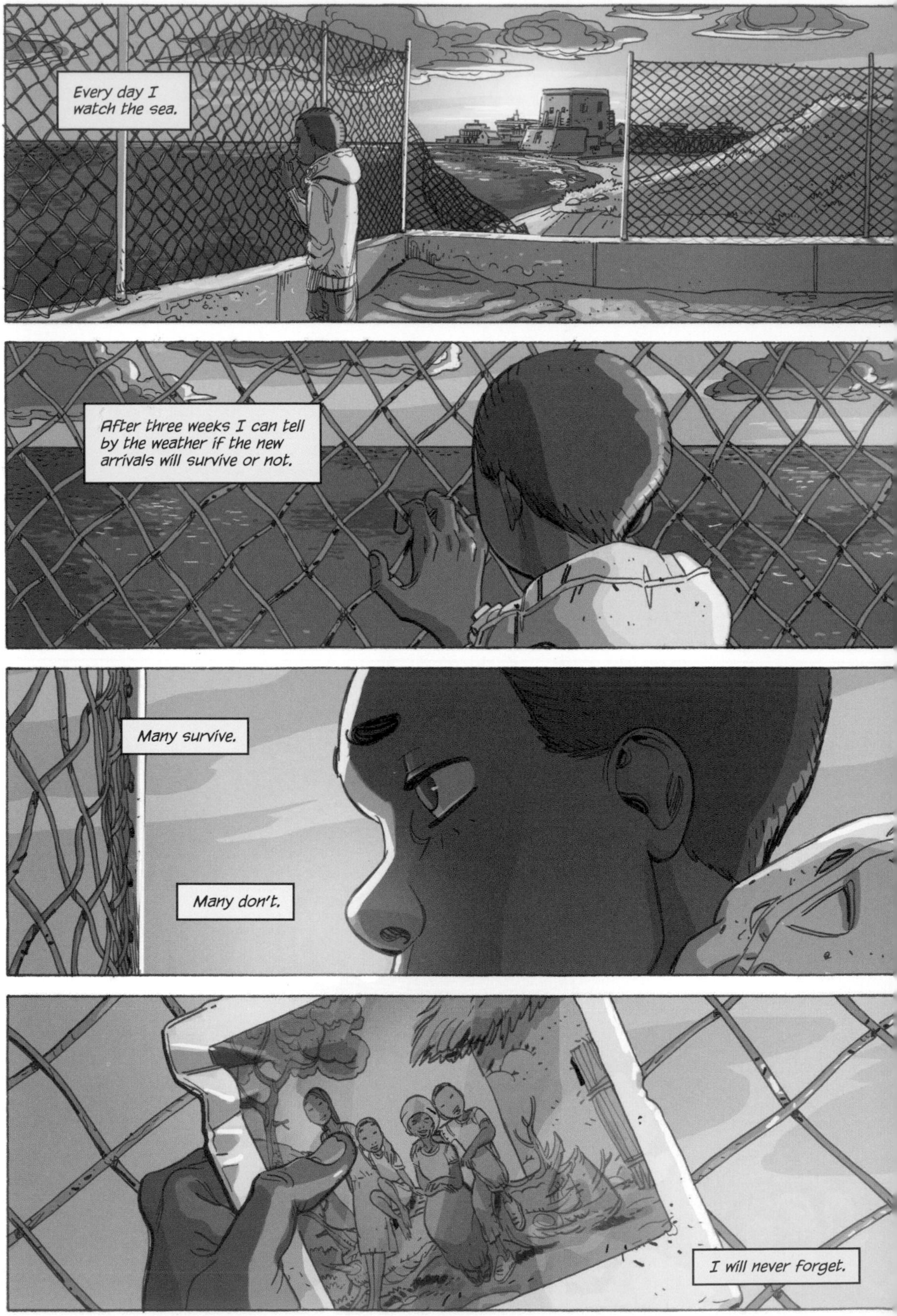
Every day I watch the sea.
After three weeks I can tell by the weather if the new arrivals will survive or not.
Many survive.
Many don't.
I will never forget.

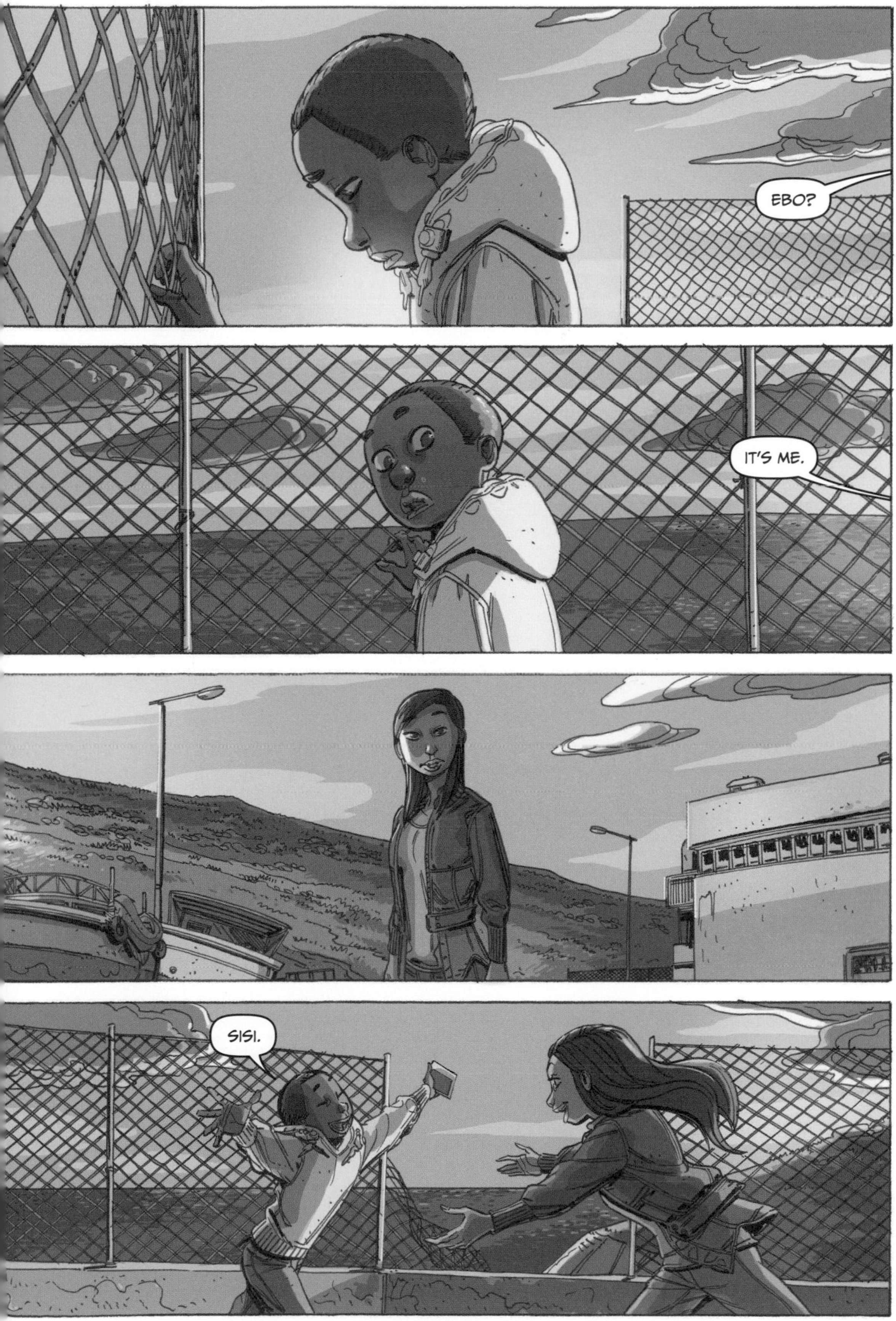
EBO?
IT'S ME.
SISI.

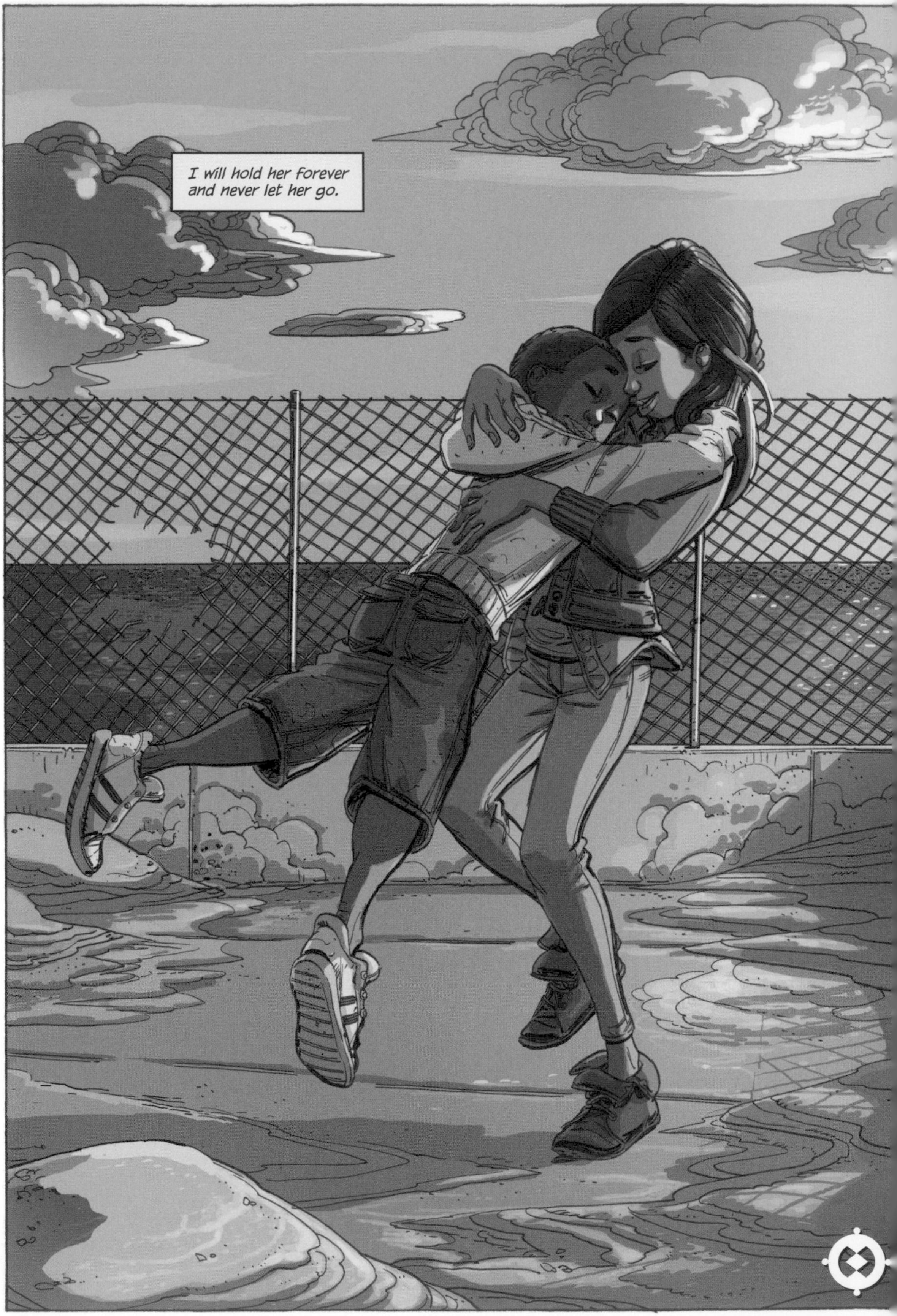
I will hold her forever and never let her go.

EBO'S JOURNEY

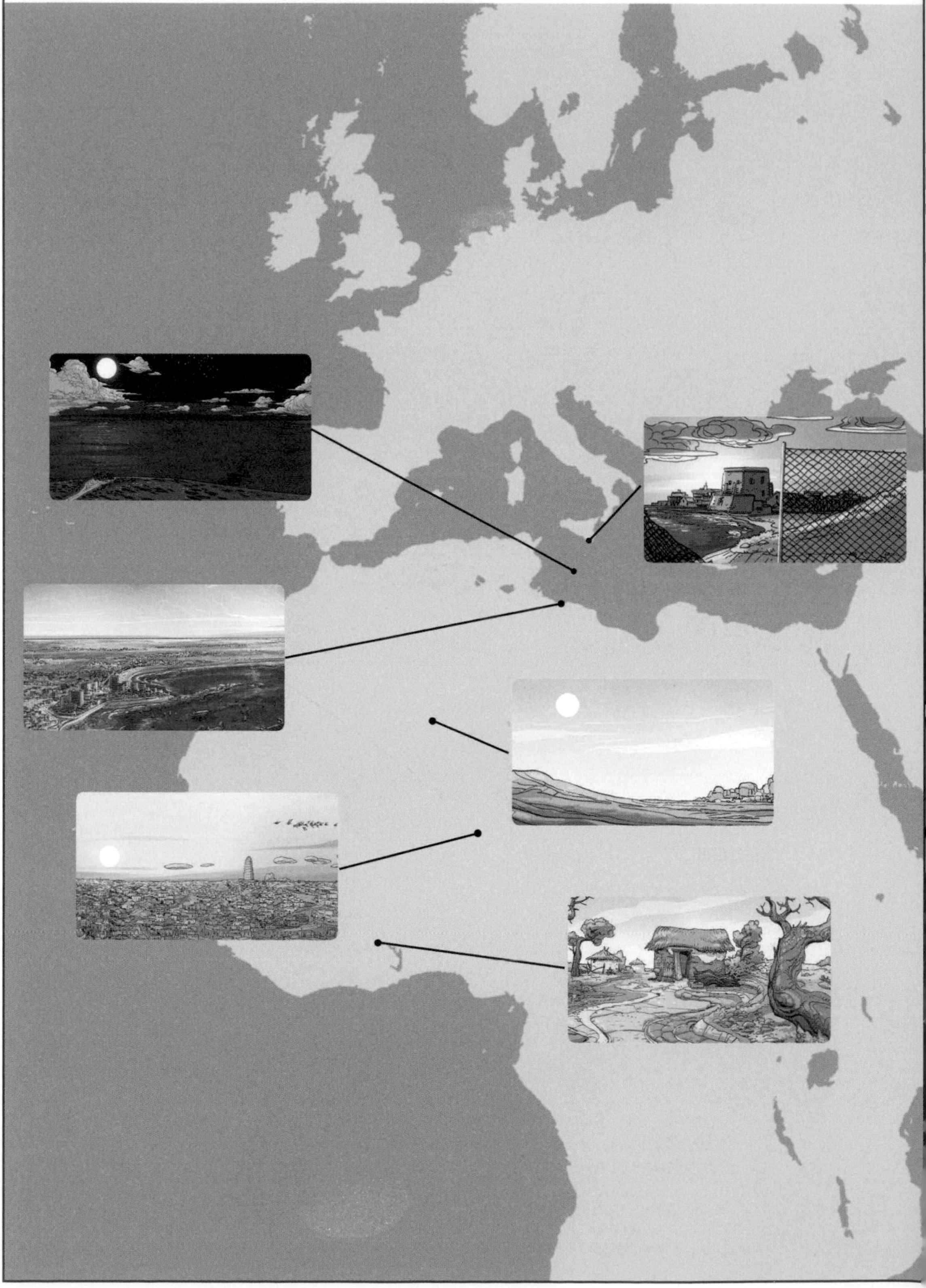

CREATORS' NOTE

The story you've just read about Ebo's journey is a work of fiction, but every separate element of it is true.

Every year, many thousands of men, women, and children risk their lives by trying to make the dangerous three-hundred-mile sea crossing between Northern Africa and Italy. They pay large sums of money to smugglers who in return provide poorly prepared, unseaworthy boats. The distances involved are formidable and the sea currents are unpredictable. The smuggling networks that run these operations make fortunes with no regard for human life. They send their victims out to sea in death traps.

Many innocents die as a result, their loss of life often unknown and unrecorded. In 2015, more than a million migrants crossed the Mediterranean Sea to enter Europe. The United Nations has described the situation as a "colossal humanitarian catastrophe" and it is still going on.

The migrants come from different countries and travel for different reasons. Some are refugees fleeing war-torn countries like Syria. Others, like Ebo, are following family members seeking a new life with better opportunities in Europe.

Most of the people trying to cross the Mediterranean Sea have already endured a long and dangerous journey. Crossing the Sahara Desert is just as dangerous as crossing the Mediterranean Sea. Broken trucks and broken promises mean many migrants lose their lives in the desert sands. Many more migrants would perish in the Mediterranean without the daily search-and-rescue operations run by humanitarian organizations.

It's not a journey to be undertaken lightly. Every person making the choice to embark on that journey has their own reasons for doing so. And every person is a human being.

Eoin Colfer
Andrew Donkin
Giovanni Rigano

JOURNEY: HELEN'S STORY

WORDS BY HELEN AS TOLD TO WOMEN FOR REFUGEE WOMEN

ADAPTED FOR COMICS BY COLFER/DONKIN/RIGANO

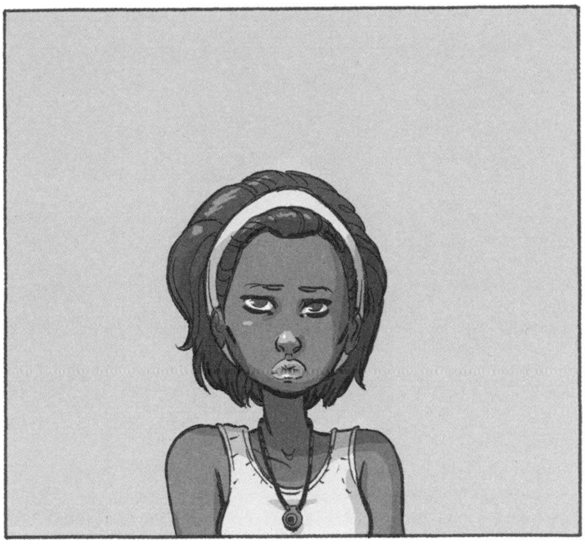

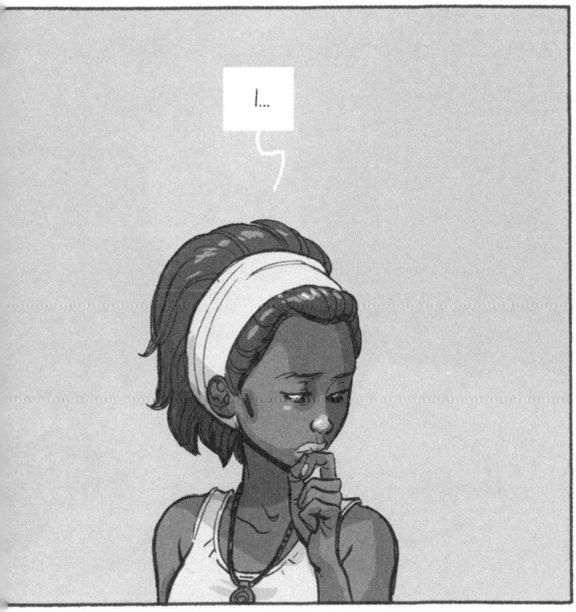
I...

I AM HELEN.

I WAS BORN IN ERITREA. MY MOTHER DIED WHEN I WAS YOUNG. MY FAMILY WERE SPLIT AND MY FATHER HAD TO FLEE. AT THE AGE OF THIRTEEN, I WENT TO SUDAN TO LOOK FOR HIM AND ENDED UP STAYING THERE MANY YEARS.

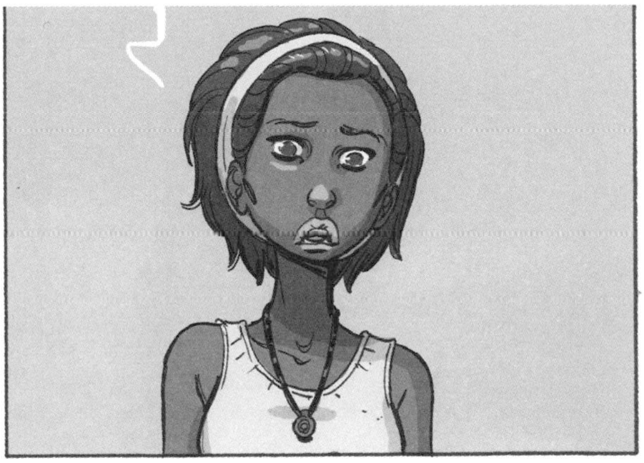

I LIVED IN HIDING, BECAUSE I DIDN'T HAVE ANY PAPERS. AN ELDERLY ETHIOPIAN WOMAN TOOK ME IN. I WORKED FOR HER MANY YEARS WITHOUT PAY BUT LAST YEAR SHE TOLD ME I HAD TO LEAVE.

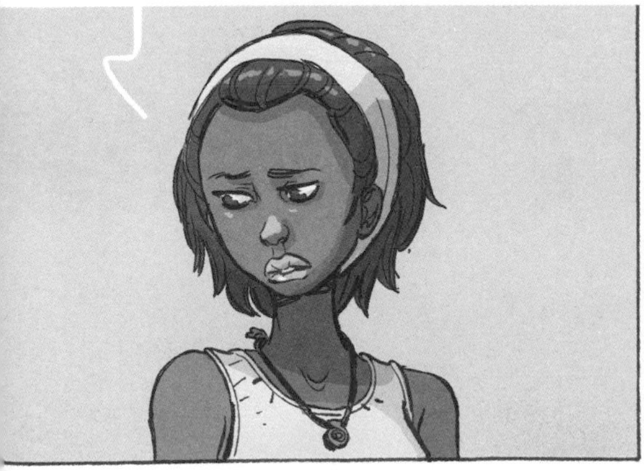

"SHE KNEW SOME TRAFFICKERS WHO SAID THEY WOULD TAKE ME THROUGH THE DESERT, THROUGH LIBYA, AND ACROSS THE SEA TO ITALY, AND SHE MADE THE FIRST PAYMENT FOR ME."

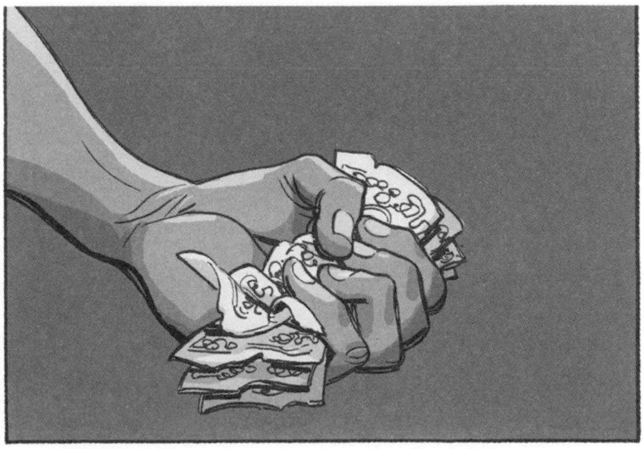

"WE CROSSED THE SAHARA DESERT IN A TRUCK, TRAVELING DAY AND NIGHT FOR FIFTEEN DAYS. IT WAS SO SANDY AND HOT."

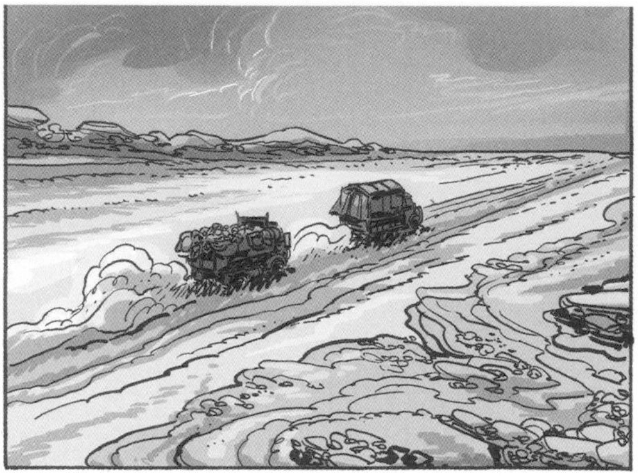

"WE HAD BROUGHT FOOD AND WATER AND WE THOUGHT WE HAD WHAT WE NEEDED. THEN THE TRUCK BROKE DOWN. THERE WAS NO SHADE—WE WERE BURNT BY THE SUN, AND THE CONSTANT HEAT MADE US MORE AND MORE THIRSTY."

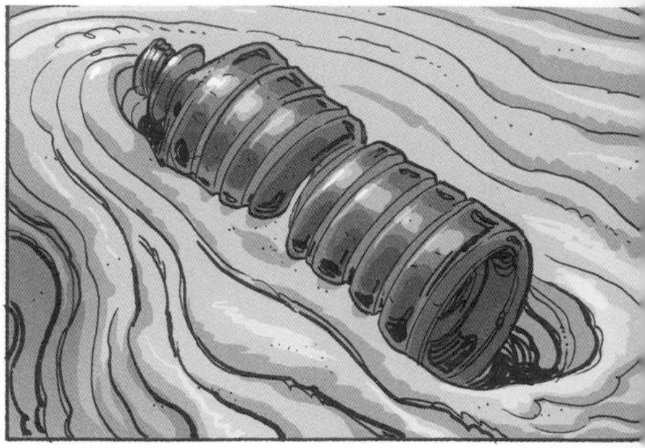

ONE MAN LOST HIS BROTHER, AND A WOMAN I HAD KNOWN IN SUDAN ALSO DIED.

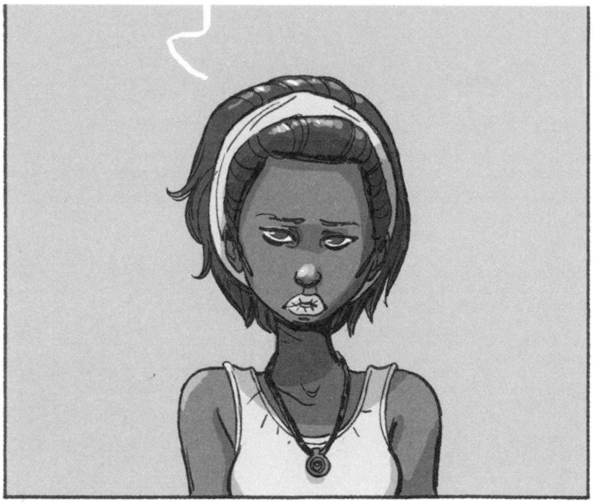

"WE TRIED TO BURY OUR FRIENDS. THE MEN DUG AND WE WOMEN WEPT. THOSE FRIENDS OF OURS WERE BURIED IN A SHALLOW GRAVE—IT WASN'T REALLY A BURIAL. THE SAND WILL NOT COVER THEM LONG."

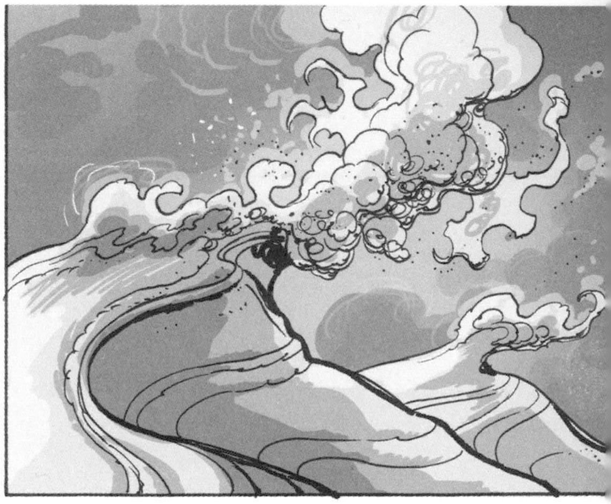

"WHEN ANOTHER TRUCK CAME FOR US IN THE DESERT, WE THOUGHT WE WERE BEING SAVED, BUT THESE MEN WERE TRAFFICKERS TOO."

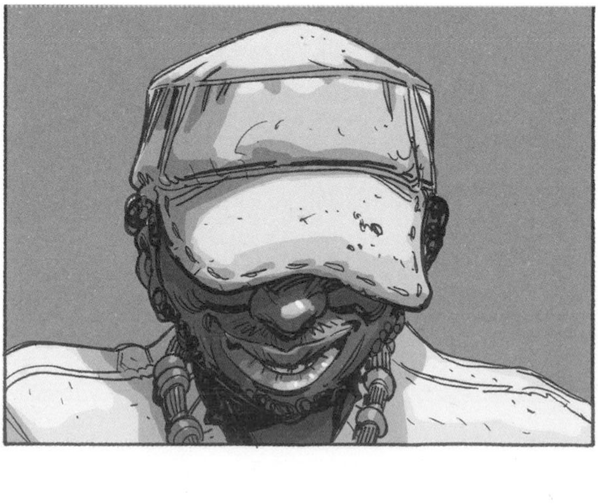

THEY TOOK US TO LIBYA, WHICH WAS GOOD, BUT THEN THEY LOCKED US UP AND DEMANDED MONEY OR WE WOULD DIE.

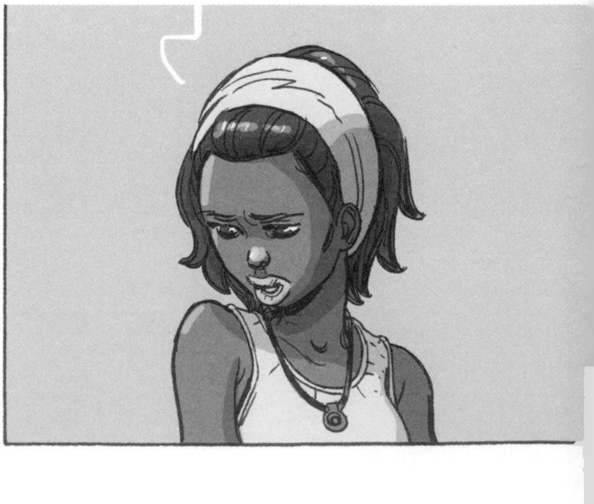

"THEY GAVE ENOUGH FOOD SO WE WOULDN'T DIE, BUT NOT MUCH—WE WERE ALWAYS IN THE BALANCE BETWEEN LIFE AND DEATH."

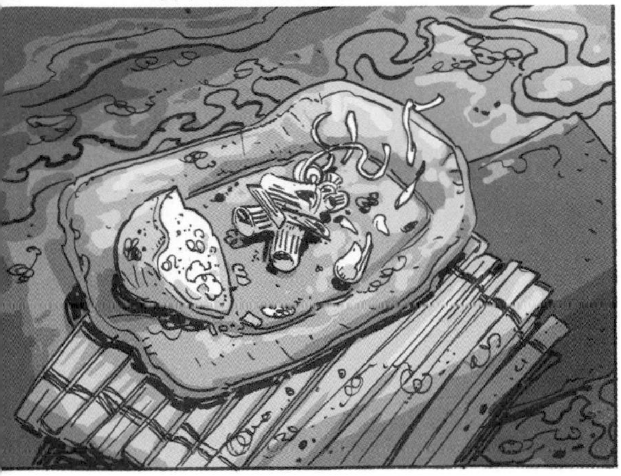

I THOUGHT I WOULD NEVER MAKE IT OUT OF THAT PRISON, BECAUSE I HAD NO FAMILY I COULD CALL ON TO SEND MONEY FOR ME TO BE RELEASED.

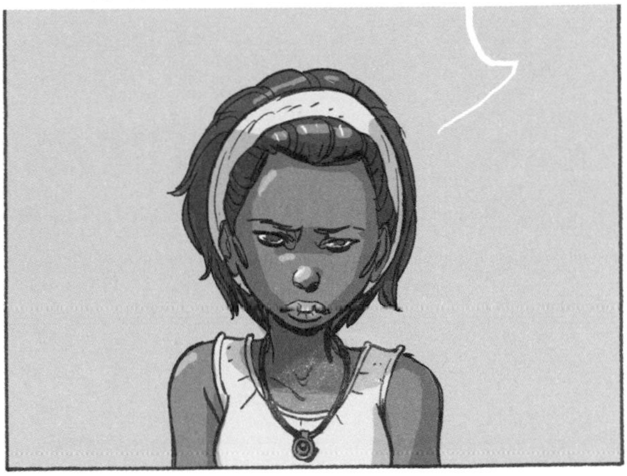

"BUT MY FELLOW PRISONERS SAVED ME. WHEN THEY WERE ASKING THEIR FAMILIES TO SAVE THEM FROM THE PRISON, THEY ALSO ASKED FOR EXTRA MONEY TO GET ME OUT OF THERE."

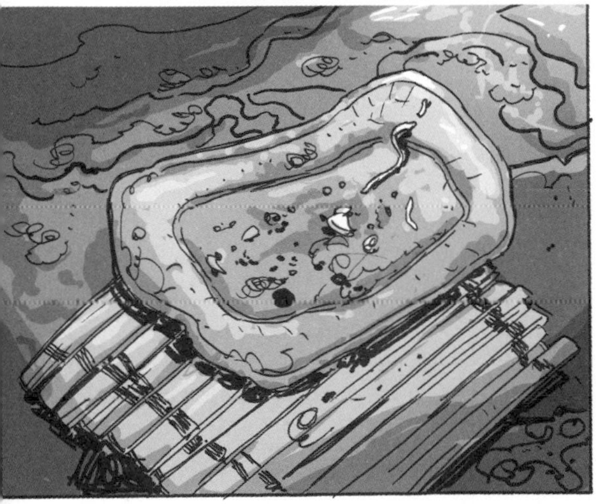

WHEN WE SAILED, WE WERE LUCKY.

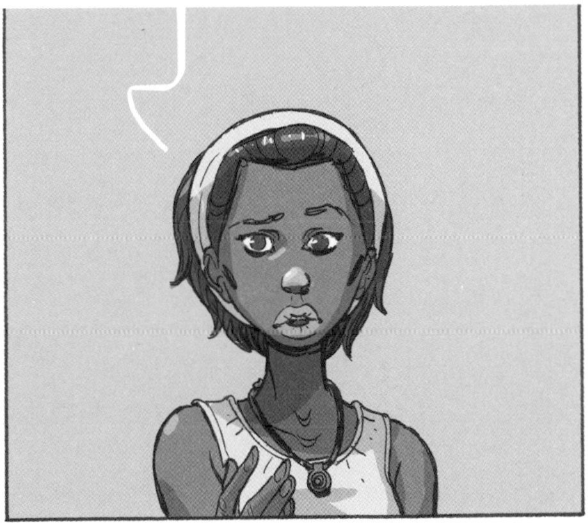

"THE BOAT BEHIND US, WHICH HAD OVER FOUR HUNDRED PEOPLE IN IT, SANK. I KNEW SOME OF THE PEOPLE ON THERE."

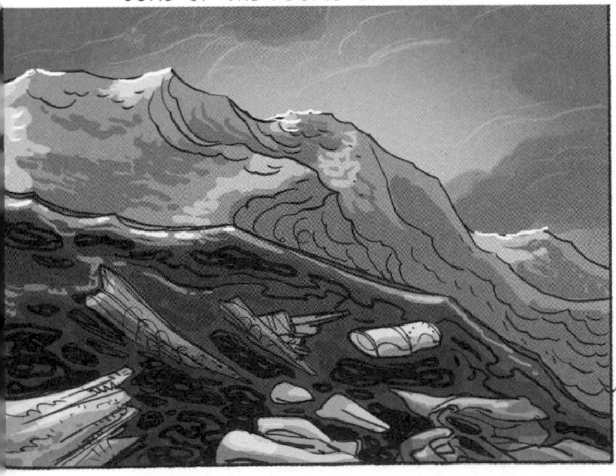

"BUT THE ITALIAN COAST GUARDS MET OUR BOAT AND TOOK US TO ITALY. A COUPLE OF THE PEOPLE I WAS WITH SAID THAT THEY WERE TRAVELING ON TO FRANCE TO TRY TO GET TO THE UK, AND ASKED ME IF I WANTED TO JOIN THEM."

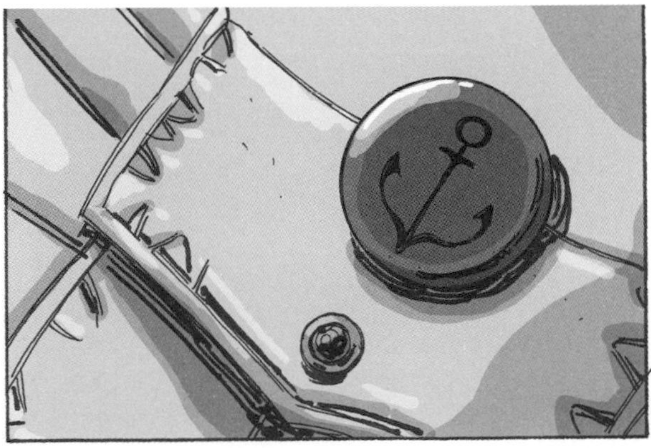

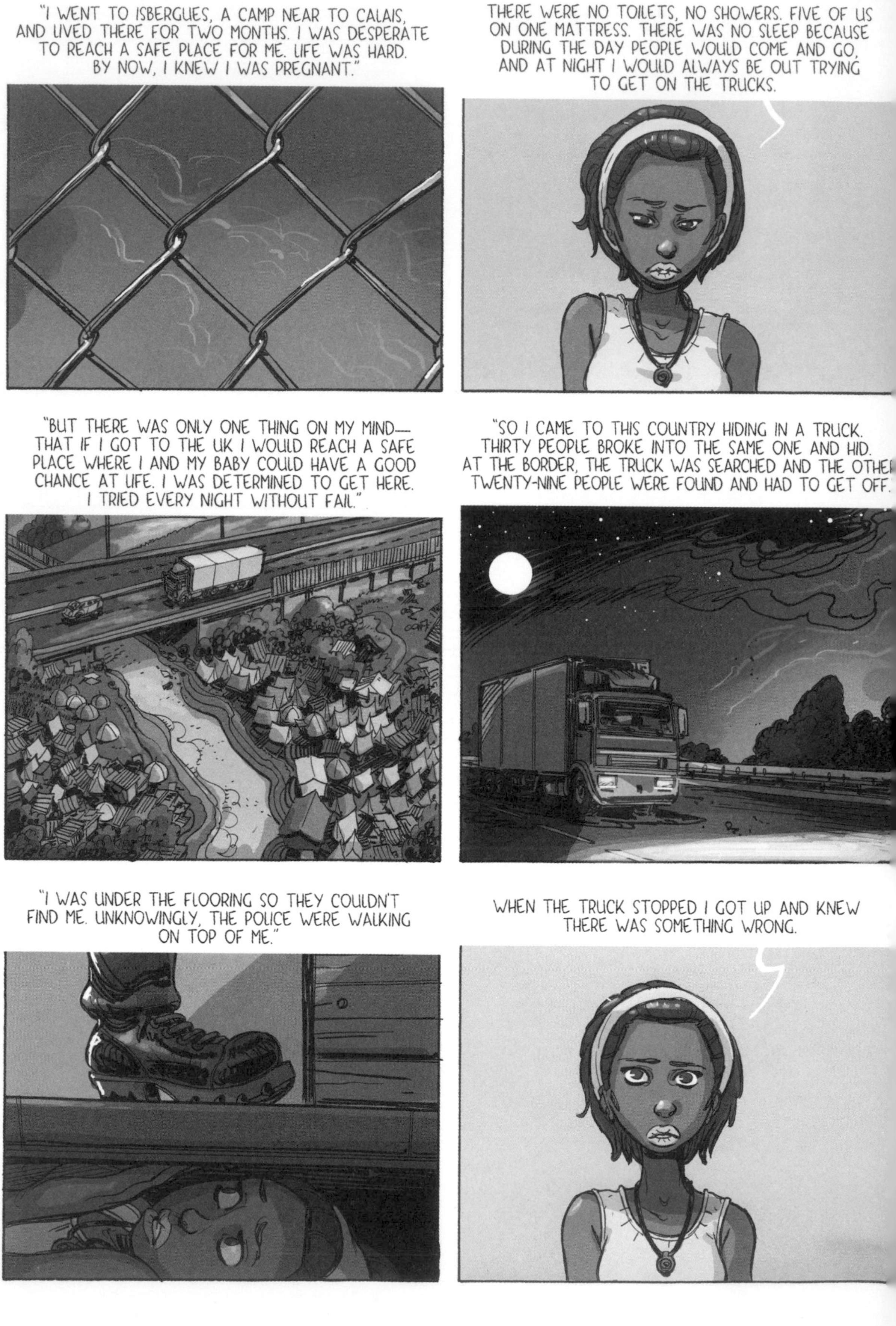
"I WENT TO ISBERGUES, A CAMP NEAR TO CALAIS, AND LIVED THERE FOR TWO MONTHS. I WAS DESPERATE TO REACH A SAFE PLACE FOR ME. LIFE WAS HARD. BY NOW, I KNEW I WAS PREGNANT."
THERE WERE NO TOILETS, NO SHOWERS. FIVE OF US ON ONE MATTRESS. THERE WAS NO SLEEP BECAUSE DURING THE DAY PEOPLE WOULD COME AND GO, AND AT NIGHT I WOULD ALWAYS BE OUT TRYING TO GET ON THE TRUCKS.
"BUT THERE WAS ONLY ONE THING ON MY MIND— THAT IF I GOT TO THE UK I WOULD REACH A SAFE PLACE WHERE I AND MY BABY COULD HAVE A GOOD CHANCE AT LIFE. I WAS DETERMINED TO GET HERE. I TRIED EVERY NIGHT WITHOUT FAIL."
"SO I CAME TO THIS COUNTRY HIDING IN A TRUCK. THIRTY PEOPLE BROKE INTO THE SAME ONE AND HID. AT THE BORDER, THE TRUCK WAS SEARCHED AND THE OTHE TWENTY-NINE PEOPLE WERE FOUND AND HAD TO GET OFF.
"I WAS UNDER THE FLOORING SO THEY COULDN'T FIND ME. UNKNOWINGLY, THE POLICE WERE WALKING ON TOP OF ME."
WHEN THE TRUCK STOPPED I GOT UP AND KNEW THERE WAS SOMETHING WRONG.

"I WAS IN PAIN."

"THE TRUCK DRIVER SHOUTED AT ME WHEN HE SAW ME, AND SAID HE COULDN'T DO ANYTHING TO HELP."

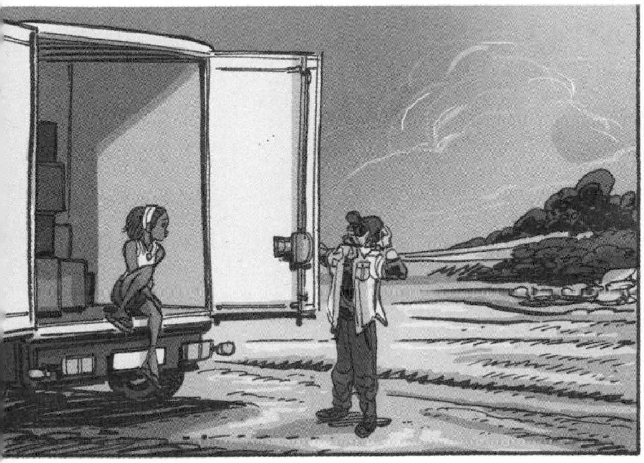

"THE POLICE TOOK ME TO THE HOSPITAL, BUT I HAD LOST MY BABY."

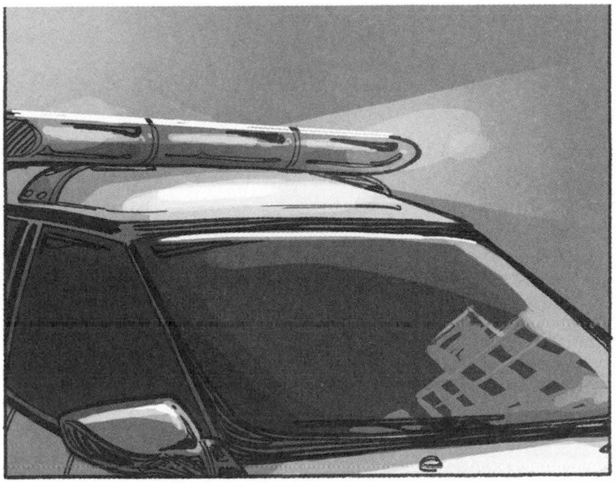

"NOW, I LIVE IN A HOSTEL IN LEEDS. I AM GIVEN MEALS BUT I DO NOT GET ANY MONEY AND I AM NOT ALLOWED TO WORK. I AM NOT COMPLAINING BECAUSE I HAVE BEEN IN SITUATIONS THAT WERE MUCH WORSE."

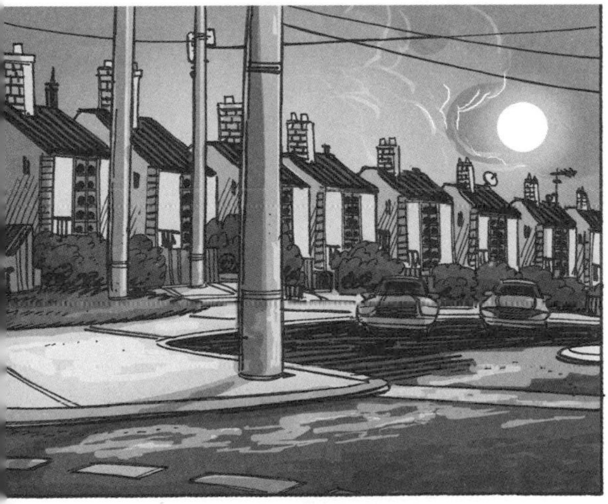

EVEN THOUGH I PASSED THROUGH ALL THAT SUFFERING, I AM HERE NOW, AND I AM THANKFUL FOR THAT.

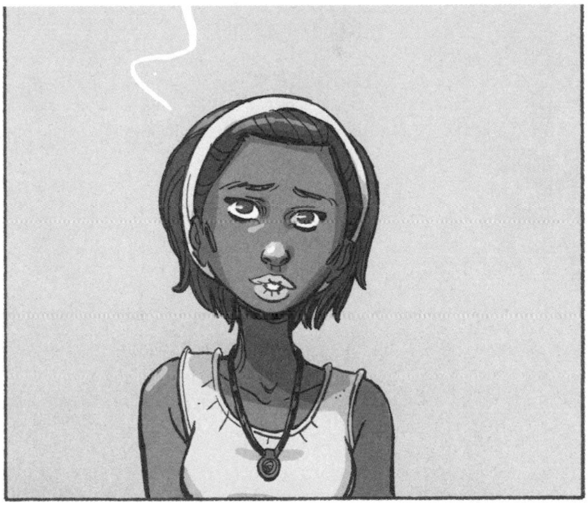

I WANT TO BE EDUCATED. I DIDN'T HAVE MUCH OPPORTUNITY FOR LEARNING IN MY COUNTRY. I STOPPED GOING TO SCHOOL WHEN I WAS TWELVE. I HOPE I CAN STUDY, BUT NOW I HAVE BECOME FORGETFUL. I DON'T REMEMBER THINGS. HOPEFULLY MY HEAD WILL START WORKING BETTER.

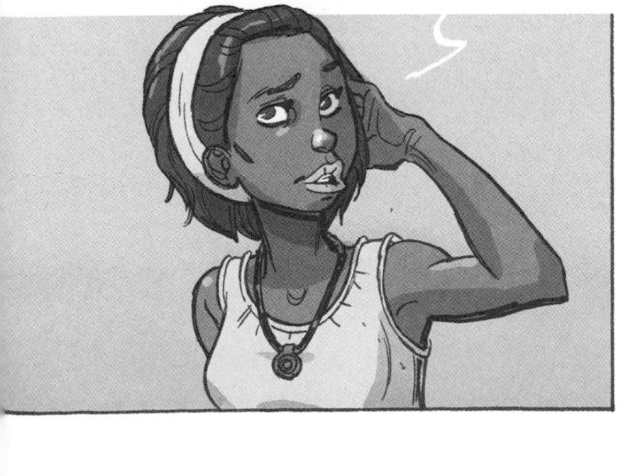

I WOULD LIKE TO BECOME A NURSE.

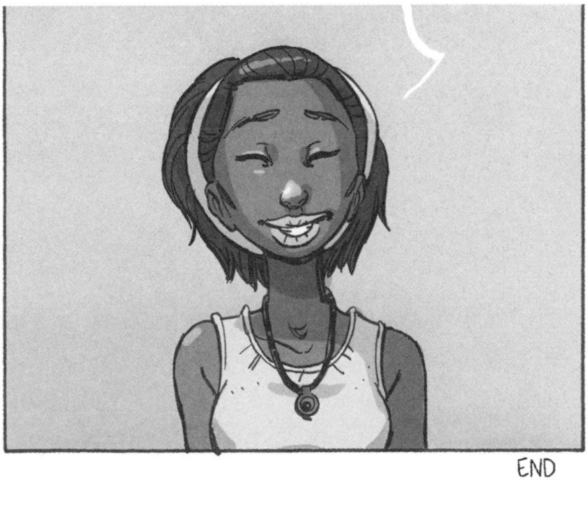

END

ACKNOWLEDGMENTS

Research consultant: Vivien Francis

Grateful thanks to all the people who have given their time and energy and knowledge to help with this book, especially:

Jo Adkins
Roberto Barrera
Sheila Brand
Jax Burgoyne
Paul Chapman
Miles Dennison
Jean Donkin
Peter Donkin
Mike Fillis
Jamie Finch
Ron Fogelman
Dr. Thomas Giddens
Sophie Hicks
Matthew Pennycook MP
Moe Redish
Antonio Scricco
Will Vunderink
Sarah Williams

The Estate of Elie Wiesel

Our lovely team at Hodder:
Anne McNeil
Alison Padley
Rachel Wade

The staff at the Cairo Library & Archive at the National Maritime Museum, Greenwich, London, England.

Special thanks to all the people who talked to us about their experiences but who wished to remain anonymous.

And a huge thank you to the following individuals and their London-based charities:

Anne Stoltenberg and Nazek Ramadan at Migrant Voice
www.migrantvoice.org

Natasha Walter and Marchu Girma at Women for Refugee Women
www.RefugeeWomen.co.uk

Helen Mead at Greenwich Migrant Hub
www.greenwichmigranthub.com

SKETCHBOOK

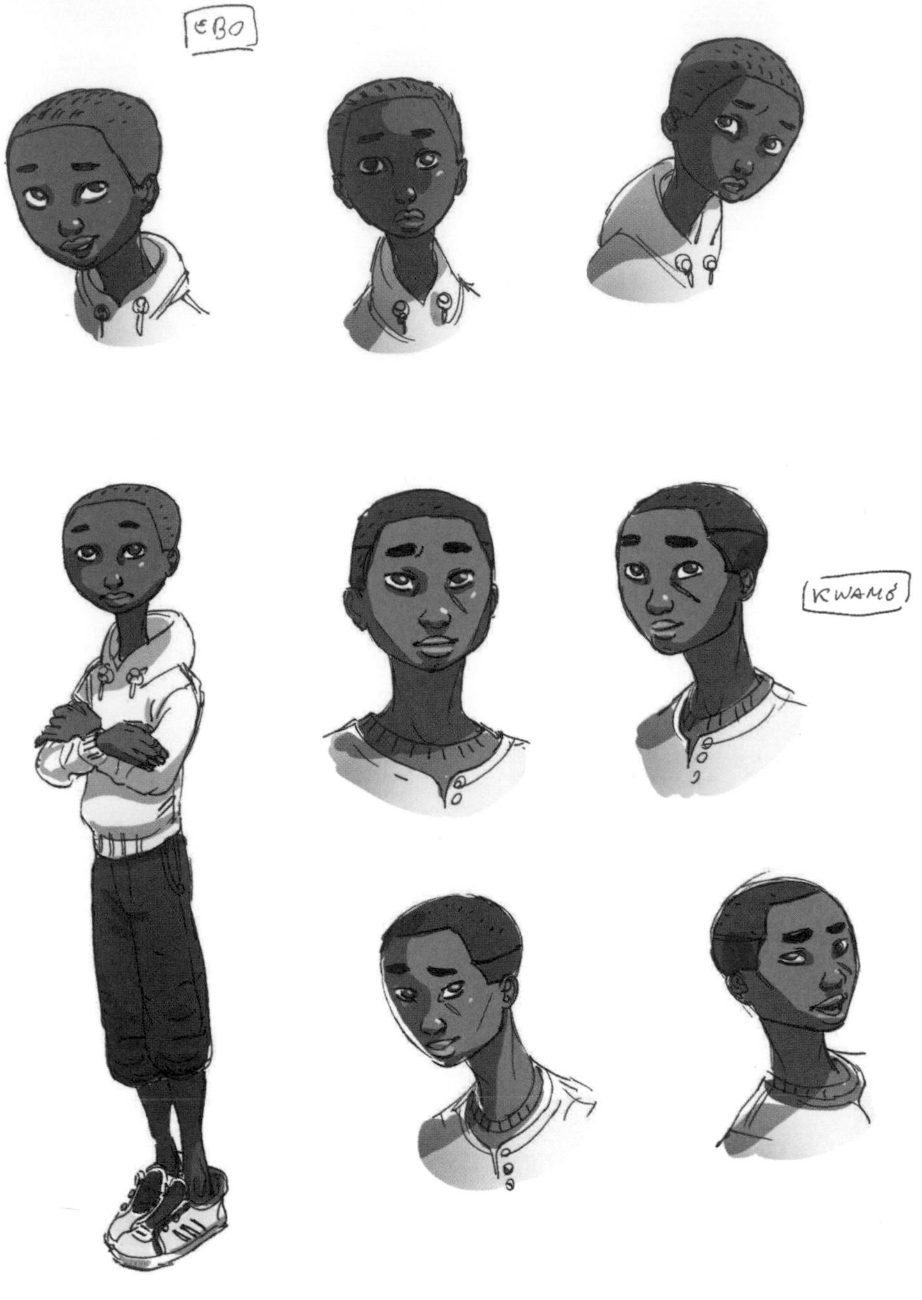
EBO
KWAMÉ

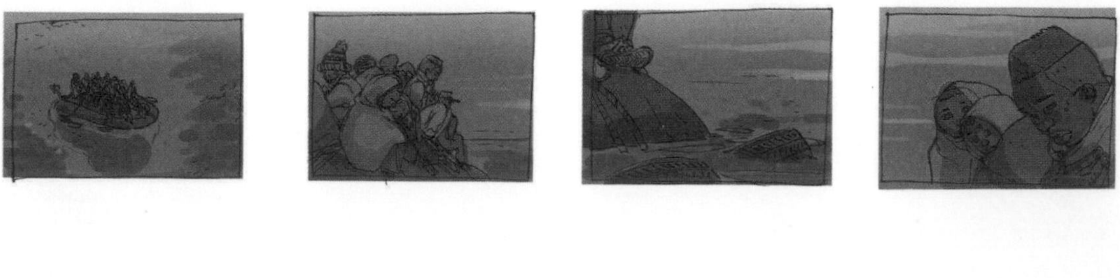

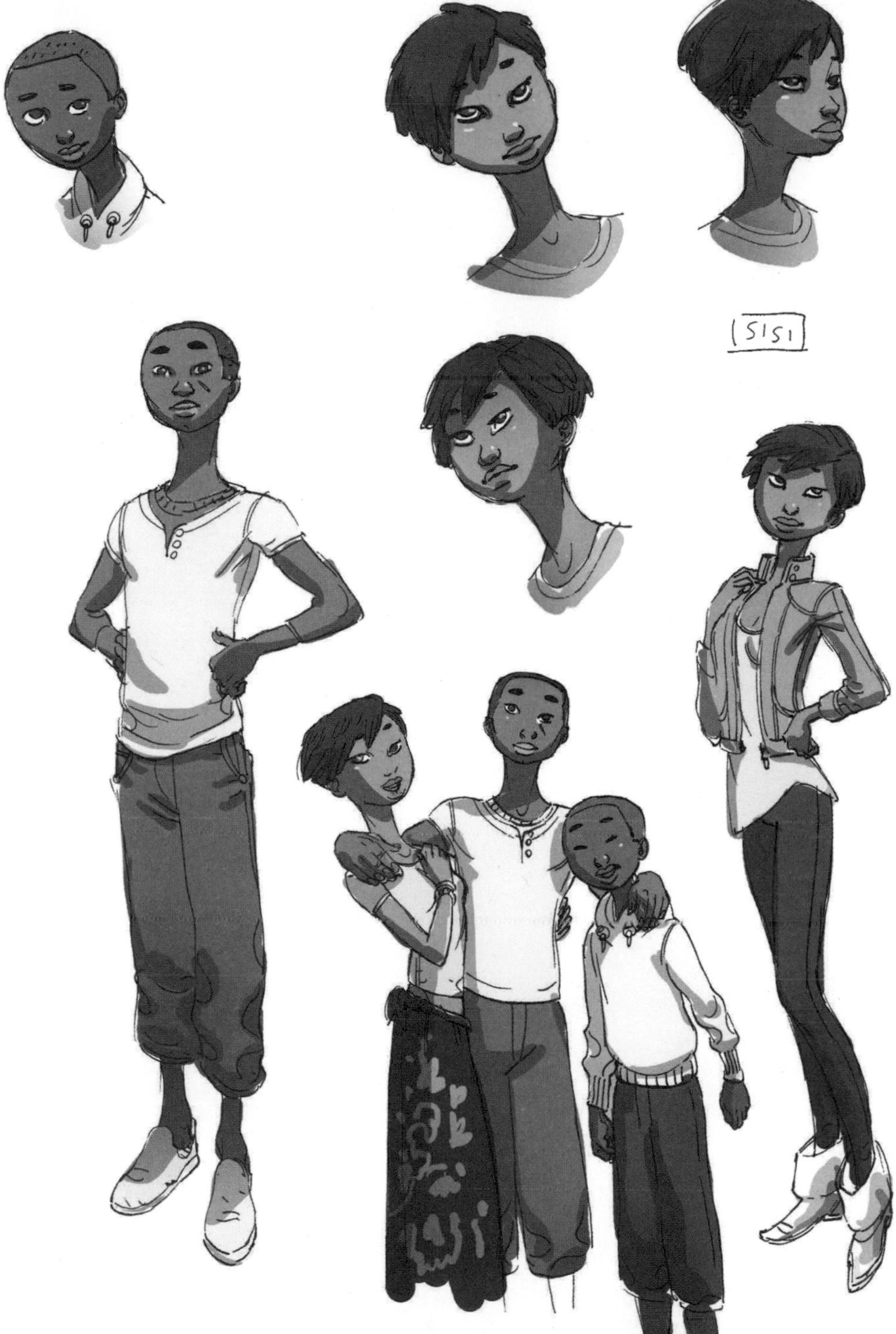
SISI

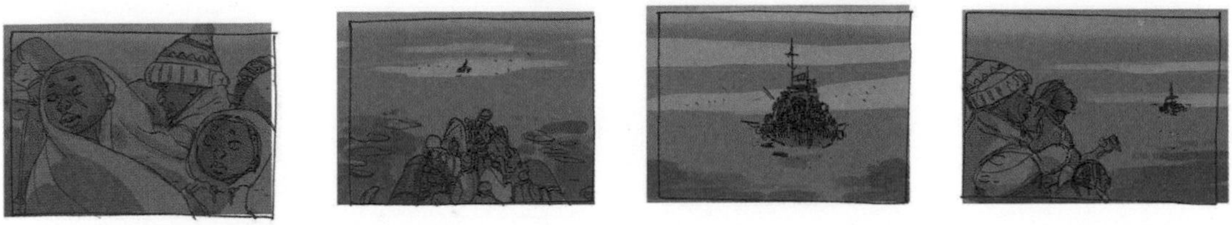

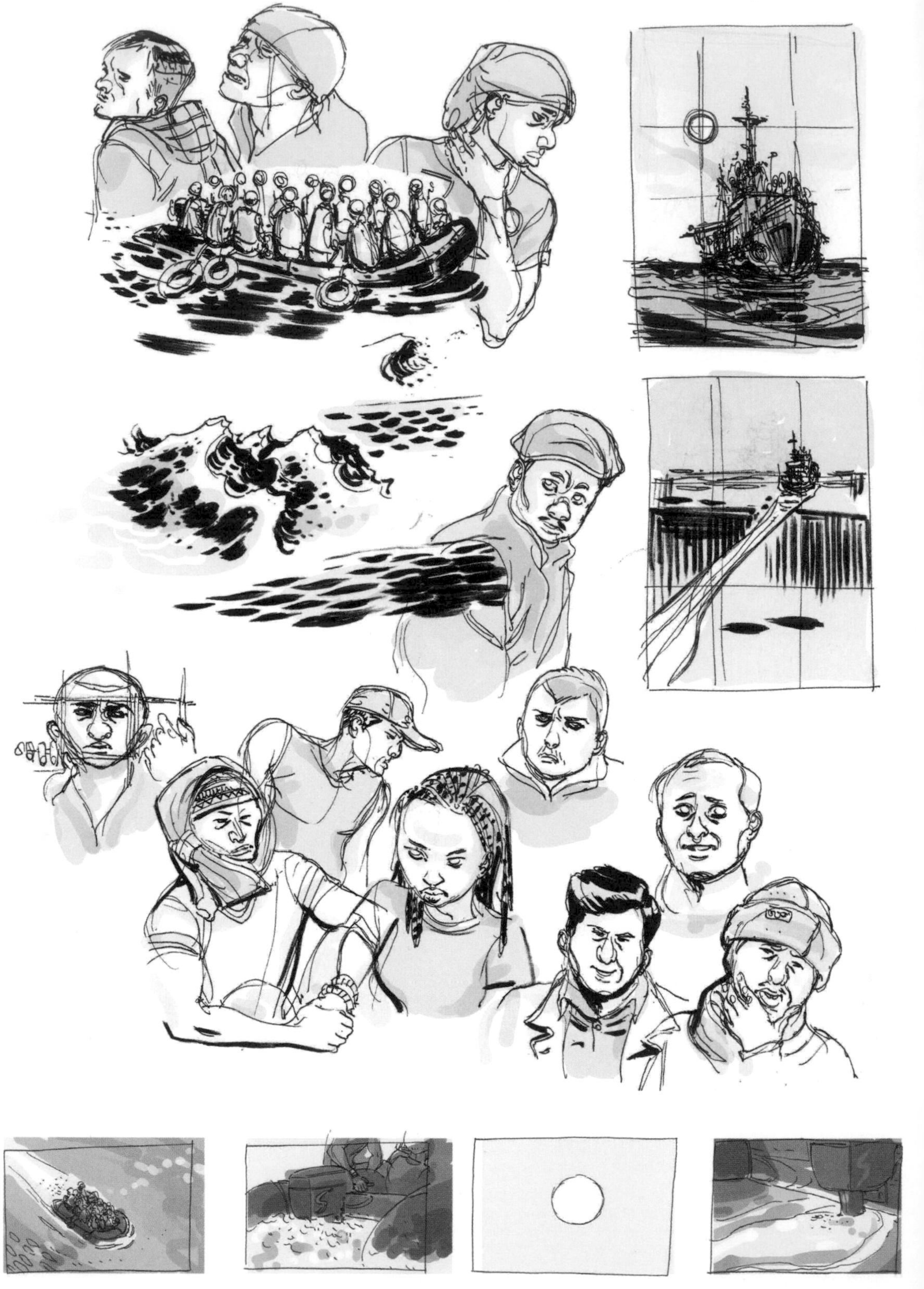

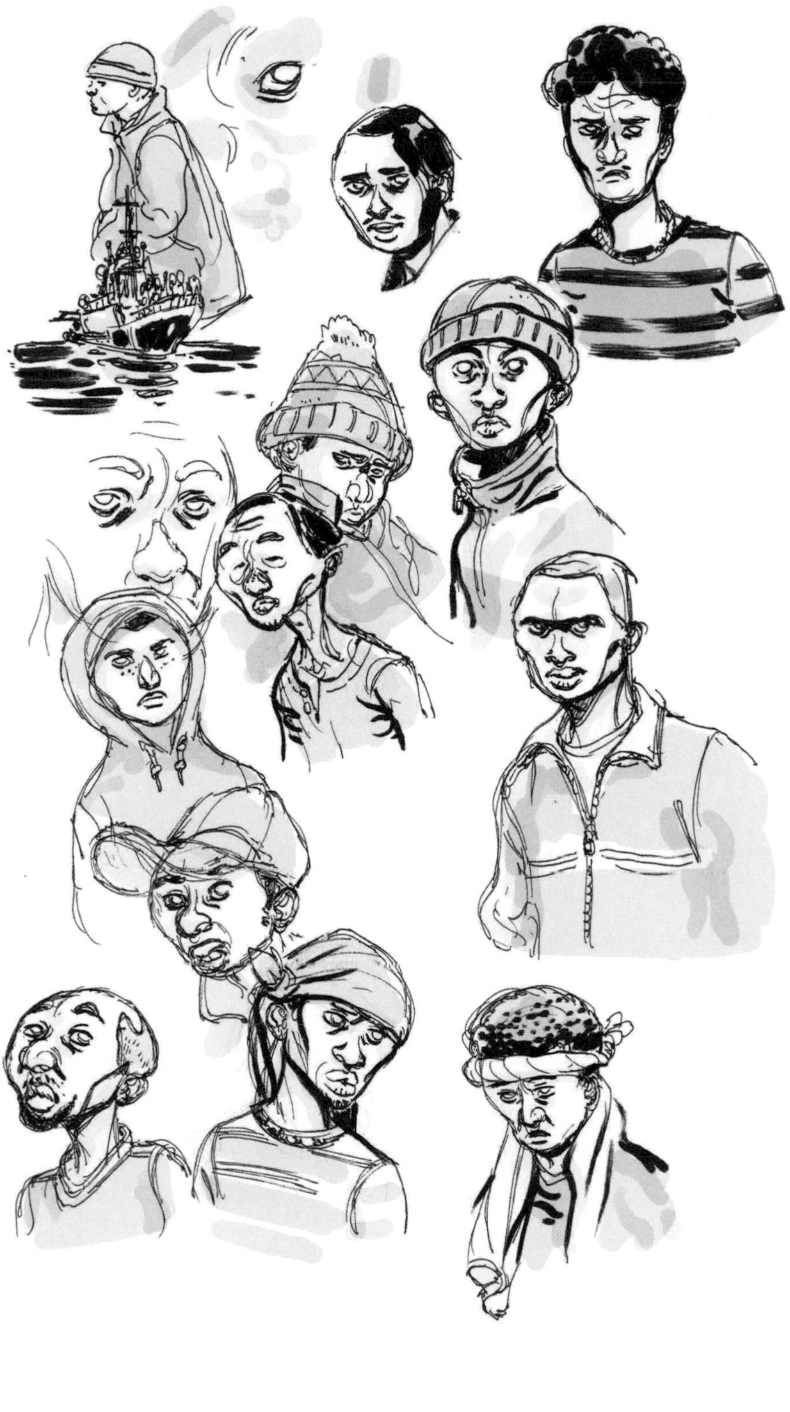

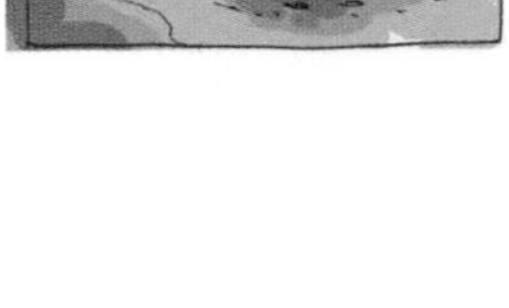
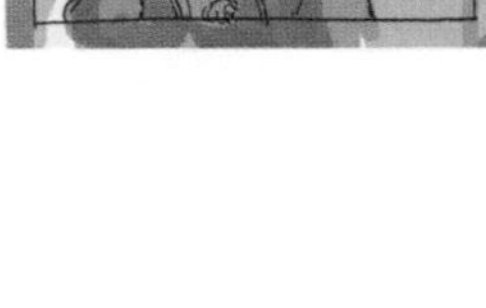
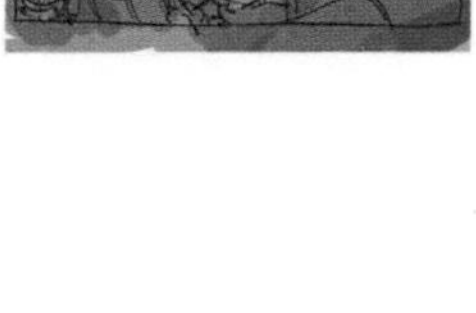
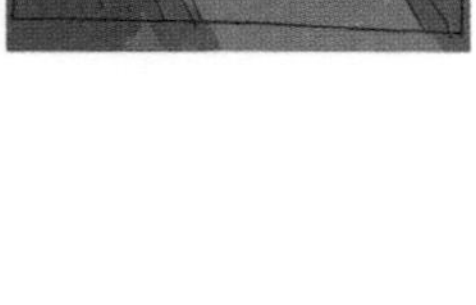

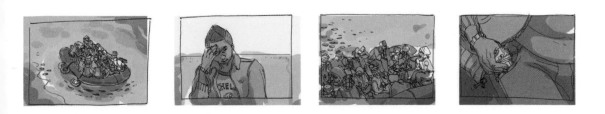

EOIN COLFER (pronounced Owen) was born in Wexford on the South-East coast of Ireland in 1965. He first developed an interest in writing when he was gripped by the Viking stories he learned about at school. After his marriage, he and his wife spent about four years working in Saudi Arabia, Tunisia, and Italy. His first book, *Benny and Omar*, was based on his experiences in Tunisia; it has since been translated into many languages. In 2001 the first Artemis Fowl book was published and Eoin gave up teaching to concentrate fully on writing. Eoin, who lives in Ireland with his wife and two children, says, "I will keep writing until people stop reading or I run out of ideas. Hopefully neither of these will happen anytime soon."

ANDREW DONKIN has sold over eight million children's books, graphic novels, and adult books. His work in comics includes *Batman: Legends of the Dark Knight* for DC Comics, and *Doctor Who*. With Eoin Colfer, he has co-written five bestselling graphic novel adaptations of Eoin's books. Andrew became interested in the issue of migrants and asylum while writing the biography of Sir Alfred Mehran, a stateless man who lived on a bench in Paris Airport for eighteen years. The resulting book, *The Terminal Man*, was described by *The*

Sunday Times (Glasgow) as "a brilliant and profoundly disturbing book." Andrew lives near the river Thames in London with his family.

GIOVANNI RIGANO is an Italian comics artist and creator of many graphic novels. He has adapted five of Eoin Colfer's novels into graphic novels, as well as Disney-Pixar's *The Incredibles*, three *Pirates of the Caribbean* novels, and his own series, *Daffodil*. He lives in Como, Italy.

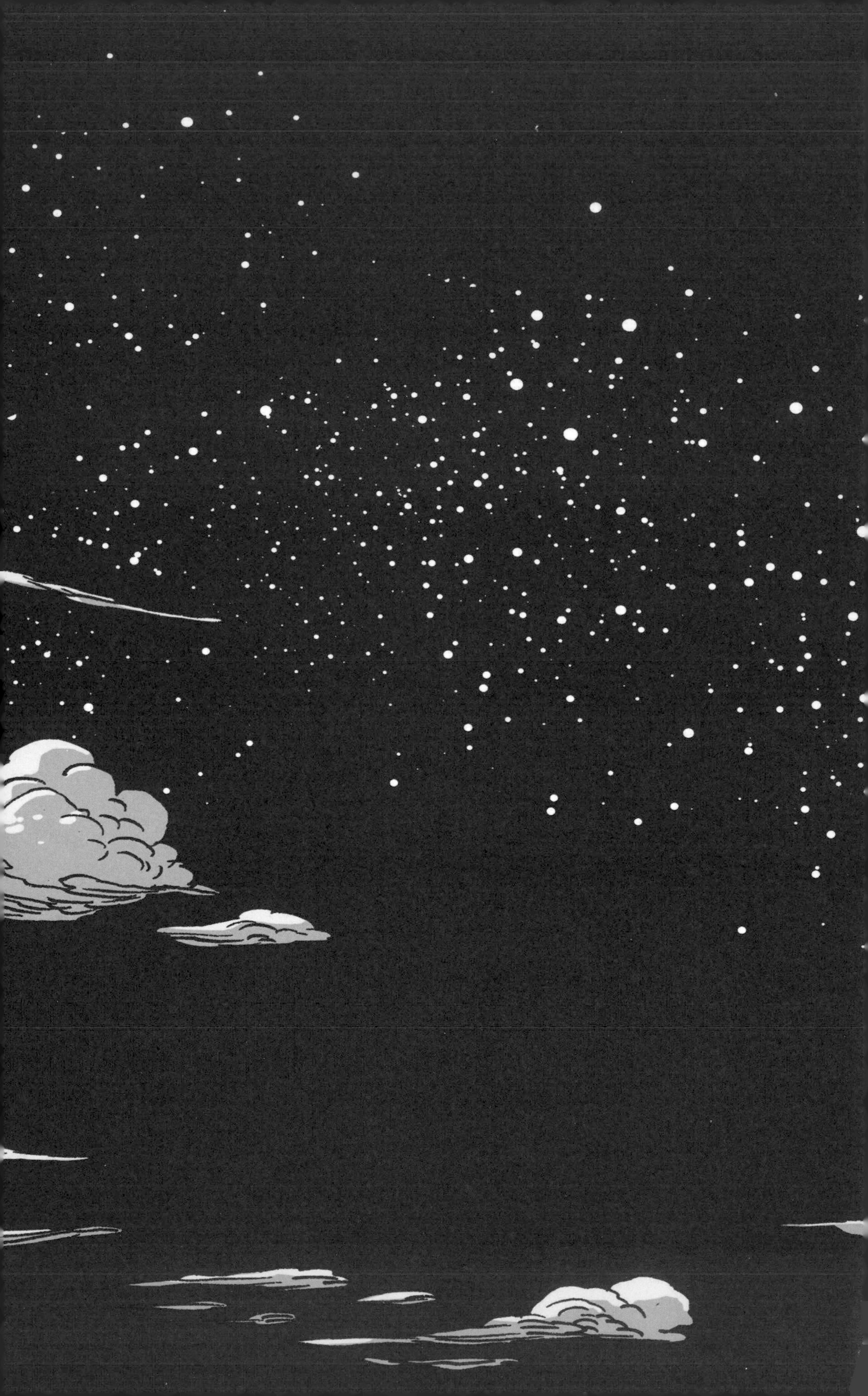